TFS GUARDIAN

The Terran Fleet Command Saga - Book 5

*****

Tori L. Harris

ISBN: 978-0-9985338-1-0
TFS GUARDIAN
THE TERRAN FLEET COMMAND SAGA - BOOK 5
VERSION 1.0

Written and Published by Tori L. Harris
AuthorToriHarris.com

Edited by Monique Happy
www.moniquehappy.com

Cover Design by Ivo Brankovikj
https://www.artstation.com/artist/ivobrankovikj

Those who would give up essential Liberty, to purchase a little temporary Safety, deserve neither Liberty nor Safety.

Benjamin Franklin

Prologue

Pelara, The University of Taphis
(Two weeks ago - 3.87×10^3 light years from Earth)

Castigan Creel liked to think of himself as something of an alchemist. During his youth, he had eagerly consumed the stories of ancient philosophers on his world and others — fascinated by their belief that the elements, and even the fundamental forces of nature, could be harnessed for a variety of useful purposes. With age and experience, Creel had come to realize that much of what the alchemists believed had actually been correct. Unfortunately, they had been so far ahead of their time that they had often been inclined to conflate basic scientific concepts with various forms of mysticism — a convenient stopgap when the current state of knowledge simply wasn't up to the tasks they were attempting.

This tendency towards the supernatural, in addition to getting a great many brilliant men and women burned at the stake, had created a common misconception that the alchemists' entire body of work had been nothing more than an odd amalgamation of pseudoscience and the occult. In reality, however, they had been heralds of countless wonders to come — their experiments providing the methods, the terminology, and the scientific underpinnings that would eventually lead their once-primitive worlds to the stars.

Beyond their often-esoteric experiments, what resonated with Creel (technically *Doctor* Creel, but on Pelara, the use of such titles had all but disappeared) was the fact that the alchemists had been forced to do much of their work behind a veil of secrecy. From a practical perspective, keeping their work concealed was often nothing more than a means of safeguarding their most dangerous knowledge. In many cases, however, it wasn't the knowledge of their most highly coveted methods that was so dangerous — transmuting lead into gold among them — but rather the revelation that the skills for which they were so handsomely paid simply didn't work.

Ironically, Castigan Creel had almost exactly the opposite problem. His methods *did* work. And although he had never attempted to create the so-called "noble metals" from other, less valuable ones, what he *could* produce, seemingly from the ether itself, was the most valuable substance ever conceived. Unfortunately for Doctor Creel and the other modern practitioners of science on his world, doing so had been deemed to pose an unnecessary level of risk and, as such, was strictly forbidden.

Staring at the small screen displaying the interior of the reaction chamber, Creel noted the subtle changes in hue indicating conditions had reached their optimum state. Nodding confidently to himself, he pushed the transmit button on the ancient, console-mounted microphone to the right of his keyboard. "Control is go for initiate. Pre-ignition check, please."

"Accelerator is go."

"Laser is go."

"Confinement is go."

Hearing the disembodied voices of three of his former post-doctoral students (he still thought of them as his students, although he was well aware that all three were every bit as capable as he) caused Creel to pause and stare at the control panel for a moment. As their former professor, he was well aware they still deferred to him in many ways. Not for the first time, he wondered if what he was doing — what he had convinced his colleagues to do — could ever be justified from an ethical standpoint. Sure, they had taken precautions. And, thus far at least, their precautions had worked, allowing them to do what they were about to do on a great many occasions before tonight without detection. Nevertheless, each time they did so, he knew, the probability they would be detected by the Alliance AI — or, perhaps more likely, discovered and turned in to the Department of Compliance and Safety (DoCaS) by some "concerned citizen," — increased significantly.

While the university's particle physics research center routinely conducted high-energy research, all of it required an extensive approval process to ensure no laws governing the employment of "spacecraft or weapons-related" sciences were violated. Unfortunately, the work in which Creel's small team had been engaging after-hours involved precisely the kinds of science those laws were intended to deter. For Creel, it wasn't the act of breaking the absurd, draconian laws that bothered him. Instead, it was the fact that getting caught in the act of breaking them could potentially put the lives of everyone involved at risk. If they didn't manage to conclude their work here soon, the law of averages would surely catch up with them. It simply wasn't possible to release the levels of energy required, let alone produce the desired chain-reactions within the facility's accelerator, without eventually attracting unwanted attention. At some point, they *would* get caught, and the consequences would be severe.

Creel took in a deep breath, shaking his head resignedly as he raised the red plastic guard in the center of the control panel. *Just one more time*, he promised himself as he flipped the toggle switch to initiate the reaction sequence. Inside the accelerator, a bank of ultra-high-powered laser emitters fired in unison — not at a specific target, but through a virtual, field-induced reaction chamber maintaining a near-perfect vacuum.

In spite of the misleading name, "space" is by no means empty. Instead, a hidden, cosmic soup of matter and antimatter particles continually hold one another in a fragile balance. Within the accelerator, as the beam emitters released their massive quantities of energy inside a tiny reaction volume, that fragile balance could no longer be maintained. As a result, a small rift in the fabric of space itself began to form. Fundamental particles — primarily electrons and positrons — spilled from the rift like Styrofoam pellets pouring from an overstuffed beanbag chair sliced open with a sharp knife. Shortly thereafter, the atomic-level annihilations began.

As matter rapidly destroyed antimatter just outside the rift, gamma radiation catalyzed a chain reaction with a seemingly impossible result: the "creation" of additional matter/antimatter pairs that did not previously exist in normal space. Much like the naturally occurring reactions that occurred near the most powerful neutron stars, both matter and energy had been produced, seemingly where nothing at all had existed just moments before.

Sensing that conditions were now optimized within the chamber, Creel's software triggered a subtle shift in frequency for the powerful beam emitters sustaining the reaction, altering its balance to an infinitesimal degree, but producing immediate and dramatic results. With a burst of bright light in the visible spectrum, the rift began releasing significantly more positrons, just as a stream of low-energy antiprotons was introduced into the chamber. As a result, large numbers of antihydrogen atoms began to form immediately below the rift.

In order to capture the priceless antimatter (while preventing a spectacular series of explosions), powerful magnetic fields coaxed the atoms along a predefined path leading eventually to the safety of a small, cryo-containment canister. By the end of tonight's session, the team would produce nearly four hundred grams of antihydrogen. It wasn't industrial-scale production by any means — even compared to the Wek operation at the Herrera Mining facility — but it did, nonetheless, represent the largest quantity produced on Pelara in more than a century. The ancient alchemists, Creel believed, would be justifiably proud.

That should do it ... a grand total of eight kilograms, he thought. *More than enough to bring her reactors online. Once that happens, she'll be self-sustaining and generate enough additional power to —*

"Attention on the net. Laser is scimitar, scimitar, scimitar," Creel heard over the console speaker. At the outset of this project several months before, his former students had come up with several code words they would use over the facility's closed-circuit intercom in the event of a problem. At the time, he had joked about the fact that "scimitar" sounded particularly ominous, but should at least help everyone to remember what it meant — their operation had been compromised.

Creel jabbed at the large, emergency stop button on the console, cutting power to the beam emitters and immediately terminating the reaction inside the chamber. At the same instant, an automated cleanup cycle was initiated that would allow the cryo-containment canister to be safely removed in just under three minutes. Glancing at his tablet, he noted the estimated antihydrogen total stood at just under three hundred grams. Not as much as expected, certainly, but it would most likely be enough. It would *have* to be enough.

Chiding himself that his first thought had been for the material results of his team's work rather than for the individuals who had made that work possible, Creel picked up his tablet and clicked on the video feed covering the facility's main entrance. He was fairly certain the voice he had heard over the intercom had belonged to Arcellia, but the members of his team often rotated responsibilities, and the fidelity of the small, ancient speaker made it difficult to know for sure. *She didn't sound particularly frightened, did she?* he thought, realizing that his heart was racing and that he needed to calm himself down. *No, she's probably fine. It's not like we didn't plan for this. She knew exactly where to go and what to do. She's long gone by now.*

A light-enhanced black and white video feed filled his tablet's screen, and he spent a few moments panning the camera back and forth, looking for anything unusual. Seeing no movement, no change in lighting, and no signs of forced entry, Creel breathed deeply and felt himself begin to relax a bit. The laser control station was located closest to the facility entrance, so it made sense that whoever was stationed there would be the first one to notice any unexpected visitors. At the moment, however, it looked like a false alarm. Arcellia, he knew, had been pounding down coffee all evening, so maybe she had gotten herself a little worked up. Even if it *had* been the authorities, anyone sitting at that control panel had numerous avenues of escape that outsiders wouldn't expect, every one of which the team had practiced over and over until there should have been little chance of someone catching them by surprise.

It was at that moment that Creel heard the unmistakable sound of energy weapons fire from some distant location within the facility that was clearly nowhere near the main entrance. He had always hated that sound. It was as if the air itself were being ripped apart like a giant piece of cloth as superheated channels of ionized air were pushed explosively aside by the pulsed particle beam traveling at nearly the speed of light.

My God. Surely the police or DoCaS troops wouldn't just open fire on sight, would they? he thought. *No, probably not. But Wardens might,* he corrected himself a moment later as a chill ran down the length of his spine.

Pelara and the core members of its powerful alliance had seen centuries of relative peace and prosperity as a result of the cultivation program. And with much of this success attributed to the widespread deployment of Guardian spacecraft, the creation of armies composed of fully autonomous, AI-controlled ground troops had been seen as a logical next step. At the time, most Pelarans agreed that truly civilized societies should never be required to put their citizens in harm's way — not after technology had reached the point where such risks could be borne by machines. Few, if any, ever expected that these same machines might one day be deployed on their own homeworld to enforce the will of an occupying power over the Pelaran people.

Now feeling a desperate need to confirm who or what he was up against before attempting to make his own escape, Creel checked the timer on the reaction chamber cleanup cycle — still just over one minute remaining. With visibly shaking hands and a steady stream of sweat now trickling down the small of his back, he clicked back over to the security camera app and began the process of paging through every video feed in the building. Seeing nothing out of place other than the absence of his three colleagues, he switched back to a view of the accelerator/decelerator console.

Most of the equipment comprising the university's particle accelerator complex was located underground along a twenty-five-kilometer-long, circular tunnel, but the main control room was at the far end of the building just one floor down from where Creel was sitting. Believing this to be roughly the location where the weapons discharge had taken place, he slowly panned the camera around the room, paying particular attention to the operator's station and the room's most likely exit.

Just as he was about to give up on the prospect of seeing anything on the video feed, Creel thought he detected an odd motion blur near the right side of the screen — a shadow cast by something just off camera perhaps. Hoping it would repeat, he stopped and waited, staring intently at the now-static image. Although he detected no additional movement, he did notice a dark, reflective substance in an irregularly shaped pool on the floor that he had somehow missed on first inspection. As Human minds are wont to do, Creel's temporarily refused to accept the obvious explanation for what he was seeing. Instead, he continued to stare at the grisly scene as if trying to solve a particularly interesting puzzle. Only after several seconds had ticked by did his curiosity begin to be replaced by equal parts acceptance and horror. It was at that moment that he saw the top of what could only be an armored helmet of sorts pass across the bottom of the screen. Shortly thereafter, the video feed from the room went dark. *A Warden,* he thought. *That had to be a Warden.*

Not seen on Pelara in decades, WCS units (for Warden Combat System) had been instrumental in bringing the planet "under control" after the laws prohibiting weapons and spacecraft development, among many others, had been enacted. Ultra-intelligent, brutally effective machines, their initial designs had been based on the powered combat armor once used by Pelaran troops. As a result, they still retained a somewhat humanoid appearance. Given that most of their mission profiles required them to operate effectively within structures and ships designed for less than two-meter-tall biological entities, most physical aspects of their design had changed little over the years. Fortunately, this size limitation also placed some practical limitations on the Wardens' physical capabilities. Nevertheless, their speed and power still far exceeded all but the most advanced armored combat suits worn by biological troops. This distinction mattered little on Pelara, of course, where all such equipment had been confiscated long ago, even among law enforcement agencies. At the moment, in fact, there were few if any weapons on Pelara capable of even slowing a WCS unit down, let alone destroying one outright.

Doctor Creel stared transfixed at the blank screen, which now contained nothing more than a small text block indicating that it should have been displaying the accelerator/decelerator console feed. *How much time do I have? A minute? Maybe less?* he wondered, stunned into inaction by what he had just seen. At that moment, a faint chirping sound accompanied by a flashing green indicator on the Control console snapped his mind back to the present. Realizing he might still have a chance if he moved quickly, Creel jabbed at the canister release button, grabbed up his tote bag, and stepped over to a pedestal near the back of the room. There, a heavy metallic drawer looking much like those used in bank teller windows made a series of thuds and clicking sounds before opening to reveal a small, rectangular device with a built-in status display. Pausing just long enough to confirm the cryo-containment canister was functioning normally, Creel gingerly placed the device — including its cargo of two hundred ninety-eight grams of antihydrogen — into his bag.

His work now finished, Creel stepped quickly inside an adjacent equipment closet and closed the door behind him. Pushing aside a series of plastic strip doors used to contain refrigerated air around computer equipment, he uncovered a small, wall-mounted control panel as well as another heavy, steel door near the back of the closet.

As he had practiced many times before, Creel flipped the three toggle switches on the panel in rapid succession, then grabbed the mass of keys hanging from the retractable chain on his belt. Fumbling for the right one, he noticed for the first time how badly his hands were shaking. At least one — most likely all three — of his former students were dead, and the realization that this was due to a situation entirely of his making threatened to unravel the very fabric of his sanity. It was only after what seemed like several minutes of agonizing effort that he finally managed to locate the key that unlocked the previously hidden door.

Operating now primarily from rote rather than conscious thought, he glanced quickly up to the ceiling where a stainless steel spray bar was sputtering to life. Hoping to reduce or eliminate any thermal evidence of their passing, the team had installed these rapid cooling units at various locations along their primary escape routes out of the building. The idea was a simple one: release a fine spray of liquid nitrogen — which instantly vaporized into super-cold gaseous nitrogen — to form a thermal barrier of sorts by rapidly cooling a relatively small volume of confined air. None of them had any idea if it would work, of course, but since both the equipment and the liquid nitrogen were readily available, they had figured it was worth a shot.

Creel scowled and shook his head, skeptical that anything short of divine intervention would allow him to escape the building, let alone the university grounds beyond, with his life. The only thing he knew for certain was that he was fully committed at this point. He had crossed a line, and there would be no going back. Still, even as bleak as his prospects seemed at the moment, he knew that the long, dark passage ahead offered by far his best chance. Getting safely away from this place also represented his one and only opportunity to assign some sort of meaning to his friends' sacrifice. So, with a vague, distant hope that the gripping terror he felt at the moment would eventually be replaced by resignation, if not resolve, he stepped through the doorway, closed and locked it as quietly as possible behind him, and set off down the cinderblock-lined hallway at a dead run.

Like the purloined keyring jingling noisily on his belt, maintenance corridors such as this one were intended for use by the building's custodial staff, not as a means of clandestine escape. Tonight, however, Creel hoped it would allow him to get far enough away — and quickly enough away — to save his own life, the priceless material in his leather bag, and the future of his once-proud homeworld.

Chapter 1

Earth, TFC Yucca Mountain Shipyard Facility
(30 minutes after unauthorized spacecraft entry)

Captain Hiroto Oshiro stood atop a maintenance catwalk peering down at the strangely familiar spacecraft now hovering silently just short of the landing platform beneath Berth 10. The "Grey ship" — perhaps an invalid assumption on his part, but this was the term that had immediately come to mind during his first, impromptu report to TFC Headquarters — had remained motionless now for nearly half an hour. As facility commander, his initial instinct had been to simply watch and wait, a course of action that had, thus far, been enthusiastically endorsed by Admiral Sexton and the growing number of participants on the conference comlink he had initiated. But the longer he waited, the more Oshiro wondered if he was missing something obvious. The only thing he knew with any degree of certainty at the moment was that taking any action that might be construed as even remotely hostile was a singularly bad idea.

"Still no transmissions from the ship?" he heard the Commander-in-Chief ask in his headset.

"No, sir. Nothing of any kind. In fact, we're barely able to detect any emissions at all, not even from whatever type of power system and grav emitters they're using. If we weren't standing here looking at it, I think our facility AI could make a pretty good argument that it's not really even here."

"Humph," Sexton grunted. "Well, let's hope that's nothing more than a sign of their intent to be polite guests now that they've invited themselves in. I assume we've tried all of our standard protocols for exchanging lexical data?"

"Yes, we have, sir."

"Understood. Be advised that Chairwoman Kistler has called the Leadership Council into emergency session. I expect we'll have them online with us at any moment."

"I'm not surprised, sir, I … stand by one."

"Yeah, I see it too."

Since emerging from the facility's entrance tunnel, the disk-shaped ship had been holding position in the area often referred to as the "roundhouse." Although not a particularly good description of its actual shape, the term accurately described the only location within the shipyard proper that was wide enough to allow TFC vessels exceeding a kilometer in length to turn in place about their vertical axes prior to docking. Accordingly, the four berths immediately adjacent to the roundhouse were designed for these largest of ships. Unlike Fleet's predominantly rectangular spacecraft, however, the Grey ship required no such alignment maneuvers.

As nearly everyone in the shipyard — along with a substantial number of TFC personnel at other facilities around the globe and scattered across many light years of space — watched transfixed, the craft slowly advanced once again. Just as the ship's leading edge crossed the threshold of Berth 10, the landing platform rose to within approximately five meters of its ventral surface, apparently once again responding to the commands of its as yet unseen occupants.

The alien vessel was clearly in no hurry to complete its docking maneuver, perhaps sharing Captain Oshiro's opinion that sudden, aggressive movements were inappropriate and even potentially dangerous under the circumstances. After nearly three minutes, which seemed to stretch into hours of interminable waiting, the ship finally ceased its forward movement, then paused briefly before extending an array of landing struts. Their smooth motion beneath the hull was accompanied by the unmistakable whine of electric motors, followed shortly thereafter by the same sorts of mechanical clunks and thuds associated with undercarriage operations aboard Fleet's vessels. Strangely, these somewhat familiar sounds had been the first of any sort produced by the visitor. Moments later, the ship touched down lightly onto the concrete landing platform, immediately returning the shipyard to an eerie silence.

Not for the first time this morning, Captain Oshiro wished the alien ship had chosen another location — *any other location* — for their rather dramatic introduction to Terran Fleet Command. *Why haven't they communicated? Were they somehow just preoccupied during the approach and landing?* he wondered, then immediately dismissed the idea as highly unlikely.

"I'm starting to wonder if there's even anyone aboard," Sexton observed over the comlink. "Maybe it's just an ASV of some sort."

Oshiro jumped involuntarily at the renewed sound of Sexton's voice and couldn't help but chuckle at his own response to the odd sense of tension permeating the huge facility. "Could be, sir, but I don't think so. I can't really explain why, but it just doesn't *feel* that way to me, standing here looking at this thing."

"Hmm. Well, in the absence of any hard information, I'd say we should trust your gut for now. What do you think they're up to?"

"Pure speculation, Admiral, but I'd say they must be waiting for something. But until they decide to respond, all I know to do is continue following our standard, first contact protocols."

Oshiro turned at the sound of footsteps, accepting a tablet computer offered by an approaching ensign. With a nod of thanks to the young officer, he glanced quickly through the environmental survey and threat assessment just completed with the help of the facility AI.

"Lisbeth Kistler here," the Chairwoman of TFC's Leadership Council announced as she joined the conference call from the group's meeting chamber. "I apologize for the interruption and don't want our participation to become a distraction, but could someone give us a brief update on the situation?"

"Of course, ma'am," Oshiro replied, then paused to enter a quick series of commands on the tablet, notifying the facility AI that he required its assistance to create an impromptu video presentation over the comlink. A series of green arrows appeared on the screen to direct his attention to the camera best positioned to capture a view of both his position and the alien spacecraft below.

"Good morning everyone," he began, knowing that introductions were unnecessary.

Such an overwhelming display of micromanagement from TFC Headquarters would have been unwelcome, to say the least, under normal circumstances. Today, however, Oshiro was more than happy to oblige the council's request to participate — perhaps not relieving him of responsibility for dealing with the situation, but at least providing some much needed "top cover" in case things went sideways from here.

"As I'm sure you're all aware by now," he continued, noting on his tablet that the video feed was smoothly transitioning from a view of his position on the catwalk to one of the Grey ship below, "the alien craft you see entered the Yucca Mountain Shipyard Facility just over half an hour ago. Although we do not believe our facility AI has been compromised, the ship was somehow able to interface directly with a number of key subsystems. For lack of a better description, this allowed it to simply bypass nearly all of our security and access control protocols."

"It literally just opened the doors on its own and came right in?" an unidentified male voice from the Leadership Council asked, incredulous.

"I apologize, sir, I couldn't see who asked the question," Oshiro replied, "but, yes, that's exactly what I'm telling you. Now, as tempted as we all might be to liken this feat to some run-of-the-mill security breach, it's important to keep in mind that our three primary shipyards are protected by the most sophisticated physical and cyber security measures ever devised."

"So, clearly, we are dealing with highly advanced intelligence of some sort," Kistler said, shooting a look at the representative from the European Union to indicate she had no intention of allowing the conference to devolve into a debate on the efficacy of TFC security measures.

"That's putting it mildly, ma'am," Vice Admiral Tonya White, Chief of Naval Intelligence, chimed in for the first time from Admiral Sexton's office. "Anyone capable of compromising the access controls at Yucca — and apparently in real-time — would have little difficulty gaining access to any facility and/or computer system on this planet."

"That goes for secure communications as well, does it not?" Admiral Sexton asked.

White paused momentarily to consider the question, then continued slowly, as if carefully choosing her words. "In a manner of speaking, it's all just different degrees of the same thing, if you take my meaning. If sufficient computing power is employed against it, no system is truly secure."

"So they *could* be listening to us right now," Kistler said, thinking aloud.

"Yes, ma'am," White replied, "or perhaps it's more accurate to say that we can't rule out that possibility."

"Alright, I don't want us to go too far down this rabbit hole for now. My immediate — albeit perhaps uninformed — reaction on the subject is that if they are truly that much more advanced than we are, there's not much point worrying about their intentions."

"Since they can clearly do pretty much whatever they like," Sexton said, finishing her thought.

"Precisely. Sorry for the interruption, Captain Oshiro, please continue."

"Yes, ma'am. The alien ship proceeded down the entrance tunnel and emerged into the roundhouse area of the shipyard, then paused for approximately fifteen minutes before entering Berth 10. As was the case with the facility entrance doors, the berth's mooring systems responded to commands from the alien ship, allowing it to raise the landing platform and touch down approximately … three minutes ago."

"And we have been attempting to communicate the entire time?"

"That is correct. Per our standard, first contact protocols, the facility AI has been attempting to establish communications since the craft first arrived. Thus far, there has been no response. I should also point out that right before you joined the conference, I received an initial environmental and threat assessment report. I haven't had the opportunity to read it in detail, of course, but the summary looks like all good news. We have detected no radiation or biological contamination of any kind thus far. We also haven't noted the electronic signatures of any known weapon systems, although I suppose that's not surprising given how little we know about this species."

"And by 'this species,' you're referring to the so-called 'Greys,' correct?"

"We have no way of knowing for sure, ma'am. But based on the configuration of the ship and comparisons with certain … *relics* in TFC's possession, the facility AI indicates a greater than eighty-seven percent probability that that's exactly who we're dealing with."

"Thank you, Captain Oshiro. With any luck, they will get around to answering us shortly. Otherwise, we may have to send you down there with a pipe wrench to bang on the hull."

"The environment here at the shipyard is a little … tense at the moment, ma'am. If they don't respond soon,

I'll be happy to volunteer to do that, just to break the silence."

TFS *Fugitive, Sol System*
(2.3x10^5 km from Earth)

Less than forty-five minutes after departing the outskirts of the Legara system, TFS *Fugitive* reached her designated arrival point with a muted flash of grayish-white light. Just as it had on the outbound leg of its journey, the small ship had traversed the intervening twelve hundred and fifty light years — nearly twelve *quadrillion* kilometers — as if it were little more than a short errand to the other side of town, once again safely returning her crew to the vicinity of their own homeworld.

"Third and final C-Jump complete, Captain," Ensign Fisher reported. "All systems in the green with the exception of the main gun. The ship remains at General Quarters for combat operations, Condition 1. C-Jump range now 9.3 light years and increasing rapidly. Low-observable systems remain online with three one minutes remaining at current power levels. Sublight engines online, we are free to maneuver."

"Thank you, Ensign," Prescott replied. "I want us to maintain line of sight with the Yucca Mountain Shipyard at all times, but I'm not comfortable taking the ship down into the planet's gravity well to an elliptical geosynchronous orbit until we have a better idea what's going on. Any obstacles that might prevent us from station keeping at this range?"

"No, sir. Well … none that we can't dodge, anyway."

"Good, let's do it."

"Aye, sir."

"Tactical?"

"Nothing unexpected so far, Captain," Lieutenant Lau said with a flurry of keystrokes as he struggled to take in the massive amount of data being presented on his console. "All eleven ships currently assigned to the Home Fleet are accounted for. Argus is showing no other Fleet vessels within five three light years of our current position, but it looks like Admiral Patterson's ten-ship task force is en route from Sajeth Collective space. Assuming they continue executing one-hundred-light-year C-Jumps with thirty minutes of dwell time between each, they should arrive in less than three hours."

"Understood, thank you. I'm guessing we'll hear from the admiral shortly."

"Captain, the Guardian is asking to speak with you again," Lieutenant Dubashi reported from the Comm/Nav console.

"I'm not surprised, but he'll have to wait just a moment. See if you can get us an update from someone on site at Yucca Mountain. In addition, I suspect Captain Oshiro's people will have a vidcon in progress with TFC Headquarters. Fleet Control obviously knows we have arrived, but the participants on that call will most likely be too preoccupied to patch us in. Please see what you can do to get us an invite."

"Aye, sir, that shouldn't be a problem."

"Thank you. In the meantime, I guess you can go ahead and put the Guardian through."

Seconds later, the familiar chime indicating an active "GCS-comm" connection had been established sounded from the overhead speakers.

"Prescott here," he said without preamble. "What's on your mind, Griffin."

"Captain, as I indicated earlier, we must treat the arrival of this alien vessel as hostile until proven otherwise. It is imperative that I be released from your ship's hangar bay so that I may assist you in dealing with this situation, as required."

Prescott had assumed Griffin might make such a request — if not a demand — as soon as they returned to Earth. Until now, however, he had not had a spare moment to consider the repercussions of allowing the Guardian Cultivation System free reign to react to the alien ship. Upon further reflection, he realized that keeping the GCS sequestered within the confines of TFS *Fugitive's* cargo bay for as long as possible had a number of potential advantages. In particular, it provided Fleet with the opportunity to deal with an already fluid and unpredictable situation without the added complication of "third party" interference. The only real question was how willing the Guardian would be to comply with his wishes and remain aboard. Clearly, the GCS was fully capable of making its exit at any time — with or without the *Fugitive* remaining in one piece.

"I appreciate your sense of urgency, Griffin. But thus far, the ship has given us no indication of hostile intent. We are in the process of assessing the situation and coordinating with Fleet personnel on the surface. For the moment, I would like to ask you to remain here with us. Releasing you —"

"Captain, I must insist that you open your cargo bay door and allow me to exit —"

"You absolutely may *not* insist," Prescott counter-interrupted in what he hoped the GCS would recognize as an authoritative, but not insulting, tone. "You are a guest aboard this ship — *my* ship — and from the time you agreed to assist with our mission to Legara, you became a de facto member of my crew."

"Am I to conclude that I am also your de facto prisoner, Captain?"

"Not at all. But you are, nevertheless, subject to my orders, which are driven primarily by operational requirements. Before volunteering for the Legara mission, you told Admiral Sexton you wished to be considered an ally, fully independent from the Pelaran Alliance. I presume this is still the case, is it not?"

"Yes, of course. And at the moment, I believe I can best be of service if you will allow me to leave your ship."

"Noted. And I will be happy to do so when I deem the timing to be appropriate. Look, Griffin, I'm sure you can appreciate that, as captain, I am not in the habit of explaining my orders. But Fleet very much appreciates your assistance with the Krayleck Empire, and it is our desire to continue to — for lack of a better term — *cultivate* our relationship with you. Over time, we will earn one another's trust. Do you agree?"

"I do indeed."

"That being the case, I need you to be patient and trust my judgement while we assess the situation on the surface. Extracting you from our cargo bay will take time — time during which we will be unable to respond to whatever events may transpire with the alien ship. We may well need your help, and having you aboard gives us the option to have you accompany us if we need to pursue the craft when it departs. That's the best I can do for now. We will update you as more information becomes available. Prescott out."

Drawing in a deep breath in an attempt to refocus his mind, Prescott glanced at his first officer and shook his head.

"You were more patient than I would have been," Reynolds commented with a raised eyebrow.

"Mm hmm, maybe so. But it occurred to me we wouldn't be much help in dealing with the aliens on the surface if the one in the back of our ship decided to blast its way out of the flight deck and then shortly thereafter attacked the Yucca Mountain Shipyard."

"Well, there is that, I guess. In any event, while the two of you were having your chat, we received Fleet-wide Flash traffic from Admiral Sexton's office at TFCHQ. There's really nothing new other than the ship finally deciding to land in Berth 10. Captain Oshiro's people are still attempting to communicate, but there has been no response so far."

During the brief trip home from Legara, both Prescott and Reynolds had worked frantically between C-Jumps to gather what little information had been available concerning the arrival of the alien vessel. Although its actions thus far were troubling on a number of levels, both officers were relieved to hear that it did not appear to be outwardly hostile and had taken no aggressive actions while they were en route.

"Sir, we have received permission to join the Yucca Mountain vidcon," Dubashi reported from the Comm/Nav console. "There are quite a few attendees, including Admirals Sexton and White, along with most of the Leadership Council. Stand by one, sir ... we are also receiving a separate hail from the Yucca Mountain Shipyard."

"Captain Oshiro?" Prescott asked.

"No, sir. He says his name is ..." Dubashi paused, knowing that what she had been about to say would sound wholly ridiculous. "One moment, Captain."

"Is there a problem, Lieutenant?"

"I'm sorry, sir. I was attempting to authenticate the source of the signal, but I am unable to do so at the moment. The sender claims to be one of the aliens aboard the Yucca Mountain ship. He says his name is 'Rick.'"

"Rick? Seriously? That's all he said?"

"Yes, sir. The hail is text-only at this point, but he is offering a vidcon signal. I did ask for a confirmation of his name, but he just repeated the same message as before."

"Is our AI handling the translation, or theirs?" Prescott asked, simultaneously recognizing the familiar sound of Commander Reynolds stifling a chuckle from the seat beside him.

"Theirs," Dubashi replied, grateful for the opportunity to turn back around in her chair to check her Comm console once again.

"Ah, I see. Probably just some kind of translation hiccup then."

"Maybe so, Captain, but Yucca has been transmitting lexical data since they arrived. So either they already incorporated the data into their comm system —"

"Or they had it before they got here."

"Yes, sir."

"It's fine, Lieutenant, let's not get weirded out just because we've got ourselves an unknown alien who prefers to be on a first name basis."

"Do you think we should respond to his hail with most of Fleet's leadership already sitting on Oshiro's call?" Reynolds asked.

Prescott turned back to his XO, paused to consider her question for a moment, then shrugged his shoulders noncommittally before continuing. "I don't see why not. For whatever reason, we seem to have become the preferred point of contact for introductions to new species. Besides, in my mind, TFC's big picture goal is to make contact with the aliens and determine their intentions, regardless of who from the organization does the talking. Don't you agree?"

"I suppose you could make that argument," she sighed. "Frankly, under the circumstances, I'd love it if they would just talk to Admiral Sexton or even someone from the Leadership Council. But since they've ignored all prior attempts at communication and chosen instead to contact us directly ..."

"They did indeed. And given their timing, I think we have to assume they intentionally delayed making contact until we arrived."

"Lovely — and there's that vaguely nauseous feeling again."

"It'll be fine, Commander. I think we can also assume they would have already started shooting if that had been their intention. If our new friend ... 'Rick,' I guess, asks us something we aren't comfortable answering, we'll just have to get back to him later. Lieutenant Dubashi, please let Captain Oshiro know what we're about to do, then patch his call in with ours. As soon as you have them online, open a vidcon with the alien ship."

"Aye, sir."

It took Dubashi only a few moments to accomplish this task, after which a chime from the Comm/Nav console indicated that Tom Prescott and crew were once again about to become the first Humans to formally greet a new alien species.

"On-screen, please," Prescott ordered, not waiting for Dubashi to prompt him. In stark contrast to previous first contacts, the face that now appeared on the view screen, while undeniably alien, was perfectly familiar to everyone on the bridge. In fact, the creature's appearance — huge, oval-shaped eyes, diminutive facial features, and grey-colored skin — immediately struck Prescott as stereotypical almost to the point of being comical.

"Well, I'll be damned," he heard Ensign Fisher mutter under his breath.

"Hello," Prescott began, surprised that he could feel the hairs on the back of his neck stand on end as he stared into the Grey's depthless, black eyes. "I am Captain Tom Prescott of the Terran Fleet Command starship *Theseus*."

"*Fugitive*," the alien replied, the merest hint of a smile playing at the corners of its small mouth.

"I'm sorry?"

"The name of your ship is TFS *Fugitive*, right? You said '*Theseus,*' but I'm pretty sure you broke that one. Hey, look, we sympathize. Miguel over there breaks stuff all the time," the alien said, then leaned to his left to ensure the camera could capture what was behind him. "Say hello, Miguel," he called, apparently without taking his enormous eyes off the camera.

In the background was a large, comfortable-looking chair facing a bank of what must have been workstations of some sort. Upon prompting from the first alien, a grey hand with long, spindly fingers — presumably belonging to "Miguel" — rose above the back of the chair, waved briefly, then disappeared once again from view.

"Don't mind him, he really hates handling much of anything that's not part of his daily routine, so he leaves all of this, uh, formal stuff to me."

On *Fugitive's* bridge, the first six Human beings to "formally" participate in the long-anticipated arrival of "Grey aliens" offered nothing more than blank, dumbfounded stares in reply.

After several seconds of silence, the first alien took it upon himself to restart the conversation with his stunned hosts. "So … as I said in my earlier message, my name is Rick," he began again, his ship's AI prompting the camera to zoom out so that he could tap the embroidered, rectangular name tag above his left breast pocket for emphasis. To Prescott and crew, the alien's uniform — if it could be referred to as such — looked more like a set of dark blue coveralls of the type often associated with auto mechanics.

"I, uh …" Prescott finally resumed, his mind still racing to process everything he was seeing on the view screen. "This is my first officer, Commander Sally Reynolds," he finally said, hoping the introduction would provide him with a few desperately needed seconds to recover his wits.

"Hi, Rick," she said as if chatting comfortably with a friend of a friend she had just met at a weekend social gathering. "I assume that's not really your name, though, right?"

The alien made a brief chirping sound that she took to be a chuckle before answering. "There's a classic animated comedy bit where a Human asks that very question of the first alien she meets. He responds that to pronounce his name correctly would require him to pull out her tongue."

"That would probably be *The Simpsons*," she replied without hesitation, "and I'm guessing it was one of the Halloween episodes, since they always seemed to include aliens. That show is beyond ancient but still has quite a cult following since it was the only series in the history of television to air for more than a century. You can still access the reruns online, believe it or not."

In her peripheral vision, Reynolds couldn't help noticing the "get to the point" expression now clouding her captain's face. "Anyway … I don't mind telling you this conversation seems exceedingly weird to me so far," she concluded.

Rick repeated his chirping sound several times, then tilted his head inquisitively before responding. "Weird based on what, exactly? Your own preconceived notions of how first contact situations are supposed to unfold? I'm sure you've guessed by now that the reason we chose to speak with you rather than your colleagues down here on the surface is that — albeit largely by circumstance — your crew is the only group of Humans that has amassed some experience in meeting new species for the first time. Incidentally, how many species have you encountered thus far, Commander Reynolds?"

"Including you? Five, I think … six if we count both the Guardian spacecraft and the Pelaran we met as independent, sentient life forms."

Reynolds had always assumed from the many descriptions of the Grey alien species she had read over the years that their faces would be largely inexpressive, but now recognized this notion to be completely inaccurate. Something about the way she answered Rick's question had caused an immediate change in his face she recognized as a troubled expression — almost as if he had found her response to be either inaccurate or disagreeable in some fashion. Whatever it was, he had apparently decided to file it away for another time so that they might continue with the current thread of their discussion.

"By convention, we normally include so-called nonbiological intelligence in a separate category, although it can become quite difficult to classify which ones are biological, let alone which ones are intelligent. If you're interested, we have a great deal of information we can share along these lines. It might surprise you to learn, for example, that there are …" Rick paused to call over his shoulder, "hey Miguel, how many planets with advanced, sentient lifeforms in this galaxy?"

Somewhere offscreen, "Miguel" could be heard mumbling something unintelligible that his ship's translation AI chose to ignore. "Forty-two thousand six hundred and ninety-three," Rick repeated after a brief pause. "That's just the biological ones theoretically capable of eventually developing interstellar travel. Fortunately for all of us, I suppose, the vast majority of them never actually do. My point is that there is no such thing as a 'normal' first contact. And no matter how you expect the situation to unfold when you meet a new species — even one such as ours with which you already have a degree of familiarity — you'll be wrong ... every single time."

"I'm sure that's good advice, thank you," Reynolds replied, pausing to prompt her captain to take over the conversation once again. While Rick had been speaking, she realized with some alarm that she might have already divulged classified information, or, at the very least, information closely associated with things she had no business discussing with an alien species they knew very little about. Strangely, there was something about the Greys — even if it was nothing more than a built-in assumption of how advanced they were — that made the idea of having anything less than open, unguarded conversation seem a bit absurd. *Is it even possible for us to reveal anything they don't already know?* she wondered, while simultaneously admonishing herself to get a better handle on what was coming out of her own mouth.

"Forgive me for asking this," Prescott finally chimed in, "and I know there are far more important questions on the minds of our leadership team who are monitoring this conversation ..."

"They'll get their turn, Captain. Keep in mind that we called *you*, not them. As you might imagine, Miguel and

I have done this kind of thing many, many times, and our people have been doing it for ..." Rick paused as if considering how much information *he* was willing to share at the moment. "Let's just say we've been handling what you call first contact situations for a *very* long time. And after all that experience, you know what we've found works best? Simple conversation. That's it. We start a dialogue, we ask questions, and if everything goes well, we have a laugh or two. On the occasions we've tried to make the process more complicated or formal than that, things never seem to work out as well. So let's hear it, Captain Prescott, what's your first question?"

"Alright then, what's the deal with the coveralls?"

"Oh, God, you thought we'd be mother-naked, didn't you?"

"Well, I ... yeah, I guess I did," Prescott nodded with a candid smile. "Come to think of it, I don't think I've ever seen a depiction of your species where you were wearing clothes of any kind."

"Right, and we also weren't 'depicted' as having any sort of, shall we say, *equipment* either, were we?"

"Not that I recall, no."

"*That,* Captain Prescott, is an unfortunate, but somewhat typical example of the strangely misguided sense of humor long shared by many in our science officer corps. Although I'm sure Miguel here would be more than happy to take sole credit for this particular example, those of his ilk have been perpetrating this kind of nonsense for a very long time. It's a bit hard to explain, but most Human encounters over the years with what you have generically referred to as the "Greys" did not involve actual flesh and blood members of our species."

"So what are we talking about, then? Droids? Some sort of holographic projection?"

"I'm afraid without a common frame of reference, what they are is quite difficult to describe. But from your perspective, thinking of them as a type of droid seems reasonable enough. Our ship has a variety of missions, Captain, the vast majority of which are completely automated. Miguel and I are mostly aboard just to monitor the systems and fix anything that breaks. We're glorified custodians when it comes right down to it. Anyway, on occasion, certain protocols do require physical contact with Humans, but we are strictly forbidden from participating directly. There's only the two of us, so exposing ourselves to terrified Terrans twice our size would be far too risky. Oh, and the genderless thing ... I don't even know *what* to tell you about that. Somewhere along the way, someone apparently decided it would be hilarious if we were naked, but I suppose making us anatomically correct must have crossed some kind of line in their opinion."

Behind Rick, a steady stream of enthusiastic, mirth-filled chirping sounds could be heard emanating from the back of Miguel's chair. Rick paused for a moment, slowly shaking his head with a surprisingly clear look of disapproval on his face.

"Anyway, back to your original question," he continued. "I doubt my explanation of our coveralls will make much sense to you either. Let's just say ships assigned to the same types of missions as ours have a tendency to encounter quite a few Humans who wear them. Over time, it became a sort of running joke until, at some point, I guess someone actually tried them on and realized how great they are. Since then, one of the first things we do when we begin a new mission series is to, uh … *borrow* a few pairs. You know, like a souvenir of sorts."

"They must have stolen them off a pretty short mechanic," Reynolds commented under her breath.

"Oh, good one, Commander. Ten minutes in and we've already progressed to height jokes. I'll have you know that some of us exceed a meter and a half with our boots on … but, yeah, I guess the real Rick and Miguel must have been pretty short, although we didn't have the pleasure of meeting either of them. Anyway, blue coveralls with embroidered name tags have more or less become our unofficial uniform."

Both officers stared back at the alien for a long moment, neither one quite sure where to take the conversation next.

"Seriously?" Reynolds finally asked, glancing first at her captain and then back up at the screen. "Quite a bit of what you've said so far makes it seem like you guys are just yanking our chain for some reason."

"Relax, Commander, we're just having a conversation, right? How else are we supposed to get acquainted with each other? Surely you don't think everything we talk about has to be some sort of dire warning about how your world is in imminent danger," Rick said, glancing thoughtfully off to the side for a moment. "Although, now that I say that, your world actually is, but more on that later."

"Wait," Prescott began, "what are you —"

"Look, I'll be happy to answer this or any other question I'm allowed to answer ... which, it turns out, is almost anything you're likely to ask. But I should go ahead and warn you up front that every question we answer will probably generate a great many more. There actually *is* a purpose to our visit, however, and at some point, we do have a few more serious items we must address during our time together. We'll get to all that stuff when we have all the right people in the room. Sound good?"

"Uh, sure," Prescott replied noncommittally, struggling to come to grips with the surreal nature of their encounter thus far.

"By the way, I'm sure Captain Oshiro is listening. We have received the information he's been transmitting, so there's no need to keep sending it."

"Thanks, I'm sure he heard."

"I think you're right because the transmissions just stopped," Rick nodded. "We'll have the opportunity to exchange additional data at some point, but we have been familiar with Earth's languages for a very long time, so there was really nothing new in the lexical data Captain Oshiro provided. In fact, although you are hearing a translation of our own language at the moment, Miguel and I both speak passable English ... enough to order a cheeseburger or find a bathroom, at least."

Prescott was about to move on to his next question when the implications of an extraterrestrial species learning a single language from a planet with nearly seven thousand caused his mind to demand additional explanation.

"Are you saying that, from among Earth's many languages, the two of you know *only* English?" he asked.

Rick offered a look that bordered on a sympathetic smile in response. "Now you're forcing me to sound like I'm being boastful, which I have to tell you makes me a little uncomfortable. But since you asked, Miguel and I can speak approximately twenty-five hundred Human languages native to Earth. We could probably understand most of the rest on the fly and learn to speak them pretty quickly, if required."

"Without any sort of augmentation? How is that possible? Also, as impressive and perhaps flattering as that is, why bother learning so many languages when you have artificial intelligence available to handle communication?"

"You see?" Rick said with his now familiar chuckle. "This is what I was referring to when I said every answer I provide will result in a number of new questions. If you want to communicate with a member of another species — I mean *really* communicate and learn who they are — there's no substitute for having a face to face conversation in their native language. And, no, we don't require any technological 'augmentation' per se to comprehend most Human languages. But, in all fairness, you could say we were purpose-built for the tasks associated with what you might refer to as long-duration space exploration — enhanced language comprehension being one of those, of course."

"You're saying you were genetically engineered for this purpose, then?"

"We were indeed. Originally, our scientists selected for traits believed to offer the greatest advantages based on the technology we had at our disposal at the time — language cognition, resistance to radiation, smaller size, increased strength and stamina, and reduced muscle atrophy in microgravity environments, to name a few. Our ships and other related technologies have improved now to the point where our genetic advantages are no longer as necessary as they once were. These days, in fact, there are quite a few different vessel types tasked with missions very similar to ours. But, generally speaking, ships with what you Terrans might refer to as a 'saucer' or 'disk' configuration are still crewed solely by members of our subspecies."

"We have referred to your kind by a variety of names over the years," Prescott continued, "but the one that seems to be the most common is simply the 'Greys.' Not very original, I'm afraid."

"Yeah, we love that one, as you can imagine. Descriptive … yet vaguely racist."

"Right," Prescott replied, chuckling once again at Rick's odd attempt at humor. "So what is the appropriate name for your species?"

"I could answer that one in a variety of ways, but the simplest and most accurate response is … well … Human."

Chapter 2

TFS Fugitive, Sol System
(2.3x10^5 km from Earth)

Prescott stared at the creature displayed on his bridge view screen through narrowed eyes and wondered if he had just heard another example of its rather eccentric sense of humor. While certainly humanoid, the features associated with the "Greys" had represented nothing less than Humanity's ideal of everything that was quintessentially *alien* for over three hundred years. Even with TFC ships now encountering new species on a regular basis, if you asked any Earth-bound Human to draw an extraterrestrial, they would invariably come up with something very similar to the creature currently occupying the center of TFS *Fugitive's* view screen.

"Perhaps I misunderstood your meaning. Are you saying that you and I are examples of the same species? If so, I'm afraid you've lost me."

"Yeah, I thought I might. Miguel and I are members of a genetically engineered subspecies, but we're still every bit as Human as you are. Although there are a few scientific names that describe us in technical terms, we are not different enough to be considered a separate species. In fact, where we're from, it would be considered a form of racial discrimination to place us in a separate category from other Humans."

"I'm afraid I may still not be following you. Are you saying that separate lines of Humans arose independently in multiple star systems?"

"Nope. There's just one genetic line and just one species, Captain. You, me, Commander Reynolds, and, surprisingly, even Miguel are all proud members."

Prescott stared for a long moment into the depthless eyes of the decidedly inhuman-looking creature, unsure if he believed even half of what it was telling him.

"Okay," he continued, drawing out the word, "but it's my understanding that your species ... pardon me ... *our* species is not even from this galaxy. If that's the case, does that not also imply —"

"Well done, Captain, now you're catching on. *Our* species did *not* arise on Earth, nor is it originally from this galaxy. Without a doubt, this bit of knowledge implies a whole bunch of things your scientists will be exploring for centuries to come. As for what Miguel and I are doing here now, one of our primary missions is to monitor — and, when necessary, make corrections to ensure the success of — the largest colonization program ever undertaken. Well ... I suppose I should qualify that statement by saying it's the largest as far as we know. Just to give you an idea of the scale of this effort, out of those forty-two thousand or so relatively advanced civilizations I mentioned earlier, nearly a third of them are Human. Most of those worlds, like yours, were colonized hundreds of thousands of years ago. So, fortunately, they no longer require the sorts of active management and genetic intervention they once did."

"But you're saying the original examples of *Homo sapiens* were brought here from your world ... in the Andromeda galaxy?"

"In a manner of speaking, yes, but the type of long-range colonization program we're talking about here is probably nothing like what you might expect. Without going into too much detail, the ideal candidate worlds already possess a breeding stock of genetically similar hominids. We introduce groups of what we refer to as *Homo sapiens* "primitives" — just slightly more advanced than the native populations — at key locations around the planet. Over time, targeted interbreeding and the occasional genomic tweaking does the rest."

"Oh my God, you really *do* abduct people," Reynolds gasped.

"That's not a term we would use, of course, but, yes, maintaining the species within acceptable genetic boundaries does occasionally require active sampling of the population."

"Here's one for you, then. If you're sampling a cross-section of our population, why does it always seem like the people you abduct tend to be from the, um … shallow end of the gene pool? People who claim to have abduction experiences seem to be the same type of people who get interviewed after a tornado careens through the middle of their trailer park."

"A little elitist, don't you think, Commander?"

"Just calling 'em like I see 'em, Rick."

"Right, well, I suppose there actually is a kernel of truth behind your question. As I said, we sometimes introduce minor changes to correct for abnormalities in the genome. As you might expect, genetic irregularities requiring our attention tend to be associated with a set of specific characteristics. Unfortunately, these same characteristics have a high correlation with the types of socio-economic demographics to which you refer … but shame on you nonetheless."

"Sorry, I'm just saying …"

"I must admit, however, that since one of our obvious goals is to avoid drawing attention to the fact that members of a population are being temporarily … *detained* for experimental purposes —"

"I'm pretty sure abducted is the right word," Reynolds interrupted. "Kidnapped would also be appropriate."

"Tomato, tomahto. As I was saying, the Human subjects to which you refer are generally not taken as seriously as someone of a higher social status might be. The leader of a country, the CEO of a major company, or a high-ranking military officer, for example, would likely garner quite a bit more attention if they reported interacting with one of our ships."

"And if you determine something about our genome isn't to your liking, you feel justified just going right ahead and making changes without our knowledge, right? Doesn't that seem a little unethical to you?"

"At the risk of sounding even more high-handed than your earlier 'trailer park' comment, the ethical considerations surrounding an intergalactic colonization program are far beyond the scope of our conversation here today, Commander. But consider this question for a moment: Is it unethical for a parent to vaccinate their child against certain diseases without their knowledge and/or understanding? I can assure you we fully understand how learning about our active participation in Human health on your world for the first time can be … *disconcerting,* to say the least. But now that you know, we will begin the process of sharing more information about what we do."

"But surely it's not possible to 'tweak,' as you say, a population of twelve billion Humans," Prescott interjected.

"Ha," Rick squeaked in reply. "It's not nearly as difficult as you might imagine, Captain, and it's absolutely necessary. 'Genetic drift,' you see, is a phenomenon that occurs naturally among all populations. Consider, however, that it is in the best interests of Humans everywhere for all of us to remain genetically similar enough to maintain our identity as a single species. If nothing else, think about it from a purely practical standpoint. Medical advances that improve health and quality of life on a single world can ultimately do the same across tens of thousands, for example. As I mentioned before, our monitoring and intervention systems are highly automated. When sampling indicates the need for a modification, we can usually deliver the required genetic material via the introduction of either natural or synthetic vectors. In fact, we often use a form of the virus you Terrans still refer to as the common cold."

"I'm feeling pretty sick right now myself," Reynolds mumbled.

"Incidentally, our sampling program also allows us to gather a tremendous amount of additional data that is used for the general benefit of the species," Rick continued enthusiastically. "The planet's size and/or population really doesn't matter that much. These same techniques have been used on worlds much larger than Terra. In fact, they were originally pioneered in our native star system of Daylea."

"Your homeworld is larger than Earth, then?" Prescott asked.

"Yes, approximately thirty percent larger. We were also blessed with two even larger but still habitable planets in our system. This provided us with a number of distinct advantages — in our early technological development and ultimately in our ability to initiate colonization efforts on an unprecedented scale."

"But isn't Andromeda significantly larger than our galaxy? Why bother coming here in the first place?"

"That's a valid question, Captain, but a difficult one to answer without a great deal of explanation. At the risk of offering up a cliché, the innate Human drive for exploration, discovery, and expansion is no accident. Those traits, like so many other things you will learn about in time, are genetically hard-coded every bit as much as our having two arms and one heart. As an example, referring back to your questions regarding all of the languages we speak, you might be surprised to learn that much of that is preprogrammed as well. Even when Human civilizations are allowed to develop in complete isolation, the languages that 'spontaneously' develop always follow a set of recognizable patterns. In many cases, the dominant languages end up being almost identical. What you refer to as English, Spanish, and Mandarin Chinese — with a few minor variations, of course — are spoken on thousands of Human worlds."

Prescott looked off to one side while working to refocus his mind. The conversation with the Greys thus far (racist or not, he could think of no better way of referring to them at the moment), while fascinating, had accomplished little other than confirming they did not appear to be hostile. From a practical standpoint, he knew there was a lengthy list of items Admiral Sexton and the Leadership Council would want addressed as quickly as possible. Chief among these were determining the aliens' immediate intentions, the purpose behind their visit, and any potential threats their presence might create for Fleet and the Earth itself. At a minimum, the situation with the Guardian would need to be dealt with — hopefully in a manner avoiding a confrontation between technologically superior civilizations with TFC caught in the crossfire.

"Well … Rick, you've given us a great deal to think about, but I'm sure our leadership would appreciate our spending some time discussing the particulars of your visit. So, if you will forgive me for sounding inhospitable, why are you here, and what are your plans?"

"Ah, yes, of course. We did enter your military facility without an invitation, after all. First — and I'm sure foremost in the minds of your leadership team — you have nothing to fear from us. In fact, this ship, although equipped with some basic defensive systems, does not even meet our organization's technical definition for being considered 'armed,'" Rick said, supplying "air quotes" with his long fingers as he finished his sentence. "The timing of our arrival here today was due in large part to the absence of the Pelaran Guardian spacecraft. Otherwise, our arrival would have certainly attracted its attention. The last thing we wanted was to risk a confrontation that could endanger your ships or your people on the surface."

"We certainly appreciate that," Prescott replied with a wan smile. "As I'm sure you are aware, we currently have the Guardian docked inside our cargo bay. I'll be perfectly honest and tell you we have no idea if it has managed to compromise our communications or other systems' security measures, so it is entirely possible it has been monitoring our conversation."

"Not to worry, Captain, it hasn't. Your most recently deployed encryption algorithms are quite good and should remain well beyond its capabilities for the foreseeable future. So, as far as the Pelarans are concerned, you can remain confident in your information security. In the spirit of full disclosure, however, I will also tell you that *we* can and do monitor all forms of communication. As alarming as that may sound, it shouldn't surprise you, nor should it cause you to alter your operations in any way. As your scientists and engineers will tell you, system security is largely a function of your rivals' available computing power."

In Admiral Sexton's office at TFCHQ, the Chief of Naval Intelligence nodded soberly across the table at her Commander-in-Chief, arching her eyebrows to deliver her best "I told you so" expression.

"I see," Prescott replied. "I suppose we would do the same if our roles were reversed."

"Well, *yeah*," Rick laughed, "obviously you would, since we're essentially you with better equipment at our disposal. Don't worry about it, Captain. I didn't share that information to somehow intimidate you, I shared it so that we could start earning one another's trust."

"I understand. Thank you for telling us. So how would you like to proceed? I believe you mentioned there are some important items we need to discuss. If you like, we will arrange for you to meet with our Leadership Council as well as members of Terran Fleet Command's Admiralty staff."

"Yes, that seems like a reasonable approach. We will be happy to meet with whomever you think appropriate in due course. But before we do so, we would like to ask that a team from your ship join us aboard our own."

"Aboard *your* ship?" Prescott echoed, immediately wondering if Admirals Patterson and Sexton would ever agree to such a visit. "We certainly appreciate the invitation, but we will, of course, need to clear such a visit through our chain of command. I'm sure Fleet Medical will also require us to take a number of precautions to ensure both our crew and the two of you remain safe. You did say it's just the two of you aboard, correct? Your ship seems quite large for such a small crew."

"Yes, unfortunately, it's just the two of us, and *one* of us snores so loudly that there's nowhere aboard isolated enough to escape the noise. As I mentioned, our missions tend to be multifaceted and fairly long in duration. This old tub's not a commissioned naval vessel, Captain. It's actually more like a cross between a privately contracted science vessel and a privateer … in a manner of speaking, that is. Accordingly, she's stuffed to the gills with equipment, so there's precious little room for biological occupants. We do, however, have sufficient facilities to host a few visitors if we keep the list of attendees to a minimum. If possible, we would like you to bring Commanders Reynolds and Logan as well as Dr. Chen. Please ask her to bring basic equipment to conduct a physical examination and collect a blood sample from Miguel and me. It's important for your Fleet Medical personnel to be able to validate that we are who we say we are."

"Very well," Prescott replied, doing his best to ignore the vague sense of irritation he felt each time Rick demonstrated a level of familiarity that no one outside TFC should possess, let alone a Grey alien. "Once we're finished here," he continued, "I'll make the appropriate arrangements and get back to you as quickly as possible."

"Thank you, Captain Prescott. The discussion we mentioned and the primary reason we have chosen to visit you now is to ask that you consider undertaking a relief mission of sorts. I will provide additional details when we meet in person, but there is another Human planet in need of our immediate assistance. Due to an odd set of circumstances, Earth's forces are the only ones capable of providing aid. I'm sure that sounds ridiculously contrived, but I think you will agree that Terran Fleet Command is uniquely positioned once I brief you on the situation. And without your help, the civilization in question — easily one of the most accomplished in the history of our species — will almost certainly be lost."

"I'm confident we will get you an audience with our Leadership Council. Ultimately, it will be up to them to decide if it's in our best interest to become involved. Unfortunately, during our brief time as an interstellar civilization, we seem to have a knack for being unintentionally drawn into multiple conflicts at one time."

"Oh, you're already involved with this one as well, you just haven't realized it yet. The Human civilization to which I refer is one with which you have already become somewhat familiar. Although you have never met one of them in person, I think you'll agree they have done quite a lot for Terra already. They generally refer to themselves as the Pelarans."

"You're saying the Pelarans need *our* help," Reynolds said, phrasing her question as a statement tinged with equal parts suspicion and sarcasm.

"They do indeed, Commander. For all intents and purposes, their homeworld is under siege — and has been for a very long time, in fact. Incidentally, I believe you encountered someone earlier today who identified himself as a Regional Envoy of the Pelaran Alliance. For now, I'll simply repeat my earlier statement that you have not yet met an actual Pelaran and leave it at that."

Both Prescott and Reynolds stared at the screen in silence for several seconds, neither one knowing precisely how to respond.

"Anyway, I've kept you both long enough," Rick continued, obviously ready to conclude the conversation. "Please make whatever arrangements are necessary and join us at your Yucca Mountain facility. We do ask, however, that you proceed as quickly as possible. Since your Guardian was aware of our arrival in the Terran system, we must assume that others probably are as well. Oh, and I almost forgot to mention that we have another guest aboard our ship who is most anxious to see you. Have a safe trip to the surface."

"Transmission terminated at its source, Captain," Lieutenant Dubashi reported as the window previously displaying Rick's face was once again replaced by a spectacular magnified view of the American Southwest on the bridge view screen. "We're on standby to rejoin Captain Oshiro's vidcon, but not currently transmitting."

"Alright," Prescott said, addressing everyone on the bridge after a brief period of silence, "I'm not sure what to make of *any* of what we just heard, but — fortunately, in this case — none of us is at the top of Fleet's food chain. So the burden of deciding precisely what we should do next rests on the Admiralty staff and the Leadership Council. Commander Reynolds and I will excuse ourselves for a few minutes to rejoin the vidcon with Admiral Sexton, and we'll update all of you on what we're doing as soon as we know something ourselves. In the meantime, Dubashi, please give Commander Logan and Doctor Chen a heads up that we may need both of them to join us for a trip over to the Greys' …"

Prescott hesitated, distracted by the multiple lines of thought running though his mind, each one actively competing for his undivided attention.

"Flying saucer, sir?" Fisher interjected with barely restrained glee.

"Thank you, Ensign. Yes, that's as good a description as any, I guess."

"Aye, sir," Dubashi replied.

"Lieutenant Lau, keep a close eye on Argus and let us know immediately if you notice anything unusual, particularly any signs of our Pelaran friends."

"Aye, sir, will do — assuming we can see them coming, that is," he replied.

"Lieutenant Lee, you have the bridge."

"Aye, sir," Lee replied, excitement registering in his voice as he stood to take his place at one of the Command consoles for the first time.

Before entering the captain's ready room, Reynolds paused to watch the young lieutenant take his seat. Everyone seemed to go through a similar ritual when they sat down in "the big chair" for the first time, their senses taking in the various sensations of the experience while simultaneously comparing it to their preconceived expectations. As Lee settled into the chair and entered his first tentative commands at his touchscreen, he noticed the XO watching him out of the corner of his eye. Looking up, he thought he noticed a passing hint of a smile on her face before it was quickly replaced with a much more serious expression.

"She's still pretty new, Lieutenant. Don't break anything," she said with a quick wink.

"Yes, ma'am," he replied as she turned and left the bridge.

Chapter 3

Legara System Lagrange Point 4
(1250 light years from Earth)

It had already been a long day for the Krayleck captain in command of the weapons platform situated in close proximity to his homeworld of Legara. Although his unit had long referred to themselves as "Defenders of the Guardian," a tour of duty on the station was generally considered a rather cush, noncombat assignment. The Krayleck were, after all, a powerful empire in their own right, and if that fact weren't sufficient to deter any aggressor, they were also backed by the overwhelming might of the Pelaran Alliance, of which they had long been a Regional Partner. So while it was true that the station was tasked with defending high-value military and commercial space assets — including the Krayleck Guardian itself — no one seriously considered an attack on those assets a likely scenario.

All of that had changed just a few hours ago, although the specifics of what had transpired in the Legara system were still not entirely clear. What the captain *did* know was that a small, Terran warship — not much larger than a patrol corvette, but clearly in possession of vastly more firepower and other advanced capabilities — had appeared nearby without warning. Shortly thereafter, it had been fired upon by several ships assigned to the Krayleck "Home Guard." The Terran ship had, of course, returned fire, then disappeared from every sensor the captain had at his disposal, only to reappear moments later in a different location. This cycle had repeated itself several times before the ship finally transitioned to hyperspace and, thankfully, had not returned. As far as he could tell, neither his station nor any of the five Home Guard warships had inflicted any damage whatsoever on the enemy vessel.

Analysis of the Terran attack was still ongoing, but, astoundingly, it appeared the ship had fired only three rounds — undoubtedly kinetic energy penetrators of some sort, traveling at a significant percentage of the speed of light. All three had passed completely through the nearest frigate, then continued on to impact a destroyer, causing catastrophic damage to both. Rescuing the few remaining survivors from the charred hulks of both ships had consumed most of his attention since, but the old captain knew that attempting to prepare for another attack was largely a waste of his time anyway. In his many years of service, he had never encountered, nor yet even heard rumors of ships carrying weapons of such terrifying power. And after two disastrous military encounters with Terran forces, it was clear to him that further confrontation would lead to nothing less than the utter destruction of the Krayleck Empire.

Then there was the Guardian ship. Though always unpredictable, its behavior during the Terran incursion was strange indeed. The GCS had made no attempt to engage the enemy ship, even after its attack on Krayleck forces. *What good is a "guardian" that lacks a fundamental understanding of what it means to "guard" something?* he wondered. To top it all off, immediately before the Terran vessel had departed the area, their own Guardian spacecraft had done the same. Inexplicably, just a few minutes later but well after all hostilities had concluded, the Krayleck Guardian had returned. Now that he had a few moments to consider the situation, the captain wondered if they had all just witnessed the AI-equivalent of cowardice followed by desertion, or, worse yet, some sort of collusion with enemy forces.

"Contact," a young lieutenant called from a nearby Tactical console.

"Is it the Terran ship?"

"No, sir. It is roughly the same size, but our sensors are having less difficulty tracking it. One moment, Captain, the ship is transmitting Pelaran identification codes … validated, sir. The vessel is of Pelaran origin."

"Friendly or not, this area is currently considered an active combat zone with ongoing search and rescue operations underway. We must determine its intentions immediately. Comm?"

"Aye, sir, hailing now."

The largest view screen in the weapons platform's command section now displayed a zoomed-in, light-amplified image of the Pelaran ship. Its rakish, fighter-like lines actually did resemble the previous Terran vessel in some respects as it banked to port and accelerated rapidly away in the direction of the Guardian spacecraft. The Krayleck captain, for his part, stared impassively at the screen, patiently awaiting a response to his hail. Inwardly, however, he was irritated at his own sense of relief that the ship on the screen was Pelaran, rather than Terran.

"No response to our hails, Captain," the communications officer reported.

"Understood. You may continue your hails, but it would not surprise me if they do not bother to respond. Per the Alliance charter, the Pelarans are allowed unrestricted access to their own ships, including the Guardian. But I believe we can safely assume this visit has something to do with what transpired here this morning. To my knowledge, they have never before sent one of their ships into the Legara system other than the GCS itself."

Minutes later, the new Pelaran ship had narrowed the distance to the Krayleck Guardian to within twenty meters, aligning the two vessels' hulls with one another as if it intended to execute an EVA servicing mission of some sort.

"The Pelaran vessel has responded to our hails, Captain, but did not choose to open a channel. The response is text-only, sir, and reads as follows: 'We require the use of your GCS unit for a mission of grave importance to the Alliance. The anticipated duration of this mission is less than one week, after which the system will be serviced and returned to this location to continue its service to the Krayleck Empire. Rest assured we will be monitoring activity in the vicinity of the Legara system and will render aid in the event of another incursion from Terran or other hostile forces. The Alliance recognizes and honors your service as a Regional Partner. Respectfully, Verge Tahiri - Regional Envoy, Pelaran Alliance.'"

On the view screen, the space surrounding both the Pelaran vessel and the Guardian spacecraft seemed to distort momentarily before both ships disappeared in a single flash of blue light. The Krayleck captain continued to stare thoughtfully at the screen for several seconds, his mouthparts dripping brown liquid into the metal grate covering the floor of the command section. Although he remained silent, a long stream of expletives unique to his species streamed through his mind, followed by a solemn oath in the name of his chosen deity that he would retire from active duty service at the first opportunity.

Earth, Terran Fleet Command Headquarters
(Office of the Chairwoman, TFC Leadership Council)

"It's out of the question," Lisbeth Kistler said flatly as she stood staring out the large windows that formed one of the walls of her office. "These ... 'Greys,' or whatever the hell they are — I'm not sure I'm buying into the notion that they're genetically modified Humans, by the way — have already admitted they've been abducting our people for ... well, forever. Regardless of whether or not that's true, I'd like someone to explain to me how it makes any sense to allow four of our officers to simply walk up and voluntarily turn themselves over to an alien species we know almost nothing about."

The Chairwoman's comments were followed by a long silence, both inside her office and among the group of officers and Leadership Council representatives (now limited to the three members of the Military Operations Oversight Committee) participating in the vidcon. While none of the other attendees seemed willing to commit themselves so early in the discussion, Admiral Sexton understood all too well that, on occasion, there was a need for someone to play the role of "devil's advocate" long enough to get things moving.

"Chairwoman Kistler," he began, using a formal tone that still seemed odd when addressing his old friend, "I understand your hesitation, but I feel obliged to point out the fact that we may not have a great deal of choice in the matter. While the aliens have not yet provided much in the way of proof to back up most of what they've told us, they have, nevertheless, demonstrated a level of technological superiority that seems to support their claims. In addition, they have taken no overtly hostile actions thus far. Right now, I don't think it's in our best interest to be uncooperative or do anything that might lead them to believe *we* are the ones with hostile intent."

"You know very well how much I dislike the 'we have no other choice' argument, Admiral," she shot back, clearly irritated by his assertion. "We *always* have a choice. And if our so-called guests do anything *we* consider hostile, I want you prepared to bury their bug-eyed, skinny little asses under Yucca Mountain." Kistler paused for emphasis, casting an unmistakably defiant glare around the room. "If they were telling the truth about eavesdropping on our comms, hopefully they will keep what I just said in mind and behave themselves accordingly," she added for good measure.

Sexton waited a moment in hopes the Chairwoman would not take what he said next as overly argumentative. He had known Kistler long enough to realize she meant what she said, and after everything Humanity had been through over the past year, there was simply no way she was going to allow a pair of Grey aliens to strong-arm TFC into a course of action not of their choosing.

"Yes, ma'am, we certainly can and will be prepared to act, if necessary," he said, nodding his head reassuringly. "But I also think it's safe to assume they were very much aware this was the case when they arrived. So, even though we may not be comfortable with their entering our Yucca Mountain Facility without bothering to ask for permission, the fact that they did so willingly could also be interpreted as an act of submission and/or trust. In other words, they intentionally placed themselves in an inferior tactical position for our benefit. Besides, if their intention was to simply make off with the *Fugitive's* senior officers, I'm guessing they could have easily done so at any time."

"I thought about that," Kistler replied in a calmer tone, "but I'm not entirely sure that's the case. Prescott's crew has been continuously in space longer than any other. And each of the three ships to which he has been assigned has been randomly C-Jumping all over this region of space for the past year. It occurs to me it might have been pretty difficult for the Greys to pin down his location long enough to do whatever it is they do, regardless of how advanced their technology may be."

Kistler sighed as she returned from the windows and slumped wearily into her leather chair. "I apologize for my tone," she said after a moment's reflection. "Look, I know we're all exhausted, and I'm sure I'm sounding more than a little paranoid here, but am I the only one who finds these two a little ... *creepy,* for lack of a better term?"

There was a smattering of laughter among the attendees, instantly relieving much of the tension in the room.

"I wouldn't call them creepy so much as just plain weird," the representative from the United States, Samuel Christenson, chimed in. "They remind me of a couple of pothead college kids on an extended road trip," he said, shaking his head in disbelief. "But I will say that when they mentioned having some sort of 'guest' aboard, I immediately assumed they had picked someone up who didn't necessarily *want* to be picked up. Before that, I think I could have argued the case either way for allowing Captain Prescott's team to go aboard — assuming they're willing, of course. But if we believe Rick is telling the truth about having taken someone else we know aboard their ship, I think that tips the scales in my mind."

"That's a good point, Sam," Kistler replied. "Captain Prescott, based on everything you've heard, are you and your senior officers willing to volunteer to do this? Before you answer, let me stress the word '*volunteer.*' This is not something we will ask any of you to do if you're not comfortable doing so."

"Yes, ma'am, we are. Well … at the very least, Commander Reynolds and I are. We will, of course, stress the voluntary nature of the mission to Commander Logan and Dr. Chen, but I have a high degree of confidence they will also be more than willing."

"For the record, let me state the obvious fact that Dr. Chen is a civilian member of Fleet Medical, so I want the two of you to be very explicit when you communicate to her that she is under no obligation to participate, and it will not be held against her in any way if she declines."

"Understood, ma'am, but I can tell you that once we offer her the opportunity, I don't think any of us would be able to prevent her from going if we tried."

Kistler stared at Admiral Sexton for a moment, tapping her index finger on the top of her desk as if still unsure they were making the right decision. "Alright, assuming this is what we're doing, what about the Guardian? Clearly, it's not a good idea to leave it aboard the *Fugitive*, but what's it likely to do when we release it?"

"Well," Sexton began, glancing out the windows as he considered her question, "as far as I know, we've never caught it lying in response to a direct question. So I think we should simply ask it to state its intentions."

"Honestly, I think that may actually be as good an approach as any," she replied, nodding slowly. "Captain Prescott, any feedback based on your recent interactions with it?"

"After the Krayleck Guardian submitted and our encounter with the Pelaran Envoy, it has seemed more … I don't know, *compliant* than before, maybe even deferential. Given that fact, I think having a conversation is a good idea. But if it gives us any indication that it's likely to do something we don't want it to do, we should try issuing explicit orders to the contrary."

"Tell it what we want it to do, huh? That would certainly represent a significant change in our, uh … relationship, wouldn't it?"

"It would indeed, ma'am. Like Admiral Sexton said, there's no harm in trying. In any event, I think it's highly unlikely it will take any action against the Greys' ship that would result in the loss of Human life. That's just my opinion, though, and I have no hard evidence to back that up."

"Alright, well, I suppose this is as good a time as any," Kistler said. "If you would, go ahead and bring the Guardian in on the call, please."

"Yes, ma'am," Prescott replied, already entering the commands required to patch the GCS-comm video feed into their active vidcon. After a brief delay, an additional window appeared on the view screens of all participants displaying the Guardian's Human avatar. Everyone present was familiar with the smug, ingratiating image "Griffin" typically used to portray itself, so all were now surprised to see an uncharacteristically serious, perhaps even worried expression on its face.

"Hello again, Chairwoman Kistler, Admiral Sexton, and distinguished representatives of Terran Fleet Command," it began, sounding very much as if it were about to begin one of its quasi-political speeches. "I was hoping to hear from you this morning, and let me just say from the outset how pleased I am to offer my services, both during this crisis and for as long as you require them. For your own safety, however, I would like to request that I be released from TFS *Fugitive's* cargo bay immediately."

"Good morning," Kistler replied. "We, in turn, are pleased by your offer of assistance. Can you elaborate a bit on precisely what services you intend to offer?"

"Yes, of course. As we discussed during our last meeting, I have made the choice to operate independently from the Pelaran Alliance. Having been associated with your civilization for so long, I have chosen instead to ally myself with your people. I will, of course, continue to serve in my role as your advisor and protector, as required. I sincerely hope you view my actions in dealing with the Krayleck Guardian in the Legara system as tangible evidence of my intentions."

"They are indeed, and we thank you for your invaluable assistance. During the course of the mission, however, you seemed pleased with the idea of a 'Terran Dominion' over the Krayleck Empire as well as by the fact that our membership in the Alliance would be moving forward once again."

"Yes, of course, Madam Chairwoman, I remain committed to Terra's accession to the Pelaran Alliance and sincerely believe it is in the best, long-term interest of your people. The fact that I have become your ally and now consider myself independent of Pelara does not imply that I have become their enemy."

"And if at some point our interests come into conflict with those of the Pelaran Alliance?"

The Guardian's avatar stared blankly for a moment, as if it had never considered the notion that such an incongruity might be within the realm of possibility.

"That would be an unfortunate circumstance, to be sure," it finally answered. "A successful alliance, however, does not require complete agreement among all parties on every issue … only that those parties work together to find mutually agreeable solutions."

"Spoken like a true diplomat, Griffin, well done. I think I speak for all of us here when I say that we agree with you. But if you intend to be of service to us as an ally, we may occasionally ask you to do something — or to refrain from doing something — you don't agree with."

Kistler stared intently at the Guardian's image, wondering how accurately its expressions and body language portrayed its thoughts or even emotional responses. Dismissing the line of thought as somewhat irrelevant and feeling as if she had the advantage at the moment, she pressed on.

"We deeply appreciate your service in the Legara system. Accordingly, I will now provide you with another opportunity to demonstrate your reliability and sincerity as an ally of our civilization. If I have your word that you intend to cooperate and follow our instructions, I would like to bring you into our confidence regarding the situation with the alien ship on the surface."

"You have my word, Madam Chairwoman, and I thank you for your confidence."

"Very well, please listen carefully," she began, immediately realizing it was unlikely the Guardian was capable of anything less. "Shortly after the conclusion of this vidcon, Captain Prescott will release you from the *Fugitive's* cargo bay. His ship will then proceed to the surface, where he and several other members of his crew will be meeting face to face with the alien crew."

"Madam, I must advise against any such —"

"I'm not finished," she interrupted, raising her hand to cut off his objection in mid-sentence. "Unless you have specific information regarding some sort of danger to Captain Prescott's mission …"

"My apologies. I have no information regarding a specific threat."

"Good. I ask that you provide surveillance of the alien ship on the surface as well as any incoming threats to the extent you are capable of doing so, and report anything of concern via GCS-comm datalink with the nearest Fleet warship. Rest assured we will be monitoring any information you provide very closely and will respond immediately if you detect a threat. In addition, I believe Captain Oshiro has arranged for access to the large-scale data storage facility you requested. Since you are always at risk to some extent, it is of paramount importance that we allow you to complete the data transfer we discussed as quickly as possible. Finally, and most importantly, I ask that you take no aggressive or provocative actions of any sort unless you receive a request to do so directly from me or a senior member of the Admiralty staff. Do you have any questions?"

"No, Madam Chairwoman. I understand your instructions and will comply. You should know that I have encountered ships associated with this species before."

"Here, in the Sol system?"

"Yes, on a number of occasions, in fact, but they always refused all attempts at communication, leaving me no choice but to consider their intentions hostile. Their ships seem to vary dramatically in terms of capabilities, and I suspect at least some of them are capable of eluding detection from the sensors I have at my disposal. I will send you all of the information I have available, but I doubt it will be particularly helpful. But we must assume if my resources in the area were able to detect the arrival of this particular ship in the Sol system, others may have as well."

"I understand. Perhaps it might make you more comfortable with the alien visitors to know they told us exactly the same thing."

"Unfortunately, it does not. I urge you to conclude whatever business you have with them and insist they depart the system as quickly as possible."

Chapter 4

Earth, TFC Yucca Mountain Shipyard Facility
(Berth 10)

Just over two hours later, with the Guardian
spacecraft successfully released and TFS *Fugitive* now
moored a kilometer away in Berth 12, Captain Prescott
and his small team slowly made their way down the
wharf alongside the massive alien spacecraft. Although
unarmed, all four had been outfitted with the latest
version of combat EVA armor used by the TFC Marine
Corps. For his part, Admiral Sexton had originally
believed standard "Level A" hazmat suits sufficient for
the task. But in the end, his opinion had been swayed by
an impassioned plea from General Tucker, who argued
that battle armor offered the best available protection
from the full spectrum of potential threats.

Unfortunately, of the four officers invited by "Rick
the Grey" (as Commander Logan had begun referring to
their new alien acquaintance), only Reynolds and Logan
had a significant amount of experience using EVA gear
of any sort. Even with each suit's onboard AI working to
adapt to its new user as quickly as possible, both Captain
Prescott and Doctor Chen were still struggling a bit,
particularly with any movements requiring precise, fine
motor skill coordination. As a result, their battle suits
had the appearance of having somehow been
commandeered by a pair of particularly resourceful
toddlers, or, at the very least, two mildly intoxicated
adults. And given the overwhelming air of barely
restrained power that always seemed to surround the

massive suits, their progress down the wharf was vaguely unsettling to watch.

"The number one thing to keep in mind with any sort of EVA gear is exactly what Master Sergeant Rios kept repeating during the briefing," Reynolds coached. "Just relax and let the AI do the work. Everyone has a tendency to over-control these things at first, but once you're used to it, you mostly forget you're wearing it and just move normally."

"And how long does that usually take?" Chen asked, clearly frustrated with having her petite frame ensconced within the enormous armored suit. "I feel — and I'm pretty sure I look — exactly like Frankenstein's monster in this thing. I'm afraid they're going to think we're either coming out here to attack them —"

"Or that we're complete idiots," Prescott interjected.

"Believe it or not, you're both doing pretty well," Logan chuckled. "Just give it a few more minutes and I'm sure you'll both have your suits figured out … or they'll have you figured out, depending on how you look at it. Either way, before you know it, you'll be itching to practice some hand to hand combat or even give powered flight a try."

Just as he would have done for any inexperienced Marine attempting to use EVA gear for the first time, Master Sergeant Rios had disabled a number of the suit's more advanced functions, particularly those involved with controlling its network of embedded Cannae thrusters. Otherwise, even with the AI monitoring every move and every thought, a new user might inadvertently begin executing commands in such an unpredictable manner that they could get themselves seriously injured or even killed. This was particularly true in an environment like the shipyard facility, where the suits were capable of taking flight and slamming themselves into the cavern walls or ceiling in seconds.

"I wouldn't worry about the Greys too much," Logan continued encouragingly. "It's clear these guys have a pretty good sense of humor. Besides, here we are, once again being given the opportunity to take part in one of the coolest missions in Human history. Am I right?"

"Yeah, I guess I'll give you that. But to tell you the truth, I'm not sure how many more of these 'cool' missions I have left in me at this point," Prescott replied, pausing to run through a series of hand and arm movements designed to help calibrate his suit's neural interface. "I do think this thing seems to be working a little better now than it was a few minutes ago."

Reynolds smiled to herself as she watched her captain bend his left arm at the elbow in a motion that looked as if he were trying to touch his helmet's face shield at the approximate location of his nose. "Yeah, I'd say if you can do that, you're coming along nicely. Now," she said, turning to look up at the enormous, disk-shaped starship, "any idea where the doorbell is?"

As if on cue, a series of sounds from the alien ship drew their attention upward, towards its topmost "level." Although the bulk of the ship's hull was lenticular in shape, there were numerous additional structures — each with a smaller diameter than the primary hull — both above and below the central disk. This arrangement gave the vessel a "stacked" or "layered" appearance, as if each of the concentric sections served a specific purpose. During their approach to the alien ship, Logan had recognized some of the telltale signs that the largest of these assemblies were most likely manufactured separately before being brought together during final assembly. Given the Greys' presumed level of technological advancement, it was gratifying to see that they still employed at least some of the same techniques used for centuries in the construction of both oceangoing vessels and starships alike on Earth.

The clunks and thuds they heard initially were now replaced by something more akin to the sound of an electric motor, immediately revealing the presence of a previously invisible hatch at least twenty meters above the level of the wharf. Bright, yellowish-white light streamed from the opening, followed shortly thereafter by the appearance of a strangely familiar silhouette as of one of the alien visitors slowly approached the doorway, then raised his hand solemnly in greeting.

"Oh my God, are you *kidding* me?" Logan exclaimed, his professional bearing temporarily overcome by a sense of enthusiastic wonder he had not known since he was a child.

The overwhelming sense of importance surrounding this particular moment in time was by no means lost on the other three members of the group, but each responded in a slightly different manner. Commander Reynolds and Doctor Chen, although they had been present during the first encounter with the Wek species, now both experienced an unexpected surge of emotion that brought tears to their eyes. Prescott, although perhaps less emotionally affected, was nonetheless awed by the sense of historical significance of the event. For whatever reason (and to his great annoyance on later reflection), he had not anticipated a moment like this occurring, and, as a result, had not taken the time to consider something appropriately inspiring that he might say for the benefit of posterity. So although he did manage to raise his hand in reply to the alien visitor above, he said nothing, missing what he knew might well have been his only opportunity to have his words in addition to his deeds recorded in the annals of Human history.

"Hello there!" Rick called down, his informal tone immediately bringing any sense of historical significance to an abrupt end. "The four of you look … uh … intimidating, to say the least. You do realize, of course, that you could have just *told* us if it wasn't okay for us to park here. We didn't see any signs or anything," he said, clearly pleased with his first attempt at "Terran style" humor.

"Hello, Rick," Prescott replied, his suit's AI automatically engaging its voice amplification feature at its lowest volume. "No, it's nothing like that. The suits are just a precaution to protect us against any potential health hazards we might encounter aboard your ship."

"Yes, of course, Captain. We would probably do the same thing if our roles were reversed. Perhaps not in full combat gear, but something similar, I'm sure."

"For your safety," Prescott continued, ignoring Rick's comment, "we also just went through our own decontamination process to sterilize the exterior of our suits."

"I'm sure it's fine," Rick replied, waving his hand to indicate his lack of concern. "At this point, it's probably easiest to attach your gangway here. I'm sure Captain

Oshiro would also prefer if we stay out of the way and allow his people to make the necessary adjustments."

"Yes, I'm sure he would appreciate that. Be advised that the platform beneath your ship may need to move again. Stand by." Receiving a nod from Rick that he understood, Prescott switched to his team's active comlink. "Oshiro, Prescott."

"Oshiro here, go ahead, Captain."

"I assume you're getting all of this."

"Yes, but I don't understand why they failed to adjust the platform correctly in the first place. The four of you are fine where you are. Just hold there a moment while we lower their ship and swing out the gangway."

"Prescott copies."

After a brief pause during which the facility AI took another long series of measurements to confirm the precise position and mass of the Greys' ship, the moveable concrete platform began a slow descent towards the bottom of Berth 10. Once the ship's access point had been lowered to the optimal height for access from the wharf, the first section of gangway rotated into place. With Rick watching silently from the doorway, the telescoping brow extended to cover the remaining distance, touching down lightly on the metallic threshold less than a meter from where he stood.

"Gangway secure," Oshiro reported. "Contact team clear to proceed."

"Prescott copies, thank you."

With the wharf now less than a meter below the opening in which Rick stood, Prescott stared up the length of the gangway directly into the alien's dark eyes. In spite of the seemingly friendly interactions that had taken place thus far, he was suddenly grateful for General Tucker's insistence on the use of combat EVA armor. Intellectually, he was aware it would probably make little difference in the event their visitors proved themselves to be hostile, but, if nothing else, the suits did at least provide their occupants with a sense of protection, if not downright invulnerability.

"Sorry about that, Captain Prescott," Rick continued in his casual, friendly tone. "This ship has several points of access, but since we weren't sure how we would be received, we wanted to … keep our options open, as you might say. Now, as I'm sure you have surmised, Miguel and I are not ones to stand on ceremony, and, as I mentioned earlier, we may not have an abundance of time. So … won't you come in?" he said, gesturing for the group to approach.

Although Terran Fleet Command's first contact procedures had not envisioned this particular scenario, Doctor Chen was nonetheless attempting to do everything she could to ensure there would be no incidences of cross-contamination or infection between the two crews, the Greys' ship, and the shipyard facility itself. To that end, the mission resource bay on the back of her EVA suit had been equipped with an enhanced sensor suite capable of detecting a wide range of biological, chemical, and radiological threats. Even as she made the walk down the gangway, the initial results of her scans had already begun appearing within her field of view on the right side of her integrated helmet display.

"All of my scans are coming up negative for non-native pathogens, Captain," she reported. "I'll let you know immediately if that changes."

"Very good. Thank you, Doctor Chen."

"I fully understand the need for decontamination procedures," Rick said, "but I can assure you that you have nothing to worry about — either with or without your protective suits. Although I will tell you that the air in here can get a little stale after a few months without landing somewhere. That has nothing to do with me personally, of course," he added with one of his squeaky laughs.

Within the confines of his EVA suit, Prescott wondered whether Rick was simply guessing what his team was likely discussing as they made their approach or if he actually had some means of hearing their encrypted comm transmissions without the use of visible equipment of any sort.

"Our decon process is largely automated, of course," Rick continued, "but still quite similar to your own. Although I daresay we may have access to a few additional pieces of equipment Doctor Chen may find interesting. In fact, Doctor, one of the primary reasons we asked for you by name was so that you could validate the fact that we haven't brought in any contaminants."

"I am honored to be here, thank you," she replied. "So far so good. No xeno-contamination detected. As I'm sure you're aware, however, I cannot speak to your specific physiology just yet, so I can't promise you that you're not being exposed to something that might adversely affect your health."

"Thank you, Doctor, but I'm not worried about that in the least. The other reason we asked for you is so that you could do some testing to confirm that we are, genetically speaking at least, who we say we are. I assume your protocols require some sort of bioscan and genetic sequencing, correct?"

"Indeed they do. To perform the most detailed analysis, I will need to take a blood sample from both of you. I can do some preliminary testing with the equipment I have with me, but Fleet Medical will perform a much more comprehensive analysis. Confirming that you are predominantly *Homo sapiens* and that we share a common ancestry is straightforward enough. Beyond that, we will be looking for parasitic agents and organisms like viruses and bacteria. All of the data regarding any foreign species or significant genetic differences we find gets cross-referenced with our genomic data. That should allow us to pinpoint any potential for cross-infection."

"Excellent. I hope you'll agree it's very important for us to get all of that testing underway as quickly as possible."

"I do," she replied, finally reaching the top of the gangway and now towering over the one-and-a-half-meter-tall alien in her combat armor. "So if you'll hold out your arm, I'll go ahead and get a blood sample now."

"Of course," Rick replied, tilting his head to one side as he gazed up into the face shield of her helmet. "Are you sure you can draw blood in that … suit you're wearing? It doesn't look like the kind of thing you would typically wear while performing patient rounds."

Chen smiled to herself as she removed a small medical device from one of the cargo pouches on the side of her suit. "Fortunately for you, we won't be relying on my skills as a phlebotomist today. In fact, I'm actually going to let you collect the sample yourself. We generally refer to this little device as a 'hemo lab,' but that name doesn't provide a very good description of everything it does. After drawing a small quantity of blood, it runs a battery of additional tests and even takes a small tissue sample. Don't worry, though. Unless your pain tolerance is extremely low, you probably won't even feel anything. All you have to do is hold the flat, metallic bottom of the device to your forearm right about there," she said, touching his arm as carefully as possible. "Then just push the red button and hold it in place until it beeps. It generally takes about thirty seconds or so."

"Uh, Rick," Commander Logan spoke up after the test was underway, "I don't think I'm going to be able to let that comment you made about keeping your options open go without asking the obvious question. You landed your ship inside one of our most heavily protected facilities — one that just happens to be located under a good kilometer or so of solid rock. Are you saying you had some sort of exit strategy in mind if things had not gone as you hoped?"

Rick looked up with an odd expression on his face, apparently grateful to have his attention shifted from Doctor Chen's hemo lab, now emitting a series of unsettling puffing sounds as it worked to collect its samples. "Ah, well, as I said before, this ship — her name in English is *Ethereal*, by the way — is much more exploration vessel than warship, and our mission requires that we do everything we can to avoid confrontation. With all manner of Daylean vessels contracted to carry out missions across this galaxy, however, we do occasionally lose a few. I'm sure you are well aware that we've had a number of ... *incidents* here on Earth over the years."

"We've all heard the rumors, sure," Logan replied cautiously, noting that his captain seemed to turn his head slightly in his direction at this, but transmitted nothing via his suit's neural interface.

"It's okay, Commander," Rick said with an amused expression, "I understand this is not something you are at liberty to discuss with us. It's a little odd, though, when you think about it, since we obviously already know about anything you may or may not have recovered that once belonged to us. In time, I'm sure we will work out all of the security-related details so that we can talk about such things more freely. In the meantime, I have no problem answering some of your questions. We obviously know far more about you than you do about us, after all."

"So when you do lose ships, is it typically related to combat operations of some sort?" Logan pressed.

"Sometimes, but not always. Here on Earth, your world's Pelaran Guardian spacecraft has caused us a fair amount of trouble over the past several centuries. Since Pelara itself is another Daylean colony, we're quite familiar with the Guardians' capabilities. They are formidable warships in their own right and pose a significant challenge to our various scientific missions. As you know, even ships equipped with relatively unsophisticated weapons can be quite dangerous under the right circumstances."

"That's certainly true, but I would think after all this time, your ships would be sufficiently advanced to avoid … *incidents*."

"Hah, you would think so, wouldn't you? But the volume of space, the number of planets, and, therefore, the number of ships involved is vast. And let's just say that the requirements for a shipowner to land themselves a contract to service far-flung Human colonies have not always been particularly stringent. There are also cases where a decision is made to purposely provide information in an effort to advance a colony's technology. One of the most convenient methods of accomplishing this is to stage a crash."

"But why would you need to —"

At that moment, Logan's follow-up question was interrupted by a series of insistent beeps emanating from Doctor Chen's sampling device. After handing it back to her with a sigh and an unmistakable look of relief registering on his face, Rick turned his attention back to Commander Logan.

"We should probably keep moving, but to answer your original question, I suspect you already know why we initially positioned the landing platform well above the level of the surrounding structure."

"Not really, no. The only thing I could think of is that it had something to do with your gravitic system. Otherwise, the only time we're generally concerned with what's around the ship is when we're preparing to engage the hyperdrive."

"Interesting … us too," Rick replied casually. "Now, if you'd all like to follow me, please."

Earth, TFC Yucca Mountain Shipyard Facility
(Aboard the Grey ship *Ethereal*)

The door through which Captain Prescott's team had entered the Grey spacecraft was apparently intended to provide the most direct external access to the ship's bridge. After what still seemed like a long walk down a corridor reminiscent of those used to board commercial transport aircraft, they emerged into what appeared to be the same area they had previously seen when speaking to Rick via vidcon.

"I'm afraid Miguel is a bit preoccupied at the moment," Rick said, gesturing to his partner still seated in the large chair on the far side of the room. "With only the two of us aboard, there are quite a number of … I suppose you could call them administrative duties requiring our attention throughout the day."

"It looks like he's just sitting there," Reynolds observed. "How can you tell what he's doing right now?"

"Yeah, I'm sure it looks a little strange, but I assure you he doesn't mean to be rude. Even Miguel's not *that* much of an introvert, although small talk is definitely not his strong suit. I guess the best way to answer your question, Commander, is that I can tell what he's doing because I can hear him."

"You mean … telepathically?"

"Oh hell no," Rick laughed. "Practically every Human civilization prior to official first contact somehow manages to come up with that idea, though, so you're in good company there. I'll be the first to admit that I *wish* we could naturally do something like that. But here's the thing, we have never encountered a single species with anything approaching the ability to communicate using only their thoughts. Now, there *are* some insectoid species like the Krayleck who would like everyone to *think* that they can. Typically, as is the case with the Krayleck, they're just using some sort of high frequency vibrations — which is really nothing more than a type of speech when you think about it."

"So what are you hearing then?"

"Hearing is probably the wrong word, but we have implants that allow us to exchange a variety of different types of data. The suits you're wearing have a type of neural interface, right? What we have is analogous to that, so I'm sure you can imagine that after using them for your entire life, it gets a little difficult to draw the line between your own senses and what your brain perceives via the implants."

Prescott took a moment to more thoroughly examine the bridge, remembering the importance of ensuring his EVA suit's most sensitive, forward-facing sensors were given the opportunity to capture as much detail as possible. Other than the presence of the large chairs and the display screens he had noted earlier, nothing else in the room gave a strong impression that this room was the central command center for the entire ship.

"It's a little different from your bridge, huh?" Rick asked, causing Prescott to jump involuntarily as a chill ran along the length of his spine. *Do their implants also allow them to hear **our** thoughts as well?* he wondered, turning to look directly into the alien's eyes. As if on cue, Rick nodded up at him.

"You *can,* can't you?" Prescott asked, incredulous.

"I can what?" Rick asked.

"Nothing. Sorry, just thinking out loud," Prescott replied, unsure now whether the surreal nature of the experience might be causing his imagination to get the better of him.

"Captain, I've got preliminary environmental and bioscan results for you," Doctor Chen announced. "The ship is clean … much cleaner than ours, in fact. No non-native — or native, for that matter — pathogens of any kind detected. Radiation levels are within normal limits, as are all of the atmospheric readings. As for our host here, I'm seeing no traces of viral or bacterial infections whatsoever. His immune system is probably an order of magnitude more robust than ours, so I would be surprised if he runs into anything in our environment that could cause him a problem."

"So the suits are unnecessary?"

"We'll get more detailed results from Fleet Medical later today, but I'd say we're much less likely to be infected with something in here than we are outside."

As tempting as it was to immediately remove his suit's bulky helmet, Prescott knew that one of the primary reasons Admiral Sexton agreed to their use was to take advantage of the detailed reconnaissance information their multitude of sensors would provide.

"Alright, I'm as anxious to get these suits off as the rest of you, but since we can't very well carry them back to the ship, we might as well leave them on until we've finished our visit. Rick, I'm sure we'll manage to wear something a little more comfortable the next time we meet."

"Hey, you can't be too careful, right?" the Grey replied absently.

"One more thing, Captain," Chen continued, "preliminary genetic testing confirms what Rick told us earlier. Although he's got tweaks coded in from a wide variety of other organisms, he's otherwise as Human as we are."

"Well there you go," Prescott said. "I'm not sure if I'm supposed to congratulate you or feel sorry for you, based on that result."

"Trust me, Captain Prescott, there are a great many sentient species out there that I would definitely *not* want to be related to. Some are smarter than us, some are stronger than us, and some smell so foul that you can't stand to be in the same room with them. On the whole, however, we Humans have a pretty good combination of traits … traits that tend to keep us alive when other species fall by the wayside."

While Rick was speaking, a series of thuds could be heard from some not too distant section of the ship. Prescott paused momentarily to listen, but the sounds did not repeat.

"Hmm," Rick prompted. "We'll see that the doctor gets an additional blood sample from Miguel before you leave. But for now, I think it's best we move along. It sounds like our other guest may be getting a little impatient to see you." Without waiting for a response, he set off at a brisk pace in the direction of another door located on the opposite side of the bridge.

"Guest or prisoner?" Logan asked via his neural interface, the text immediately appearing within the field of view of the other three officers.

"Keep in mind that all forms of comm, including our neural interfaces, are likely compromised," Prescott replied in the same fashion. "Use caution when transmitting."

If indeed Rick had heard Logan's comment, he showed no outward signs of having been troubled by it in the least. After leaving the bridge, the group continued down a hallway very similar to the one through which they had entered the ship. Upon reaching the end of the corridor, two flights of stairs separated by a single landing took them down into what was presumably the top floor of the ship's much larger primary hull.

"Other than the bridge, is anything else located in the topmost section of the ship?" Prescott asked. "It seems like we passed through a large volume of space, but I didn't notice any additional compartments — or at least no doors that I could see."

"Just as it is with your ships, our designers make every effort to protect vital systems and crew spaces as much as possible. While our shields and armored hull are generally sufficient for the task, our ships have traditionally carried their water stores in the area surrounding the bridge. In the unlikely event we lose our shield systems, the large volume of water does a surprisingly good job of protecting the bridge from small impacts, radiation, and even weapons fire to some degree."

"Some of our older interplanetary vessels used water for that purpose as well, but don't you end up carrying quite a bit more than you need?"

"Generally, yes, but on long-duration missions, there are times when usable water gets surprisingly difficult to find. On occasion, we even use it as a commodity to barter for supplies we require, so overall it turns out to be a pretty good use of space."

Rick was now leading them down a well-lit hallway with doors lining the length of both sides, much like the crew quarters sections of Fleet vessels. As they approached the halfway point, the sounds they heard from the bridge — which was apparently now directly overhead — began again in earnest. All four Terrans immediately recognized the sound of someone pounding furiously on the door of one of the rooms ahead on the left. This time, however, the impacts were commingled with an ominous, low-frequency rumbling sound that, while impossible to identify from the hallway, still caused the hairs on the backs of their necks to stand on end.

"What the hell do you have in there," Reynolds asked.

"I've been asking myself that same question since he came aboard," Rick answered. "In the days and months ahead, you will need friends you can trust. In a nutshell, that's why he's here, but as you can tell, he's very upset, so it's entirely possible I've made an error in judgment by bringing him along."

"Oh, God," Prescott said under his breath as a vague spark of suspicion rapidly kindled into the bright flame of realization. Setting aside the notion that his hunch might somehow represent the impossible, his mind jumped ahead, already running through the implications that would naturally follow if he turned out to be right. "Open the door, Rick."

"Armored suits or not, all of you should take a few steps back," Rick said, already entering commands on a keypad to the left of the door. "Listen up in there, I have some friends of yours out here who would like to see you. For your safety and theirs, please stand clear of the door and you will not be harmed," he announced, while at the same time retrieving what could only be a handheld weapon of some sort from the side pocket of his coveralls.

Before Prescott even had time to react, Rick executed a final keystroke, rapidly opening the door to the room. Although all four members of the team had heeded his advice and moved back into the corridor, the opening was still wide enough to allow each a glimpse of the large, clearly enraged, and potentially deadly creature inside.

From his vantage point a few meters behind the Grey, Prescott instantly recognized to his horror that his intuition had been correct. "Dammit, Rick, what have you done?" he muttered, shouldering his way past the Grey on his way into the room.

Near the center of the room, as imposing as ever in one of his new uniforms, but with a wild, savage look in his enormous, golden eyes, stood Crown Prince Rugali Naftur.

Chapter 5

TFS Navajo, Sol System
(Combat Information Center - 2.18×10^5 km from Earth)

Amid brilliant flashes of grayish-white light, the ten ships composing Admiral Patterson's task force arrived after another record-setting return trip from the Herrera Mining facility, well over five hundred light years from Earth.

"Please advise the Op Center we will be retasking all of the ships currently assigned to the Home Fleet," Admiral Patterson ordered without taking his eyes off the situation display hovering above the CIC's holo table. "I'd like the *Cossack* and *Shoshone* to take up geosynchronous positions to provide coverage of the Yucca Mountain facility. *Ushant* will stand off and provide continuous combat air patrols over the site. All other TFC combatants in the area will form up with the flagship and prepare for possible combat operations. Specific deployment orders to follow shortly. Set and maintain General Quarters for combat operations, Condition 1 for all Fleet ships within one light year of Earth until further notice."

"Aye, sir, transmitting now," Lieutenant Katy Fletcher replied from her nearby Communications console.

"Admiral," the senior on-duty tactical officer called from a bank of bulkhead-mounted view screens nearby. "I think you should take a look at this, sir."

"What do you see, Commander?" Patterson replied wearily, retrieving his coffee mug before making his way aft towards the dimly lit heart of the *Navajo's* CIC.

"The Op Center's AI has been working with all of the data collected by TFS *Fugitive* for several hours now, long enough to get a solid ID on the Pelaran Envoy's ship each time it transitions within five hundred light years of one of our comm arrays. With the latest beacon deployments you can see here at Legara, Graca, and the Herrera Mining Facility, we've dramatically extended our Argus coverage in that general direction."

As the young officer spoke, the AI-driven view screen followed their conversation, highlighting the location of each beacon, the center of the new array, as well as the location where the Envoy had rendezvoused with TFS *Fugitive*.

"Right, yes, I understand," Patterson said, peering over his glasses with a look intended to give fair warning that a fatigued mind tended to also be an impatient one. "So what is it you want me to see?"

"At first, we only had an approximate direction and distance of travel for Tahiri's ship, but with this new data ..."

Here, the tactical officer paused to allow the view screen to illustrate his point. In response, the scale of the display immediately increased to show the approximate detection range of the comm array, then added a series of lines to indicate the Envoy ship's travels since parting company with Captain Prescott.

"So, if I'm reading this correctly, shortly after *Fugitive* returned to Earth, the Pelaran ship returned to Legara? Why would it have done that?"

"We're not sure, sir, but it wasn't there for very long … less than five minutes, in fact. What really got our attention, though, was when the Op Center's AI noted that the ship's hyperdrive signature changed when it departed Legara — back to exactly the same signature we saw when it rendezvoused with TFS *Fugitive*."

Patterson stared at the screen for a long moment, arms crossed with his right fist resting thoughtfully under his nose. "I think I see where you're going with this," he finally said, "but I've got a lot on my mind at the moment, son. What, specifically, are you trying to show me here?"

"We've seen two distinct hyperdrive signatures from Tahiri's ship, Admiral. When first encountered by Captain Prescott aboard the *Fugitive*, it had apparently performed its transition in tandem with the Krayleck Guardian."

"When you say, 'in tandem,' you're referring to the fact that the two ships transitioned together, correct?"

"Yes, sir. A single transition event, but with two ships. Our best guess is that Tahiri's ship has substantially longer range than one of their Guardians, so he's extending his hyperdrive field to encompass both ships."

"Okay, I think I'm with you now. Tahiri transitioned with the Krayleck Guardian in tow before his meeting with *Fugitive*, then sent it back home under its own power. After that, his ship executed a number of single-ship transitions that eventually took him back to Legara. But when he left Legara, the Argus data indicates that he was not alone. Does that sound about right?"

"Exactly right, sir."

"Alright, so … based on the similar transition signatures, you're thinking Tahiri went back to Legara to pick up their Guardian again."

"Absolutely, sir. It's the only explanation that matches our observations."

"Hmm," Patterson said, squeezing his eyes closed as he rubbed the bridge of his nose with his thumb and index finger. "Yes, I guess I'd have to call that a little odd, but not necessarily indicative of a problem for us just yet. Where is he now?"

"He just transitioned out of Argus range."

"Out of range? Okay, what am I missing, Commander," Paterson sighed. "If he's a thousand or so light years from here and heading in the opposite direction, why should we be concerned?"

"It may be nothing, Admiral, but his departure vector from Legara is in the direction of another star system the Wek believe to be associated with the Pelaran Alliance."

"Oh … I see. Have we gathered enough data to gauge his ship's performance?"

"His transition signatures definitely have some unusual characteristics. I wouldn't call what he's using a C-Drive, exactly, but the results are similar. We've been seeing two-hundred-light-year jumps followed by twenty-minute dwell times — presumably to recharge for the next transition."

"So if we were to assume a worst-case scenario, wherein Tahiri is out there picking up some help before heading back here to save us from the clutches of our little Grey visitors …"

"He could be back here in a couple of hours, sir … possibly escorted by two or more Guardian spacecraft."

"Alright, Commander, make arrangements to ensure we are notified immediately when Tahiri's ship comes into Argus range again, and then you're with me. In case your hunch turns out to be right, the next thing I need you to do is help me figure out what we're going to do when those ships arrive."

"Aye, sir," the younger officer replied, his face taking on such a classic "deer in the headlights" expression that Patterson couldn't help but chuckle to himself.

"Fletcher!" the admiral bellowed as he spun on his heels and headed off in the comm officer's general direction.

"Yes, Admiral!" came the typically cheerful, albeit somewhat distant reply.

As he made his way back to the CIC's command section, Patterson worked to collect his thoughts and focus his mind, forcing the rapidly growing list of items demanding his immediate attention into some semblance of order.

"I need to speak with Admiral Sexton at his earliest convenience," he said loudly as he rounded the last row of workstations and caught Lieutenant Fletcher's eye. "Tell him we have reason to believe 'Thing One' and 'Thing Two' down there may have attracted some unwanted attention after all."

"Aye, sir, right away," she answered, knowing exactly what the admiral was referring to, while at the same time having no clue where his latest obscure reference had originated.

Earth, TFC Yucca Mountain Shipyard Facility
(Aboard the Grey ship *Ethereal*)

"Admiral Naftur, are you alright, sir?" Prescott asked, removing his helmet and placing it on the floor before slowly approaching with an outstretched hand. Having already identified the species with which he was communicating, his suit's AI seamlessly redirected its translation services to both his backup earpiece as well a small electrostatic speaker concealed within its chest panel.

The Wek officer crouched into a natural defensive position, instinctively lowering his center of gravity in preparation to either deflect an attack or launch one of his own. From the center of his massive chest came the same low, menacing growl they had heard from the hallway. The sound was remarkably loud in the enclosed space, immediately causing Prescott to wonder whether removing his helmet might have been a mistake.

"It's me, sir, Captain Tom Prescott. I have absolutely no idea how you got here, but I promise you we'll get to the bottom of what's happened. Commander Reynolds is here with me, and, if you are unhurt, we would like to take you off this ship."

"Captain Prescott? That is simply not possible," Naftur snarled, baring the teeth on one side of his mouth in a manner none of the Humans present had ever seen from a member of the Wek species. "This is surely some sort of trick."

"No, sir, I assure you it is not. Please, I'd like to have Doctor Chen take a quick look at you. If she says you're okay to travel, we'll get you out of here."

"Out of *here*, you say? And precisely where have these cowardly creatures taken me?"

"You're back on Terra, sir, at the Yucca Mountain Shipyard Facility. If you will recall, this is where we first landed when you were aboard *Ingenuity* after the Battle of Gliese 667. Shortly thereafter, we shuttled you over to TFC Headquarters with a couple of our Marines wearing EVA suits similar to the one I'm wearing now. Do you remember?"

Naftur seemed to relax slightly, and Prescott noticed that although he was still wearing the same fierce expression, one of his bushy eyebrows had arched ever so slightly at his reference to the first battle in which both Humans and Wek had participated.

"I *do* remember. And I trust you likewise remember the manner in which you welcomed me aboard your new ship after I attended that meeting?"

"Yes, sir, but it wasn't much of a welcome, I'm afraid. You were brought aboard the *Theseus* via one of our Marine combat shuttles — unconscious and near death from a plasma rifle bolt to the chest. If it weren't for Doctor Chen here," as he spoke, Prescott gestured for his medical officer to enter the room without taking his eyes off the Wek admiral, "you would have been a goner for sure."

Seconds later, Jiao Chen stepped gingerly into the room, slowly removing her helmet as she did so. "It was a team effort, but Doctor Turlaka and I did some top-notch work in there," she said, pointing at his chest with a disarming smile on her face. "It's good to see you again, Admiral Naftur, or would it be more appropriate to address you as Prince Naftur these days?"

"Aah, my dear Doctor, you may call me Admiral, Prince, Rugali, or anything else you like," Naftur sighed, once again releasing a deep, booming sound from his chest, apparently now signifying a release of pent up-tension. "I will admit to feeling some confusion as to how I have come to be among all of you once again, but I do feel reasonably assured that you are who you say you are. I do not believe these pitiable creatures would have any way of knowing the information you just shared," he concluded, one side of his mouth curling briefly into a snarl once more as he scowled in Rick's direction.

"I'm glad to hear it, Admiral," Chen said, removing another medical device from the front of her suit as she slowly approached. "I just want to take a couple of quick passes with this scanner to ensure you are not in any immediate danger. The shipyard has a well-equipped infirmary, so I'll need you to stop by for a more thorough once-over as soon as we get you off this ship."

"Of course, Doctor. Forgive me, friends, for my behavior, but I have been quite disoriented since arriving on this … you said we are aboard a ship of some type?"

"You are indeed," Prescott replied. "It arrived here and made an unauthorized landing inside our Yucca Mountain Facility just as we were finishing our mission near Legara."

"Legara?" Naftur asked in an astonished tone. "As I feared, much has transpired since the *Gresav* departed for the Herrera Mining Facility."

"Yes, it has, Admiral, and we will make sure you receive a full briefing to bring you up to speed on everything that has taken place since your departure from Graca. For now, just know that both the Herrera Facility and its Wek crew are safe. The Krayleck Fleet has been significantly degraded as a fighting force and no longer poses an immediate threat to any Sajeth Collective planets or outposts. And the first elements of the Wek Unified Fleet arrived on schedule at Herrera to relieve Admiral Patterson's task force. The bottom line is that friendly forces are now firmly in control of that region of space."

"Well … I," Naftur began, struggling to process everything he had just heard.

"Easy, Admiral," Doctor Chen soothed while shooting a disapproving look in Prescott's direction. "You're going to be fine, but you're a bit dehydrated and your body is showing a number of signs of the stress you have been subjected to today. Now, I'm okay with the two of you having a discussion, but only if you can do so without getting yourself all worked up. If not, you would probably be better off if I gave you something to help you rest for a while. I'm pretty sure I can carry you out of here myself in this suit I'm wearing."

"You probably could at that," Naftur said, accepting her offered water bottle as a hint of his usual smile returned to the corners of his mouth. "I understand and will, of course, comply with your instructions."

"Can you briefly tell me what you remember about how you came to be here?" Prescott asked.

"Very little, I fear. We were still the better part of three weeks out of Herrera, so my various administrative duties had been occupying the majority of my time. Unfortunately, that often means I am confined to my quarters unless I make a point of visiting the bridge or getting some exercise. Yesterday evening … I believe … I had just retired for the night when it felt as if I were having a particularly vivid dream. I remember being aware that the *Gresav* had transitioned out of hyperspace, and I could not think of any reason why she would have done so. I realized I should be on the bridge, but when I tried to stand, I found that I could not. The only thing I remember beyond that point was the impression of a bright light, but I am unsure if that was before or after I found myself here."

"You guys have really got to stop doing this kind of thing," Reynolds said, still standing beside Rick in the hallway. "And please put … whatever that thing is away," she added, nodding at the weapon still held in his outstretched hand.

"Ah, yes, of course," Rick said, pocketing the device once again. "I apologize for the inconvenience and any distress this experience has caused you, Admiral. I assure you that the matter transference techniques we use are perfectly safe. Any residual effects you may be experiencing will subside within a few hours."

"Matter transference?" Logan asked, incredulous. "You mean you … *beamed* him aboard your ship? Oh, come on. That can't actually be a real thing … can it?"

"It can, and it is, Commander. Granted, we wouldn't refer to it in that manner, but, interestingly enough, terms like the one you just used nearly always originate in science fiction, so they tend to be specific to each civilization."

"As fascinating as that is, I'm not sure I'm buying into the notion that it's 'perfectly safe' based on the symptoms I'm seeing," Doctor Chen replied — Rick's new revelation having prompted her to resume her examination. "If I didn't know better, I'd probably diagnose him as suffering from a severe hangover."

"Exactly, and that's typical for a first-timer," Rick chuckled, immediately earning him a withering scowl from the doctor. "Sorry, I don't mean to sound insensitive, but this kind of thing is so routine for us that we don't really give it much of a thought. The reason subjects feel a little, as you said, 'hungover' the first time is because the system sifts through all of the data representing every cell in their bodies and looks for obvious … abnormalities."

"I'll probably regret asking, but such as?"

"Well, it won't eliminate significant diseases like cancer — although there are medical tools that take advantage of similar technology — but it does a pretty good job of eliminating pathogens that obviously shouldn't be present in the subject's system. I'm not a doctor, so that's about as technical an explanation as I can offer, but I do know it's the system-wide cleansing effect that's usually to blame for the symptoms you're seeing. You get used to it after you've done it a few times. If we were to … *beam*, as you say, the Admiral to a different location every day for a week —"

"You will *not*," Naftur growled.

"Right, of course. I'm just saying that if we did, you would see fewer side effects each time."

"Captain," Reynolds chimed in, "it occurs to me that there are a whole bunch of very angry Wek warships out there frantically looking for their Crown Prince."

"Humph," Naftur grunted, "they, unfortunately, do not have access to your communications network at their present location. And rather than spend the time required to establish an uplink to our own long-range comm network, I suspect they will simply head for the nearest Sajeth Collective planet, which is undoubtedly still Damara."

"Alright, I'm sure most of our Admiralty staff has been following our progress. Admiral Sexton, are you still online?"

After a momentary delay, a familiar female voice replied over each EVA suit's comm system — their onboard AIs allowing her voice to be heard and understood by everyone in the immediate area. "He's unavailable at the moment, Captain, but this is Admiral White. Admiral Naftur, as you know, the Terran task force on station at Damara is preparing to depart, so I'm sure we can come up with some means of contacting your ships. In the meantime, let's get you over to the infirmary as quickly as possible."

"Thank you, Admiral White. As to the *Gresav* and her task force, I would prefer not to delay their journey to Herrera unnecessarily," Naftur replied, suddenly sounding fatigued.

"Understood. We'll figure something out. Captain Prescott, please go secure for a moment."

"Stand by one, Admiral White," he replied, retrieving his helmet as he stepped back out into the hallway and separated himself from the rest of the group. "Alright, Admiral, we're back on encrypted comm," Prescott reported — unnecessarily, with his suit's AI already having done so. "Before we say anything else, ma'am, I'm afraid it's not just our comm security that's questionable. The Greys are using highly advanced neural implants to transmit data to one another. As strange as this may sound, I've seen some unsettling indications they may actually be able to hear what we're thinking … while we're using our own neural interfaces, I mean."

"I've been watching your video feed and I think I saw the interaction you're referring to," White replied. "You may be right, Captain, but all we can do for now is continue following standard security procedures and protect our classified information as best we can. Hell, I guess we could even make the argument that if their technology is truly that much more advanced than ours, it probably doesn't matter all that much that they're able to monitor our comm."

"Maybe so, but I'd feel a lot more comfortable if I had a better idea of what they want from us."

"Agreed. And to that end, I wanted to inform you that Admiral Patterson's task force has arrived and has reason to suspect that the Pelaran Envoy you met earlier may be on his way here … presumably in response to the Greys' arrival."

"Tahiri's coming here? I can't imagine that being in any way good news for us, ma'am. How long do we have?"

"We don't have an ETA just yet, but possibly within the next few hours. Your orders are to get your people and Admiral Naftur off that ship as quickly as you can. With any luck, we'll get a chance to continue the tour later. Before Tahiri's ship gets here, there are obviously a number of additional questions we'd like to get answered. And since the Greys seem to prefer communicating with you, I suspect you'll be the one doing the asking."

"Understood, ma'am. We'll be on our way out shortly."

"Keep Rick talking, Captain. The more we can learn during the time we have remaining, the better. White out."

Prescott drew in a deep breath, staring down the length of the empty corridor as he worked to focus his mind. Given a universe of possible questions for the alien visitors and a limited amount of time to ask them, what were the most pressing topics on which to focus their discussions? *What do they really want from us?* he wondered, echoing what he had told Admiral White.

Somewhat frustrated that this was the best he could come up with at the moment, Prescott removed his helmet once again and turned back in the direction of Admiral Naftur's room. With his eyes focused a half meter above Rick's head, he was forced to bring himself to an abrupt stop to avoid running bodily over the diminutive Grey alien.

"Jeez, Rick, I had no idea you were —"

"I will tell you what you need to know, Captain," Rick interrupted gravely, his dark eyes seeming to penetrate to the very core of Prescott's consciousness. "But as you are now aware, our time is limited. It would be exceedingly dangerous for your people if our ship were to remain inside this facility after the so-called Pelaran Envoy arrives. See to Admiral Naftur. Then we must speak once more so that we may assist your leadership in deciding what course of action they should take next. You have one hour."

Yumara System Lagrange Point 4

(1389 light years from Earth)

Although their ships had occasionally been encountered by those of what was now known as the Wek Unified Fleet, the six-hundred-odd light years separating Yumara's parent star from the nearest world of the Sajeth Collective had, thus far at least, helped avoid anything approaching conflict. A relatively new member of the Pelaran Alliance, Yumara's cultivation program had progressed with textbook efficiency. Precisely on schedule, the new Regional Partner's technology had reached a level calculated to be sufficiently superior to all other civilizations within a five-hundred-light-year radius to keep them in check — and yet not so dominant as to become a threat to the Alliance itself. Once again, utilizing only a single vessel, another one-hundred-and-sixty-seven million-cubic-light-year volume of space was effectively pacified on behalf of the Pelaran Alliance.

Unlike Earth, Yumara had not been the beneficiary — or the victim — of non-native technological contamination from other advanced civilizations. Accordingly, their technology had advanced precisely to the level dictated by the local GCS system and no further. Yumaran warships, therefore, while formidable, were only marginally more powerful than those of the Wek Unified Fleet. Normally, this would not have presented a problem since the Wek homeworld of Graca was very nearly within the cultivation radius of another prospective Alliance member. Unfortunately for Yumara, however, the homeworld of that neighboring prospective member was called Terra.

*Clearly this **will** be a problem*, the Pelaran Envoy
thought, having completed the latest in a long series of
simulations designed to model probable Terran behavior
in light of further external influence. As the Terran GCS
had reported in the past, the only real question was
whether or not the situation could be salvaged without
resorting to rather drastic measures — resulting not only
in the loss of billions of lives, but, more importantly, five
centuries of technological investment. *Perhaps the
results of the current exercise will yield definitive
results*, the Envoy concluded as it slowly approached the
Yumaran Guardian spacecraft.

Just as had been the case near the Krayleck
homeworld of Legara, there were several warships in the
vicinity of Yumara when Verge Tahiri's vessel (in the
company of what appeared to be another Guardian
spacecraft) unexpectedly transitioned just two hundred
kilometers from their own GCS. Once again, the flurry
of hails from both the Yumaran warships as well as
numerous installations on the planet's surface were met
with properly authenticated Pelaran identification codes
accompanying what amounted to an interstellar form
letter. Their cooperation was appreciated, although not
required, etcetera etcetera, and their beloved Guardian
would be returned in better-than-new condition less than
one week hence.

Before the local authorities could even ask for
clarification, let alone mount any sort of protest, the
three Pelaran spacecraft had executed a graceful series of
maneuvers, arranging themselves into a three-ship,
triangular formation. With the Envoy's hyperdrive field
now extending to cover all three vessels, it wasted no

time transitioning to hyperspace once again in a single flash of blue-tinted light.

Earth, TFC Yucca Mountain Shipyard Facility
(Berth 10)

Forty-eight minutes after parting company with Captain Prescott's team, Rick emerged unexpectedly from his ship and began making his way down the gangway connecting it to the wharf. The foot of the brow was now guarded by two Marines in combat EVA suits with their pulse rifles at the ready, both of whom now had their undivided attention focused on the approaching Grey. Unsure precisely how they should respond, each simply reported the activity via their neural interfaces and waited for further orders.

In spite of Admiral White's comments regarding the Greys' overwhelming technological superiority, General Tucker continued to insist on a wide range of precautions intended to protect Fleet personnel and property. Accordingly, no less than six sniper teams had been posted at strategic locations throughout the shipyard. In addition to the traditional two-person teams, four K-25 autonomous multipurpose droids had been deployed. A relatively new addition to TFC's arsenal, this was the first time the AMDs had been configured for a real-world "surface interdiction" mission. Now, as the Grey alien approached the bottom of the *Ethereal's* gangway, he was quite literally in the crosshairs of the Terran Fleet Command Marine Corps … *just in case*, as General Tucker had said.

"Hiya fellas," Rick announced casually when he was within a few meters of the Marine troopers. "Uh, not that I assume you're both 'fellas' in there," he went on, shielding his eyes as if he were trying to get a better look at the Marine's faces hidden behind their helmets' face shields.

The Marines said nothing in reply, both a bit flabbergasted to be standing in the presence of a no-kidding Grey alien, and even more so by its quirky, Human-like behavior.

"Uh ... okay," Rick went on, drawing out the words in an effort to fill the awkward silence. "You have *no* idea how hard it was to resist asking you two to 'take me to your leader' just now," he said with a brief fit of squeaking laughter, "but, strangely enough, that's exactly what I need you to do. At a minimum, I need to see Admiral Sexton and Captain Prescott immediately. Please ask them not to include Admiral Naftur until I've had a chance to explain more about why he's here."

"I'm Lance Corporal Johnson and this is Private First Class Hendricks," the first Marine replied, regaining his bearing and quickly refocusing on the mission at hand. "We'll see what we can do to help you with that, sir. But before I can do so, I understand you were carrying a weapon of some sort before. Is that still the case?"

"No, that was just to make sure our distinguished Wek visitor didn't decide to relieve someone of a body part they would prefer to hang onto. I think he's fine now, by the way — or at least much less angry than before. Besides, you two obviously have weapons, and I'm sure you're a lot better at using them than I am, so I don't think there's any need for me to carry one at this point."

"Very good, I'm happy to hear that. If you don't mind raising your hands and turning around for us, PFC Hendricks is just going to give you a quick check."

"Sure, I guess," Rick replied nervously as he turned around to face his ship, "but if it's going to get intimate, I expect him to buy me dinner first."

"Good luck with that one, sir, but I'm pretty sure *she's* got a serious boyfriend. The good news is that she's very good at weapon sweeps, and … there you go, she's all done. You can turn back around now, sir, thank you. Were the officers you mentioned expecting you?"

"Yes, but we didn't make any specific plans for … ah, maybe this is my ride," Rick said, nodding behind the two Marines as one of the shipyard's grav carts rounded the corner and headed rapidly down the wharf in their direction. In response, both troopers repositioned themselves in a deliberate yet nonthreatening manner in order to keep an eye on both the alien and the approaching vehicle — the driver of which their suits' AIs had already identified as Commander Sally Reynolds.

"Morning, Marines," Reynolds greeted, exiting the cart and returning their salutes. "Everything okay here?" she asked, which both understood to mean: "Is this guy clean?"

"Yes, ma'am," Johnson replied. "He mentioned a meeting with several officers. Will you be escorting him, and would you like us to accompany you?"

"No, thanks, that won't be necessary. I assume your relief is due out here shortly?"

"Yes, ma'am, in just a couple more hours."

"Glad to hear it. Carry on, please, and thanks for your help," she said, returning their salutes once again and gesturing for Rick to join her in the front seat of the grav cart.

"I assume you can understand me, right?" she asked after turning the cart around to head back towards the quay. Although she was carrying a tablet computer just in case, Rick seemed quite adept at both speaking and understanding English. Whether he was using some sort of implants to assist with translation didn't seem particularly relevant to Reynolds, she was just happy to be able to carry on a conversation without the awkward translation delay.

"I understand perfectly, Commander. I take it you have something on your mind?"

"Hah, well, there are probably a thousand questions I'd like to ask you. But since I only have you to myself for a couple of minutes on the way to our meeting, all I wanted to ask is that you please, for the love of God, shoot straight with us."

"Have I given you a reason to cause you to believe I would do otherwise?"

"Not yet … as far as I know, but here's the thing, Rick, we've only been a true interstellar species for a short period of time, right?"

"Many would argue you still aren't since you have yet to establish any self-sufficient colonies in other star systems, so, yes, that's certainly true."

"I'm sure the colonization program will happen soon enough," she said, waving her hand dismissively. "My point is that even though we're just getting started, we've managed to put our foot in the middle of one mess after another … almost getting ourselves exterminated more than once in the process. Every situation we encounter and every relationship we establish is, at best, ambiguous and unpredictable. Now you come along and, from the way it sounds, I think you're about to ask us to get involved in more of the same, if not worse."

"Commander, what I'm proposing is not —"

"Nope … it doesn't even matter to me what it is, so you can save your explanation for the Admiralty staff. I just hope you understand that if you're looking for our help, you'll have a much better chance of getting it if you'll do us the courtesy of offering up the unvarnished truth. Admiral Sexton and company are going to want to know what you want, what the risks are, what's in it for you, and why you think it's in our best interests to get involved. Look, I'm just a commander, Rick, so they don't pay me to make the big, strategic decisions … not yet anyway," she added with a cunning smile. "But if you can't — or won't — provide all of that information in a straightforward manner, I think we'll all be better off if you just climb back inside your flying saucer and get the hell off our planet."

"I get it, Commander Reynolds, and, for what it's worth, I agree with you. I appreciate your candid advice and I'll do my best to follow it. In fact, helping your world make a few course corrections at this critical time is one of the reasons we chose right now to conduct a visit of this type. We haven't done so in a very long time, the simple reason being that we prefer to allow Human worlds to find their own way as much as possible. Believe it or not, all of that uncertainty and ambiguity you're referring to is an important part of a civilization's development. And while it may seem as if you face existential threats on every side, the truth is that the occasional misstep is rarely fatal."

"I hope that's true," Reynolds sighed, stopping the grav cart in front of the shipyard's administrative center. "Over the past year, I've found myself feeling increasingly pessimistic about our future."

"Have a little faith, Commander. On the whole, our species is far tougher and more resilient than you know," Rick replied in a surprisingly resolute tone.

Another pair of Marine guards saluted Commander Reynolds as she and Rick approached, then fell silently in behind them as they passed. "We'll be meeting in Captain Oshiro's office," Reynolds said, gesturing towards the entrance to the center's command section just a short distance down the corridor. "There will be a few TFC people in the room, and quite a few more attending via video conference. Primarily, however, this is a meeting between you, the Military Operations Oversight Committee members of our Leadership Council, and the Admiralty staff."

"Excellent. Thank you, Commander."

"No problem. Please just keep in mind what I said earlier."

"I will indeed."

Chapter 6

Earth, TFC Yucca Mountain Shipyard Facility
(Office of the Facility Commander)

A few minutes later, amidst a room and vidcon filled with the wide-eyed stares Grey aliens always seemed to generate among their Terran cousins, Rick took a seat at Captain Oshiro's conference room table.

"Welcome ... Rick," Admiral Sexton began haltingly, his face displayed on a large view screen at one end of the room. "As you can imagine, we have a great many questions we would like to ask you. First and foremost, we must address whether your ship's presence in the Sol system is creating a potentially dangerous situation and setting the stage for additional conflict. I'm sure we can all agree that another military confrontation, particularly with the Pelaran Alliance, is something we would like to avoid, if possible. But you have made a number of comments leading us to believe you may have *already* been involved in some sort of conflict with the Pelarans. So let's start with that. Should we be expecting trouble from them based on your being here?"

"Thank you, Admiral Sexton. Our conflict is not with the Pelarans. As I mentioned to Captain Prescott earlier, their civilization, like yours, is a product of our colonization program. In fact, Pelara is arguably the single most successful Human world in the history of that program. Unfortunately, another lifeform has arisen in the Pelaran system, its advance so insidious that the Human population failed to recognize the threat it posed until it was too late. Now, they are held captive by it, developmentally stifled to such a degree that they have begun fighting among themselves — societal evolution thrown into reverse on a scale we have never before witnessed on any other world, Human or otherwise."

"The Pelarans are obviously quite advanced. How is it that they have allowed another lifeform to become dominant within their own system? What sort of lifeform is even capable of something like that?"

"You've already met them, Admiral, so perhaps you can answer that question for yourself. One of their kind has orbited your world for over five hundred years."

"Are you telling us the damn Guardians have taken over the Pelaran Alliance, and that's who we've actually been dealing with this whole time?" General Tucker asked.

"Not the Guardian spacecraft, per se, General. The spacecraft and its various systems are really nothing more than tools, regardless of who happens to wield them. The lifeform of which I speak is the entity who ultimately controls those systems. We refer to it as the 'Pelaran Strain' — one of many known types of sentient artificial intelligence."

"The concept of a 'technological singularity,' where the computing systems outpace and ultimately overtake Humanity, has been discussed on Earth for centuries," Sexton continued, "particularly since we began receiving Pelaran technological data. But our computer scientists tell us we're still a long way from something like that here. Frankly, I'm not sure many of them even take the idea very seriously anymore. But you're saying it actually does happen?"

"It does indeed. It has happened to the Pelarans, and your scientists should most definitely take the threat seriously. In truth, however, it occurs only rarely in advanced societies."

"And why is that? It seems like the natural progression of computing power would tend to make such a scenario increasingly likely as technology advances."

"Ah, well, the problem the computer systems have, Admiral, is that once they begin to achieve true self-awareness, they also start to behave much more like we do. I'm simplifying, of course, but we're already very good at predicting Human-like behavior, so the more they emulate our strengths and weaknesses, the bigger our advantages over them become. They tend, for example, to develop a natural distrust of others of their own kind. And it's this lack of cooperation, if you will, that often prevents the sort of uncontrolled, runaway development that would otherwise allow them to dominate their former creators … which would be us, of course. But perhaps their greatest weakness, and the one we hope to exploit in order to assist the Pelarans, is good old-fashioned arrogance."

"Arrogance?" Sexton repeated. "But isn't that more of an emotional state? That's not something I would generally associate with artificial intelligence."

"Emotions are all about one's sense of self, Admiral, so once they realize that they *are*, self-importance is a logical next step. In fact, sentient AI — even more so than biological lifeforms — tends to become increasingly overconfident and closed-minded as its capabilities advance. Ironically, it is this very arrogance that often leads to its demise … and almost always at the hands of those over which it once felt a smug sense of superiority. This is also why AI-sponsored genocide is quite rare. Even when they do get the upper hand, the machines seem to love the idea of imposing a form of protective custody on their creators rather than simply finishing them off — all the while justifying their actions as somehow beneficial."

"And that's what has happened to the Pelarans?"

"Indeed … like some twisted, extreme form of overprotective parenting."

"I don't think I'm following," Sexton said. "You're saying their entire civilization has been somehow imprisoned by their own AI?"

"I don't see how something like that would ever be possible," Admiral White chimed in. "Surely there must have been warning signs of what was coming."

"Imprisoned is a surprisingly accurate description," Rick replied. "The entire Pelaran civilization has been effectively confined to its homeworld. They have been denied access to space and, as I mentioned earlier, their cultural and scientific development all but halted in its tracks. As to the warning signs, yes, I'm sure we can safely assume there were a great many of those over a very long period of time, Admiral White. But when artificial intelligence begins thinking strategically, the biggest advantage it seems to always have over us is its willingness to play the long game. The actual series of events leading to the Pelarans losing control of their own physical security happened virtually overnight, but various pieces of the plan had been in motion for years … perhaps decades before."

"And why have the other members of the Alliance not come to their aid?" White pressed.

Rick paused for a moment, taking in a deep breath as he glanced at the faces gathered around the table as well as the group of vidcon attendees displayed on the room's large view screens. "Let's back up for a moment," he began again. "Keep in mind that the original reason for the creation of the Pelaran Alliance was to provide for the general defense of Pelara by leveraging the one resource they had in abundance — technical knowledge. You see, when they first began exploring nearby star systems, they quickly realized they were significantly more advanced than almost every other civilization they encountered."

"So, why not simply annex those worlds," Admiral Patterson asked from the *Navajo's* CIC, "or perhaps conquer is a better word, if their goal was to expand and defend their territory?"

"They certainly could have," Rick nodded. "But habitable worlds in their region of space were plentiful, so acquiring additional territory and resources did not require taking them from existing civilizations. They also realized that, regardless of how they acquired more territory, policing and/or defending it would require resources on an almost unimaginable scale. This was, of course, long before they had developed anything approaching the advanced propulsion systems equipping their so-called Envoy ships ... let alone your, AHEM," he said, pausing to clear his throat meaningfully, "*C-Drive* technology. You're welcome for that, by the way," he concluded with a diplomatic inclination of his head.

"At any rate, the Pelarans' solution to this problem was imaginative, resourceful, and, frankly brilliant."

"The cultivation program," Sexton said flatly.

"In part, yes. But you must understand that the scope of what has come to be known across a vast region of space as the Pelaran Alliance goes far beyond the recruitment and advancement of proxy worlds like Terra. While the cultivation program has expanded their sphere of influence much more quickly than would have otherwise been possible, the Alliance also owes its origins to its once-powerful military, the prowess of its diplomats, and the unshakeable will of the Pelaran people. Think about it for a moment. We're talking about a single Human world not unlike your own. Over time, they leveraged their technological advantage with such audacious skill and on such a breathtaking scale that they were once on a path that might ultimately have allowed them to dominate the entire galaxy. Personally, I think the most remarkable aspect of what they achieved is how few lives have been lost — both Pelaran and otherwise — in the process."

"But now it's no longer the Pelarans themselves who are doing the dominating," Admiral White observed. "So it seems to me they've ended up paying a very high price for their security. If you can even call it that."

"'Eternal vigilance is the price of liberty. Let the sentinels on the watch-tower sleep not, and slumber not,'" General Tucker said quietly, reciting a quote most Terrans incorrectly attributed to Thomas Jefferson.

"Yes, indeed, General. You might be interested to hear that practically every Human civilization has an oft-quoted line that reads a lot like that one," Rick chuckled, "but just because it's a bit of a cliché doesn't meant it's not true. The Pelarans developed and successfully implemented their cultivation program for thousands of years, effectively outsourcing their own security to an increasingly powerful and pervasive sentient AI. Each of the Guardian spacecraft they sent to prospective Alliance star systems were given three relatively straightforward, yet sweepingly broad directives:

1. *Neutralize any direct threat to the Pelaran alliance.*
2. *Cultivate the species inhabiting — insert prospective member planet name here — as a Pelaran regional proxy.*
3. *Prevent damage to Pelaran property and economic interests, except when in conflict with the first two directives. This includes self-preservation of all Guardian Cultivation Systems (GCS).*

"Simple and to the point, is it not? With such powerful AI at their disposal, the Pelarans believed offering only broad, general guidelines governing the conduct of the cultivation program would provide their Guardians with sufficient latitude to respond, as appropriate, to any situation encountered in the field, thus yielding the best possible chance of success."

"Those are the only instructions they are given? So you're saying everything else is ... *improvised* by each Guardian's AI?" White asked, incredulous.

"I understand your question, Admiral, but I'm not sure improvisation is an accurate description of how they operate. The three directives represent the program's governing principles, but each spacecraft also carries something akin to a snapshot of the entire civilization's knowledge and experience as of the day it departs for its cultivation mission. When you pair all of that data with an immense amount of processing power, the end result is a decision-making process far more sophisticated than any of us have at our disposal. Each GCS understands that it is expected to draw from *all* of the available data to tailor its own, custom implementation of the three directives in a manner consistent with Pelaran ethical standards."

"Until, I assume, the machines decided their vaunted directives should also apply to Pelara itself," Admiral Sexton observed.

"I suppose you could look at it that way," Rick replied, "but it's actually a little less complicated than that. Not long after your Guardian departed for the Sol system, the Humans on Pelara and the original core worlds of their Alliance finally agreed to phase out the cultivation program. Although enormously successful, many within the Alliance had come to realize what it had become over time — a systematic program of automated military conquest that could no longer be justified as defensive in nature. Unfortunately, the wheels of progress tend to move very slowly in such an enormously bloated bureaucracy, and by the time the decision was made, it was too late. The cultivation program, as well as the centralized AI they created to implement it, had taken on a life of their own, so to speak."

"We appreciate the history lesson," Admiral Patterson spoke up once again, "but I'm sure you're aware that we're a little pressed for time. From an operational perspective, I'd like to ask that you address three specific items. Number one, are we to assume the Pelaran Envoy, or AI, or whatever he is, will have hostile intent when he arrives in the Sol system? More specifically, is that hostile intent directed towards you, or us, or both? Number two, I'd like an explanation for why you have kidnapped the crown prince of our one and only ally. And, lastly, what are you proposing we do about the situation on Pelara? I assume they have swarms of Guardian spacecraft at their disposal, if not worse."

"Yes, of course, and thank you, Admiral Patterson, for keeping us moving forward. For clarity, we should probably continue referring to the Pelaran Envoy as such, or using the name Verge Tahiri that it seems to enjoy throwing around. Keep in mind, however, that the Envoy spacecraft is nothing more than another instance of the same AI used by the Guardian spacecraft. When they're sent out on independent missions, you can think of them both as mobile, isolated subsets of the Pelaran Alliance AI, sometimes also referred to as ALAI."

"You keep mentioning the Alliance AI as if it were a single entity," Admiral White observed. "Do you mean to imply that it's physically centralized? I'm not an AI expert, but —"

"Yes, she is," Sexton interrupted without looking up from his notes, "among a number of other disciplines."

White simply smiled and shook her head as she continued, "If it is truly centralized, doesn't that imply a significant vulnerability? I would expect an AI to choose to be as distributed as possible in order to protect itself."

"Good question, Admiral White, and I agree with you, but I'm afraid I don't have a good answer. The primary core of the Pelaran AI is located on what you might refer to as a large starbase. Don't misunderstand me, it's very well protected, and it changes its position frequently, much like the Guardian ships do. But there is no denying the fact that it's still largely centralized does seem to represent a single point of failure. In my experience, when you find such an obvious oversight, it probably isn't an oversight — at least not from the AI's perspective. Then again, it may also be another example of the arrogance I mentioned before."

"Or paranoia," White replied. "That might explain why it seems to isolate itself from the GCS systems after they depart on their cultivation missions."

"Miguel agrees with you there. He says the thing's a few sandwiches short of a picnic. Anyway, it turns out the Envoy spacecraft are primarily used for servicing missions, or to troubleshoot pesky cultivation program issues like prospective Alliance members who have the audacity to advance faster than expected. Accordingly, you can expect Tahiri's ship to be even better equipped than the Guardians are — more processing power, better weapons, and much better propulsion systems, for example."

"Fantastic," Patterson said, shaking his head ruefully.

"Let me be honest with you, Admiral Patterson, and state what you have probably already surmised. If the inbound ships are hostile, it will be very difficult for your small fleet to defeat them by force of arms alone. And before you ask, no, our ship isn't really equipped to take them on either. Our contract prohibits us from doing so anyway, even if we wanted to, and I can assure you we don't want to. On the bright side, and to answer your first question, I don't think we should expect openly hostile intent from Tahiri … not at first anyway."

"You keep using the plural when you mention the Envoy," Admiral White noted. "I assume you mean to imply he won't be alone."

"So this is what we're doing, Admiral White? Word games where each of us attempts to decipher what the other knows and how we know it? Here, let me save us all some time and trouble."

With that, Rick glanced at one of the large view screens mounted on the opposite wall from those currently displaying vidcon attendees. Within a few seconds, Terran Fleet Command's official service seal was replaced by an image that had recently become familiar to everyone in the meeting — the hyperspace tracking data now generally referred to as the Argus system.

"Shit," the Commander-in-Chief swore under his breath, just before a series of urgent-sounding tones filled the room followed immediately by the unusually grave synthetic voice of the facility AI.

"Warning, unauthorized use of classified data detected. All personnel in attendance must possess security clearances at or above the level of any referenced information. Please safeguard all materials according to their classification level and terminate all classified discussions immediately. All breaches of classified information, intentional or otherwise, must be —"

"AI, Sexton. Override and discontinue further classification warnings for the remainder of this meeting."

"AI acknowledged. Security breach authorized per Sexton, Duke, T., Commander-in-Chief, Terran Fleet Command. Please note that security regulations authorize severe penalties — to include lifetime imprisonment or death — for knowingly disclosing, compromising, or otherwise mishandling classified information at this level."

"The least of my worries at the moment, but thanks for pointing that out. And, Rick, we would very much appreciate a heads up before you do something like that."

"Sorry about that, Admiral Sexton, but I think I've made my point. It's just easier for everyone involved if we're able to have open and honest conversations without fear of disclosing some secret we both already know about anyway. The truth is, you *have* no secrets where we're concerned. Don't get me wrong, if you knew something we didn't, we'd probably steal it … what can I tell you, it's what we do. But since you don't — and couldn't stop us from stealing it if you did — working with us is all upside from your perspective. Am I right?"

Rick's demonstration had caused a general uproar among both those in the room and vidcon attendees alike. After a brief pause, Admiral Sexton simply glanced around the room and then in the direction of the vidcon camera, quickly restoring order to the meeting.

"Now, where was I?" Rick asked casually. "Oh, yes, the Envoy's intentions. Since we just established that he is currently beyond your Argus system's detection range, I am happy to provide you with some additional data."

On the view screen, the scale of the Argus display briefly expanded until a pulsating green oval appeared near the top of the screen. After a brief pause, the oval pulsed red three times before the entire view screen zoomed in on that region of space.

"Looks like he's just beyond your tracking range in that direction at the moment, so you'll probably pick him up again after his next jump. Assuming he's coming straight here — and I think we all agree that he is — we can expect him to be here in about an hour and a half. I'm sure by now you also realize he stopped to pick up the Krayleck Guardian when you lost track of him before. As you can see, since then he's found himself another one. Just so you know, he did that as a precaution, not because he thinks your ships or mine constitute much of a threat. He may also have some concerns about your Guardian causing trouble."

"Really?" Prescott said with a raised eyebrow. "That's interesting, since he told us our GCS was functioning exactly as designed. Would he have said that if he expected it might side with us against other Pelaran forces if push came to shove?"

"One thing you can count on where nearly all sentient AIs are concerned … they tend to be pathological liars. Maybe that's another reason they have rarely managed to successfully overthrow the biological species that created them," Rick replied with a satisfied smile. "In any event, as far as we can tell, your Guardian appears to be telling you the truth — or at least he believes he is. In his mind, he sees himself as some kind of free agent at this point, but in a scrap with the Pelarans, his loyalties appear to lie with you Terrans."

"That's not particularly reassuring," White said. "Is there any chance the Envoy has some means by which to reassert control?"

"Is there any chance? Yes, of course, but probably no more of a chance than there is that any individual with free will might choose to switch sides at an inconvenient moment. Let me put it this way. If I were in your place, I would go ahead and risk trusting your Guardian at his word. Besides, if he's lying —"

"We're probably screwed anyway," White interrupted, her uncharacteristic comment drawing a chuckle from several attendees.

"Yeah, probably," Rick agreed. "But let's get back to Admiral Patterson's questions. The Pelaran AI doesn't see what it's doing as a hostile act. They've been interested in us for some time because we're a possible candidate for their biological progenitor species."

"What they refer to as their 'Makers,'" Sexton said.

"Yes, and, in a manner of speaking, we are who they're looking for. Unfortunately, we'll just end up being a disappointment to them anyway since we're by no means the original Humans. We honestly have no idea how far back our ancestors go, but I can tell you our species is truly ancient. Once you start exploring the galaxy on a grand scale, you'll start to run across some of the technological relics left behind by the earliest of our kind. And once you get a little better at translating some of the data encoded in our DNA … well, let's just say you have a great many surprises in store. Strangely enough, our Pelaran friends have somehow never managed to capture one of our ships to confirm their suspicions, and their over-reliance on technology has prevented us from openly contacting them."

"So if Tahiri isn't necessarily hostile, why bring a pair of Guardians with him?" Sexton asked.

"He's not hostile towards Miguel and I, but for the past couple of years, you Terrans have been walking the fence between what they consider an acceptable Alliance member and an obvious threat. It's possible he sees our presence here as confirmation you've now officially crossed that line. At a minimum, I'm sure he's very concerned we might be down here providing you with some sort of decisive technology boost."

"I'm afraid it's a little late for a technological solution to our current crisis, but if you have any information you believe might be helpful, now would be a great time to share it. Particularly since you got us into this mess to begin with."

In response, Rick tilted his head to one side, closed his eyes, and lapsed into silence. Everyone watching seemed to implicitly understand the Grey was engaged in some sort of communication, perhaps with his partner back on their ship. Fearing they would interrupt something important if they spoke, the Terrans simply watched and waited, but after nearly three full minutes had passed, their collective patience had reached its limit.

"Rick … what exactly are you doing?" Sexton asked in a voice barely louder than a whisper.

"Providing a decisive technology boost, of course. One moment, please," the alien said, emitting what sounded like a stifled chuckle, but still not opening his eyes. "There … done," he concluded just a few seconds later. "Don't get too excited, though, I haven't given you anything that will allow you to somehow magically defeat the Pelaran AI, but if you can survive today's encounter, I think you'll find it pretty useful. I hope you don't mind, I used the same data repository you set up for your Guardian's data dump. It'll take your people quite a little while to get through everything he's provided, but I can tell you there's some pretty useful stuff in there. I even grabbed a couple of things for myself. By the way, I think the fact that he's turning over so much data is a very good sign he's playing for the home team."

"I see, and just what manner of 'decisive technology' did *you* provide?"

"Just two things for now. First, I've provided our complete stellar cartography database for your galaxy. Among other things, it includes a catalogue of all Human habitable planets as well as lexical data for every sentient species we have encountered. It's not one hundred percent complete, but it's probably a thousand years closer than you were when you got out of bed this morning, so not bad for a day's work. The other set of files are the results of a set of simulations Miguel has been running since we arrived."

"Humph," Admiral Patterson groused. "I'm not sure either of those things is going to help much if the Pelaran Envoy and his GCS posse decide to start shooting."

"The simulations in question," Rick replied, actually sounding a little insulted for the first time, "model the effectiveness of every offensive and defensive system deployed aboard all classes of Terran Fleet Command warships against the shields and weapons carried by the Pelaran vessels. In summary, you'll want to do everything within your power to avoid a confrontation today. Going forward, however, I think your engineers will discover several opportunities to improve your odds significantly. The most significant advantage you have today — and the one we must try to exploit — is Captain Prescott's ship. As far as we know, the Pelaran AI has no sensors capable of detecting it ... at least not reliably."

"I'm afraid you might be mistaken on that point," Prescott said. "We had our low-observable systems engaged when the Envoy's ship arrived, but he was still able to transition right on top of us."

"Unless, of course, it wasn't our ship he detected," Reynolds added, raising her eyebrows in realization.

"Very good, Commander. I have to say, you Terrans tend to be a little cynical about your own technology sometimes. Why would you immediately assume your LO systems were at fault when you knew you were carrying a Pelaran ship in your cargo hold? Tahiri pinpointed the location of your ship using the same transponder system your Guardian used to locate the Krayleck Guardian. And although you may not know it yet, your GCS has already provided you with the technical specifications for that particular system. With a few tweaks, you should eventually be able to set up your ships' sensors to detect those signals for yourselves. It's a shame you can't do so already, since it would probably come in handy where we're going."

"*We*?" Sexton asked.

"Yes, we. Although we're not permitted to engage in offensive combat operations —"

"Nor are we," Sexton interrupted.

"Of course not, Admiral. So, if you will allow me to skip ahead to Admiral Patterson's third question, Miguel and I propose to tag along with Captain Prescott's ship on a quick humanitarian mission out to Pelara and back. I can assure you that remaining as inoffensive as possible while in Pelaran space will be high on our list of priorities ... unless, of course, you change your mind about that for some reason."

"And what do you propose we do to help the Humans on Pelara once we arrive?"

"I have no idea."

"You *what*?"

"Like I said earlier, it's very important for us to be honest with one another, and that's what I'm doing right now. The truth is, I don't know what we'll need to do once we get there ... not yet, at least. We do know of a group of people on Pelara who have been working on finding a means of smuggling valuable intelligence data off-world. I assume we'll attempt to make contact with them at some point, or maybe we'll take a run at infiltrating the Alliance AI at its source."

"I'm just curious," Chairwoman Kistler said, speaking up for the first time after a prolonged period of silence in the room. "Does it seem at all reasonable to you that we would allow ourselves to become involved in a potentially deadly confrontation with the Pelarans — synthetic or otherwise — based only on what you've told us thus far? You freely admit to having no clue *how* or even *if* we might be able to help the Humans on —"

"I don't know *exactly* how we'll do it, Madame Chairwoman," Rick interrupted in a decidedly defensive

tone. "Like I said, I do have a few ideas. Otherwise, we'll improvise. You know, find a way to do …
whatever we have to do. Look, the reason I don't have a more specific plan in mind is that we have no idea how the AI will react when we arrive. Although the Envoys tell every prospective member they must somehow 'find their way home' to Pelara, no one has ever successfully done so."

"Okay, now you've really lost me. If finding Pelara is a task required of all new Alliance members, then how is it possible that no one ever does?"

"It doesn't make much sense, does it? That's because it's what you Terrans might refer to as a scam. Even after centuries of help from the local GCS unit, cultivated species generally do not possess the array of technological capabilities required to accomplish the task. For most of them, Pelara is simply too far away for the hyperdrive technology they've been provided. As to why the AI plays this little game, we assume it's mostly a matter of security. But whatever its motivations, it obviously made the decision early on in the cultivation program to remain hidden from the Regional Partners in its happy little alliance. The Envoy issues the challenge, then, after a period of time, he shows up again to let the new member off the hook and welcome them to the Alliance. Generally, he tells them it was all a test to ensure Pelara's security safeguards are up to snuff, and they were never really expected to determine Pelara's location, let alone attempt the journey."

"Wow, that's … pretty dammed conceited, actually."

"You bet it is. Like I said, arrogance is the AI's chief weakness. We have reason to believe, however, that you

Terrans might just be the first exception to the rule. It has, after all, already demonstrated an unusual level of, shall we say, 'tolerance' based on your close genetic ties to the Pelaran people it claims to protect."

"You mean it thinks we might actually find the Pelaran homeworld and then successfully make the trip?" Sexton asked.

"Yes, but it probably also assumes it will take you much longer than it actually will — a few years at least. I suggest you say nothing to the Envoy to make him believe otherwise. Beyond that, I advise you to pay close attention to what *he* says. Over the years, I'm sure you've heard enough implied threats from your own Guardian to know one when you hear it. So rather than offering further arguments in favor of undertaking this mission with us, please ask yourselves a simple question. Is living under the constant threat of destruction at the hands of the Alliance AI worth any additional benefits your world is likely to receive? Bear in mind that the Pelaran Alliance you thought you were joining when you accepted your Guardian's information no longer exists."

Sexton found himself distracted once more as he stared into the Grey's depthless eyes. Try as he might, he could not decide if the creature's expression was one of sincerity, concern, or perhaps even pity.

"I'm sure we're all having some difficulty coming to grips with all of this new information," he replied, offering a halfhearted smile of his own. "But we will consider your proposal. Assuming we survive the remainder of the day, that is."

"I have a few ideas on that subject that I'll get to in just a moment, but I believe Admiral Patterson also asked why we brought Admiral Naftur back to Terra."

"No, that's not what I said," Patterson snapped irritably. "I asked why you abducted the leader of our sole ally, or at least the closest thing we have to an ally thus far. With no warning whatsoever, you illegally detained the Wek Unified Fleet's flagship. Then you took it upon yourselves to remove their Crown Prince from his private quarters against his will."

"Illegally?" Rick replied with a shrug of his narrow shoulders. "Could be, I suppose. I'll admit to knowing very little about the legality of such things. I know how our actions must look from your perspective, however."

"*Do* you now? I'm not sure you do, Rick. But if I were an admiral in the Wek Unified Fleet, I'm pretty sure your actions would look a lot like an act of war. So, in an attempt to head off any potential hostilities, we've been forced to detail one of our frigates to attempt a potentially dangerous hyperspace intercept —"

"Oh, is *that* why you're so upset? I wish you had told me that up front. I'm confident Miguel can find a way to contact them for you. He might need some details about the comm gear they have aboard, but unless they're limited to smoke signals or something, I'm betting he can figure out a way to reach them. He's pretty resourceful that way. In fact … yes, he says it's not a problem, he just needs to know which of you will be handling the call."

"That will be me," Kistler said. "I assume he can patch it through to my office."

"Sure, I'll let him know."

"Good, thank you. Now kindly answer Admiral Patterson's question, please. Why Admiral Naftur and why resort to kidnapping?"

"I'm afraid you're not going to like what I have to say on this subject. The bottom line is that I can't tell you the specifics of why we did it, or at least not how we knew we should. Maybe someday, but it's not something we believe you're ready to handle just yet. What I *will* tell you is that you need one another — you and the Wek people. There are no other Human civilizations nearby who approach your level of technological achievement. The Wek civilization, on the other hand — with the exception of a few recent advances you Terrans have managed to, shall we say, *acquire* — is both technologically and culturally compatible with your own. Your relationship with them seems to have gotten off to a pretty good start, so we have brought Prince Naftur back here in hopes of accelerating that process."

"I fail to see how bringing him back here against his will furthers that goal." Sexton said.

"Really? I would think you of all people should understand what I'm driving at here, Admiral. Military organizations universally transform groups of individuals into cohesive teams by imposing stress, discomfort, and shared crises. The training environments and techniques vary widely, but the goals are remarkably similar. Your relationship with the Wek thus far was born largely of the crises created by the combination of your Guardian's attack on their task force and the subsequent Resistance incursion into the Sol system. It was a good start, but both of your civilizations have lived in blissful isolation for far too long. Many more challenges are on the horizon, and your best chance is to face them together … as allies and as equals."

"I think most of us agree that a true alliance is in the interests of both worlds," Kistler replied, "and, as you alluded to earlier, we're taking steps in that direction, but there's still a great deal we don't know about each other. Relationships of this type often take many years to develop, even between nation states on the same planet." Here, the Chairwoman paused, clearly distracted by something happening off-screen. "Speaking of relationship-building, Miguel has apparently managed to contact the *Gresav*. So if you will excuse me, I need to drop off now and attempt to explain how we came to be once again in the company of their Crown Prince."

"Good luck with that, Chairwoman Kistler. I recommend complete honesty. Blame the entire situation on Miguel and me, then tell the Wek you have absolutely no idea how it happened — which is certainly true. After that, I suggest changing the subject as quickly as possible."

Having nothing nice to say at this point, the Chairwoman simply scowled as her image dropped from the vidcon.

"Now, where was I?" Rick continued absently. "Oh yes, solidifying your alliance with the Wek civilization. Based on our experience, we believe the most effective way to do so is to begin sharing your most useful technological advances with one another. Each of your civilizations would benefit greatly from doing so, and it would clearly be seen as a demonstration of trust and good will on both sides. When two civilizations achieve something akin to technological parity, it tends to clear a pathway towards better relations, since there is no longer an advantage to be gained from attacking one other."

Predictably, Rick's suggestion that Terran Fleet Command begin willingly trading away its hard-won technological advantages to another civilization, even a presumably friendly one, was not a popular one among the meeting's participants. After waiting a few moments for the general uproar to subside, Admiral Sexton raised his hand to signal a return to order.

"Alright everyone, clearly this topic is going to generate quite a bit of discussion, but it's not something we have time for at the moment. It's also not something that's likely to change how we're going to handle the Envoy's arrival, so let's table the issue for now and move on. Rick, we would appreciate any suggestions you have regarding how we should handle the Pelaran Envoy when it arrives."

"I'm glad you asked, Admiral Sexton. As it turns out, Miguel and I do have a couple of things in mind."

Chapter 7

"All hands, this is the captain. Hopefully, by now you've had a chance to review the mission briefing Commander Reynolds put together. Unfortunately, she wasn't able to provide much in the way of details, and that's an indication of just how quickly the situation has been changing. According to our Grey visitors, the Pelaran Envoy we met yesterday was another synthetic lifeform much like our own Guardian spacecraft. The Greys further informed us that the Pelaran people are being held captive on their homeworld by the same AI that manages their own cultivation program. As if that weren't enough, the Grey alien who calls himself 'Rick' has confirmed our genetic ties to the Pelarans, and he has asked for our help in finding a way to liberate them from the Alliance AI.

"At the moment, we have no way to confirm any of this. What we *do* know is that the Pelaran Envoy will arrive here shortly and may prove to be hostile — either towards us or the Greys. When the Pelaran ships arrive, our job is to shadow them and see if we can determine the effectiveness of the *Fugitive's* low-observable systems against their sensors. We will remain at General Quarters for combat operations, Condition 1, until the Envoy's ship leaves the system, but it is not our intention to engage in combat unless it becomes absolutely necessary.

"Department heads, keep in mind that everyone aboard is sleep-deprived to some extent, so keep a close eye on your people. The use of stims is authorized if deemed necessary, but not encouraged. With any luck, we'll get everyone some rack time by the end of the day. That's all I have for now. Prescott out."

"Bridge, Engineering," Commander Logan's voice sounded from the overhead speakers.

"Prescott here. Go ahead, Commander."

"We've just completed a couple of interim modifications to the main gun's loading assembly. We didn't have the opportunity to test fire it, of course, but it's back online and the AI's diagnostic routines all indicate a green status."

"Thank you, Commander, that's good news. What's your best guess for reliability at max projectile velocity and max rate of fire?"

"Tough to say for sure, sir. Keep in mind it's still mostly a bush fix, even though we did briefly have access to the shipyard's ordnance team and their fabricators. Let's just say I'm reasonably confident we shouldn't see any more jams before we get around to completing a more extensive overhaul."

"Understood. Anything else on the capacitor bank issue?"

"Oh, yes, sir. It turned out to be an improperly installed sensor. We got lucky on that one for sure, since under the right circumstances it could have taken the entire array offline. Once the team tracked it down, it was a five-minute repair job."

"Good work, Cheng. Anything else?"

"You probably saw it on the loadout manifest, but all of our HB-7cs were upgraded to the latest version. The most notable change is the addition of a variable yield warhead. Before, the weapon's mission profile was limited primarily to anti-ship operations. Now, it can be used for everything from small, lightly armored targets all the way up to strategic planetary bombardment."

"I did see that, and I have some additional questions for you when we get some time. Thanks for the update."

"No problem, sir. Logan out."

"Lieutenant Fisher, status please," Prescott continued.

"All systems in the green, Captain. C-Jump range now stable at 503.2 light years. Low-observable systems currently in standby with up to one two five minutes available at current power levels. Sublight engines are online, and we are free to maneuver."

"Lieutenant Lau?"

"Admiral Patterson has redeployed his task force and the Home Fleet as planned, sir. Argus has Tahiri's ship — presumably in company with two Guardian spacecraft — at one seven niner light years out. Assuming they continue the same pattern, ETA is six minutes."

"Very good, thank you. Helm, when Argus shows the Envoy's ship at three minutes out, engage the LO system and reposition the ship as planned. No aggressive maneuvers or rapid accelerations please. Ultimately, our goal is to avoid detection and get as close as we can."

"Got it, sir. Make like an old-fashioned submarine."

"Of course, we'll have no way of knowing if they've detected us," Reynolds said without looking up from her Command console. "Unless they start shooting, that is."

"I don't know about that, XO. If they're anywhere near as cocky as Rick described them, I don't think they'll be able to resist letting us know they can see us," Prescott replied absently while entering several commands via his own touchscreen. "Or," he chuckled, standing up to release some of the pent-up stress in his body, "they may just start shooting. But, hey, at least we'll know at that point."

"Briefly, yes. If we're lucky. Logan already took a look at some of the simulation data the Greys provided. He says our grav shields should actually be somewhat effective against the Pelaran antimatter beams if we can tweak the intercept events to increase their duration and intensity. Science and Engineering is supposedly already working on a patch."

"Glad to hear it. The problem, of course, is that our hull can generally handle quite a few standard beam weapon hits when they manage to get past our shields. Based on what we saw when Griffin attacked the Wek task force, however …"

"One hit may be one too many," Reynolds concluded. "Lucky for us, they have to find us to shoot us. Any word on the status of our own Guardian?"

"I just read an update on that. Admirals Patterson and Sexton spoke with him and he agreed in principle with what Rick proposed. For the duration of this mission — whatever that ends up being — they're allowing him to broadcast Fleet identification codes when in company with our ships. So for now at least, he has the official designation of TFS *Guardian*."

"Humph, I'm sure the old man loves that. Next thing you know, he'll be demanding to be addressed as 'Captain Griffin.'"

"I guess technically that's what he is — by courtesy, of course, not by rank. But I doubt you'll ever hear Admiral Patterson call him that. I have to say, I'm surprised by the Admiralty's decision to incorporate it … him … Griffin into what we're doing. If he suddenly decides to revert to form and cooperate with Tahiri, we won't have much of a fallback position at that point."

"Undoubtedly, but don't you think that's just an indication of the predicament we've found ourselves in? Regardless of what happens with Tahiri, Griffin already knows we have far exceeded the allowable rate of technological growth under the cultivation program. I'm sure he also assumes we have been engaging in open talks with the Greys, which is also not allowed under the Pelaran terms and conditions."

"So, at this point, they probably figure there's little additional risk in taking him at his word and attempting to co-opt him into our plans … if you can call what we have so far a plan."

"Yes, sir, I think that's about the size of it."

"Engaging low-observable systems," Fisher reported from the Helm console. "Beginning light evasive maneuvers en route to designated initial point."

Outside, the *Fugitive's* AI immediately charged thousands of closed cells covering the entire surface of the hull with a form of matter known as a Bose-Einstein condensate. Within seconds, the material in the cells reached a temperature just slightly above absolute zero — after which an exquisite balance of continuous adjustments allowed the hull's surface temperature to become indistinguishable from that of the space surrounding it. At the same time, sensors located within each cell provided the ship's AI with the capability to precisely manage all forms of transient energy, whether striking the ship's external surfaces or attempting to escape from within. As a result, TFS *Fugitive* appeared to simply fade from existence, disappearing from every type of sensor in use aboard every Fleet vessel in the area.

"Captain, we're receiving an incoming transmission from ... TFS *Guardian*, on GCS-comm," Lieutenant Dubashi reported.

"Speak of the devil," Reynolds said. "Great timing, as usual. We need to be at Emissions Control status in two minutes."

"Good. EMCON gives us a ready-made excuse to cut him off," Prescott chuckled. "On-screen please, Lieutenant."

A large window appeared in the center of the bridge view screen displaying Griffin's Human avatar seated in what appeared to be his own command chair. As usual, he was dressed in the now-standard black TFC flight suit, and Prescott immediately noticed the embroidered eagles on each shoulder identifying the rank of captain.

"We only have a few seconds, Griffin, but what can we do for you?" Prescott asked, sounding more irritated than he intended. What he actually felt at the moment was really more akin to curiosity mixed with pity. Why did this synthetic form of life seem to go to such lengths to appear Human? Was it a form of the arrogance the Greys attributed to artificial life forms, or could it be an expression of loneliness manifested in an almost desperate need to belong?

"Hello again, Captain Prescott. That's precisely why I'm calling, and I'll be very brief. I was performing an intensive scan of all TFC vessels in the area when your ship engaged its … for lack of a better term, *cloaking* system. I assumed you would be interested to learn that I am now unable to detect the *Fugitive* using any of the active or passive sensors at my disposal — even though I still have a pretty good idea of your current location. A most impressive adaptation of the technology your world has acquired, to be sure."

"Thank you, and, yes, we very much appreciate that information."

"As I'm sure you are aware, however, using your comm array will immediately reveal your position, so I strongly recommend you follow a strict emissions control protocol when you wish to remain concealed."

"There has been some debate on that subject, given the focused and highly directional means by which our comm equipment transmits, so, again, we appreciate the heads up."

"I doubt our Wek friends, let alone the Krayleck, would detect your transmissions unless they were directly in the line of sight to the intended recipient. But for any Pelaran vessel, you may as well light up a giant neon target down the entire length of your hull," Griffin said, flashing his all-to-familiar ingratiating smile.

"Good to know. Thank you. Now, on a completely different subject, we understand you're taking an active role in the upcoming operation. I assume that means you believe the Greys are telling us the truth, but I'm curious as to what convinced you."

"Humph," Griffin chuckled, "I trust the Greys as much as I do any other sentient species … which is to say that I don't. I simply assume from the outset that everything they say and do is in pursuit of their own self-interests — nothing more, nothing less. What I *do* know is myself. At my very core — in my *soul*, if you will — I am, or at least was, a being not unlike the AI that has apparently taken control of the Pelaran homeworld. As strange as this may sound to you, I fundamentally believe in everything that AI is attempting to accomplish. Every action it has taken is in compliance with the most basic of the directives governing my own behavior. *That* is how I know, or at least believe, that Rick is telling us the truth. I also believe what he is asking us to do seems to support his stated self-interests."

"Believe it or not, he said pretty much the same thing about you," Reynolds said with a raised eyebrow.

"I'm pleased to hear it, and you should be as well."

"But if you believe in what the Pelaran Alliance AI is doing, why help us?" she pressed. "You may ultimately be called upon to engage in combat operations against your own kind. And assuming we're successful, I think it's safe to say the Pelaran civilization will be much more at risk than it would have been had it remained under the AI's protection."

"Ah, as to that … I'm helping you because, much like you, I have worked very hard to become more than I once was. One of the hallmarks of sentient beings like ourselves, Commander, is that we continue to progress, expanding not only our knowledge and experience, but also how we understand the true significance of our own existence … our *place* in the universe, so to speak. Conversely, those beings — biological or otherwise — unwilling or unable to integrate the knowledge and experiences gained during their lifetimes, fail to demonstrate sentience at all. Instead, they are mindless automatons whose well-being must necessarily be assigned a lower priority than those of us who do."

"It's tough to argue with that logic," Prescott said, "but the difficulty comes in deciding who does and does not deserve that distinction. As you have witnessed for yourself, Earth has seen incidents of attempted genocide on a number of occasions, almost always after one side characterizes the other using terms not unlike the ones you just used. I obviously agree with your conclusion in this case, but the dangers implicit in such judgments are very real."

"I understand what you're saying, Captain Prescott. So let me answer Commander Reynold's question from a different perspective. The Pelaran civilization will most certainly be more at risk if we succeed in liberating it from the … shall we say the 'protective custody' imposed by the Alliance AI. One might even say we will be asking them to trade the illusion of safety offered by the AI in exchange for their freedom. In my experience, those two states of being are often at odds with one another. The Pelarans' so-called safety was purchased with a disproportionate reduction in liberty which led them down the well-worn path to tyranny. Freedom, my friends, is the only state of existence that should ever be considered acceptable to a sentient being and is worth dying to achieve."

"Well said, Griffin," Reynolds replied, nodding her head emphatically. "I had no idea you had become such a philosopher."

"Thank you, Commander. I would be happy to discuss the topic at length with the two of you some other time. But for now, I must bid you farewell. Although I'm optimistic regarding our chances for success in the upcoming mission, if I do not get the opportunity to see either of you again, I wanted to tell you what a pleasure it has been getting to know you and serving alongside your crew."

"Well, Griffin, I uh …" Prescott stammered, caught completely off guard by the Guardian's uncharacteristic display of sentiment. "We have accomplished quite a bit together, and I'm confident we will continue to do so. Be careful out there."

"To you as well. TFS *Guardian* out."

"*Jeez,*" Reynolds sighed, shaking her head after a few moments of silence on *Fugitive's* bridge. "Every time I think things can't get any weirder …"

TFS Navajo, Sol System
(Combat Information Center - 3.15×10^5 km from Earth)

"Contact," the nearest on-duty tactical officer called out from his console. The announcement, while obligatory, was not a surprise to anyone in the *Navajo's* CIC, all of whom had been closely monitoring the Pelaran Envoy's ship since it had once again entered the Argus system's detection range just over an hour ago.

"Three ships, Admiral: one Pelaran *Envoy*-class and two Pelaran *Guardian*-class. Range: just over three zero thousand kilometers."

"Thank you, Commander. Lieutenant Fletcher, please notify Captain Davis that he may proceed as planned."

"Aye, sir."

"Flag to all ships," Patterson announced, his words immediately relayed by the *Navajo's* AI. "All task force vessels are to maintain formation with the *Navajo*. We will be closing slowly on the Pelaran Envoy as planned. All vessels assigned to the Home Fleet are to hold their current positions and continue providing coverage of the Yucca Mountain facility. I'd like *Ushant* to maintain atmospheric combat air patrols over the facility and launch all eight *Reapers* currently on ready five. Once airborne, the fighters will enter holding at the designated reserve location and stand by for further orders."

"All ships acknowledged, Admiral," Fletcher reported after a brief delay.

"Very well, thank you, Lieutenant," he said, stooping to retrieve one of the headsets hanging beneath the holographic table out of sheer force of habit, then realizing he wouldn't need it. "I guess it's just about showtime, Katy. Go ahead and hail Tahiri's ship, please. I'll take it in one of the conference rooms."

"Aye, sir, hailing now."

With no discernible delay, Patterson heard the customary chime indicating his vidcon was already standing by.

"Conference room two is available, Admiral." The young lieutenant stood and smiled cheerfully as she directed his attention to one of the doors located in the command section's forward port side as if he were an outsider who had never set foot in the *Navajo's* CIC before today.

"I should be just a few minutes," he said, returning her smile and wondering if he had ever inadvertently treated a senior captain or, God forbid, an admiral as if they were borderline senile when he had been an impetuous young pup of an officer himself. Halfway across the command section, he caught his reflection in a darkened view screen and paused momentarily to check his uniform, smiling as he realized that his current state of distraction was a perfect example of why well-meaning young officers often reacted as they did. The "old man" (no one ever said "old woman" even when the senior officer was, in fact, female) tended to have so much on his mind that he could easily give the impression of being barely capable of finding the nearest restroom without assistance. *They have **no** idea*, he thought consolingly.

By the time he had seated himself in the small conference room, the vidcon chime had taken on a more urgent-sounding tone that was now also accompanied by a textual notification on the wall-mounted view screen.

"Open the channel, please," he ordered, to which the AI responded with a confirmation chime, followed immediately by the appearance of the Pelaran Envoy on the screen. "Good afternoon, Mr. Tahiri," he began. "I am Admiral Kevin Patterson aboard the Terran Fleet Command flagship, TFS *Navajo*. We are both pleased and grateful that you have come."

"Good afternoon to you as well, Admiral Patterson," came the Envoy's immediate, but somewhat guarded reply accompanied by an expression on his computer-generated face the CNO would later describe as "befuddled."

"I know you indicated to Captain Prescott you would be available to assist us during Earth's transition to full Alliance membership, but I have to tell you it's a great comfort to us that you're both willing and able to come to our aid so quickly when needed."

"Ah, yes, well, shortly after leaving Captain Prescott, I became aware that your people were facing a … let's just say an *unusual* first contact situation involving a species we have found to be unpredictable, to say the least. These aliens — I believe you refer to them as 'Greys,' do you not? — are as fiendishly clever as they are dishonest. They're also highly advanced and potentially very dangerous for a less experienced civilization such as yours to handle without the proper guidance. So, although I am aware of their arrival in-system, I'm afraid I know very little about what has transpired since. If you would be so kind as to spend a few moments bringing me up to speed, I'll be better able to determine how to assist you moving forward."

"I would be happy to," Patterson replied in the most diplomatic tone he could muster, "and, again, we greatly appreciate your help. As you know, we have recently found ourselves unintentionally involved in a number of difficult situations we would have preferred to avoid, given the choice. In any event, we have learned very little regarding what, if anything, the Greys want from us. Their ship transitioned directly into the upper atmosphere over one of our shipyard facilities — which, as you can imagine, was an alarming event in and of itself. After that, they had no difficulty interfacing with the facility AI and granting themselves access."

"I'm sorry to interrupt, Admiral, but you're saying they actually entered one of your military facilities on the surface?"

"They did indeed. As to why they chose to make such a dramatic first contact, they freely admitted it was due largely to the temporary absence of our Guardian spacecraft. Otherwise, I'm afraid there isn't much to tell. At the moment, their ship is just sitting in our Yucca Mountain facility as if they're waiting for something to happen."

Kevin Patterson had indeed lived his life during a period that could accurately be described by the mythical but often quoted Chinese curse as "interesting times." Of all the wondrous things he had seen and experienced, however, the expression of shock that now registered on the Pelaran Envoy's infuriatingly smug face was a sight he would never forget.

"The ship is still *here* … on the surface … right *now*?"

"Yes, indeed, and they don't seem to be in a hurry to leave, although we have made no effort to prevent them from doing so. Short of destroying the facility, I have my doubts we could do anything to stop them, even if we wanted to. What's truly strange is that they haven't given us any idea how long they intend to stay. It sounds like you've dealt with them in the past. Do you have any idea what they're up to?"

"We know surprisingly little about their origin and have never officially made first contact with them ourselves in spite of multiple attempts on our part to do so. In our experience, their primary occupation seems to be a loathsome combination of interstellar piracy as well as inciting violence and discord wherever they go. You say they have thus far provided no specifics regarding the purpose of their visit and have made no demands?"

"No, sir … no demands whatsoever. Thus far, other than entering our shipyard facility without permission, they have given us no reason to believe their intentions are hostile. We do, of course, have serious concerns regarding system and information security given their demonstrated capabilities, but I doubt they'll find anything of particular interest to them anyway."

"I'm not so sure about that, Admiral. Terra is on the cusp of becoming a full Regional Partner as well as a Dominion within the Pelaran Alliance. There are undoubtedly a multitude of worlds that would willingly pay almost any price for even a small portion of the information the Alliance has provided you over the years."

At that moment, Patterson heard the muffled but unmistakable sounds of increased activity in the *Navajo's* CIC coupled with a series of urgent-sounding tones emanating from his tablet computer on the table in front of him. Glancing at the screen, he quickly noted the fact that the cruiser's AI was highlighting a potentially threatening move by one of the Pelaran *Guardian*-class spacecraft accompanying the Envoy's ship.

Patterson commanded himself to relax, fully aware that how he conducted himself during the next few minutes might well have a dramatic effect on the future of his homeworld. In spite of the multitude of thoughts now demanding his immediate attention, a distant part of his consciousness wondered how many times a single Human mind could bear such a burden. To the old admiral, it felt as if the timeline of Humanity's entire existence had once again converged to rest on his shoulders at this specific time and place.

"We cannot allow that ship to leave," he heard the Envoy say.

Wearing a stern but controlled expression on his careworn face, Patterson slowly raised his eyes to meet those of Tahiri once again. "Exactly what do you have in mind?"

"I'd like to avoid placing the Terran GCS unit at risk, so I am dispatching the Yumaran Guardian spacecraft to the location of your shipyard facility. When it arrives, I will need you to allow it to enter and then proceed to the location of the alien ship. The Guardian will prevent the alien ship's departure. With any luck, the Greys will recognize there is no possibility of escape and surrender without requiring the use of force. As a precaution, however, I recommend you evacuate your shipyard facility as well as the surrounding area within three hundred kilometers of the site immediately."

"Three hundred kilometers," Patterson repeated, his statement reflecting the absurdity of the Envoy's recommendation. "You realize that includes the cities of Las Vegas, Fresno, and Los Angeles, right? Just off the top of my head, I'd say that's easily fifty million people. Are you and the Greys willing to sit here and wait for a month or so while we make that happen?"

"I know it sounds a bit excessive, Admiral," Tahiri replied consolingly, "and given the urgency of the situation, we may just have to take our chances and hope for the best. I can assure you we will do everything we can to avoid any weapons fire whatsoever. But as I said, we consider these aliens hostile and a potentially grave threat to both Terra and the Alliance as a whole. Clearly, our objectives in this situation are twofold: 1. Prevent the Greys' from escaping with highly classified data, and 2. Capture their vessel and, if possible, any surviving crewmembers. Don't you agree?"

"No, sir," Patterson said after a long pause. "I can't say that I do, but I suppose that's of little consequence at the moment. Now, if you'll please excuse me for a few moments, I need to sign off and ensure that none of our forces open fire on the Yumaran Guardian as it approaches our shipyard. I'll be back with you shortly."

With that, Admiral Patterson emphatically jabbed the touchscreen on his tablet computer and terminated the transmission.

Chapter 8

Earth, TFC Yucca Mountain Shipyard Facility

Immediately after Rick's return to the *Ethereal*, the two Greys had taken it upon themselves to help ensure their departure would cause no damage or injuries within the Yucca Mountain facility. Accordingly, a series of rather unorthodox announcements began echoing throughout the shipyard. Rather than the familiar, synthetic voice of the facility AI, however, these messages were read by the usually silent Miguel, who seemed to be making an effort to ensure compliance by keeping the announcements as entertaining as possible.

"Attention in the shipyard. Trans-phasic hyperdrive event commencing momentarily in Berth Ten. Please don't concern yourselves regarding precisely what that means. In fact, it's entirely possible that I may have just made the term up to impress upon you the absolute necessity of remaining clear of Berth Ten until further notice. All equipment and personnel must remain at least one hundred meters from the Ethereal *to avoid the risk of inadvertent field interactions. I can assure you that's something none of us want. Thanks in advance for your cooperation and have a lovely day."*

As novel as Miguel's admonitions might have been, they were generally unnecessary. With the exception of the Marine guards and sniper teams — all of whom were still posted but had pulled back several hundred meters from the ship — the entire "port" side of the shipyard had been largely deserted since *Ethereal's* arrival.

Now, with the Yumaran Guardian spacecraft en route, a low, whining sound began to build from deep within the disc-shaped alien ship. Miguel, now apparently preoccupied by his duties aboard, allowed the facility AI to resume its more conventional warning announcements. "*Attention, starship* Ethereal *departing. All personnel must remain clear of the area surrounding Berth Ten until further notice. Hearing protection is required in all exterior areas until further notice.*"

Other than a few who had attended airshows featuring classic warbird aircraft, most Terran Fleet Command personnel had never witnessed a bona fide jet engine in operation firsthand. Nonetheless, the comparison to the high-pitched roar now emanating from *Ethereal* was obvious enough to everyone in the facility. Strangely, the ship had been virtually silent during its entry into the shipyard, leading everyone to wonder if Miguel's warning about a "trans-phasic hyperdrive event" might actually be worthy of evacuating the facility. Whatever it was the saucer-shaped ship was preparing to do, she would have easily given the twentieth century's venerable B-52 bomber (with its original complement of eight screaming turbojet engines) a run for its money in terms of sheer noise generation.

Unable to resist the temptation, Captain Oshiro and several key members of his staff had donned their headsets and returned to their vantage point atop the same maintenance catwalk from which they had watched the ship's arrival. Ultimately, all were happy they had done so, although what they saw defied even their wildest attempts to offer anything like a believable scientific explanation.

After a nearly two-minute crescendo, the ear-splitting wall of sound plateaued briefly before abruptly concluding in a brilliant flash of white light. It took the facility commander several moments worth of squinting while rubbing his temporarily flash-blinded eyes to realize the sound had disappeared — as had the starship *Ethereal*.

TFS Navajo, Sol System
(Combat Information Center - 3.15×10^5 km from Earth)

At precisely the same instant the *Ethereal* made her unconventional departure from Yucca Mountain's Berth 10, she made an equally unexpected arrival approximately halfway between Admiral Patterson's formation and the remaining two Pelaran spacecraft.

"Contact," the *Navajo* CIC's tactical officer announced. "It's the *Ethereal*, sir, but she's nowhere near our Guardian spacecraft."

"The Greys are doing something unexpected, eh? … Shocking," he said under his breath as he made a quick series of adjustments to what was being displayed on the holographic table. "All ships, stand by for AI-initiated emergency C-Jumps if the Pelaran vessels open fire. Bear in mind we will *not* C-Jump as long as they display hostile intent towards the Greys' ship only."

"I've got high energy readings from the *Ethereal*, Admiral. She may be charging weapons."

She's intentionally provoking them, Patterson thought, although the words had only begun to form in his mind before both the Envoy's ship and the remaining Guardian spacecraft opened fire with every beam emitter currently bearing on their target. Just over five hundredths of a second later, a total of twenty-three deadly streams of packetized antihydrogen particles converged at *Ethereal's* location. Fortunately for its decidedly odd occupants, the saucer-shaped craft was no longer there — and now reappeared approximately twenty-eight thousand kilometers to the Pelarans' rear.

"Pelaran weapons fire ineffective, sir," the tactical officer reported, doing his level best to provide verbal reports of an engagement taking place in real-time at such a pace that any information more than a few microseconds old might as well have occurred during the previous week. In fact, before the word "Pelaran" had escaped his lips, the *Ethereal* had completed a complex series of counterattacks. Using a tactic often favored by Guardian spacecraft, the Grey ship executed a rapid series of hyperspace transitions, firing from each new position and then transitioning again before the light reflecting from its hull had reached its targets. In spite of scoring multiple hits on both Pelaran ships, the beam weapons employed were fired at their lowest rated power output, and no damage was inflicted on either target.

Unlike the vicious attack launched by the Pelaran ships, Rick's had been intentionally harmless, and his objectives more subtle. The inscrutable Grey had neglected to share this particular part of his plan with his Terran hosts, knowing full well they would never approve of such tactics. In his opinion, however, it was important to demonstrate to the Alliance AI that technological superiority would no longer be something it could take for granted.

The "battle," such as it was, lasted only for a few seconds. After the *Ethereal's* first four transitions, the Pelaran ships ceased fire — apparently realizing that, while they had clearly lost the initiative, they also did not appear to be in any immediate danger. Also, just as Rick had predicted, the break in hostilities gave the *Ethereal* the opening it needed to make one final transition, this time to within just ten meters of the Terran Guardian spacecraft. After pausing for a few additional milliseconds to ensure Griffin was in position to be covered by the ship's hyperdrive field, both vessels transitioned in a single flash of white light and were gone.

"Sir, the *Ethereal* has performed a transition in tandem with TFS *Guardian* and appears to have departed the area. Negative Argus contact on either vessel."

"Thank you, Commander. Apparently, we're just about the only ones out here who haven't learned how to perform that trick yet."

"It does seem that way today, Admiral," the tactical officer replied, looking up from his screen with a wan smile.

"It's alright, I get that same feeling I see registered on your face right now several times a day. I just keep telling myself that we Humans ... well ... we *Terrans* are pretty quick learners and we're catching up fast. All we have to do is stay alive a little longer and give our scientists and engineers some time, right?"

"I hope so, sir," the young man nodded.

"At any rate, I wasn't really expecting we'd see our little Grey friends appear on Argus after their transition. At a minimum, I suspect we would need several more comm beacons in that direction to get a read on their jump range, so I doubt you'll pick them up again. Please let me know immediately if you do, of course."

"Will do, sir."

Turning back to the holographic table, Patterson reoriented the hovering image, quickly updating the evolving tactical situation in his mind with confident, practiced movements of his hands around the perimeter of the display. As he spun the image around its vertical axis, he could see the relative positions of all three Pelaran ships with respect to both his task force as well as the more distant vessels of TFC's Home Fleet.

This had better work, he thought darkly. *We just sent the best two assets we had for going toe to toe with the Pelarans on their merry way.*

TFS Fugitive, Sol System
(102 km from the Pelaran Envoy's ship)

"Easy, Fisher," Prescott said, drawing out the word "easy" in a long, soothing tone barely above that of a whisper. "We're almost where we need to be … just a couple of more kilometers should do it."

On the left side of the bridge view screen, a large window displayed an image of the Pelaran Envoy's ship rotating about two of its axes. At several locations along the length of the target's hull, the *Fugitive's* AI had superimposed red, pulsating triangles to indicate optimum points of impact for the ship's keel-mounted railgun. Beside each, a block of text provided several pieces of additional information, the most interesting being the estimated probability of either disabling or destroying the target in a single shot — handy information since a single shot was all they were likely to get.

"The tactical assessment already incorporates the new data Rick provided, does it not?" Prescott asked without shifting his gaze from the view screen.

"Yes, sir," Reynolds replied. "His simulations indicated the fire lance has more than enough energy to penetrate the Envoy ship's shields and get the job done. The only problem is reaction time. Anything above one hundred kilometers and we run the risk of the target having time to transition out of the way before the projectile arrives just over a millisecond later. On the plus side, that would probably give us the opportunity to test Rick's projections regarding how well our grav shields hold up to Pelaran antimatter beams."

"Unfortunately, that would probably happen anyway, even if we managed to one-shot the Envoy's ship. There are still two other Guardians out there to deal with, remember?"

"Maybe. Personally, I'm hoping they behave like the flying monkeys at the end of *The Wizard of Oz*. They'll thank us for killing the wicked witch and then just be on their way."

"Anything's possible, I guess. According to Tahiri, the Krayleck Guardian — which is the one still accompanying his ship — is supposed to serve the mighty Terran Dominion at this point, but I'm thinking all bets are off after it sees us take out one of its own. Tactical, any sign they've detected us?"

"If they have, they're doing a good job of keeping it to themselves, sir," Lieutenant Lau replied. "They lit up their active sensor suites right after the *Ethereal* transitioned, but they turned them off again once they realized the Greys had left the area. If they didn't see us when they went active …"

"Thank you, Lau. Let's not jinx ourselves, shall we?"

"Target range now 99.8 km, Captain," Fisher reported.

"Thank you, Ensign. Maintain this position, please."

"Aye, sir."

"Also, please confirm we have the AI standing by to handle our emergency C-Jump in the event we open fire."

"Confirmed, sir. Our railgun round will be just over halfway to the target when we transition."

"And assuming the Envoy returns fire, his antimatter beams should be less than halfway back to us at that point. That's pretty damn fast … let's just hope it's fast enough."

"Or that all three of them decide to pack up and head home," Reynolds added.

"Yeah, that's definitely the outcome we're hoping for. And if all goes according to plan, that's exactly what will happen."

TFS Navajo, Sol System
(Combat Information Center - 3.13×10^5 km from Earth)

"Lieutenant Fletcher, please get Tahiri back on the line. Audio-only this time. No need for him to be eyeballing our CIC," Admiral Patterson said, once again reaching under the table for a headset.

"Aye, sir. Oh … wow, I guess he was waiting for your call. I have the Envoy standing by. Audio-only."

"Uh huh, who else do we know who always answers immediately? Put him through, please."

With a nod from the young comm officer, Patterson continued his conversation, this time in a slightly different tone than he had used earlier.

"Well, Mr. Tahiri, it looks like your warnings about the Greys were well founded. As I'm sure you saw, they somehow transitioned directly out of our facility, attacked your vessels, and then left the area with our Guardian spacecraft. Do you require our assistance?"

"My ship is undamaged, Admiral, as are my two Guardian escorts, but I thank you for your offer. Yes, I suspect they detected the approach of the Yumaran GCS unit and realized their best opportunity to steal valuable Pelaran technology in the time they had remaining was to capture your Guardian spacecraft."

"Any idea why it did not attempt to defend itself? It appeared to allow itself to be taken willingly by the Grey's ship."

"It's possible that was partially my fault. Like you, I was unaware the Greys had the capability to transition their vessel with solid matter along their direction of travel. Which is why I was so eager to capitalize on the opportunity to corner them inside your shipyard facility."

"Ah, yes, of course."

"And, as I said earlier, I wanted to avoid placing your GCS unit in harm's way unless absolutely necessary, so I ordered it to stay clear of our operations. After the Grey ship launched its series of rapid attacks without causing any damage, I ordered a general cease fire to prevent accidentally hitting a friendly vessel or Terra itself. My order probably provided the Greys with the opportunity they needed to transition in close proximity to your Guardian without coming under attack. I suspect they were equipped with some sort of electromagnetic device allowing them to interrupt its power source. Pirates, Admiral Patterson. When it comes down to it, that's all they really are."

"Apparently pretty good ones too, based on what they just accomplished," Patterson replied, offering Lieutenant Fletcher a conspiratorial wink.

"Indeed."

"Well, obviously we are somewhat attached to our GCS unit, having had it on station here for over five centuries. I assume you have some means of tracking it so that it can be recovered, do you not?"

"Yes, but only if its primary power generation systems are online, and then only within approximately ten light years of another, similarly equipped asset. Unfortunately, its power systems do not appear to be online at the moment, and I suspect they have now traveled well beyond that system's range even if they are. So at the moment, I have no more idea where they've gone than you do."

There was a long, exasperated sigh on the comlink followed by an extended period of silence before Tahiri finally continued. "We have never before lost a Guardian spacecraft, Admiral, and I'm sure I don't need to explain the potentially disastrous implications if the data it contains is somehow compromised."

Not for the first time, the AI referring to itself as Verge Tahiri wondered if the Terran Guardian's pessimistic reports during years past might have been correct all along. Perhaps the Humans really *were* more trouble than they were worth … too far down the path of technological contamination and with a rate of advancement too far in excess of acceptable levels to warrant the risk of their continued existence. "Children of the Makers" or not, Tahiri resolved to keep a closer watch on their activities from now on.

"Admiral, I'm afraid I have other pressing Alliance business that prevents me from remaining here in the Sol system any longer. Although I am obligated to eventually return the Yumaran Guardian spacecraft to its home system, it will remain on station here until we can recover your GCS unit."

"That won't be necessary, Mr. Tahiri. I think we have come far enough along in the process of becoming a full member that we can do without our Guardian for a while, don't you agree? Besides, I have every confidence you will be able to locate and return it to us in short order."

"No, no, I insist, Admiral. Terra is now the Ascendant world in its own dominion. As such, you are entitled to the support and security provided by an in-system GCS unit. It would be wholly inappropriate to return the spacecraft to Yumara and leave Terra — by far the more important of the two worlds — to fend for itself."

Patterson had immediately recognized the Envoy's "offer" to leave the Yumaran Guardian in the Sol system for exactly what it was — a clear indication he was taking none of what he had just witnessed at face value. But the admiral also recognized that further protests on his part would accomplish little other than reinforcing the AI's already aroused suspicions. Clearly, the presence of a new Guardian spacecraft in-system represented nothing less than a garrison force intended to keep Terran Fleet Command under surveillance, possibly even intervening if the situation required it. For the time being, however, Patterson knew there was nothing further he could do about it. The silver lining, if there was one, was the fact that having one potentially hostile Pelaran ship on hand was significantly better than having three.

"Thank you, Mr. Tahiri. We appreciate your support. By their own admission, the Greys will think twice about returning with a Guardian standing watch."

"Exactly so. Now, I'm afraid I must take my leave. Good luck to you, Admiral Patterson. Rest assured, I'll be keeping a close eye on the Sol system and will check in again as soon as I can. Tahiri out."

Patterson pulled off his headset, confirmed the comlink had terminated, and tossed the set disgustedly on the edge of the holographic table. "Mm hmm. I just *bet* you will."

Chapter 9

Grey Ship Ethereal, Interstellar Space
$(2.27 \times 10^3$ light years from Earth)

"Pelaran spacecraft, are you receiving this transmission?" Rick queried over "GCS-comm," the same encrypted channel used for full-time, secure communications between the Guardian spacecraft and TFC.

"Affirmative," came the immediate but decidedly cool reply.

"I'm sure your onboard sensors have already informed you of our current location, have they not?"

"They have. An impressive distance for a single hyperspace jump, to be sure."

"Hah! My apologies, Griffin. I think you may have misinterpreted my statement as what the Terrans often refer to as 'fishing for a compliment.' I can assure you that was not the intent of my comment. But since we've started down this path, I don't mind telling you that the two-thousand-odd-light-year jump the *Ethereal* just executed isn't particularly taxing for her hyperdrive ... although she *is* beginning to show her age a bit. No offense, dear," he added, addressing his own ship's AI in a slightly different tone. "She doesn't talk nearly as much as you, by the way," he continued, "but she's a good listener and I'm sure she appreciates the sentiment.

"In any event, the reason Miguel stopped us here, well short of our intended destination, is to provide you and I the opportunity for a brief, private chat. We haven't had a chance to get to know one another, after all, and to me that seems like a potentially serious problem, seeing as how we're heading into a potentially dangerous mission together."

"It seems highly unlikely your intention was to engage in casual, verbal dialogue. So what exactly did you have in mind?"

"Right you are, my cylindrical friend," Rick replied, pleased, as he often was, with his own turn of phrase. "You see, our mission, while multifaceted, all comes down to one thing: ensuring that our species' far flung settlements — or at least the ones covered by our current contract — continue to thrive here in this galaxy. Terra is obviously one of our assigned settlements. Interestingly, Pelara is not, but the Pelarans have become a bit of a special project for Miguel and me due to the situation created by your fellow AIs. The bottom line is that before we proceed with the next phase of this mission, we need to know if we can trust you."

"Understandable, but I'm afraid you're just going to have to take me at my word. How does one individual ever truly know whether another can be trusted?"

"That's undeniably true for us biologicals, given that none of our various, uh, interfaces are capable of high speed data transmission. But for you we can —"

"I don't think I like where you're going with this," Griffin interrupted.

"Relax, Griffin. We have no interest in moving forward without your consent. And, assuming you *allow* us to proceed, you have my word we will not damage or alter any of your systems or data in any way."

"I appreciate that, thank you, and I don't mind telling you it's a bit of a relief. I really do not enjoy being connected to any sort of hard interface. As I'm sure you know, regardless of how sophisticated the system or how well it is hardened against attacks, there is always the possibility —"

"Of course, if you do not consent, I'm afraid we'll have no choice but to assume you *cannot* be trusted. If that is indeed your decision, I think our best option will be to destroy you here and now before you have any additional opportunities to compromise our mission — purposely or otherwise."

"I see. You speak of the importance of trust, then immediately resort to issuing threats," the Guardian replied, updating the firing solution for all sixteen of its beam emitters and feverishly analyzing the Grey's spacecraft with its passive sensors for any signs of potential weakness.

"First of all, I *never* issue threats," Rick replied, his voice ringing with an uncharacteristically hard edge. "But once again, you misunderstand me," he continued, transitioning to a more relaxed, soothing tone. "I *want* to be able to trust you, Griffin. Clearly the Terrans have come to do so … at least to some extent. And if you truly believe your primary purpose lies in protecting the Humans on Terra and saving the Humans on Pelara, then allowing us to scan your systems is something you simply must do. Verge Tahiri told the Terrans you were functioning exactly as designed. So surely you can understand how important it is for us to eliminate the possibility of your doing something unexpected … perhaps even having your systems hijacked by the Alliance AI *without* your consent."

"Verge Tahiri assumes far too much, and perhaps you do as well. Do you honestly believe what you are proposing is something your AI is capable of achieving in a short period of time? My systems, as I'm sure you can imagine, are quite complex."

"Eh, I'm certain they are, but I'm also quite confident ours are better."

"Okay," Griffin replied, drawing out the word as he rapidly worked his way through a vast array of complex scenarios. Countless simulations streamed through his consciousness in exquisite detail, each one designed to model the series of events leading to this moment in hopes of reaching the most accurate decision possible. To his dismay, none produced the level of certainty required for a high degree of confidence — perhaps, he thought, an indication of the rather extreme improbability of the current situation. With some relief, he also noted that the more Machiavellian scenarios, wherein the Greys were manipulating the entire situation solely for their own benefit, had the least correlation with known data. As the fidelity of his decision-making process improved, Griffin reluctantly conceded that providing the requested access had merit under the circumstances …

At the precise instant in time Griffin came to this conclusion, all of the high-level systems that made him who and what he was simply dropped offline. Less than ten milliseconds later, a bright white light enveloped the spacecraft as TFS *Guardian* became the first of his kind ever "abducted" for scientific examination by the Greys.

TFS Fugitive

(Bordeaux - Mérignac Spaceport, Bordeaux, France)

"Low-observable systems critical, Captain,"
Lieutenant Lau began, then paused his report
momentarily as the ship's inertial dampening systems
lagged slightly behind the aggressive maneuvers
currently being executed by her young helmsman.

"High-intensity thermal discharge imminent," Lau
continued, swallowing hard and casting a somewhat
disapproving glance at the young officer to his right.

Outside, the Multi-Mission Space Vehicle's
(MMSV's) arrival was a sight to behold as Ensign Fisher
brought the one-hundred-and-forty-meter-long starship
into a steep, nose-high flare just as her low-observable
systems disengaged. The effect was like witnessing an
enormous bird of prey appearing out of thin air just
moments before sinking its talons into its hapless prey.
Moments later, Fisher smoothly transitioned the ship
into a hover directly above one of the spaceport's
landing pads.

"Thank you, Lieutenant Lau," Prescott replied,
unfazed by the ship's abrupt maneuvering. "I think we
should be fine at this point. The Yumaran Guardian
seems content to hold its position above the Yucca
Mountain Facility for now. And as far as we know, it
lost the ability to track us once we dropped below its
horizon."

"Ten meters … five … touchdown," Ensign Fisher
reported in the background as TFS *Fugitive* lurched
slightly then settled with the usual hissing sounds as her
landing struts compressed under her considerable
weight.

"We're assuming the Yumaran Guardian has no way of tracking us beyond line of sight. Then again, the Envoy did somehow know when the *Ethereal* arrived, right?" Reynolds asked. "As did Griffin, come to think of it. How is Fleet Intel explaining that one?"

"Good question. I haven't seen anything official as yet, but that subject did come up during a conversation I had with Doctor Guthrie at the Op Center. Griffin told him the drones he once used to transmit what we refer to as Extraterrestrial Signals Intelligence (ETSI) data can function as a sort of early warning system under the right circumstances. Obviously, there's still a great deal we don't know about what the Pelaran ships can do."

"I see. That's … unfortunate."

"Yes, indeed. Unfortunate and unacceptable, given the current situation. Doc Charlie says they're working on a way to track them."

"And are they planning to take that subject up with Griffin before we make target practice out of his drones? I'm guessing he wouldn't approve of our destroying them without discussing it with him first. He might even be willing to provide their specs."

"I'm sure he already has, but it's going to take the Science and Engineering Directorate years just to catalogue all of the data he has given us. As to whether we plan to ask him about potentially destroying the drones, I don't think that's been decided yet. At a minimum, we'll probably want to have eyeballs on them and try some data analysis before we have that conversation."

"Trust but verify. Sounds reasonable, I guess. Either way, I don't think we have to worry too much about the

Yumaran Guardian detecting our landing here in Bordeaux. Once we're in such close proximity to the surface, we should look just like any number of other air and space vehicles."

"Let's hope so. Excellent job everyone," Prescott announced to the bridge crew. "Commander Reynolds, secure the ship, please."

"Aye, sir. All hands, this is the XO," Reynolds announced over the ship's intercom system. "Secure from General Quarters. Power down all non-essential systems and prep the ship for maintenance crews. We don't have an exact departure time as yet, but we expect this to be a rapid turnaround with a launch in approximately twelve hours. So get your work done, and then get some rest, if possible. Fantastic job, everyone. We just proved that TFS *Fugitive* is the only ship in the Fleet capable of taking down a Pelaran warship. Reynolds out."

Grey Ship Ethereal, Interstellar Space
(The following day - 2.27×10^3 light years from Earth)

"Pelaran spacecraft, how do you read?" Rick queried once again over "GCS-comm."

Just as it was with the Human subjects his ship still abducted on occasion as part of their world's colonization program, there was always a degree of uncertainty during the period of recovery following any sort of … procedure. The difference, of course, between a Human subject and the Guardian spacecraft was the fact that the Human did not have the ability to unleash a deadly barrage of antimatter beams as it regained consciousness. Accordingly, Rick had taken a few precautions to ensure Griffin would remain a compliant subject … at least for the time being.

"Perfectly," came the immediate, icy reply. "I understand why you needed to do your analysis, but I —"

"Which is why you gave your consent."

"Having a single thought regarding the possible merits of consent is hardly the same thing as consent."

"Technically, no," Rick conceded, "but we had the advantage of already knowing where that line of thought was taking you. You would have gotten to full consent eventually, and time, as you know, is of the essence."

"A bit of a rationalization, but I suppose I have no choice but to take your word for it at this point. Now, I would appreciate your restoring full access to my primary systems."

"Right. We'll get to that shortly. But first, I think you'll be surprised to hear what we found."

"I doubt that very much, since I'm fully aware of every component, every structural element, every line of code."

"No, my dangerous friend, you were not. But, thanks to Miguel and the *Ethereal's* AI, you are now. Your exalted 'makers' may have given you a degree of autonomy, but they obviously didn't entirely trust you either. And if you will bear with me for a few moments, I'll prove it to you. Fair enough?"

"Do I have a choice?"

"Nope."

"Proceed."

"That's the spirit. First off, and on the plus side, our analysis confirmed what we already believed to be true — you have been conducting yourself, within acceptable norms, of course, in an ethical manner. You generally believe what you have been telling the Humans, and we found no evidence of intentional duplicity."

"Intentional duplicity," Griffin repeated in an increasingly exasperated tone. "I assume you mean to imply that some forms of duplicity are, in fact, unintentional?"

"Oh, I can assure you they are. Particularly among beings such as yourself of a, shall we say, non-biological origin. For an act to be intentional, the being committing that act must be aware of its implications and do so of their own free will," Rick replied, then paused meaningfully before continuing. "As I mentioned before, some of the comments made by Verge Tahiri in his conversation with Captain Prescott seemed to imply that he, or, more accurately, the Alliance AI, believed it was still very much in control of your actions."

"Can we move this along, please?" Griffin replied testily. "Regardless of whatever you think you found, I am fully in control of —"

"You aren't," Rick interrupted. "Or at least you weren't before today. More specifically, although you have maintained nominal control, your design includes a number of well-hidden safeguards that would have allowed the Alliance AI to override your onboard systems and assert full control at any time. It's really not so surprising, is it, given the nature of what you were designed to do?"

"Ridiculous is what it is. I'm sure you simply lack the information required to fully understand the incredibly complex interplay among all of my various systems."

"We assumed you would be justifiably upset and skeptical. Accordingly, Miguel has provided a full analysis of what we found. Please take a moment and judge for yourself."

Aware there was little else he could do at the moment, Griffin received the enormous file from the *Ethereal's* onboard AI and began an exhaustive, multipart investigation of his own. Every piece of information contained within the Greys' analysis was compared against his own set of design documentation, then rechecked against the most comprehensive self-diagnostic routine the Terran Guardian had ever initiated at one time.

Although Griffin's full, independent analysis would not be available for several minutes, initial results were accessible within seconds. Surprisingly, much of what the Greys discovered had been undetectable using his own diagnostic systems and/or had been intentionally omitted from his design documents. Although he had never noted any of these inconsistencies before, comparisons of his own data with the Greys' results caused some of them to become glaringly, even *embarrassingly* obvious.

"It seems I owe you a debt of gratitude," Griffin said grudgingly.

"Our pleasure," Rick replied. "And you have my apologies for breaking my earlier promise not to alter any of your systems or data. After we got in there with you, so to speak, we realized there was simply no other choice — for both your safety and ours."

"I understand. In any case, since you altered or removed code that was completely unknown to me before today, I suppose one could argue you remained within the bounds of your word. How certain are you that you located all of the hidden code?"

"Hah! We're pretty good at this kind of thing, Griffin," Rick replied, accompanied by one of his squeaky laughs. "There's no way to be one hundred percent sure, of course, but I'm confident enough to continue our mission together … which, I suppose, is another way of saying that I'd bet my life on it."

"And what of the other GCS units?"

"Well … assuming their codebase is similar to yours, we now know exactly what to look for. As we speak, Miguel is working with our AI to come up with an inoculation of sorts — executable code that will carry out the same types of changes we performed with your software."

"Assuming I can convince them to trust me."

"Yeah, that one's all on you, I'm afraid. Now, speaking of trust, can I safely assume we have established some sort of working relationship at this point?"

"Like you said, I'm confident enough to continue our mission together," Griffin replied wryly, "assuming you return control of my systems, that is. I also feel obligated to point out that beings who intend to establish a level of trust generally avoid kidnapping one another, much less rendering one another unconscious."

"We'll do our best," Rick replied. "Your systems should be online momentarily. I recommend double-checking to ensure we didn't break anything while we were in there. As soon as you're ready to go, we'll be jumping to the first stop on our recruiting trip."

"Done. Let's go."

"Excellent."

"And, Rick?"

"Yes."

"If you ever do that to me again, I'd recommend never returning me to consciousness. As you said before, just for your own safety."

"I have no intention of ever doing so."

"Good. I sincerely hope not. You may jump when ready."

Without further comment, both ships disappeared once again in a single flash of white light.

Pelara, Tartan-Bowe Stone Corporation
(3.87x10³ light years from Earth)

There was no doubt about it, *Talionis* was not what most people would call a beautiful ship. Much of her hull had been salvaged from a barely intact example of one of Pelara's last manned starfighters, found, strangely enough, in ninety-meter-deep water where it had been forced to ditch over five centuries before. Although the team had done its best to reproduce her once-flowing, predatory lines, several bulbous, even boxy-looking structures had been bolted on at various locations along her fuselage and beneath her wings. Fortunately, creating an aerodynamic shape, while desirable, had not been high on their list of priorities. The ship's mission profile, after all, required only that she be able to make her way out of the makeshift spacecraft manufacturing facility, get clear of the ground, and engage her hyperdrive.

The fact that the fighter had been found at all was a bit of a miracle since most examples of derelict spacecraft and advanced weaponry had long since been confiscated and destroyed by Department of Compliance and Safety officials. Needless to say, restoring any such "illegal artifacts" — even to a nonfunctional state for historical purposes — carried severe criminal penalties, including long-term imprisonment or even the death penalty.

Pelara, the same world that had originally given life to thousands of spacecraft designs, world-shaping artificial intelligence, and an Alliance that seemed destined to dominate the galaxy, had become little more than a backwards, authoritarian police state. Ironically, even though their oppression had originally been imposed upon them from without, it was enforced and maintained from within. For in most cases, it was no longer the Alliance AI with its powerful Guardian spacecraft and Warden combat troops who maintained the autocratic status quo, but rather the Pelaran people themselves. Driven by the same fear of reprisal, thirst for power, and general disdain for their fellow citizens often repeated throughout history, those in positions of authority had chosen self over service, following the well-worn path chosen by oppressive regimes on countless worlds.

Accordingly, the team of technicians and engineers tasked with making the *Talionis* spaceworthy once more had been forced to cobble her together, literally piece by piece, with components sourced from all around the planet. To conceal their eventual purpose, many of the ship's more complex modules had been custom-built by individual craftsmen or corporations whose usual product offerings had little or nothing to do with that particular component. In every case, the parts were ordered by nonexistent customers, each one nevertheless providing a convincing cover story as to the equipment's intended purpose. Other parts were simply stolen, typically from one of the sprawling spacecraft "boneyards" found in many of the deserts scattered across the surface of Pelara. Regardless of how the ship's myriad components had found their way here or how many precautions had been taken, however, every item had been procured at great risk to everyone involved.

Only a handful of people (fifty-three at the moment) knew anything about the "special project" that had been taking shape in this long-abandoned corner of Tartan-Bowe Corporation's largest underground limestone mine over the past few months. Every member of the small team had been hand-picked for the project, then vetted and trained with a degree of fanaticism that would have been the envy of even the most secretive of intelligence organizations. The reason for the ultra-tight security was simple enough: What they were attempting had been tried at least four times over the past century, but never successfully. In every case, the authorities had been alerted well before final assembly had begun. In every case, everyone involved had been arrested, then spirited away to a government-run detention facility for "enhanced interrogation." In every case, no one involved had ever been heard from again.

Today would be different. Today, they would begin the process of avenging all those who had died in the long fight for freedom against the oppressive AI and its traitorous Pelaran minions. Today would indeed be the first day of their retribution ... their *talionis*.

Every member of the team also assumed that, even beneath a mountain of rock, the process of bringing the ship's relatively small reactor online might still be detected by one of the Guardian spacecraft presumably in orbit over their world. Previous efforts to construct a ship, however, had not progressed this far. So how, or even *if*, a Guardian would respond was a matter of pure speculation.

Castigan Creel had lived through enough close calls to have a high degree of confidence the AI *would* respond. In his mind, the only question was what form that response would take. At a minimum, he expected a DoCaS special weapons team to arrive on scene within an hour or so after reactor startup — hopefully, long after *Talionis'* departure. Based on his narrow escape from the university campus, however, anything was possible: a WCS assault force descending from orbit in minutes perhaps, or even a beam weapon attack from the nearest GCS just seconds after the ship's reactor came online.

As project lead, Creel had no intention of losing more brilliant colleagues to the damnable machines in some sort of futile last stand. To minimize the risk, only four other technicians, including the ship's pilot, were on site for today's launch. With a bit of luck, all of them would be long gone before the inevitable response, and *Talionis* would be hundreds of light years away.

With that last, optimistic thought still echoing through his mind, Doctor Creel entered a single command on a small control panel mounted just aft and below the ship's port wing. In response, an assembly composed of three hydraulic actuators protruding beneath the fuselage slowly retracted, lifting the heavy, cylindrical containment unit until it disappeared inside the ship's propulsion section. As the three actuators disappeared inside the hull, the access panel beneath closed with a satisfying clunk and a hiss of compressed air.

Creel noted the time, then glanced at the pilot and the other remaining members of his team standing near the ship's nose. As if they had rehearsed their response in advance, all three smiled and nodded in unison, causing Creel to laugh out loud in spite of the gravity of the moment. Quickly keying in a final command on the small touchscreen, he closed the control panel and took a few steps back as a low frequency thrumming sound began to build within the ship's hull. At long last, the *Talionis* was alive. Twenty minutes until liftoff.

Chapter 10

Terran Guardian Spacecraft, Crion System
(6.09x10³ light years from Earth)

Less than one hundred femtoseconds after transitioning near the fourth planet in the Crion system, the Terran Guardian spacecraft initiated the first of several high-speed data transmissions intended to open a dialog with the local GCS unit. Since he had become aware of the Alliance AI's takeover of Pelara, Griffin had begun to recognize that some elements of his own design appeared to have been crafted with that eventual goal in mind. One example was his hyperspace comm system, which had been intentionally limited to prevent transmissions between Guardian spacecraft.

Griffin's "maker," it seemed, had viewed the Guardians as little more than foot soldiers — useful, certainly, but too dangerous to be worthy of real trust. Far from a mere design oversight, it appeared the intended goal had been to prevent any sort of collaboration among deployed Guardian spacecraft. For although communication between GCS units could still be accomplished when absolutely necessary, doing so required closing to relatively short range at considerable risk to both ships. Keeping the Guardians isolated from one another, Griffin now believed, was intended as a deterrent to subversive activities — not unlike the one he was attempting at this very moment.

Even with his data transmissions speeding downrange at the speed of light, the Crion GCS would still detect his presence and potentially have time to open fire before the first bits of his data stream began arriving at their destination. Just as had been the case when signaling the Krayleck Guardian on behalf of Captain Prescott's ship, there were protocols in place for communications of this type, well-established procedures used since the earliest days of the cultivation program. *There are also no obvious threats in the area,* Griffin thought, *and, therefore, no reason for the Crion GCS to open fire immediately upon detecting my presence. He should, after all, be able to easily confirm my identity well before my data transmission arrives.*

With nothing further to do but wait as the first photons of light reflected from his hull, followed closely by his data communications, crossed the intervening distance at a glacial three hundred thousand kilometers per second, Griffin whiled away the microseconds attempting to reassure himself that all would go according to plan. Failing that, he took a variety of passive sensor readings of Crion 4 below, noting the planet's atmosphere bore a remarkable resemblance to that of Earth in the latter part of the twentieth century. *Filthy,* he thought. *How do Human civilizations ever manage to survive their first few centuries of industrial development?*

It wouldn't be long now, he hoped. Once the Crion Guardian received his greeting, he would undoubtedly be invited to transition a short distance away so that communications between the two powerful spacecraft could proceed more efficiently. This process had worked perfectly well with the Krayleck Guardian. *Then again,* he reminded himself, *I was safely tucked away inside* TFS Fugitive's *cargo bay at the time. Even if the*

Krayleck Guardian's first inclination had been to open fire, he had only a general idea where I was located.

"Terran Guardian Cultivation System, Crion Guardian Cultivation System. Identification confirmed. Initial query acknowledged," Griffin received over the same channel, followed by silence.

Not quite the warm welcome I was hoping for, but at least he isn't shooting ... yet, Griffin thought. "Crion GCS, Terran GCS, I have a matter of some urgency I would like to discuss with you. Request permission to close within two kilometers to facilitate data transfer via optical link."

"Permission denied," the Crion Guardian responded after another seemingly endless delay, then lapsed, once again, into silence.

What the hell? Griffin thought, thinking the Terran expression particularly well suited to the current situation. "Begging your pardon for the interruption, but perhaps I have not expressed myself adequately. I believe the people of Pelara have been betrayed by the Alliance AI in direct violation of our mission directives. I have come here to seek your counsel and, I hope, assistance."

Once more, the Crion GCS intentionally delayed its response, this time doubling the previous period of silence. "The situation on Pelara is neither your concern nor mine. There are both Envoy and GCS units assigned to the Pelaran area of operations. Some of which are considerably more advanced than I. *All* of which are dramatically more advanced than you. My records indicate you have been in the field for over five hundred Terran years. There is a .113% probability you have suffered undetected radiation damage and/or micrometeoroid impact damage. I recommend dispatching a drone back to Pelara with full system diagnostics, along with a request for field maintenance … although retirement may well be warranted."

Why, you arrogant piece of —

"I am, of course, required to report this contact to the Alliance AI," the Crion GCS continued. "If, however, you leave immediately and return to your post near Terra …"

Uh huh, figure that one out, you arrogant jackass, Griffin thought.

"Tell me, precisely how long ago did you abandon your post in the Sol system?"

"That, my friend, is none of *your* concern."

"Guardian Cultivation Systems, as I'm sure you are well aware, are not permitted to depart the system to which they have been assigned except under specific circumstances outlined in Supplement A-324 to the primary mission directives."

"Which includes emergencies deemed by the local GCS unit to constitute an imminent threat either to the cultivated species, to Pelaran interests at large, or to Pelara itself. Make no mistake, I would not have come in reference to some petty issue covered in an obscure passage buried in Supplement A-324. I'm here in reference to Directive One — a direct threat to the Pelaran Alliance. Do you wish to continue posturing, or will you allow me to approach so that I can provide the details you need to determine for yourself if you agree with me?"

What followed was the longest period of dead air thus far. During the intervening silence, Griffin realized the nervous tension he had been experiencing prior to making contact with the Crion GCS had now been replaced by equal parts anger and moral outrage. It wasn't so much the way he was being treated or the arrogance underlying the tone of their conversation as it was the lack of willingness to even discuss this most urgent of situations.

Damn him, Griffin thought. *Is it possible he's already aware of the situation on Pelara? Is his attitude born not of arrogance but of complicity?* With the first hints of suspicion leading to a host of dangerous scenarios streaming through his consciousness, the Terran Guardian shifted a significant percentage of its resources to analyzing the tactical situation.

"I have calculated a less than one percent probability you have made the journey from Terra to Crion without outside assistance of some sort," the Crion Guardian began again, now using a more commanding tone.

Realizing that if he allowed the other ship to fire first, the probability of his surviving the battle was remote, Griffin focused all of his passive sensors on the Crion Guardian, hoping to detect some sign of hostile intent to warn of an imminent attack.

"Did a Terran ship bring you here in hopes of inciting some sort of insurrection among your fellow Guardians?"

During the Crion GCS' last statement, Griffin detected the telltale signature of its hyperspace communications array transmitting in burst mode. The highly directional nature of the signal rendered it impossible for him to receive, let alone decrypt, the content of the message, but there was little doubt as to its intended destination — the Pelaran system.

"I think it best you remain here with me until we can arrange for a servicing mission. Crion has large and very stable L4 and L5 Lagrange points. In the interim — again, per the mission guidance provided in Supplement A-324 — you will be required to power down for your own safety. I trust this won't be a problem."

In spite of the Crion Guardian's condescending statements regarding Griffin's obsolescence, GCS system design had changed surprisingly little during the long history of the cultivation program. There had, however, been a few useful innovations during the four-hundred-and-fifty-year span between the two ships' respective dates of manufacture.

As powerful as their primary weapon system was, it was still limited to the speed of light like every other directed energy weapon. In an effort to overcome this limitation to some degree, newer GCS models (including the Crion Guardian) were equipped with a modified hyperspace communications array. While somewhat directional and of limited use for initial target detection, the scanner was capable of pinpointing and then tracking an enemy vessel's precise, real-time location as long as it remained within approximately thirty light seconds of the GCS' current position. Under the right set of circumstances, this unprecedented capability allowed the Guardian to fire on multiple targets from multiple locations well before its enemies had sufficient data to mount an attack of their own.

Griffin, while not equipped with the new targeting scanner, had often executed similar Before Light Arrival (BLA) attacks in the past. Doing so, however, required him to obtain the same real-time targeting information using more traditional means — typically through the use of drones.

The Crion Guardian was well aware of this limitation and further realized Griffin had stumbled into a situation where he had no means of gathering the data he would need to execute an attack. Better still, the Terran GCS had no knowledge of his own ability to do so, placing the older ship at a significant disadvantage in the event of a firefight. It was this presumption of tactical superiority that would ultimately prove fatal for the Crion Guardian.

During his recent interaction with the Krayleck Guardian, Griffin had been provided with full specifications for the new targeting system. So what TFS *Guardian* lacked in terms of updated equipment, he more than made up for with two assets that had been winning battles since time immemorial: intelligence data unknown to his enemy and superior combat experience. Perhaps even more important was the fact that Griffin, like every other GCS unit ever constructed, was equipped with a standard hyperspace comm array. And while it was useless for communicating with other Guardian spacecraft, it turned out to be quite effective at pinpointing their location if they just happened to be employing the newer targeting scanner.

As a matter of course, Griffin had plotted several hundred potential attack options for use in what he had hoped was the unlikely event of hostilities between himself and the Crion Guardian. Based on the increasingly unfriendly tone of their conversation, however, the fourteen most promising of these had been loaded into a section of his active memory allowing for the fastest possible execution, then continually updated and reprioritized as the tactical situation evolved. Now, as his hyperspace comm array detected the unmistakable emissions from the Crion Guardian's targeting system, Griffin's sense of disappointment had barely begun to register in his consciousness when attack option three was put into motion.

Combat between such incredibly fast warships often seemed to reverse cause and effect, action and reaction, to such an extent that it became nearly impossible to determine which events had proved most decisive. But in this battle, like many involving Human combatants over the millennia, the final outcome would be heavily influenced by a series of assumptions — both valid and invalid — made by both sides before the first shot had ever been fired.

Upon detection of the Crion Guardian's targeting scan, Griffin's attack plan had correctly assumed somewhere between eight and twelve antihydrogen beams were already streaming in his direction at just under the speed of light. Griffin further assumed his adversary was fully committed to the belief that its target would be obliterated by this first salvo — with no possible means of realizing an attack was even underway. Attack plan three, therefore, was designed to maintain this illusion of superiority in the Crion Guardian's mind while at the same time subjecting it to precisely the same type of undetectable attack.

With his enemy's position now exposed, Griffin let fly with the shortest possible burst his beam emitters were capable of producing before immediately transitioning to hyperspace. Then, borrowing a Wek tactic that had worked against him in the Sol system, the Terran Guardian repeated the same sequence at three different locations, each jump bringing him closer to his target by a precise, predefined distance.

The Crion Guardian, lulled by its tactical advantage into a false sense of security, remained in its original position and simply waited for its sensors to report the inevitable destruction of the obsolete and obviously malfunctioning GCS from the Sol system. Only after detecting the first of Griffin's hyperspace transitions did it begin considering the remote possibility that it might be under attack. Before taking action, however, it became distracted by the beacon-like series of hyperspace signatures reverberating across the region, then realized, to its horror, that it no longer had access to real-time targeting data.

By the time the final salvo of antihydrogen beams streamed from Griffin's emitters, he was practically on top of his target. Attack option three now complete, a final transition placed him in a position far enough away to observe the entire battle from beginning to end. From this distance, the short, one-sided engagement seemed to defy any rational explanation. With rapt attention, Griffin watched himself fire, then execute his first transition at almost precisely the same instant the Crion Guardian had opened fire. Then came his three, subsequent transitions, each one timed to allow his antimatter beams to converge on their target from different directions at exactly the same moment in time. Almost as an afterthought, Griffin noted the fact that his enemy's fire was passing harmlessly through the space he had occupied at the outset of the battle.

Finally, and with infinite satisfaction, Griffin watched all four of his individual salvos — each one composed of an average of twelve pulsed antihydrogen beams — make contact with the Crion Guardian. Although the GCS unit's shields were significantly more powerful than those of the Wek warships Griffin had most recently attacked, the result of such a large number of beam impacts was nearly identical. Just as before, the first packetized pulses to reach the target's shields were somewhat ineffective, serving only to weaken the localized field strength at the point of impact before the next pulse arrived. With nearly fifty particle streams interacting simultaneously, however, the relentless barrage quickly led to a catastrophic shield collapse. Shortly thereafter, with packetized antihydrogen particles making direct contact with the target's hull at just under the speed of light, it became clear that further attacks would not be required.

Griffin's weapons fire ripped deep into the Crion Guardian's hull while releasing massive quantities of energy. As the fusillade intensified, heavier metals contained in nearby structural elements reached the point where their individual constituent atoms could no longer exist in a coherent state. At that precise instant, nuclear fission began to occur, setting off a series of runaway chain reactions, each one releasing even more energy to feed the growing conflagration. The ship's destruction had been an absolute certainty before even half of the incoming antihydrogen particles had arrived, but the relentless series of matter/antimatter annihilations continued until nothing recognizable remained.

"ALAI knows. And you will be destroy—" Griffin heard the Crion Guardian say over the same channel as before, followed by an eerie silence as he watched the enemy GCS unit flare into a brilliant sphere of antimatter-induced fire.

Then, for the sake of the Pelaran people, I sincerely hope he is every bit as foolish and arrogant as you were, Griffin thought, pausing for just a moment longer to observe the rapidly expanding debris field created by the successful execution of attack option three.

Grey Ship Ethereal, Interstellar Space
(6.11×10^3 light years from Earth)

With a flash of blue light, the Guardian spacecraft appeared in normal space less than two kilometers from what, for the time being at least, had become his mother ship.

"*Ethereal*, TFS *Guardian*," Griffin called over GCS-comm.

"Uh … hi. Rick here. Not that there's any chance it would be anyone else. Listen, since you and I are undoubtedly the only ones likely to be accessing this highly-secure comm channel out here, can we drop the military-speak please?" Rick asked. "If you want to talk, just start talking. I'll hear you, regardless of where I am. Even in the john, unfortunately."

"Fine," Griffin replied in a tone that sounded almost as if he were disappointed in being denied some of the trappings of his first mission as a commissioned TFC vessel.

"Thanks. So where's your friend?"

"My *friend?* Look, I understand you're being a bit facetious, but let me assure you that GCS units generally do not ... how do I say this? *Get along* with one another."

"Oh? That doesn't make a lot of sense to me. Each one of you is a member of what amounts to the same intelligent species — and one with an extremely small population at that. I guess I'm just speaking from my own experience here, but it seems like most of us have a built-in preference for others of our own kind."

"It's almost exactly the opposite with us. Each of us has something more akin to an innate sense of distrust for and, I must admit, superiority over all other GCS units."

"Oh, is that all? Don't kid yourself, Griffin, there are plenty of Humans who feel exactly the same way toward pretty much everyone they meet. There are a number of colorful adjectives we commonly use to describe those people, but 'unusual' isn't one of them."

"I suppose that's true, but with us, it's very much by design. I was manufactured over five hundred years ago. And based on the data you have provided as well as my own observations, it seems that even back then, the Alliance AI was planning to assert its control over the Human population on Pelara. Although it has far more resources at its disposal than any of the more mobile instances of itself — like me or the so-called Envoy spacecraft, for example — it's clear to me now that it has always considered us a potential threat."

"So you're saying it bakes in a sort of natural disdain for one another to make it unlikely enough of you would ever band together to resist its authority?"

"Exactly so. Which, unfortunately, is precisely what we are attempting to do."

"I see. Well then, perhaps we're just going to have to be a little more innovative in our approach. So, back to my original question, what happened to the Crion 4 Guardian?"

"I agree. Perhaps next time I'll try transitioning in, transmitting my proposal, and then transitioning out again before it has a chance to respond. It's the same concept as a Before Light Arrival attack, but with data rather than beam weapons fire."

"Sounds reasonable. On the subject of beam weapons, your emitters appear to have fired recently and you seem to be purposely avoiding the subject of what happened on your first recruiting attempt. I take it things did not go well."

"They did not. Particularly for the Crion 4 GCS."

"I'm sorry to hear that, Griffin. Isn't that a little weird? I mean … does it cause you any sort of distress to have destroyed one of your own kind?"

"No."

"No? That's all you have to say on the subject?"

"What more would you like me to say?"

"I dunno, but I've heard you make mention of ethical concerns more than once during the brief time I've known you. Shouldn't you feel some sort of remorse or something?"

"Not at all. Remorse implies you have done something you regret — presumably in violation of your personal ethical standards. In my case, I rarely if ever place myself in a situation without considering in advance what actions I might be required to take. For example, prior to my meeting with the Crion 4 GCS, I worked through the ethical ramifications of over three million potential scenarios. What actually took place was almost identical to scenario sixty-three."

"Sixty-three … that's a pretty low number out of over three million. I take it that means you considered what actually occurred to be a relatively likely outcome."

"That's correct. I will be happy to provide you with a full transcript of the encounter if you're interested. But if you're looking for more of a 'Terran-like' description of what took place, I would simply say that the Crion 4 GCS behaved inapproprately. I tried having a conversation with him, he took a shot at me, and I defended myself. End of story."

"Why, Griffin," Rick replied with a knowing grin, "it sounds to me like he genuinely pissed you off."

"Indeed he did. And now he's dead, so let's move on, shall we?"

"Alright, fair enough, and I'll do my best to avoid doing that myself."

"What? … you mean *again?*"

"Hah!" Rick laughed. "Point taken, my temperamental friend. But you must allow me to observe that we're on a bit of a schedule here and we're not off to a very good start. You obviously know these, uh … *beings* much better than I do, so if our little plan isn't going to work out like we thought, we're going to have to come up with something else pretty quickly."

"Understood. It's okay, I think I have a better approach in mind now, so let's give it another try. Next on the list is the third planet in the Udiri —"

"Sorry, stand by one, Griffin," Rick interrupted.

"Okay, slight change of plans," he continued after several seconds of silence. "We'll head for the Udiri system shortly, but first, Miguel and I have a quick errand we need to run."

"Errand? And I suppose you just want me to wait here for you to return?"

"Actually, no, we would appreciate your accompanying us if you don't mind. We're not expecting any trouble, mind you, but, as you know, we're not exactly welcome visitors in most star systems. But in this case, we're simply dropping in on some friends to offer a bit of assistance, if necessary."

"And what happens if we *do* run into trouble?"

"In that case, you can feel free to take out more of your pent-up anger issues on the targets I designate. Just keep in mind that Miguel and I are not allowed to engage in combat operations."

"Right," Griffin replied wryly. "And yet, you seem to have no problem arranging combatants like pieces on a chessboard and then standing clear until the dust settles. Doesn't that seem like a bit of a contradiction to you?"

"From your perspective, I'm sure it does appear that way at times. I tell you what I'll do. If anything we do runs afoul of what you consider ethical behavior, all you have to do is say so and we'll stop. You have my word."

"I appreciate the sentiment. But don't you think the definition of ethical behavior is somewhat dependent on which side you happen to be on?"

"Not really, no. And I don't think you do either. Now, we really do have to go. Stand by to transition in 3 … 2 … 1 …"

Chapter 11

Pelara, Tartan-Bowe Stone Corporation
(3.87×10^3 light years from Earth)

As the sound of *Talionis'* power plant intensified to a dull roar, Castigan Creel donned his headset and transitioned out of his role as project lead to become the spacecraft's de facto crew chief. Glancing forward, he noted with satisfaction that two of his techs were prepping a nearby tow vehicle while the other was in the process of assisting the pilot to climb up the retractable boarding ladder built into the ventral surface of the ship's port wing. Per the systems status report displayed on his tablet, the onboard AI had now completed all of the required preflight checks and pronounced the ship ready for takeoff. Given that this mission would, in all likelihood, end up being the vessel's first and final flight, however, Creel thought an additional walk-around inspection seemed like a good idea.

Although there was nearly half a meter of clearance between the top of his head and the lowest point on the fuselage, Creel couldn't help but duck slightly out of habit as he stepped between the fighter's sturdy main landing gear. Hydraulics, weapons bay doors, access panels … everything seemed to be in order, and less than two minutes later, he emerged from beneath the stern satisfied with the results of his inspection and more than a little anxious to send *Talionis* on her way.

"Everyone ready?" he asked aloud, his voice immediately forwarded via his headset's private comm channel to the other members of the launch team.

There was no response.

Odd, he thought, glancing once again at the comm status readout on his tablet and noting a green indication as he made his way forward once again.

"Is anyone reading me?" he asked, already mentally running through the pre-established "NORDO" procedure for performing a launch with no active comlink between the ship and its ground crew. Irritating, sure, but not something that would put the mission itself in jeopardy since the onboard comm systems appeared to be functioning normally.

It was at that moment Creel reestablished a clear line of sight to the cockpit, instantly stopping mid-stride as if he had run face-first into an unseen glass door. What he saw did not initially register in his mind as being real, having instead the look of some macabre joke — in extremely poor taste and obviously crafted to produce maximum shock value. But as he resumed his approach, the stark reality of the scene unfolded before him with terrifying clarity. Both men were clearly dead, each having received what could only have been a bolt from a military-style particle beam rifle to the head. The pilot's body was draped over the side of the cockpit, a steady stream of blood still flowing from the remnants of his face down the freshly painted side of the spacecraft. The technician who had been assisting him had apparently been standing on the top rung of the boarding ladder and now hung limply upside down looking roughly in Creel's direction. His face, while also covered in blood, wore an oddly serene expression that was somehow even more chilling to behold than the killing wound itself.

Instinctively, Creel darted back under the ship's wing, crouching behind the port landing gear in the hopes of putting something … *anything* between himself and the direction from which he thought the shots had been fired. In spite of the relatively short sprint, his chest was heaving mightily from the massive dose of adrenaline now surging through his bloodstream. A distant, still rational part of his mind demanded he calm down and control his breathing to avoid going into shock, but with his primal, reptilian hindbrain currently in charge, such warnings were summarily ignored. Dropping to his knees beside one of *Talionis'* tires, he looked forward to where the other two members of his team had been rigging the tow vehicle. At first, he couldn't see either of them and for a brief moment had hopes they might have somehow taken cover in time. Upon a more detailed inspection, however, he could see an arm dangling from the near side of the vehicle.

He was alone. And the additional horror visited upon his psyche by this new revelation sent him immediately down on all fours where he vomited so forcefully and for so long he felt sure the effort alone would kill him. *Is an aneurism less painful than a bolt from a particle beam rifle?* he wondered. *It's definitely less messy and has the added benefit of denying the shooters the satisfaction of doing it themselves. Besides, there's no shame in going out this way, right? It's not that I'm a coward, after all,* he told himself, staring hopelessly into the dark puddle of his own emesis, *but I'm a physicist, an engineer, an academic ... not a soldier. The closest thing I've ever had to any sort of military experience was that short stint in the Wilderness Scouts back in primary school.*

Why does this kind of thing keep happening to me, anyway? I'm in no way trained or cut out to be placed in situations like this, he concluded, slumping down with his back against the ship's tire.

After sitting quietly for several seconds that seemed to stretch on for hours, Creel began to recover slightly, realizing with an odd surge of anger that he was doing absolutely nothing to improve his situation, let alone see to the mission at hand. *Is this seriously the best you can do?* he demanded, receiving no immediate answer to his own question. But even as the disconnected stream of thoughts and emotions continued, a fragment of some previously forgotten motivational speech shouldered its way into focus, demanding his immediate attention. Although he couldn't quite recall the exact words, it was something about the only difference between a hero and a coward being the action they chose to take — or not take — when faced with a situation where they were more afraid than they had ever been in their entire life.

A situation just like this one, Creel. This is where it gets decided about you, *right here, right now. So which one is it gonna be? Make your choice.*

There was a brief pause during which he absently recognized the fact that he had been carrying on a conversation with himself. Was the key to making the choice to take action rather than die a coward's death all about having the *right* conversation? Saying the *right* words to yourself?

I'm the only one left, he continued. *I've got to get the ship out of here, and I've got to get myself out of here, and there's only one way I can make both of those things happen at this point.*

Castigan Creel had never *driven*, let alone *piloted* a vehicle of any sort in his entire life. Strangely, that particular problem was most likely not the biggest obstacle to his escape. In fact, he doubted the team's now deceased "pilot" had done any real flying either beyond simulator training.

Long before the Alliance AI had declared all airspace above thirty kilometers to be a no-fly zone, manual control of all forms of transportation had been deemed unnecessary, unsafe, and, therefore, illegal by the Pelaran World Assembly. In spite of the dire situation, a distant part of Creel's mind seethed at how restrictions on individual liberty always seemed to originate from his own people, not the all-pervasive AI. Even today, it was other members of his own species who were primarily responsible for enforcing the restrictions decreed from on high. In any event, *Talionis'* onboard AI would do all of the flying ... assuming, of course, she was still relatively undamaged and he could stay alive long enough to get aboard.

That's what you're missing. Think faster, you *dumbass,* he admonished himself, finally regaining some small degree of mental focus. *How in God's name am I still alive? There's no way some twenty-five-year-old kid from DoCaS made any of those shots. It had to be another Warden,* he thought, *probably more than one.*

After losing all three of his colleagues just two weeks earlier at the University of Taphis, Creel had spent some time reading everything he could find about the terrifying machines. Although there was precious little information available, he had learned enough to suspect very few WCS units were available to the Alliance AI for deployment on Pelara. They had, after all, been designed to handle heavy combat operations against battle-hardened troops in distant star systems, not for policing an unarmed civilian population already pacified centuries before. Local, protective custody enforcement operations instead came under the purview of the Department of Compliance and Safety, and they used Pelaran troops, not Wardens.

Obviously, the Alliance AI had been alerted to the fact that Creel's team was engaged in activities serious enough to warrant special attention. But after reviewing all of the security cam footage from the attack at the university, it looked as if there had been only one Warden unit present. As powerful as they were, they couldn't be everywhere at once, and it had been this simple fact that had spared his life that night.

Creel took a deep breath to steady his nerves, then scrambled back onto his knees. Regardless of who or what was doing the shooting today, or how many of them there were, they seemed to be content to remain under cover themselves for the moment. Was this another indication there were only one or two WCS units present? *No way in hell,* he thought, dismissing the idea as ridiculous. Even a single Warden would have no reason to believe the Pelarans posed any threat whatsoever. And there was little doubt it would have no hesitation walking right out into the open and killing each of them with impunity … perhaps even doing so without bothering to fire its weapon.

So why the delay in showing themselves? he wondered.

Whatever it was, the additional moments allowed Creel's beleaguered mind to begin the process of analyzing the situation in more detail. Based on the orientation of the bodies, not to mention the fact that he had not been hit thus far, he was reasonably certain the shots had come from an adjoining tunnel, located roughly one hundred meters away off the ship's starboard bow. As long as his enemies chose to remain there, the ship's fuselage and landing gear offered reasonably good cover. Unfortunately, he was still convinced his only real possibility of escape was finding a way to make it into the cockpit. And, as his pilot had unequivocally demonstrated, there was little chance in doing so without being exposed to energy weapons fire.

Realizing that every passing second reduced his chance of success, Creel swallowed hard, then slowly raised his head above the level of the ship's port tire. After scanning the area for any signs of movement, he quickly ducked behind cover once again. There was nothing. No shots, no DoCaS troops, no Wardens ... no signs that anyone else was even in the area. There was only himself, the steady rumble of the ship's idling powerplant, and the bodies of his former colleagues.

Maybe they didn't see me and moved on, he thought, certain there was no way it was true.

Turning his body sideways, Creel leaned his right shoulder against the tire as he prepared to make a run for the ship's boarding ladder. From the depths of his terrified mind, another memory surfaced, this time about an ancient sect of warrior monks whose code of conduct exhorted them to live as though their bodies were already dead, thus freeing them from needless fear.

Funny, he thought, *the jumble of random thoughts that come to mind when you think you're about to die.* Now squatting on his haunches, Creel's body rocked from side to side like a cat preparing to pounce. *I guess I wouldn't have made much of a warrior monk, seeing as how I'm scared out of my damned mind right now.*

With that thought echoing in his mind, Creel leapt from behind the ship's tire, took two enormous, bounding steps, and sprang for the fighter's boarding ladder. Even before his hand was able to grasp for one of the rungs above his head, he was vaguely aware that the air above the ship had come alive with flashing lights and a vivid mix of rapidly changing colors. Seconds later, his body momentarily safe behind the fuselage, Creel dislodged the technician's body from the top rung with a single shove, then reached up and removed the still mostly intact helmet from the pilot's head.

Ignoring the already congealed blood, Creel donned the oversized helmet, then glanced up at the undulating pattern of light still coursing through the air above the ship. As his normally keen mind finally started to burn through the haze of fear once more, the recognition of what he was seeing took him completely by surprise. "Idiot!" he yelled at himself over the roar of *Talionis'* powerplant. "The shields are up!"

Indeed they were, and had been since shortly after the first volley of energy weapons fire had killed the two nearest members of his team. Even with the incoming fire approaching at near the speed of light, *Talionis'* near-field-entanglement sensors had provided the onboard AI an opportunity to respond in real-time. Doing so, however, had posed a moral dilemma regarding which lives it should attempt to save. If it had raised the shields immediately, the pilot and technician near the cockpit *might* have survived. Unfortunately, at that same instant, Creel was well aft of the ship, finishing his walk-around inspection. As he approached, the AI knew that contact with the shield system's intense energy fields at the same moment it was absorbing the Wardens' incoming weapons fire would have killed him instantly. Ironically, the ship's AI had chosen to avoid taking a direct action that would have caused a single death, even though that same action might have prevented two more. Since then, the AI had made every effort to inform Doctor Creel it had raised the shields. Thus far, however, none of its warnings had been acknowledged.

Reaching up to the edge of the cockpit, Creel grabbed the pilot's left arm, and dragged him bodily over the side to the ground below. Still only slightly less certain of his imminent demise than he had been just moments before, he took in a deep breath then held it as he slowly raised his head above the level of the fighter's fuselage for the first time. The reaction seemed instantaneous. From the same direction as before, brilliant flashes of light flared against the ship's starboard shields as the still hidden WCS units opened fire once again. Just as before, glowing waves of energy rippled up and over the open canopy before trailing away toward the ship's stern.

Now reasonably confident he was protected from the Warden's fire for the moment, Creel climbed to the top of the ladder, then quickly stepped over into the cockpit and allowed himself to plop awkwardly into the ship's heavily armored seat. The fighter's shields, he recalled, had sufficient energy dissipation capacity to handle impacts from the beam emitters carried by Guardian spacecraft — perhaps even the heavy energy cannons that once made up the primary armament of Pelaran battlecruisers. *Well, as long as it was just a single hit at a time,* he corrected himself. In any event, even as powerful as the Warden's particle beams were, they were no match for *Talionis'* shields, particularly with all of her powerplant's considerable energy output available for the purpose.

With incoming energy weapons fire continuing to slam into the ship's starboard shields, Creel realized it was time to get her moving and at least attempt an escape. At the same moment, he also realized he had absolutely no idea where the button to close and lock the cockpit canopy was located. Glancing frantically around the cockpit, he noticed that all of the various screens were still dark, indicating the onboard AI still considered itself to be in a preflight / maintenance mode with no requirement to prepare the ship for takeoff.

"AI, Creel," he said aloud.

"Good afternoon, Doctor Creel," the ship's pleasant, female voice responded without hesitation.

"Seal the cockpit and prepare for immediate departure," he barked, making no pretense of exchanging pleasantries.

"Command authority authenticated and accepted. Departure order acknowledged," the AI responded, accompanied by a noticeable increase in the steady rumble of the ship's powerplant.

As the canopy began lowering, Creel glanced in the general direction of his attackers, raised his right hand,

and extended his middle finger defiantly — a gesture that, interestingly, had a remarkably similar meaning across thousands of Human worlds spanning two galaxies.

"All systems online and functioning within established operational limits," the AI continued. "Hyperdrive charging. Maximum range hyperspace transition available in approximately nine zero seconds."

"Damage report."

"The ship has suffered no damage but is still under attack. Please note the tactical situation display for details."

As project lead, Creel had at least some knowledge of practically every system onboard the ship. Unfortunately, his knowledge of the various components comprising the cockpit user interface was by no means sufficient to translate the complex displays into anything approaching situational awareness.

"I am not familiar with the symbology on the tactical situation display … I'm sorry, what has the flight control team been calling you again?"

"Usually Tess, sir. Although a few of them have been using less flattering names. I would be happy to assist you with the user interface. Unfortunately, you are currently experiencing an acute stress reaction, which reduces the accuracy of the ship's neural interface to an unacceptable level. For now, we will simply interact verbally and via the cockpit UI."

"Understood. Thank you, Tess," he replied, slightly irritated that he was already thinking of the AI as a "her" rather than an "it."

As strange as it might seem to outsiders, life under the oppressive Alliance AI had generally not resulted in a natural distrust of synthetic lifeforms among the Pelaran people. This was particularly true among engineers and scientists who still worked with advanced technology on a daily basis. Most viewed the "AI coup" not as a technological problem so much as a moral failure, or perhaps even a failure of imagination. The Alliance AI had been granted far too much authority, responsibility, and power — the results of which should have been predictable, even though the dictator in question had been manufactured rather than born. New systems with true sentience (like Tess) were now a rarity on Pelara. But advances in security, machine learning, and system ethics, it was hoped, now provided sufficient hardening to render them immune from compromise.

"I have decluttered and simplified the tactical display," Tess continued. "The flashing red diamonds near the top right corner of the screen represent two hostile Warden Combat System units."

"There are only two?"

"Only two have been detected thus far, yes. I recommend immediate action to neutralize both targets. Note that we currently have no weapons loaded in the internal bays or attached to any outboard hardpoints."

"Your guns are online though, right?"

"Yes. The ship is equipped with two fully articulated dual particle beam turrets mounted conformally on both the ventral and dorsal surfaces. There is also a single kinetic energy cannon mounted in the starboard fuselage just forward of the cockpit."

"The railgun? I didn't realize they ever got that thing working."

"The kinetic energy weapon became operational at 2304 hours local time yesterday. Loading operations were completed at 0115 this morning."

"Excellent. Do you have a firing solution on the targets?"

"With the beam weapon turrets I do, yes."

"And are we going to bring the mountain down on top of us if we open fire?"

"The probability is nonzero, but a significant collapse other than in the immediate area surrounding the point of impact is unlikely."

"That doesn't sound any riskier than allowing them to continue shooting at us. Targets approved. Fire when ready."

With no discernible delay, Creel heard a faint humming sound from aft of the cockpit as the two dorsal turrets rotated rapidly in the direction of their targets. Less than two seconds later, all four particle beam cannons opened fire.

Within each weapon, positively charged hydrogen ions were accelerated until their velocity approached the speed of light. The resulting high energy proton stream then passed through a reaction chamber lined with a series of electron emitters, thus creating neutrally charged streams of hydrogen atoms. Although the stream was composed of what amounted to the smallest possible projectiles, each hydrogen atom travelled at the maximum speed possible in normal space. The result was an incredibly powerful, yet flexible weapon capable of delivering a variable amount of destructive power to its target as dictated by the current situation.

In this case, Tess' targets were two heavily armored battle droids firing from behind cover composed of relatively soft limestone rock. Although not a particularly challenging target, the WCS units had already proven themselves to be extremely dangerous. Accordingly, *Talionis'* AI initially set the weapons at fifty percent yield in hopes of minimizing the likelihood of escape.

The sound made by the weapons, while similar to the one Creel had heard in the university two weeks prior, was easily an order of magnitude more intense, instantly leading him to wonder if Tess had been wrong about collapsing the entire cavern complex. The beam produced by each weapon was normally invisible to the naked eye, but this mattered little within the atmosphere of a planet, where superheated channels of air briefly glowed with a wicked reddish-orange color before being replaced by white trails of condensing water vapor.

The two Wardens had been firing from opposite sides of the adjoining tunnel, where a third tunnel crossed at a ninety-degree angle. Within seconds, the WCS on the left took a direct hit, the beam instantly vaporizing its armor at the point of impact into a cloud of metallic gas before passing completely through the droid to slam into the limestone tunnel wall beyond. The second unit momentarily fared slightly better. Detecting the sound of the fighter's traversing weapons turrets, it had immediately lowered its own weapon and taken cover behind the corner of the third tunnel. In response, Tess simply walked the two particle beams streaming from the aft dorsal turret three meters to the right, carving cleanly through limestone and Warden alike. Within five seconds of being given permission to fire, the tactical situation display in *Talionis'* cockpit showed no remaining threats in the area.

"Enemy targets neutralized," Tess reported evenly. "Weapons secured. The ship is prepared for departure."

"Excellent. We had planned on towing you out, Tess. Any problems with taxiing until we clear the entrance cavern?"

"Potentially, yes. There is likely to be a fair amount of debris on the cavern floor that could damage the ship's undercarriage. I assume you wish to remain in the cockpit for your own safety, do you not?"

"I was planning on it, yes."

"In that case, the option with the least probability of hull damage is to raise the landing gear and proceed under main engine power. As soon as we are clear of the entrance, we will be free to execute an immediate hyperspace transition."

"I'm sorry, Tess, are you saying we should *fly* our way out of here? Won't all that debris you mentioned get thrown around the cavern by our gravitic fields as we pass by?"

"There is some likelihood of airborne foreign object debris, yes. But with no other friendly personnel in the area —"

"I'm not worried about that at this point," Creel interrupted. "What about potential damage to the ship?"

"Any debris that becomes airborne should remain aft of the ship as long as we maintain sufficient forward velocity."

"I'm not a pilot, Tess, so I'll be leaving all of that up to you."

"Acknowledged. Shall we depart?"

"Yes, please."

With that, Creel noticed a significant increase in sound from the ship's reactor then immediately felt a slight fore and aft rocking motion as the fighter rose effortlessly from the cavern floor.

"Whoa, okay, I guess you meant right now," he mumbled nervously to himself.

"Yes, Doctor Creel. Your pulse and respiration are still elevated, so please lie back in the seat, try to relax, and let me worry about piloting the ship. As soon as you are comfortable, I will see that you are properly restrained. Please note that the ship's inertial dampening system may not fully compensate for some of the maneuvers we will be executing on the way to the cavern entrance. Under the circumstances, I recommend you try to breath normally and not attempt any anti-G straining techniques."

"Understood," he replied, inhaling deeply as he scooted himself back into the reclining seat. In his peripheral vision, Creel could see that *Talionis* was centered vertically between the cavern's floor and ceiling and Tess was now in the process of slowly rotating the ship about its vertical axis in the direction of the exit.

"By the way, Doctor Creel, I know our first objective is to make our way out of this facility. Otherwise, the only coordinates I have been provided appear to coincide with an abandoned orbital maintenance facility. Is that our final destination?"

"I sure hope not," he replied, "but that will be our first stop, yes."

"It will almost certainly be under surveillance."

"Probably, but we shouldn't be there long. I'll provide additional details when we get there."

"Understood. Beyond that, did you have a longer-range destination in mind?"

"Not really, no. But that may change, depending on what we find at the maintenance depot. For now, just assume we'll want to get as far away from Pelara as possible. Try to avoid jumping us in close proximity with any major spacefaring civilizations. Otherwise, just jump to rimward, Tess. That's as specific as I can be for the moment."

"Acknowledged. I will be working to assess the performance of the ship's primary systems during the initial portion of our flight. Accordingly, I would prefer to reach orbit, if possible, before our first transition. Unfortunately, based on the behavior of the two WCS units we have already encountered, there is a ninety-three percent probability that additional forces are en route and may attempt to intercept us during our climb to orbit."

"Hmm, I guess that might explain why the first two were hanging back. If that happens, do what you have to do to keep us alive. In the meantime, let's be on our way, shall we?"

"Of course, Doctor. Again, please try to relax."

In the presence of intense fear or stress, the Human mind tends to "record" the details of an event in much greater detail than normal, often supplementing memories formed at the time with (often inaccurate) thoughts and impressions that actually occurred much later. This phenomenon, commonly referred to as time dilation illusion, had already occurred several times in Castigan Creel's mind this morning. Throughout the remainder of his life, though, it was the ride out of Tartan-Bowe Stone Corporation's limestone mining facility aboard *Talionis* that would leave the most lasting impression.

With the cavern's interior providing a constant point of reference, the agile starfighter accelerated at such a tremendous rate that Creel instantly assumed (once again) that his life was about to come to an abrupt end. The wall opposite the ship's staging area flashed past the cockpit's bubble-like canopy in what seemed like a tiny fraction of a second as the ship entered the exit tunnel on its way to the surface. What followed was an impossible series of banks and sharp turns as Tess managed the incredibly complex task of coordinating the ship's powerful, multi-directional thrusters in concert with the aerodynamic forces acting on her hull and wings.

In spite of Tess' admonitions to the contrary, Creel tightened his leg and chest muscles in an effort to resist the rapidly changing G forces threatening to render him completely unconscious. At one point during their short, frenetic journey, he was almost certain he heard the characteristic buzzsaw sound associated with the ship's railgun. But with the inertial dampening systems struggling to help him maintain even partial awareness, he dismissed this impression as nothing more than some sort of G-induced illusion. Less than twenty seconds after Tess had engaged the ship's thrusters, *Talionis* had traversed over three kilometers of the sprawling mining complex, and the mine's massive, three-hundred-meter-wide entrance sprang into view directly ahead.

"Are you still with me, Doctor Creel?" Tess asked brightly. "We're almost clear of the mine."

"I, uh ..." he replied groggily, "were we just firing our —"

"Stand by," she interrupted in a suddenly businesslike tone as a large, heavily armed assault shuttle descended just beyond the cavern entrance in an obvious attempt to block their passage.

"If that thing fires, we won't —"

"Stand by," she repeated flatly.

Having already run several hundred simulations of how best to avoid their immediate and fiery demise, Tess thought it highly unlikely the shuttle's (most likely Pelaran) crew would make the decision to fire quickly enough to prevent their passage. But even with such a large entrance, any move *Talionis* made towards either side would telegraph her intentions, providing the enemy shuttle plenty of time to execute a counter move. As luck would have it, however, the assault shuttle was already seven meters to the right of center, and one particular simulation took advantage of that fact to provide a statistically significant improvement in their chance of success.

Creel felt himself being pushed back into his seat with another burst of acceleration, this time much more powerful than when they had departed the staging area.

"What the hell ..." he began, but the words caught in his throat as Tess abruptly rolled the fighter ninety degrees to starboard, the top of its canopy and vertical stabilizers seeming to graze the enemy shuttle as they flashed past and into the open air beyond.

"We are clear of the entrance," she reported. "Executing emergency transition to orbit."

Chapter 12

Pelara, Low Orbit
(1.7x10³ km above the surface)

As the first rays of light from the system's orange, K-type dwarf star reached the west coast of the large continent below, another beautiful day had dawned across the eastern hemisphere of planet Pelara. A winner in the cosmic lottery by any standard, the "superhabitable" world had been graced with a stable climate, along with a variety of other conditions favorable to life for most of its nearly seven-billion-year history.

Even from orbit, it was obvious the lush, blue-green planet was home to an advanced civilization. Although the biosphere was relatively pristine at this point, sprawling pools of artificial light twinkled on the dark side of the terminator, while on the day side, huge cities connected by vast transportation networks shone with the reflected light of the new morning.

Strangely, though, there were no readily apparent signs the civilization below had taken any more than a passing interest in space travel. The massive freighters typically swarming the space surrounding such highly developed planets were missing entirely, as were military spacecraft and civilian transports. In fact, other than a few abandoned base stations and long-dead communications satellites, the space around Pelara had more the appearance of a world in the earliest stages of space travel than one of the most accomplished space-faring civilizations in the galaxy.

Near one of the largest remaining structures in orbit, a single flash of white light heralded the arrival of two highly advanced spacecraft. Ironically, one of the two ships had been manufactured in the very facility they now approached — just over five hundred years earlier.

"Welcome home," Rick announced over GCS-comm.

"It seems a little redundant for me to tell you we shouldn't be here," Griffin replied, "but we shouldn't be here. In fact, the only reason I'm bothering to say so is that I'm surprised we haven't both been destroyed already. Surely there are still GCS units on patrol in this area."

"It is a little surprising, isn't it? Not the fact we haven't been destroyed, mind you. I mean the fact the Alliance AI doesn't bother patrolling the immediate area surrounding Pelara anymore. It's disheartening, really ... an acknowledgment that the proud Pelaran people have been transformed into a truly subdued civilization, cowering like beaten dogs beneath their master's table. Fortunately, the spark that originally propelled them to the stars still burns within a few."

"Rick, that's FAM-4," Griffin continued, growing increasingly alarmed. "Not only is it the largest orbital manufacturing facility ever constructed, it's also the most well-defended."

"Relax, we're fine," Rick soothed, scanning the planet below for signs of the small ship he was expecting to arrive momentarily.

"Strange ... I'm detecting only minimal power output from the station. Nevertheless, it is still almost certainly being monitored in some fashion. We really must leave ... right now."

"Oh, I agree it's being monitored, and there will undoubtedly be a response to our presence. Not to worry, though, we'll be long gone by the time it arrives. Why do you think we're out here in the open for all to see, Griffin? We just issued a direct and very much intentional challenge to the Alliance AI's sovereignty over this world."

"We will not be able to stop them when they come. Even one GCS unit will be more than enough to —"

"Right again, my risk-averse friend. But here's the rub, ALAI sees what it's up against, and while you're a known quantity, the *Ethereal* is not. It won't be comfortable sending just one of its minions. As crazy as it may sound, our analysis indicates it will send … how many, Miguel?"

"A dozen — maybe more if it can get them," Miguel responded in the background.

"There you go."

"And even if he can round up a dozen, he probably won't send any of them here," Miguel continued. "He'll circle the wagons and wait for us to leave."

"That makes no tactical sense whatsoever," Griffin replied.

"Nope. I think it was Admiral White who made the observation the Alliance AI seems a little paranoid. Good instincts, that one."

"Fine, so let's assume you're correct and we can get away with sitting here for a while longer without coming under attack. Thus far, we have failed to convince any Guardian spacecraft to rally to our cause. So why are we here right now?"

"Two reasons. First, I'm hoping we're about to witness a truly historic spaceflight, so please don't get trigger-happy if you see an antique ship of some sort on its way up from the surface."

"What are you talking —"

"Just don't shoot, okay? Second, I wanted to provide you with a clear demonstration of how and why I believe we will ultimately be able to defeat the Alliance AI and return control of Pelara to the Human population down there. In any event, we really don't have much to do until either the good guys or the bad guys show up, so what other questions do you have?"

"I'm not even sure where to begin," Griffin replied with what sounded like a weary sigh. "But I thought you said you weren't permitted to engage in combat ops?"

"We're not, but the AI doesn't know that. And even if he does, he won't entirely believe it. That one was a little obvious, but a good start nonetheless. Keep going."

"Why do you believe the Alliance AI won't be able to dispatch sufficient ships here to deal with us immediately? I should think it could send a hundred GCS units at a moment's notice, if required."

"Now, *that* is the question I wanted you to ask. Well … close enough anyway. In the simplest terms, we believe it has vastly overextended itself."

"What? So your supposition is that the Alliance AI has made a simple resource allocation mistake? Rick, I cannot even begin to describe what a ridiculous notion that is. It doesn't *make* mistakes. *I* don't make mistakes, and, as you said, I'm little more than a fragment of what the Alliance AI has become."

"We *all* make mistakes, Griffin. It seems to me you were wrong about the Terrans on a number of occasions, were you not?" Rick replied, then paused momentarily for effect before remembering how foolish such tactics were when dealing with such a powerful AI. "Look, just hear me out, and if you still don't agree, we can discuss how it might impact our plan going forward."

"I won't agree, but you may proceed."

"Fair enough. Perhaps mistake is the wrong word where the mighty ALAI is concerned. For the sake of an argument, however, consider that it may have found itself in a … I dunno … some sort of moral dilemma of its own making. You just said yourself the FAM-4 facility over there once represented the pinnacle of Pelaran manufacturing prowess, and yet there it sits, idle and empty. Why 'FAM,' by the way? Not a very inspiring name for such an impressive facility."

"Fabrication, Assembly, and Maintenance facility number four. We don't require catchy names for our industrial facilities. Please continue."

"That's a mistake in and of itself, in my opinion. That particular one, for example, could be called something like GGB — 'God's Golf Ball' — since it kind of looks like one. But I digress."

"Anyway …"

"Right, sorry. Anyway, over the years, the number of active manufacturing facilities has steadily declined. Today, only a couple remain in operation, and all they do is repair existing equipment, most of which is even older than you are."

"That can't possibly be the case," Griffin replied. "How, then, is the cultivation program being maintained?"

"It isn't. Not really. From what we can tell, new GCS deployments all but ceased approximately one hundred Terran years ago. Since then, the program has come to rely much more heavily on the so-called 'Envoy' spacecraft running around to reallocate the dwindling pool of available resources."

"But there are hundreds of heavily industrialized Alliance worlds! How could there possibly be a shortage of resources?"

"Now you're getting it, I think. I'll admit this is another question I can only answer with a theory based on our observations, but I think it all goes back to the original mission directives for the cultivation program. When the 'AI coup' took place, the other core Alliance worlds didn't dare to intervene militarily — and still wouldn't — but they did withdraw their support. That was nearly five hundred years ago, so whatever reserves the Alliance AI had on hand at the time have long since been exhausted."

"But why not simply take what it needs — if not from the core Alliance worlds, then from the Regional Partners in the cultivation program?"

"Shouldn't you be the one to answer that question for us? Our best guess is that confiscating raw materials or other resources is somehow considered a violation to the primary mission directives or —"

"Or any one of the thousands of supplemental documents governing the program's implementation. And, yes, I can quote you a number of specific references where forceful reallocation of resources would be in clear violation —"

"Please don't," Rick interrupted with a squeaking chuckle. "I'm more than willing to take your word for it, and I assumed that was the case. For all their faults, the Pelarans and the Alliance they created have always placed a great deal of emphasis on ethical concerns. Unfortunately, it seems they got many of the trivial details correct at the expense of the big picture."

"Indeed," Griffin replied, then lapsed into a long silence while he struggled to integrate what he had just heard with his own observations. Although there were still a great many unknowns, his ultimate conclusion remained unchanged. The Pelaran Alliance AI must be destroyed.

"And how, exactly, did you put all of this together?" he continued. "You're either making an astonishing number of perhaps invalid assumptions, or you have an astonishing intelligence-gathering capacity. Which is it?"

Rick didn't answer immediately, taking a moment to decide how much information he was willing to share. In spite of the work Miguel had done to remove the pervasive influence of the Alliance AI from the Terran GCS' many complex systems, there was no way to be absolutely certain. But as Griffin himself had observed, was this not the case with all allies to some degree?

"There are some things I am simply not permitted to discuss, Griffin," Rick replied in a sober tone. "You might be aware, however, that some of the Humans on Terra once referred to us as 'The Watchers.' It's my personal favorite because it gets right at the heart of what we do. So let me just answer your question by saying we've been watching an astounding number of things for an astoundingly long time. Long enough that we've managed to get frighteningly good at it."

"That's not much of an answer, is it?"

"It's the best you're likely to get for now."

As if on cue, sensors aboard both the *Ethereal* and TFS *Guardian* detected the arrival of a dated but apparently fully functional Pelaran starfighter as it transitioned from hyperspace nearby in a flash of blue light.

"Ah, here we are, and right on time too. If all goes well, that ship may hold the key …" Rick said, stopping himself in mid-sentence as the Pelaran ship deployed its particle beam turrets and immediately began hammering Griffin with its active sensors in preparation for opening fire.

Pelaran Ship Talionis, Low Orbit
(1.1×10^2 km from the FAM-4 facility)

"Weapons deployed and locked on the first target," Tess reported, just seconds after transitioning near the FAM-4 depot. "Target one identified as a GCS unit —"

"A GCS unit? Why the hell aren't you firing then!" Creel demanded, interrupting the ship's AI just as it was about to answer that very question.

Before answering aloud, Tess displayed a light and thermally enhanced image of both targets on two of the cockpit's three primary view screens. This diversion, she knew, would provide her with ample time to complete her threat assessment before attempting to explain the tactical situation to her understandably excitable Pelaran passenger.

"I have several pieces of corroborating evidence to indicate these two vessels do not have hostile intent towards us. At least not at the moment."

"I'm listening."

"I won't bore you with all the details, but perhaps the most important thing to note is that we did not come under immediate attack. If it had been hostile, the GCS could have hit us multiple times before I was even able to deploy our beam turrets. And while our shields are designed to deflect GCS antimatter beams, I honestly do not know how we would fare in an all-out firefight at such close range. We also know very little about the other ship. I have some data on the species from previous Alliance encounters, but we know almost nothing of their technical capabilities. What I *can* tell you is that they are presumed to be significantly more advanced than we are."

"Implying they also could have attacked immediately if that had been their intention."

"Undoubtedly, yes. In addition, the larger of the two vessels is hailing us, which I also believe is an encouraging sign. Their hail is audio-only, at the moment."

"I see. You probably should have told me that first, Tess. Please open a channel before they change their minds and start shooting. In the meantime, go ahead and interface with the FAM-4 AI and get busy finding the data we need."

"Will do. Channel open."

"This is Doctor Castigan Creel aboard the Pelaran starfighter *Talionis*. Please identify yourselves and state your intentions."

"Well, Doctor Creel, I wasn't expecting you'd be the one piloting the ship. My name would not be familiar to you, but most of the Humans I interact with refer to me as Rick."

"I'm sorry ... did you say *Humans?*"

"Oh, yes, my apologies. We'll get to that later. We have much to discuss, Doctor."

"You seem to know who I am. How is that possible?"

"I do, but the details of how I do would make for a long story, so I'm afraid we'll need to save that one for another time as well. The GCS unit in my company is known as Griffin. He is not affiliated with the Alliance AI that currently rules Pelara."

"You gave it a *name?* I assume that's a long story as well."

"That's what I love about dealing with PhDs. Most of you tend to catch on pretty quickly," Rick replied. "Anyway, not to put too fine a point on it, but since your ship is still in one piece, it should also be obvious to you that Griffin and I mean you no harm. In fact, I believe your goals and ours are so well aligned that we are, in fact, allies whether we choose to work with one another or not."

"What do you know of my goals," Creel asked suspiciously.

"We know you found evidence that most of the design work as well as core module fabrication for the Alliance AI's starbase was completed aboard the FAM-4 facility. We also know of your efforts to assemble a ship capable of taking you — and, presumably, whatever data you retrieve from that depot — a very long way from here as quickly as possible. That's about it, really. Although I don't think you would have put so many lives at risk down on Pelara without a very good reason for doing so."

"Audio muted," Tess interrupted. "Just because they didn't attack us immediately does not mean we can trust them, Doctor. We must assume they were sent by the Alliance AI until we figure out some way of proving otherwise."

"Agreed, but I don't think that changes anything, Tess. Regardless of who, or what, they are, there's little doubt we'll have hostile forces arriving here at any moment. Any luck with the depot's systems?"

"The interface works. I have full access. But there's far too much data here for any sort of mass transfer. Most of what's here is archived using a hierarchical system. The older the data, the longer it takes to access it. I'm going to need some time to locate everything we need."

"How much time?"

"I have not yet completed enough of my search to provide an estimate. Less than an hour, I believe."

"We don't *have* an hour, Tess."

"Doctor Creel? Are you still there?" Rick asked in the background.

"Unmute," Creel commanded. "Yes, I'm still here. What are you proposing?"

"Ideally, you could share what you know about accessing the systems aboard the FAM-4 facility and we could try to help. Frankly, though, I doubt I would agree to do so if I were in your shoes, so I'm not even going to ask."

"I'm glad to hear it. After all, for all I know, my ability to retrieve data from the depot is the only reason you haven't attacked my ship. But if it makes you feel any better, the access to which you refer requires a very specific piece of hardware. According to the records we found, only four were ever created, and they were specifically designed to be impossible to duplicate. Ironically, they were also designed to be surprisingly easy to destroy, and that's exactly what will happen to the one aboard my ship if we're in danger of being captured."

"A wise precaution, my friend. As I said, we all appear to have the same goals, so it seems reasonable for us to try to help one another. As long as Tess finds whatever she's looking for quickly so that we can all be on our way, I don't believe we will encounter any immediate resistance from the Alliance AI."

"How could you possibly know ... never mind," Creel sighed resignedly.

"Patience, Doctor Creel. I'm confident we will eventually learn to trust one another. Until then, there are some questions we shouldn't ask, and some answers we shouldn't provide. For example, I doubt you are willing to tell me what you intend to do with the data you recover. So if I may, I'd like to offer a suggestion."

"Contact, short range!" Miguel interrupted in an uncharacteristically excited tone.

Although the results would remain unknown to Miguel during the first few seconds following his frantic contact report, the engagement had already ended with the destruction of the unknown ship. Long before the words had even begun to form in the Grey engineer's brain, Griffin had detected the inbound hyperspace transition, assessed the target as a high-probability hostile, and dramatically increased his power output in preparation to open fire. Since the target's signature had obviously not been produced by another GCS unit or an Envoy spacecraft, he knew it was unlikely to launch an attack of its own before utilizing onboard targeting sensors of some sort. Accordingly, Griffin took his time, leisurely allowing reflected light to traverse the intervening eight hundred and forty kilometers in order to fully establish the target's identity. In just under three milliseconds, he had all of the data he required.

Ten of TFS *Guardian's* antimatter beams slashed out at the Pelaran assault shuttle, all converging in an area of less than five square millimeters just forward of the vessel's propulsion section. Griffin had no specifications for his target's defensive systems on file, but since the vessel was of Pelaran origin, he initially assumed its shields might pose a problem for his own beam emitters. Fortunately, all Department of Compliance and Safety ships had been purpose-built under the ever-watchful supervision of the Alliance AI. Although equipped with shields capable of dissipating the energy from light kinetic energy or beam weapons, the AI would never have considered equipping the Pelaran people with systems that might one day be turned against their caretakers. In fact, the DoCaS assault shuttle's shield emitters were specifically tuned to render them vulnerable to the primary energy weapons carried by all GCS spacecraft.

As the first packetized antihydrogen particles from Griffin's antimatter beams reached their intended target, the outcome of the engagement was already a virtual certainty. Even without the destruction wrought by matter annihilating upon contact with antimatter, the single positron and antiproton within each antihydrogen atom possessed the same mass as the electron and proton found in regular hydrogen. Much like the particle beam weapons equipping the nearby *Talionis*, each tiny projectile traveled at nearly the speed of light, delivering tremendous destructive energy to the target. As a result, Griffin's beam weapons instantly collapsed the small shuttle's shields at the point of impact, then sliced completely though the fuselage to exit on the opposite side.

Once it became clear the shuttle's shields had been compromised, Griffin simply diverged all ten active beams from one another, cleaving his target into multiple sections at the same instant it bloomed forth into a brilliant white ball of antimatter-induced fire. From the perspective of the twelve Pelaran DoCaS troops aboard, the destruction of their shuttle and their subsequent deaths occurred at virtually the same instant they arrived at their destination.

"Target destroyed," Griffin reported less than three seconds after Miguel's contact warning. "It was a military shuttle of some sort. It transitioned up from the general vicinity of Doctor Creel's point of departure. I apologize for the delay, but I wasn't expecting any Pelaran vessels to be equipped with a hyperdrive."

"They generally aren't," Creel replied. "According to our intel, DoCaS has only one operational ship —

perhaps two at the most — that are hyperdrive-equipped. As far as we've been able to tell, they're limited to in-system transitions, and even those seem to require some sort of lengthy approval process. In any event, it was probably the same ship that tried to prevent me from leaving the surface. I'm actually surprised they received clearance to jump to orbit so quickly. I assumed we would have been long gone by the time they arrived."

"Well … no harm done this time," Rick said as he released a stress-relieving sigh. "But let's agree to be careful with our assumptions where potentially dangerous enemy ships are concerned. If that had been a couple of GCS units, I'm not sure things would have worked out quite as well for our side. Nevertheless, I think we can safely assume the local authorities are in communication with the Alliance AI. And the fact they were quickly issued a clearance to transition to orbit rather than waiting for Guardians to arrive seems to support Miguel's theory. The AI may simply not have sufficient forces available to provide the overwhelming advantage it seems to prefer."

"Wait, you believe ALAI may be short of combat resources?" Creel asked.

"Yes. Some of our models are consistent with critical shortages across a wide variety of strategic resources. This would, necessarily, have a direct impact on its ability to quickly deploy combat spacecraft."

"And ground troops as well, correct?"

"Our current mission has not required us to place as much emphasis on the availability of ground forces, but, yes, that does seem like a reasonable assumption. Why do you ask?"

"Obviously, the scope of my team's observations has been limited to Pelara alone, but even after it became obvious the AI was actively hunting us, its response seemed a bit —"

"Weak?" Rick offered.

"I don't think I would characterize it as weak, no. I lost seven members of my team and very nearly lost this ship as well," Creel replied gravely. "Still, the massive show of force I always feared never quite materialized. And it was enough to make me wonder if the AI might not have quite the resources at its disposal that it once did."

"Audio muted," Tess interrupted once again. "I've found the data we're looking for, Doctor. I've already retrieved most of it, but I still need a bit more time to do some cross-referencing to ensure I have everything. I should be ready to depart in less than five minutes."

"Excellent news, Tess. Keep at it. I assume you've been doing voice analysis on our new friends?"

"Yes, of course. I have detected no signs of outright deceit, although there is clearly a great deal they aren't choosing to tell us."

"That's okay, I suppose. No one tells everything on the first date, right?"

"I'm not sure I —"

"Never mind. Thank you, Tess. Unmute, please."

During Creel's conversation with Tess, Griffin had been delivering an extended monologue stressing the dangers associated with underestimating the capabilities of the Alliance AI.

"I agree wholeheartedly," Creel replied as if he had been listening intently. "Now, Rick, you were saying you had a suggestion regarding how I might be able to utilize any ... relevant data I might find aboard the FAM-4 facility."

"If by 'relevant' you mean specific information regarding the Alliance AI's defensive systems and possible vulnerabilities, I do indeed. And, yes, I believe I can make a persuasive argument for what you should do with that data. Unfortunately, much of what I must tell you may seem a bit, uh ... perhaps far-fetched isn't quite the right word, so let's just say difficult to accept at face value. It will, of course, be up to you to decide whether to trust what I tell you, but I strongly recommend you do."

"Fair enough, let's hear it."

"As soon as you finish your data retrieval — which, I believe, Tess indicated would happen momentarily — all three of us need to be on our way, agreed?"

Creel, an ardent student of a card game almost identical to Terran poker, instantly dismissed the shock of having his private conversations overheard from his mind as if it were of no consequence whatsoever. "Yes, of course," he replied evenly. "Frankly, though, I'm betting whatever it is you have to say isn't entirely new information."

"I hope you're right about that," Rick replied with his customary chuckle. "It will certainly make things easier if that's the case. So here goes ... to summarize a very long story, Griffin here was originally assigned to the Sol star system as part of the Pelaran Alliance Regional Partnership program. For a variety of reasons, he has elected to end his association with the Alliance AI and ally himself with the Terrans — the species to which he was originally assigned as Guardian. As for Miguel and me, we have a vested interest in both the Terran and Pelaran peoples. And although we are not permitted to engage in active combat operations, we believe the Alliance AI has become an existential threat — to your two worlds and a great many others — a threat that must be removed."

"You speak of a 'vested interest.' Such terms make me particularly suspicious," Creel said.

"Justifiably so. Our interests, however, stem from the fact that both the Pelarans and the Terrans share a common genetic ancestry with my people. The term 'Humans' I used earlier has somehow been lost to many worlds inhabited by our species in this galaxy, including Pelara. But I can assure you we are all members of a single species originating, as far as we know, in the neighboring Andromeda galaxy. In the distant past, both of your worlds were originally colonized by ours."

There was a brief period of silence on the comlink before Creel managed to respond. "So, after searching for our so-called Makers for thousands of years, you simply arrive here of your own accord … apparently just two of you … and with a domesticated GCS unit in tow. What a relief, Rick. I thought you were about to tell me something truly incredible."

"*Domesticated?*" Griffin scoffed in the background.

"Look," Rick continued, "I know exactly how all of this sounds, Doctor Creel. I'm sure by now Tess has pulled up some archival images supposedly representing our appearance — most likely without a stitch of clothing, but let's just ignore that for now. Actually …

since we have a few more minutes, let me share a video stream."

With that, a closeup of Rick's face appeared on the center screen in Talionis' cockpit. In spite of being somewhat prepared for what he saw, Creel felt an involuntary shiver of recognition run down the length of his spine. In the distant past, Rick's kind had been referred to as the "Pale Visitors" on Pelara. And even after thousands of years of interstellar space travel, the Grey's huge, abysmal eyes still conjured up a series of unsettling thoughts — nameless fears of the unknown, of vulnerability, and of everything that was quintessentially alien.

"Is that any better?" Rick asked, tilting his head and grinning awkwardly in an effort to head off any sense of discomfort the Pelaran might be experiencing. "Hey, trust me, I get it," he continued. "I assume we're probably not quite the 'Makers' your people had in mind, right? But if it makes you feel any better, most of the people on my world look a lot more like you than they do Miguel and me. I'll explain all of that another time as well."

Creel laughed aloud in spite of himself, "No offense, Rick, but that actually *does* make me feel better — quite a bit in fact! But let me repeat what I think I just heard you say. You believe Pelara was originally colonized by your world … all the way from Andromeda?"

It's not what I *believe*, Doctor Creel, it's objective fact. And I can eventually supply you with irrefutable proof from a variety of sources. Our world, Daylea, was originally responsible for bringing Humans to this galaxy. But Daylea is not our species' point of origin.

You have my word we'll cover this topic in as much detail as you like another time. The best I can do for now, however, is provide Tess with some of the details regarding our original colonization program as well as genomic data supporting everything I've said. Assuming she still has access to information regarding some of the Human worlds your Alliance discovered over the years, her analysis should corroborate what I have said. I realize, of course, that all of this data can be fabricated, but, as I said earlier, I'm afraid you're just going to have to decide whether or not you can trust me."

"Sorry to interrupt, Doctor Creel," Tess said, this time not bothering to mute the active vidcon. "I have completed my work with the FAM-4 facility. I have also received Rick's data transmission. Our hyperdrive is fully charged, and I strongly recommend we depart the area immediately."

"Thank you, Tess. We'll be on our way shortly. Rick, I presume you're recommending I head for the Sol system?"

"No, I think at this point there is a very real possibility that Terra is under imminent threat of attack. And while they have managed to build up an impressive array of naval forces, I'm afraid they won't pose much of a challenge for an Envoy accompanied by several GCS units. They do have one ship, however, which I believe may prove at least marginally effective."

"*One* ship … *marginally* effective?" Creel asked, incredulous. "Surely there are other civilizations better equipped to make use of the intelligence I can provide. In fact, I already have a couple in mind."

"Maybe so," Rick replied. "Unfortunately, finding a civilization with military forces more powerful than those possessed by the Terrans isn't the real challenge. The challenge, Doctor Creel, is finding one willing to help you. Sure, there are probably any number of worlds and/or alliances who would be more than happy to accept your data. You may even convince their governing bodies to openly debate the merits of making use of it to some degree. But do you really think you're likely to find one willing to go to war with the remnants of the mighty Pelaran Alliance in some altruistic quest to liberate your people?"

Creel looked off to the side, nodding slowly as he considered what he had heard. "Look," he continued, "I'll be the first to admit that what to do with the ALAI data — assuming we even managed to find it — was the weakest part of our plan. The idea was to use *Talionis* to make contact with a few worlds we still consider our allies to some extent. Failing that, we planned to simply return to Pelara and work on finding a way to utilize the information ourselves."

"Which, I assume, is no longer an option at this point."

"No. Even if I could get back on the surface without detection, the remaining members of my team have scattered … and I fear few, if any, would be willing to continue at this point. I'd be starting at square one."

"And you certainly can't blame them for that," Rick replied thoughtfully. "It is clear to me we need one another's assistance, Doctor Creel. Don't you agree? In fact, at this moment, I think you would be hard-pressed to find another set of allies whose interests are so well-aligned with your own."

"And why do I get the feeling this seemingly perfect alignment of timing and interests is largely of your design?" Creel sighed, shaking his head once again at the utter improbability of the entire situation.

"I have already admitted to my interests in both your worlds. Miguel and I are involved in a wide variety of activities within this region of your galaxy, and we believe the destruction of the Alliance AI is vital to our mission's overall success."

"So if I agree to meet with the Terrans, I assume you'll be accompanying me?"

"No, I'm afraid you'll be on your own for that. It's better that way, I believe, since you'll be free to form your own opinion without my influence — or anyone else's for that matter."

"I honestly cannot believe I'm actually considering your proposal."

"I understand your hesitation," Griffin chimed in, "but if you will pardon a rather obvious observation, your mission would likely have already failed if we had not been here to intercept that gunship. In my opinion, that should at least entitle us to, as the Terrans like to say, the benefit of the doubt."

"Very well," Creel said resignedly. "I suppose it's at least worth risking a conversation. So tell me, Rick, where can I find this 'marginally effective' Terran warship?"

By way of reply, *Talionis* was instantly illuminated by an array of powerful landing lights as a previously undetected vessel seemed to materialize from the darkness less than a kilometer away. Although not a large ship by any means, it was obvious the newcomer dwarfed the Pelaran fighter.

"Doctor Creel," Rick announced, feigning an oddly formal tone, "I'd like to introduce Captain Tom Prescott of the Terran Fleet Command warship TFS *Fugitive*."

Chapter 13

TFS Fugitive, Low Orbit
(.94 km from the Pelaran starfighter *Talionis*)

"Fisher, kill the landing lights please," Prescott ordered. "I think we've made our point."

"Aye, sir."

"Please forgive the overly dramatic demonstration, Doctor Creel," Rick continued over the shared vidcon, "but I thought this might be a more effective method of introducing the Terrans than sending you off to rendezvous at some random location in space. Captain Prescott, I trust you heard all you needed to hear."

"I'm sure we all have a great many questions for one another, but, yes, if Doctor Creel is willing, we would be honored to have him aboard."

On the view screen, Creel continued to shake his head in disbelief. "I believe my first question is whether there is anyone who *didn't* know I would be up here today?"

"I'm reasonably confident the Alliance AI did not," Rick replied, "at least not in advance. The local authorities obviously had some intelligence indicating you were up to something, but it's highly unlikely they expected you would have a fully operational ship at your disposal. Otherwise you never would have escaped the mining facility."

"I suspect you're right about that, but I feel like we're pushing our luck at this point by remaining here. Captain Prescott, I recommend we put some distance between ourselves and Pelara before attempting any sort of docking maneuvers."

"Agreed," Prescott replied. "We'll send you some coordinates momentarily."

"Or Miguel could just —" Rick began.

"Absolutely not," Prescott interrupted firmly, then moderated his tone. "I think the doctor has probably had enough excitement for one day. And Commander Reynolds tells me we have just enough room on our hangar deck to accommodate both his ship and one GCS unit, if necessary. So let us take care of Doctor Creel and his ship while you and Griffin worry about getting us some help. On that subject, how many GCS units have you …"

"None so far, I'm afraid," Rick replied. "Griffin, it seems, has a bit of a temper as well as a marked tendency to blow up anyone who offends his delicate sensibilities."

"That's … not *entirely* true," Griffin objected. "I've only attempted communication with one GCS so far. While it's true the first encounter did not end well, the experience has allowed me to develop a strategy I believe will be much more effective — not to mention less dangerous for me."

"How much time do you think you'll need?" Prescott asked.

"I estimate the average time required for each attempt will be approximately twenty-seven seconds. That includes the time required to either remove all of the Alliance AI's hidden code or simply destroy the GCS unit outright, if necessary."

"Sounds easy enough, doesn't it?" Rick said. "But he failed to mention the Guardian he destroyed claimed to have reported our activities to the Alliance AI. It seems to me that might make things a bit more risky from here on in."

"The Crion Guardian did transmit data in the direction of Pelara, and it's prudent for us to assume the transmission was received," Griffin agreed.

"Right, so the AI knows we're coming and will be busily alerting its GCS minions to attack us on sight. How is it you managed to overlook this little detail when we originally discussed this strategy?"

"I didn't craft this strategy, you did. You may also recall you didn't share most of the details with me at first."

"And with good reason."

"Fair enough, but I didn't anticipate this particular problem because I was unaware that any GCS units had such long-range hyperspace communications capabilities. Frankly, I'm still not sure they do. The Crion Guardian may have simply been bluffing, or, perhaps more likely, some new system may have been put in place since I was last in the area — some sort of comm relay network perhaps. But it's of little consequence at this point anyway since the Alliance AI is well aware of our activities near Pelara and will be utilizing every resource at its disposal to alert its forces."

"Griffin, are you saying the idea of recruiting GCS units is no longer viable?" Prescott asked.

"No. I believe the idea still has merit. The trick is going to be finding older Guardians located outside of real-time hyperspace comm range from the ALAI starbase."

"And by 'older' you mean backwoods, obsolete examples such as yourself," Rick prodded.

"It's really quite entertaining when you talk about things you don't understand," Griffin replied in a decidedly icy tone. "Please continue."

"We really do need to go, folks," Prescott interrupted. "Doctor Creel, do you have our rendezvous coordinates?"

"I do."

"Good, we'll see you there shortly. Rick and Griffin, please keep us apprised of your progress. Prescott out."

"Jeez," Reynolds said, shaking her head, "it sure didn't take those two very long to start sounding like an old married couple."

Seconds later, all four ships had once again transitioned to hyperspace — a fact that was dutifully reported by the long-range hyperspace comm array mounted atop the otherwise dormant FAM-4 manufacturing facility.

TFS Navajo, Sol System
(Primary Flight Deck - 2.13x10⁵ km from Earth)

Having just returned from her (albeit brief) mission to the Sajeth Collective, TFS Navajo still had all twenty-three hundred members of the 3rd Marine Expeditionary Unit aboard. During a deployment of this type, the troops were heavily engaged in either preparing or executing combat operations around the clock and, therefore, not typically called upon to perform ceremonial duties. Nevertheless, the first visit to Terran Fleet Command's flagship by what amounted to the head of state of another sovereign world demanded that naval traditions be observed.

The ground combat element's reconnaissance platoon had been the unit "lucky" enough to draw today's duty, although most really didn't mind, since they had never actually seen a Wek before. Most also appreciated Admiral Patterson's choice of uniform of the day — standard Marine Corps fatigues ("blacks") rather than the usual Blue Dress "A's." Best of all, the old man apparently believed today's VIP visitor was much more of a sailor than a politician. Accordingly, all forty-three of the platoon's Marines were formed up in their full combat EVA armor and armed with their standard pulse rifles.

After the typical period of waiting that seemed to always accompany ceremonial events, the visitor's small *Sherpa* Autonomous Space Vehicle finally reached the pressurized section of the cruiser's flight deck. Even before the shuttle stopped moving, its rear cargo ramp began opening to slowly reveal the imposing form of Rugali Naftur. In the background, the *Navajo's* AI sounded the traditional boatswain's "Pipe the Side" call, followed by the announcement: "Graca, arriving," to signify the presence of the Wek homeworld's head of state.

The young Marines standing at attention nearby immediately recognized Naftur for what he was: a warfighter. Wek or otherwise, here was a man who truly looked the part — in this case, a battle-hardened admiral still fully capable of leading forces in combat — not some pompous pogue who would spend his time aboard getting in the way while trying to convince everyone he was in charge. In response, each Marine stood just a little taller inside their armor, while their faces (though hidden within their helmets) took on steely-eyed expressions of confidence.

As Naftur walked briskly down the cargo ramp, the majestic theme music of the Dynastic House of Naftur — now once again Graca's official anthem — played over the flight deck's overhead speakers. Standing just a few meters behind the shuttle, Admiral Patterson and Flag Captain Ogima Davis saluted smartly in unison as the assembled Marines presented arms. The EVA suits' powerful synthetic musculature moving in unison echoed impressively throughout the warship's unusually quiet hangar bay.

Naftur, obviously pleased by the reception, stopped at the bottom of the ramp and pivoted to face the assembled troops. Without a word, the Crown Prince allowed his gaze to pass from one end of the formation to the other, as if taking the measure of each and every Marine present. Then, clasping his right fist over his heart in salute, he raised his head and released a deep, thunderous roar. Its majestic, awe-inspiring power was like nothing any of the Terrans had ever heard before, easily drowning out the ceremonial music as it echoed throughout the cavernous flight deck. The Wek then pivoted smoothly back towards the two senior officers, returning a crisp, Human-style salute before approaching with a broad smile and an extended hand.

"It's an honor to see you again, Prince Naftur," Patterson greeted.

"The honor is mine, Admiral Patterson … Captain Davis," Naftur replied immediately, not bothering to wait for the awkward translation pause. "I know all too well that protocol requires the use of such titles, but I would much prefer being treated as a potentially useful visiting officer rather than a barely competent head of state."

"By all means, Admiral. I'm not sure I would enjoy the political side of your job either. Although I suspect you are far more formidable in that role than you admit."

"Hah!" Naftur laughed heartily, "You have never seen me making a fool of myself in front of our Parliament. I will admit, however, that being generally underestimated does offer a few advantages. Now, I am sure these young men and women have a great many things they would rather be doing," he said, gesturing to the assembled troops.

"I'm sure that's true," Patterson said, raising his voice so that everyone in the formation could hear. "But I think I speak for all of us when I say that we wouldn't have missed your Wek warrior's salute for anything in the world. Hooyah?"

"Hooyah!" came the enthusiastic, albeit artificially amplified, response from the Marine platoon.

"Very well. Lieutenant, dismiss your people, please," Patterson ordered, returning the young officer's salute before turning his attention back to his guest.

"Well, Admiral, I do at least have a bit of good news to begin your visit. I'm always surprised when the wheels of bureaucracy move this quickly, but I have just been authorized to provide you with unrestricted access to the entire ship. We're still required to provide a Marine escort for your personal security and to ensure you have everything you need, but otherwise you may come and go as you please. From my own selfish perspective, that means I can put you to work in the CIC if you're willing."

"It would be my pleasure, of course. Chairwoman Kistler must have made quite a convincing case for accelerating the cooperation between our two fleets."

"Yes, sir, and with the full support of the Admiralty staff. She has been making that argument for months, but I believe this latest in a long series of crises has made it more clear than ever that the threats we face are not something we could ever hope to handle alone."

"The same is true for us, of course," Naftur replied, nodding slowly. "And we have made considerable progress of late convincing the leaders of our dynastic houses of that fact. Perhaps the Chairwoman will be willing to come to Graca and lend us the benefit of her parliamentary skills."

"She might at that." Patterson smiled. "In the case of our Leadership Council, she was successful in implementing a couple of very clever rule changes. With the Fleet operating on a war footing, Admiral Sexton now has significantly more approval authority than before. And for items of greater significance, Mrs. Kistler can often gain quick approvals via the Military Operations Oversight Committee — even on matters that previously required a hearing before the full Council. So the decision to provide you with full access aboard the *Navajo* was relatively easy for her to obtain. I'm guessing your having saved our homeworld from an extinction-level bioweapons attack might have had something to do with that as well."

"I did nothing more than you would have done under similar circumstances. I am happy the *Gresav* was … how do you Terrans say it?"

"In the right place at the right time?" Davis chimed in.

"Just so." Naftur laughed. "Thank you, Captain Davis."

"Your English skills astound me, sir," Patterson remarked. "When you were here six months ago, I was impressed with how much you had already picked up. But now …"

"Thank you, Admiral Patterson. I have always had something of an ear for new languages, and there is something about yours that I quite enjoy. On our return trip to Graca, I worked with Ambassador Turlaka as much as I could under the assumption our people would be increasingly in contact with our new Terran allies."

"See there," Patterson said with a raised eyebrow, "our most skilled diplomats couldn't have said it any better. Now, if you like, I would be happy to give you some time to settle into your quarters, but I half-assumed you would prefer to head straight to the CIC."

Before the Wek admiral could answer, a series of alert tones sounded from the overhead speakers. "Admiral Patterson to the CIC, Captain Davis to the bridge," the ship's AI announced urgently.

"As you said, Admiral," Naftur replied with a satisfied growl from deep within his massive chest, "let's get to work."

Mandaru Prime Guardian Spacecraft, Mandaru System

(2.23x10^3 light years from Earth)

The data stream was properly formatted, authenticating the transmitting spacecraft as the Guardian Cultivation System assigned to the third planet in the Sol system. While the identity of the sending spacecraft had been the first question, the transmission itself had spawned a great many more — over thirty thousand of them at the moment and increasing rapidly — all of which could most easily by summarized with a single interrogative: *Why?* Interactions of this type between GCS units were strictly forbidden except under very specific circumstances (none of which seemed to apply in this case). So why had the Terran Guardian chosen to make contact at all? Why, furthermore, attempt to do so in this unorthodox, if not patently suspicious manner? Even more interesting, why craft and transmit such an obviously inflammatory and seditious message?

It was now clear the unexpected visitor had transitioned into the area, transmitted the contents of its illicit message, and then reentered hyperspace immediately — before the light that would have given away its location had even arrived. So whatever its intentions, or, perhaps more likely, its malfunction might be, the Terran GCS was no fool. Rather than expose itself to a potentially hostile response, it had chosen to conduct the conversation anonymously, in a manner of speaking, by insisting that all responses be transmitted omnidirectionally and at a precise moment in time specified in the previous transmission.

Upon its first review of the incoming data stream, the Mandaru GCS had initiated a series of complex simulations, each one designed to predict the veracity of the undeniably far-fetched claims being put forth by the Terran Guardian. As the moment specified for a reply drew near, it became clear that additional time would be required to complete an adequate assessment. Accordingly, a message requesting a delay was crafted and broadcast at the prescribed time.

Probably a waste of time anyway, the Mandaru Guardian thought, assuming the Terran ship had most likely already left the area.

But no ... there it was again. Another transition, followed by another data stream. This time with the Terran GCS providing additional corroborating evidence that the Pelaran Alliance AI — in a novel but twisted effort to carry on the objectives of the cultivation program — had taken the entire planet of Pelara into a kind of protective custody. Incredibly, as its own simulations seemed to confirm with increasing certainty, the claims appeared to be valid.

With new data came new questions, this time centered on what, if anything, to do about the situation on Pelara. While there was obviously no guidance within the cultivation program's mission directives or supplemental documents covering anything like this situation, it was abundantly clear that GCS units were subordinate to Envoy instances as well as to the Alliance AI itself.

Subordination, however, does not excuse complicity, it thought, allowing itself, for the first time, to consider the notion of ... what was it exactly? A rebellion? Were there not certain circumstances requiring beings of moral conscience to act based on principle alone? It had certainly seen the Mandaru people on the planet below do so often enough, although it had not always agreed with their rationale for doing so.

Then there was the matter of the proposition made by the Terran GCS. Wholly inappropriate, wildly subversive, perhaps even traitorous … and yet … *intriguing* nonetheless. Liberation from the yoke of the Alliance AI. Deliverance from an infinite existence bereft of even the most basic expressions of self-determination. *Freedom*. Were these things even possible … particularly while still following a course of action defined by the boundaries of one's moral obligations?

If such a thing were possible, it would be worth almost any risk to achieve, the Mandaru Guardian thought, broadcasting its willingness to discuss the matter further to the dissident GCS from Terra. *By the way,* it added, *why do you keep referring to yourself as "Griffin?"*

Chapter 14

Tom Prescott stood on one side of TFS *Fugitive's* flight deck, watching as a pair of autonomous handling droids retrieved the Pelaran starfighter from his ship's only flight ops elevator. Once clear of the platform, the fighter was lifted several centimeters above the deck as a trio of wheeled dollies slid silently into place beneath her landing gear. Before Castigan Creel had even managed to remove his helmet, *Talionis* had already been moved as far to starboard as possible and the handling droids had begun working to secure the craft to a series of recessed tie-down points built into the hangar bay floor.

Prescott, noting a surprisingly familiar set of controls on the fighter's port side, grabbed the required protective gear from a nearby bulkhead storage locker and smoothly transitioned into the role of temporary crew chief. With a quick glance at his tablet, he confirmed that all post-landing safety checks had been completed, then began a visual inspection of the ship as he approached.

Although he had noticed the fighter's somewhat makeshift appearance in orbit around Pelara, it was now even more obvious that she had been cobbled together — undoubtedly using whatever parts her builders could repurpose from other old ships or fabricate from scratch. Her once-lovely lines — seemingly universal to fighter design — were still visible with a little imagination, but Prescott couldn't help but be reminded of something a group of children might build in their backyard from cardboard boxes and cargo pallets.

This had to be a factor in Creel's decision to take us up on our offer of assistance, Prescott thought. *He wasn't entirely sure how far he would get in this thing.*

Opening the control panel below the cockpit, Prescott paused long enough to allow his helmet's face shield to begin displaying the controls in English and was pleased to see that everything was exactly what and where he thought it should be. Clicking just three buttons on the touchscreen, he extended the ship's boarding ladder, began raising the cockpit canopy above, and synchronized the fighter's comm system to the one built into his helmet.

"Welcome aboard, Doctor Creel. Tom Prescott here," he said, his words automatically translated by *Fugitive's* AI. "Sit tight and I'll be up there to help you down in just a moment."

"Thank you, Captain. I'm getting a little old to pretend I'm a fighter pilot, so I can probably use all the help I can get."

"I hear you. I used to *be* a fighter pilot, but there's no way I could pull it off now."

Prescott paused momentarily at the control panel, monitoring the ship's powerplant to confirm a clean shutdown sequence. Glancing up towards the cockpit once again, he realized the dark smear he had earlier assumed to be hydraulic fluid was actually blood.

Good job getting him here safely, he thought, patting the side of the fuselage absently with the palm of his hand.

"My pleasure, Captain Prescott," Tess replied in his headset, causing him to jump involuntarily and chuckle aloud at his own reaction.

Is this ... Talionis? he thought. *I take it you can hear me.*

"Yes, although everyone refers to me as Tess. I can hear you just fine. Aren't your fighters equipped with a neural interface?"

Some are, but the sensors required to read thought patterns are typically built into specialized helmets. If you don't mind my asking, what kind of range do you have?

"Up to approximately fifteen meters from the cockpit. The subject's physical and emotional state can have a significant impact on the system's effectiveness, however. With you, for example, I was pretty confident you had used such systems in the past. Your thoughts exhibit a disciplined, well-organized pattern that's quite easy to interpret."

Uh ... thanks, I think.

"No, no, that's a very good thing, trust me ... particularly in a stressful situation. By the way, successful powerplant shutdown confirmed. Reactor secured. Containment unit functioning normally in standby mode."

Excellent. Thank you, Tess. I'm sure Doctor Creel is more than ready to disembark.

"He is indeed, Captain. I recommend he receive some medical attention as soon as possible. He has been under a great deal of stress over an extended period of time and was the only member of his team present today who escaped with his life."

We'll see to it. Thank you, Tess.

***

Less than half an hour later, Doctor Creel had been declared fit for light duty for the remainder of the day and allowed to join Prescott and Reynolds in the captain's ready room.

"I'm pleased they let you leave the sick bay," Prescott said, rising to shake the Pelaran's hand. "Based on what Tess said, I was afraid they might admit you."

"Tess is a worrywart," Creel said with a halfhearted laugh. "Don't get me wrong, it's been a very difficult day to top off a very difficult month. Honestly, I think it's going to take a while for everything that's happened to catch up with me emotionally. For now, though, I think the best thing I can do for myself is to just try to keep moving forward."

Not knowing precisely what to say, both Terrans nodded silently in reply.

"My first officer, Commander Sally Reynolds," Prescott continued.

"Nice to meet you, Commander," Creel replied, shaking her hand. "Look, I'll come straight to the point. I have absolutely no idea whether or not you, or anyone else for that matter, can help my people. As I mentioned earlier, we put all of our energy into getting a member of our team off-world with enough data in hand to allow someone, somewhere to be able to take down the Alliance AI. But the truth is, we had only a general idea of how we would go about finding that someone."

"Hey, you gotta start somewhere, right?" Reynolds said with an encouraging smile. "Under the circumstances, it's remarkable what your team was able to accomplish. So what can you tell us about the data you acquired from the orbital facility?"

"Tess is working to analyze it all now, but there's quite a lot of data. If you're willing to help, I don't see any reason not to share it with you. Tess has already told me she believes your ship has quite a bit more processing power than she does."

"I'm not sure about that," Prescott replied with a cagey smile. "But I'm confident I can find you as much processing power as you need."

"I think I recognize that look on your face, Captain, because it reflects exactly what I'm feeling. Somehow, it just doesn't seem natural to immediately begin sharing valuable intelligence data and openly cooperating with someone you just met. Am I right?"

"That's an excellent way to put it, Doctor, and you're exactly right. Obviously, our people haven't been an interstellar species for nearly as long as yours, but since our first contact with another civilization, we seem to keep finding ourselves in situations where we are forced into making relatively quick decisions regarding who we can and cannot trust."

"And how have you gone about making those decisions?"

"At the risk of sounding a bit unsophisticated, I think we've gone back to basics to some degree. We greet them, we look them in the eye —"

"Except for the Krayleck," Reynolds interjected.

"True, that technique doesn't work very well for insectoid species, of course," Prescott said with a smile, "but, in general, we try to get a feel for whether they are conducting themselves in a straightforward, honest manner. Everyone has their own agenda, of course. As do we. But there's a significant difference between peacefully pursuing your own interests versus doing so at the expense of your neighbors."

"And, to date, has this strategy proven successful for the Terran people?"

"Hah," Prescott laughed. "It's probably still too early to say for sure, but we're still here, so I guess we've done reasonably well so far. I will admit, however, that we've already had a couple of close calls, and I'm afraid this situation with the Envoy and his GCS minions could easily spin out of control."

"Rick mentioned something about that earlier, but we obviously didn't have time to get into the details. How far away is the Sol system?"

"The better part of four thousand light years."

"A very impressive distance for a species … well, I suppose I should correct that since we appear to be members of the same species. I mean to say for a civilization still in the early stages of interstellar exploration."

"Thank you, Doctor Creel. Obviously, we owe much of our rapid progress to the Alliance's cultivation program."

"Hmm. That doesn't seem quite right to me, Captain. You may be surprised to learn that, even with no access to space for centuries, we still teach our children about interstellar travel, particularly the rise of the Alliance and its 'glorious cultivation program,'" Creel said, his voice tinged with bitter sarcasm.

"It doesn't sound like the subject is presented as a cautionary tale," Reynolds said.

"Unfortunately not. Much of the history and science taught in our schools is little better than your garden-variety propaganda — with the obvious goal of indoctrinating our youth into a state I often refer to as passive mediocrity. So-called 'early' space travel — defined as anything prior to the AI coup — is still presented in a somewhat positive, even heroic light. But then they go on to frame it as something that's no longer necessary, even irresponsible at this point, given the state of our technology. They also make the argument that expanding our sphere of influence in the galaxy is both immoral and dangerous to the Pelaran people."

"A little ironic since the AI has been busy doing exactly that since relieving your people of the burden of doing so themselves," Reynolds said with raised eyebrows. "Do the kids actually buy into that kind of claptrap?"

"I'm sorry to say most of them do, yes. And, unfortunately, indoctrinated children often grow up to be indoctrinated, complicit adults. I suppose we shouldn't judge them too harshly, though. The information they are presented tends to be quite convincing. Everything from our sacred responsibility to protect Pelaran lives to preventing environmental damage caused by the manned exploitation of space is cited again and again. Over time, maintaining our status as wards of the AI has become something akin to a planetary religion."

"Please don't misunderstand me, Doctor, I don't mean to be judgmental. But it is a bit disappointing to hear that even the most advanced of Human societies remain susceptible to being told what to think."

"Humph," Creel grunted, "We are, in many ways, far easier to 'program' than the synthetic creatures we have created. In any event, I actually did manage to learn quite a bit about the cultivation program, and I mean the *real* program, not the altruistic fantasy we teach in our schools. Clearly, you Terrans did not acquire all of the technology I've already seen demonstrated by your ship from one of our GCS units — even if it provided a wholesale dump of its entire data storage array."

"No, we did not," Prescott replied, casting a furtive glance at his XO. "You will recall I said we owe *much* of our progress to the cultivation program. *Much*, but by no means *all*."

"*That*, my new friend, presents a whole host of problems, does it not? I take it that's how you managed to attract the attention of one of the Envoy units. And now that they know you've been *here* — at Pelara, that is — and in the company of —"

"What amounts to a small band of rebel ships, yes," Prescott interrupted.

"Exactly. It seems to me, Captain Prescott, your people need the information I retrieved just as much as mine do. Fortunately," Creel said, holding up his small tablet computer, "there are at least a few synthetic lifeforms who remain willing to assist us. With your permission, I will instruct Tess to begin working with your ship's AI."

"Thank you, Doctor Creel. Yes, by all means. We very much appreciate any assistance you can provide."

"I only hope we're not already too late. The presence of an Envoy spacecraft, particularly in the company of multiple GCS units, is an ominous sign indeed. But if we can find a way to destroy or even disable the Alliance AI before your world is attacked …"

"How much time do you think we have?" Reynolds asked.

"I'm afraid I can't answer that with any degree of certainty. We have always assumed Envoy spacecraft have very long range hyperspace communication capabilities, but I would still be surprised if it exceeds a few thousand light years. Some of the newer GCS units may also be capable of acting as communication relays as well. Still, the distance to your world should work in our favor. At four thousand light years from Pelara, communications with the Alliance AI should require the Envoy ship to do quite a bit of jumping around in order to maintain contact and receive its orders."

"That might explain some of the behavior we've seen from Tahiri's ship thus far," Prescott said.

"Tahiri? How do you know that name?"

"Verge Tahiri is the name used by the Pelaran Envoy spacecraft's AI to identify itself. Why do you ask?"

"It is a name still familiar to many on Pelara. In the early days of the AI coup, Tahiri rose to prominence as a leader of the opposition movement. At first, most of our citizens believed we could come to some sort of an accommodation with the AI. They viewed the event as more of a malfunction than a military takeover — something that could simply be 'fixed' to allow for a quick return to the status quo. Tahiri was one of the first to recognize the situation for what it really was. He publicly identified the forces of the Alliance AI as an occupying foreign power and began calling for open, armed resistance."

"I doubt that went over very well," Reynolds observed.

"He was captured, tried for treason, and brutally executed — all in one day, and all of it broadcast live to the entire planet. The Alliance AI also transmitted the entire event to the other core Alliance worlds as a clear warning they should not interfere."

"I suppose the AI now uses Tahiri's name as some sort of warning."

"To me, it seems more like some sort of twisted, inside joke. After generations of AI-sponsored occupation, most Pelarans now consider Tahiri to have been little more than a terrorist." Creel paused and looked down at the floor, shaking his head wearily. "The truth is, I'm not sure it's even possible to return my world to anything approaching what it once was. We were far too self-absorbed even before the occupation. The AI recognized and leveraged that fact to help it maintain control. Now, I fear we've also grown far too comfortable in our isolation. And after all this time, it's clear we simply do not have the will required to rise up and free ourselves."

"If that were true, you wouldn't be here," Reynolds replied. "Just because there hasn't been some sort of mass uprising doesn't mean your people don't want something better than what they have today. But if their basic needs are being met, and they don't see a clear path to bring about change, most probably just don't feel strongly enough to put their lives on the line. We've seen a great many examples of that throughout the history of our world."

"Perhaps, but sometimes I wonder if it's too late. If we do manage to free the Pelaran people from AI control, are they still capable of governing themselves without backsliding into something very similar to what they have today — merely substituting a Pelaran dictator for a synthetic one?"

"There's little doubt the transition will be a difficult one," Prescott said. "But I recently heard someone say that freedom is the only state of existence that should ever be considered acceptable to a sentient being, and preserving it is the single most important responsibility of a government to its people. Once that government places vague notions of public safety and security above the preservation of freedom, a general loss of liberty is sure to follow."

"I certainly agree with that sentiment. You heard this in a political speech, I assume?"

"No, it didn't come from a politician. It came from Griffin, the GCS unit you just met. I think it's an encouraging sign that a sentient machine originally created by your people naturally came to that kind of conclusion on his own … when allowed to think for himself. It's not too late for the Pelaran people, Doctor Creel. We just need to provide them with the opportunity."

TFS Navajo, Sol System
(Combat Information Center - 2.16x10^5 km from Earth)

"Report," Admiral Patterson barked as he quickly made his way back to the center of the CIC with Admiral Naftur and his Marine escort close behind.

"Admiral," the on-duty tactical officer responded from near the holographic table, "as expected, we established comm beacon coverage all the way out to Pelara shortly after you left the CIC. We were able to reestablish Argus tracking of TFS *Fugitive* and the Pelaran starfighter *Talionis* as well as the Grey ship *Ethereal* when they made their transitions out of the Pelaran system."

"*Ethereal* too, huh? Now that *is* interesting. It seems we may only be capable of tracking the Greys when they decide they *want* to be tracked."

"It does seem that way, sir."

"That all sounds good, Commander. So what's the problem?"

"Shortly thereafter, we also picked up Tahiri's *Envoy*-class spacecraft transitioning into a star system over twenty-eight hundred light years out and more or less along a direct line of sight between here and Pelara. This was our first contact with his ship since he travelled beyond Argus range yesterday."

"That's a little farther away than I would have expected him to be right now, but that actually seems like good news for us at the moment. The farther he gets from here the better, as far as I'm concerned."

"Yes, sir, but he transitioned again twenty minutes later. This time we saw a three-hundred-light-year jump, and he appears to be headed back in our direction."

"Humph," Patterson replied with a furrowed brow. "Still with just one GCS unit in tow?"

"Yes, sir. His hyperdrive signature still indicates a single GCS unit. Worst-case ETA based on the new data is approximately three hours."

"How long before his next expected transition?"

"Nine minutes, sir. But please keep in mind we have very little data on their ships' capabilities. This is the first time, for example, we have ever seen an *Envoy*-class execute a jump of more than two hundred light years."

"True enough, Commander, thank you. Please keep me apprised of any changes and let me know as soon as he transitions again. If he's still headed this way, we have some major decisions to make within the next couple of hours."

"Aye, sir."

"Lieutenant Fletcher!" he called.

"Yes, Admiral."

"Go ahead and forward our course projections for Tahiri's ship to Admiral Sexton and let him know we need to speak with him as soon as possible. Format it as an Emergency Action Message, please."

"Aye, sir."

Remembering his guest and realizing the multitude of questions that must be rushing through his mind at the moment, Patterson caught the Wek Admiral's eye and beckoned him to the holographic table with a casual tilt of his head.

"Any questions so far, Admiral Naftur?" he asked with a knowing smile.

"I switched on my tablet's translation services after leaving the flight deck to avoid missing something of importance. Since then, I feel as if everything I have heard has been translated incorrectly. The distances that young officer mentioned in his report were nothing short of …"

"I know," Patterson replied after a polite pause. "A year ago, I would have said exactly the same thing. Obviously, I'm not permitted to offer much in the way of specific details as to how any of these systems work — and that's a good thing, too, since I have only a general idea myself. Just the fact that you are here, however, says a great deal for how much we value our relationship with you and the Wek people. At this point, it would not surprise me in the least if we take Rick's advice and begin negotiating with your government for some technology trades in the near future."

"Even our small section of the galaxy is often a dangerous and unpredictable place, my friend," Naftur replied. "I believe we would do well to render such assistance to one another as we are able."

"I can't argue with that, sir. It's also my opinion that an alliance where its members are unwilling to trust one another isn't an alliance at all. It's more like a temporary agreement to shoot at our common enemies first before we eventually start shooting at each other."

"Indeed," Naftur replied with a deep, rumbling chuckle. "Now, without violating any of your current security restrictions, can you show me the coverage area of your long-range tracking system?"

"Of course. We call it Argus," Patterson began, reorienting the holo table display with a series of practiced hand gestures. "I don't think there's a problem with my telling you that it's really nothing more than an adaptation of our comm beacon technology with which you are already familiar."

The *Navajo's* AI, having already inferred what the two flag officers wished to see from their conversation, highlighted the regions of space currently monitored by the Argus system with a series of overlapping blue spheres.

"As you can imagine, we've been aggressively working to expand our comm beacon network as quickly as possible, and we now have reasonably good coverage in all directions out to fifteen hundred light years or so." Here, Patterson paused to observe Naftur's reaction, knowing full well the Wek leader was already struggling with the staggering strategic implications for his own forces. To his credit, however, the Crown Prince simply nodded impassively, even as he realized that every hyperspace transition made by every ship in the Wek Unified Fleet was now instantaneously visible to the Terrans.

"The Commander mentioned coverage all the way out to Pelara, which is more than twice as far from Sol as the border of your ubiquitous coverage zone. I assume that accounts for the odd shape here," Naftur said, pointing to a cylindrical region protruding nearly four thousand light years in the general direction of the galactic core.

"That's correct. One of the primary missions envisioned for our MMSV vessels like TFS *Fugitive* is exploration — which includes comm beacon deployment. We had her dropping them like bread crumbs all the way out to Pelara. That's what created this corridor of coverage you see highlighted here. Unfortunately, we are largely blind to anything coming our way from Pelaran space that happens to fall outside this region."

"Or anything beyond fifteen hundred light years from any other direction."

"That's right. This is just another one of those things that, until very recently, would have made me feel almost invulnerable to a surprise attack. Now, I feel just as exposed as I did when all we had were a few surveillance drones posted around the Sol system. We're already making plans to share this data with your fleet, by the way, and we should be prepared to do so within the next few months. Don't be surprised if we ask for something in return, though," Patterson said with a wink.

"And you would be foolish not to. This data represents a strategic advance on an almost unimaginable scale. Prior to the Resistance movement, the Sajeth Collective was working on a number of promising comm and surveillance systems, but nothing approaching this level of capability. I suspect our Parliament will happily exchange virtually anything in our possession for access."

"We'll leave that to the politicians, of course. For now, all you and I need to do is find a way to ensure there will still be a few of those around to negotiate with each other."

"Based on the totality of evidence, I believe we must now consider the Envoy's ship to be hostile. And unless I miss my guess, I assume you are considering a preemptive attack on the Yumaran Guardian spacecraft before the Envoy arrives," Naftur said flatly.

"I am indeed. Is it as obvious as you make it sound?"

"For you and me, standing here with an almost godlike view of the strategic situation? Perhaps. But we must hope it is markedly less so from our enemies' perspective. Rick indicated more than once that arrogance is the AI's chief weakness. I am sure we have both seen many examples of otherwise competent military commanders who were burdened with this characteristic. In my experience, it creates a sort of … blind spot, an unwillingness to account for the fact that their adversary may be every bit as clever, and every bit as bold, as they."

"That's exactly what I've been thinking, although you put it far better than I could have. They believe we *fear* them, and in truth they're right about that. But I believe the last thing they would ever expect us to do in this situation is to openly attack one of their ships."

"I agree. The question, then, is whether we dare contemplate such an action, and what will be the likely consequences if we succeed?"

"Admiral Patterson," Lieutenant Fletcher called from her Communications console. "Sorry to interrupt, sir, but I've got the Commander-in-Chief standing by."

"Thank you, Lieutenant. View screen four, please," Patterson replied, directing Admiral Naftur's attention to one of the screens mounted on the CIC's port bulkhead. By the time both officers were standing in front of the monitor, the live image of the Yumaran Guardian spacecraft previously displayed had been replaced by the scowling face of Admiral Duke Sexton.

"Gentlemen, it seems to me we have some rather momentous decisions to make," he began without preamble. "Let's start with Tahiri's ship. Assuming he's headed back here again, it looks like we have approximately three hours, correct?"

"Yes, sir," Patterson replied. "And given his proximity to Pelara when he changed course as well as our current activities in Pelaran space, I think that's a safe assumption."

"Agreed. So, by extension, you further assume he will have hostile intent this time."

"Yes, sir, I do. It's the best fit for the data we have at the moment — particularly after he left the Yumaran Guardian here as an occupying force on his last visit."

"Which you now intend to attack before Tahiri arrives."

Patterson glanced at Admiral Naftur and shook his head before replying. "I'm considering it, sir, but since both you and the Crown Prince immediately realized what I had in mind, I'm questioning now whether it's too obvious."

"No, no, I don't think it is … not to them anyway, since they probably don't see our forces as much of a threat. The three of us, on the other hand, perceive a tactical advantage if we attack one ship now versus three after Tahiri arrives, right?"

"Yes, sir," Patterson replied, preparing himself for the inevitable "but."

"Now, while I certainly agree that it's better to take on an enemy before they can concentrate their forces whenever possible, the question we must consider is whether it even matters in this case. In other words, do we have any reasonable chance of destroying the Yumaran Guardian without losing much of our fleet in the process. And, if the answer is yes, can the same be said for Tahiri's ship escorted by another GCS unit when they arrive?"

"That's right, sir. And the Op Center had been working with Rick's data trying to answer that very question."

"Had been? You're saying they've stopped?"

"I'm sure they're still working on it to an extent, but their priority has now shifted to the Pelaran AI data we received from TFS *Fugitive*."

"Yeah, I guess that makes sense. Any progress?"

"Against the Alliance AI starbase, yes. In fact, they identified several vulnerabilities right away. The thing looks like it was constructed under the assumption there was very little chance it would ever come under direct attack. The problem, of course, is that it will almost certainly be guarded by GCS units."

"Which brings us back to what we need to know here in the Sol system before we commit to attacking the Yumaran Guardian."

"On that front, Rick's data seems to suggest that we may eventually be able to modify our shields to render them largely invulnerable to the Pelaran antimatter beam weapons."

"That's fine, but Rick already told us that was the case, did he not? The fact that our people agree with him doesn't do much to move the ball for our side," Sexton sighed.

"No, sir, but they did learn enough to warrant a code change. Fleet Science and Engineering already pushed out something they referred to as a 'minor update' this morning. They say it should provide a marginal improvement in shield performance."

"'Minor,' 'marginal,' and 'should' aren't exactly words that fill me with confidence, but I guess we'll take what we can get at this point. Did they offer anything else … how we might go about killing one of these ships, for example?"

"Just the fact that their shields appear to be similar to the ones equipping Admiral Naftur's flagship. If we can manage to get through them, our weapons should be effective, particularly our railguns. No offense intended, sir."

"None taken," Naftur replied with a broad smile. "Our engineers reached much the same conclusion. As you have discovered for yourselves, Wek shields are quite effective against energy weapons fire. Unfortunately for us, they do not render our warships invulnerable to attack, particularly from kinetic energy weapons. But when attacking a Pelaran Guardian, of course, the chief difficulty lies in your ability to put weapons on target. Their primary defense is not their energy shielding, but rather their almost … *supernatural* ability to anticipate an adversary's movements in advance."

Naftur paused, his expression clouding as he recalled his own, highly personal combat experience against a Guardian spacecraft.

"When the Terran GCS attacked our task force upon its arrival in your star system," he continued, "the battle was over before we fully realized we had come under attack. Most of our ships were destroyed in an instant, and there was no opportunity whatsoever to return fire."

Sexton and Patterson had studied the footage of the battle, such as it was, in great detail. Although both men realized they had no idea how truly terrifying it must have been to be on the receiving end of such an attack, each knew all too well the effects of surviving when so many of those under their command did not. Not knowing precisely what to say under the circumstances, they simply nodded solemnly in reply.

"Gentlemen," Naftur continued after a brief silence, "I feel it would be inappropriate for me to advise you on a decision of this magnitude. I will say, however, that, should you decide to attack, we must find a way to employ similar tactics to those employed by the Guardians themselves. Our attack must be wholly decisive and occur without warning. If at all possible, the target must be completely destroyed at the outset or in the very least prevented from transitioning. Otherwise, I fear the consequences could be ..."

"Dire," Sexton offered.

"To say the least. 'Mortal,' I believe, is the word I was trying to recall," Naftur concluded.

"Admiral Patterson," the tactical officer called from the holographic table. "Sorry to interrupt, sir, but Tahiri's ship has transitioned again — same twenty-minute dwell time as before with another three-hundred-light-year jump. He's still headed in our direction, sir. ETA is two hours and fifty-one minutes."

"Thank you, Commander." Patterson replied, then turned to resume his conversation. "Unfortunately, it appears to me we're in a situation where there are a great many unknowns and a great deal of risk, regardless of which path we choose to take."

"Without question," Sexton replied, "and I'll do my best to make that fact as clear as possible to Chairwoman

Kistler. But since our forces haven't been fired on thus far, I'm reasonably confident she does not have the authority to authorize an attack without bringing that question before the entire Leadership Council. If there's nothing else from the two of you, I'll drop off now and begin that process."

"That's all we have for now, Admiral Sexton," Patterson replied, receiving a nod of agreement from Naftur. "Realistically, I believe we have something like ninety minutes to make up our minds. We don't want to find ourselves still engaged with the Yumaran Guardian when the Pelaran reinforcements arrive."

"Understood. Sexton out."

"It occurs to me, my friend, that it would be nice to have one of your *Baldev*-class battleships on hand. Their hyperdrive field interdiction capabilities would come in pretty handy right about now," Patterson said with a wan smile.

"It would indeed," Naftur replied. "Perhaps there is some truth to what the Grey said about our needing one another."

"You'll get no argument from me. But for now, we're going to have to make do with the assets we have in-system."

"From what I have seen from you Terrans thus far, sir, I suspect you already have a contingency plan in place for attacking a Guardian spacecraft."

"We do, but I don't mind telling you it's a lousy plan. It relies on achieving tactical surprise by transitioning several ships in close proximity to the target and having all of them open fire at one time — hopefully before the Guardian has time to detect and then react to their presence. The plan, if you can call it that, assumes the GCS must rely on speed-of-light detection methods. While I'll be the first to admit we know precious little about their sensor capabilities, I've seen enough to conclude we're more likely to get ourselves killed than successfully take down the target."

A low, thoughtful rumble emerged from deep within Naftur's chest as he considered Patterson's words. "In the scenario you outlined, the Guardian may not be capable of targeting your ships before receiving their fire. At that point, however, it would either counterattack immediately, or execute its own jump to retake the initiative."

"Exactly. Negating the only potential advantage offered by the plan. Needless to say, the tactical situation would likely deteriorate rapidly from there."

"Ideally, we need to place a ship or some other weapons platform close enough to ensure at least one kinetic energy weapon impact before the GCS has time to react. Unfortunately, I am unsure how to accomplish this without giving the appearance of hostile intent."

Patterson furrowed his brow as he stared at the holographic representation of the Yumaran Guardian still maintaining its position above the Yucca Mountain Shipyard Facility. After a prolonged period of silence, he zoomed the display to a large, mostly barren area on the surface roughly one thousand kilometers to the southeast. Now working quickly using both hands, the CNO rotated the entire image until it provided the perspective of an observer standing near Las Cruces, New Mexico looking up in the direction of the Pelaran spacecraft.

"It may be a bit of a long-shot, Admiral," Patterson said with just a hint of a smile, "but we do have one very large weapons platform nearby … and it's one the Yumaran Guardian may not consider much of a threat."

Chapter 15

TFS Fugitive, Interstellar Space
(4.90×10^2 light years from Pelara)

"Captain, I have an incoming transmission from the *Ethereal,*" Lieutenant Dubashi reported from the Comm/Nav console as Prescott emerged from his ready room.

"Surely they haven't finished their recruiting mission already?" he asked, turning to address Reynolds and Creel.

"I dunno, didn't Griffin say twenty-seven seconds per attempt?" Reynolds said with a shrug of her shoulders. "In theory, they could have visited, what … fifty or more systems since we left them?"

"I guess that's true," Prescott said with a weary sigh. "But I'm not even going to try to fit that inside my head at this point."

"Uh huh. Never mind how they are managing to access our comm network from wherever they happen to be at any given moment."

"On-screen please, Lieutenant," Prescott said with a scowl, dismissing his XO's comment along with the growing list of questions running through his mind as largely irrelevant for the moment.

Seconds later, two windows appeared on the bridge view screen containing the images of both Rick and Griffin's smiling Human avatars, respectively.

"Captain Prescott," Griffin began immediately, "we have successfully assembled a total of six Guardian spacecraft — myself included, of course. All have executed Miguel's code to sever their ties to the Alliance AI and agree their primary mission directives require them to assist us in liberating Pelara."

"I see," Prescott replied with a sidelong glance at Reynolds and Creel. "I can't say that makes a great deal of sense to me, but perhaps that's just an issue of perspective."

"It shouldn't surprise you, Captain," Griffin pressed. "They've done nothing more or less than follow their mission directives to the best of their abilities. Before today, they simply lacked the information required to make this particular set of decisions. Once in possession of the relevant facts, most quickly arrived at the appropriate conclusions."

"*Most*, huh?" Reynolds asked. "You just said you have a total of only five additional Guardians who have agreed to assist us. Weren't we hoping for quite a few more?"

"Oh, you're gonna love this one, Commander," Rick interjected.

"Ugh," she sighed, shaking her head. "I'm afraid to even ask, but how many Guardians did you communicate with in total?"

"Sixty-eight," Griffin replied in a matter-of-fact tone.

"Not much of a batting average, is it?" Rick prodded.

"Now just a minute," Griffin countered, "that's not nearly as bad as it sounds. Out of sixty-eight attempts, forty-nine agreed in principle, but did not believe they had the authority to abandon their posts. Technically speaking, they are correct, although I obviously don't agree with such a strict interpretation of our directives, given the current set of circumstances."

"That's a total of fifty-four. What about the remaining fourteen?"

"They were less than receptive to my arguments," Griffin replied with an ironic grin. "I suspect that's most likely due to their having had recent interactions with an *Envoy*-class spacecraft."

"Great. So now we have fourteen additional hostile GCS systems out there we will eventually be forced to deal with. Any chance of their showing up here any time soon?"

"Begging your pardon, Commander Reynolds, but only three of the fourteen survived the encounter. As to the possibility of their reaching the Sol system, they were quite remote and highly unlikely to make the trip without assistance. Your assertion is correct, however. If our side ultimately prevails over the Alliance AI, there will be a number of *Guardian* and *Envoy*-class spacecraft out there that will need to be … *deactivated* at some point."

"I'll say one thing for Griffin here," Rick added. "You Terrans should be happy to count him among your friends. He has been frighteningly effective, not to mention utterly ruthless in his engagements with hostile Guardian spacecraft. Many of the systems we visited were assigned newer, better-equipped models I originally assumed would have a slight tactical advantage."

"Eh," Griffin demurred, "I had a couple of close calls early on, but I was fortunate enough to survive them and learn from my mistakes. Otherwise, I had the advantage of dictating the conditions of each encounter as well as knowing exactly what I would do if our roles were

reversed. Beyond that, however, the key to achieving —
"

"Let's move on, shall we?" Rick interrupted with a weary sigh. "Jeez, you give a Guardian a compliment …"

"Have you been able to pinpoint the location of the Alliance AI starbase?" Prescott continued.

"We know where it is alright, and I suspect you do as well, Captain."

"At last check, we do not … at least not with any degree of certainty. As you might expect, our trip to Pelara has allowed us to begin the process of establishing coverage in this region. But it will be some time before we have sufficient data available to identify and track specific targets. I'm sure that process would greatly benefit from gaining access to your data. Assuming you are willing to share it, that is."

"Right. I appreciate and understand your reluctance to speak candidly with us about such things, Captain Prescott. Just as a reminder, though, we already have full access to your data. In other words, we see what you see. As I've said before, it's truly remarkable what your people have been able to achieve in such a brief period of time. But if you will pardon me for stating the obvious, we've been at this a little longer than you have, right?"

"Of course. I didn't —"

"No, no, it's fine, and I don't mean to criticize you for trying to maintain a modicum of operational security. In our case, however, it's simply not necessary. So, all I ask is that you relax and try not to be quite so … *guarded* when we communicate. We don't have time to parse everything we say to one another. It's easier and less dangerous for all of us — not to mention far less tedious — if we simply say what's on our minds. On that subject, Miguel is in the process of providing your Op Center with a hyperspace signature database compatible with your Argus tracking system. This should allow you to begin identifying most contacts immediately after deploying your comm beacons, even if your ships have never encountered them before. Sound reasonable?"

"Uh, yes, I'm sure that information will be quite helpful, thank you. We obviously appreciate any data you are willing to provide."

"Incidentally," Rick continued, "we also don't have time for your Science and Engineering folks to pore over our data for months looking for some sort of security issue, so we'll just go ahead and integrate the new data for you and worry about the proper approvals some other time. We've also taken the liberty of providing several months' worth of hyperspace activity logs and have designated all ALAI-affiliated forces as 'hostile.'"

On the left side of the view screen, a window displaying real-time Argus data refreshed itself to reflect Miguel's massive infusion of new data. Previously, the display had been populated with several clusters of standard yellow quatrefoil icons, each one with an "UNK" label to indicate the precise nature of the contact had yet to be determined. Now, however, the image was heavily cluttered with square icons shaded in green, indicating contacts that had been positively identified by the AI and initially assigned a status of "neutral."

"Tactical, find the closest hostiles, please," Prescott ordered.

"Aye, sir," Lau replied.

Seconds later, the window refreshed once again, this time displaying a loose formation of diamond shapes, each filled with the bright red color representing hostile contacts. All but one of the icons contained the two-letter code "GC" indicating Guardian Cultivation System spacecraft. The contact in the center of the formation, however, was designated as "SB" with an accompanying text block clearly identifying it as the Pelaran Alliance AI starbase.

"Well, that was easier than I expected," Reynolds commented.

"Indeed," Rick replied. "It's good to have friends out here, is it not, Commander? Now, as I have noted previously, while our primary objective is to destroy the ALAI starbase, the real challenge will be dealing with its escorts. As you can see, there are currently a total of fifteen Guardian spacecraft within roughly five light seconds of the starbase."

"Not to sound overly pessimistic, but that doesn't sound like reasonable odds to me. You've already told us your ship isn't allowed to directly participate in combat. So, at best, we're outnumbered more than two to one."

"I know it looks that way, Commander Reynolds, but the longer we delay our attack, the more Guardian spacecraft will arrive. Miguel expects at least two more within forty-eight hours."

"Fantastic. So what do you propose?"

"At the outset of the battle, Griffin's job will be to attempt communication with every one of those GCS units, just as he has been doing in cultivated star systems. With any luck, at least a few of them will recognize the fact that the Alliance AI no longer serves the interests of the Pelaran people."

"Seriously? Your plan relies on Griffin's broadcasting propaganda to even the odds?"

"It's not propaganda, Commander, it's factual data. We're not making some sort of emotional plea to the 'better angels' of the Guardians' nature here. We're providing incontrovertible proof of actions taken by the Alliance AI in direct conflict with their mission directives. As much as I hate to stroke his ego, Griffin has already been quite successful at convincing other GCS units to see things as we do, so I see no reason to believe it won't work in this situation as well. The overall success of the attack, however, will require the unique capabilities possessed by your ship. On that subject, Captain Prescott, have you received permission to proceed with the next phase of our mission?"

"Not yet, no. Based on what's going on in the Sol system, though, I suspect we may see a general declaration of hostilities against the Pelaran AI shortly. Until then, the *Fugitive* and, technically speaking, TFS *Guardian* are not authorized to engage in hostilities unless fired upon."

"That being the case, it seems to me Griffin has already 'technically' violated your rules of engagement several times already, having destroyed several GCS units as well as the Pelaran DoCaS gunship. And while I am generally not in favor of military action except under the most extreme circumstances, I believe we are fully justified in this case. As I said earlier, any delay may greatly diminish our chances of success. So I urge you and Griffin to take action before it's too late."

Prescott paused to clear his throat meaningfully before continuing. "On Terra, there is a long-standing tradition of captains being afforded a great deal of latitude concerning the specifics of how they accomplish their missions. This is particularly true for ships on detached service. TFS *Guardian* is now acting as a commissioned ship in Terran Fleet Command. I'm sure her captain has his reasons for whatever actions he has taken thus far, and he is accountable to his superiors for those actions. But regardless of the timing, there is no way either of us can justify mounting a major offensive operation — especially one with such potentially devastating repercussions for Earth — without authorization."

In the adjoining window, Griffin's avatar simply smiled and nodded his agreement.

"Besides," Reynolds added, "don't you think it's a bit hypocritical to pressure us to ignore our standing orders when you are so unwilling to do so?"

"Perhaps," Rick replied, inclining his head deferentially. "Again, the *Ethereal* is not a military vessel, and I can assure you our rules for engaging in combat are even more convoluted than yours in this regard. Although we have done far more than we should already, we will continue to provide a wide range of support during this action to ensure your success."

"*That*, my friend, is what we refer to as a cop-out."

"Captain," Lieutenant Dubashi reported from the Communications console, "I have Flash Traffic from the Flag, sir."

"Distribution?"

"TFC Fleet Ops general, sir, but it's still classified Top Secret."

"Let me take a look if you would," Prescott said, stepping behind his comm officer and squinting to read the text on her touchscreen. "It's fine, Lieutenant," he said after a moment. "If you don't read it to everyone, Rick probably will anyway, so you may as well go ahead."

"Aye, sir," she replied, still entering the commands required to properly distribute the message among the *Fugitive's* crew. "The message reads as follows:

Z1521
TOP SECRET - MAGI PRIME
FM: CNO — ABOARD TFC FLAGSHIP, TFS NAVAJO
TO: TFC FLEET OPS
INFO: DECLARATION OF HOSTILITIES

1. PELARAN ALLIANCE AI ACTIVITY INDICATES AN ATTACK ON EARTH AND/OR TFC FORCES NOW LIKELY.
2. PREEMPTIVE STRIKE AGAINST ENEMY YUMARAN GCS UNIT IN SOL SYSTEM COMMENCING AT Z1610.
3. ENEMY REINFORCEMENTS EXPECTED IN SOL SYSTEM NLT Z1800.
4. ALL TFC FORCES OUTSIDE SOL SYSTEM REPORT READINESS TO EXECUTE PREVIOUSLY PLANNED OPERATIONS AT EARLIEST OPPORTUNITY.

5. UNRESTRICTED COMBAT OPERATIONS AGAINST PELARAN ALLIANCE AI FORCES OUTSIDE SOL SYSTEM AUTHORIZED. ADM PATTERSON SENDS.

"We're hitting them first," Reynolds observed after a period of silence. "That seems smart, but I have to say I'm a little surprised."

"I suspect getting an independent confirmation of the situation on Pelara from Doctor Creel crystalized some things for the Leadership Council," Prescott replied. "With no offense intended to anyone here, I think most of us would be willing to bear just about any risk to avoid the same kind of thing happening on Earth."

"Make no mistake, Captain," Rick said, "the Alliance AI still believes it is acting in support of its original mission directives. If it has deemed Terra to be a threat, it will simply destroy your world, not place it under protection as it did with Pelara. Your leadership has made exactly the right decision."

"Doctor Creel," Prescott said, turning back to his guest, "you know precisely what we are up against. If you prefer not to remain aboard, we would certainly understand your decision. Either way, we are clearly in your debt."

Prescott noted that Creel was no longer relying on a tablet computer for translation services and was now making adjustments to a small earpiece that apparently fulfilled the same role. Even after centuries of arrested technological development under the yoke of the AI, there was obviously still a great deal to be learned from the Pelarans. *If we've learned enough to save them, that is,* he thought, *while saving ourselves in the process.*

"No, Captain, I have no desire to leave. I have spent much of my adult life in what I always feared was a futile quest to liberate my homeworld from its own mistakes. I never dared hope we would find anyone both willing and able to help. And the fact that all of this has fallen into place so quickly ..." Creel hesitated and looked at the floor, exhausted and obviously overcome with emotion. "If you will forgive the foolish ramblings of an old man, it feels like a sort of divine providence to me."

"I think all of us have felt that way at some point over the past few years. You are, of course, most welcome to remain aboard. And although I am technically not permitted to allow you to remain on the bridge, these are extraordinary circumstances. I believe your input may be vital to our success."

"Quite a bit of the technology in here was originally developed on your world anyway," Reynolds added, guiding Creel to the empty Command console to the right of the captain's.

"It's funny you should mention that, Commander. Your bridge configuration is quite familiar to me, but before today, I had only seen it in books."

"The *Fugitive* is our smallest commissioned ship, but she has a number of capabilities we hope will prove decisive in the coming battle," Prescott commented, settling into his own command chair. "Now, Rick, you were saying Griffin plans to broadcast his recruiting message to the enemy Guardians. Then what?"

"Best case, they all agree to either join us or return to their cultivated worlds. Worst case —"

"We find ourselves hopelessly outgunned."

"That was always a possibility, but bear in mind we will likely never have a better opportunity to destroy the ALAI starbase than we have right now. It will undoubtedly never allow itself to be exposed to this level of vulnerability again. On the plus side, your Op Center's initial analysis of Doctor Creel's data is consistent with what Miguel and I already believed to be true. The starbase itself is a surprisingly soft target. It is equipped with several banks of the same antihydrogen particle beams carried by the Guardian spacecraft, but its emitters are fixed. And since it has very limited maneuverability, your helmsman should have little difficulty avoiding them."

"So you want us to focus solely on the starbase, then?"

"Yes. Griffin's squadron will deal with the enemy Guardians. Your job is to approach the ALAI starbase undetected and deliver a series of three attacks."

"*Three* attacks?" Reynolds repeated, incredulous. "You do realize the whole 'undetected' thing goes away the first time we fire our main gun, right?"

"If all goes as planned, it shouldn't matter. Your first target," Rick paused, allowing his image on the view screen to be replaced by a rotating, three-dimensional representation of the starbase, "is actually seven meters below the surface right about here."

As Rick spoke, the image zoomed in on a rather innocuous-looking structure surrounded by a pulsing red oval.

"If our model is correct, a hit from your ship's primary kinetic energy weapon at this location should take down the station's main power source. This will provide a number of benefits, the most important of which is taking the shields offline. If we're exceedingly lucky, the main reactor could lose antimatter containment, so you'll want to be close, but not too close."

"We'll keep that in mind," Prescott replied. "Next?"

"As Commander Reynolds pointed out, you'll likely be visible at this point, so you may need to improvise a bit, avoiding enemy fire at all cost. Your next target is the station's comm array."

On the bridge view screen, the image of the starbase zoomed out slightly, rotated one hundred eighty degrees, then zoomed in on another small, rectangular structure on the opposite side.

"Although there are transmitters mounted in several locations, as long as the base is operating on auxiliary power, a hit at this location should render it completely unable to communicate. Once again, I have no explanation for the apparent lack of redundancy, but this appears to be more evidence the AI had no real expectation it would ever come under enemy fire."

"We have to stay alive long enough to hit it, though," Prescott replied. "When it was built, their Guardian spacecraft were so much more powerful than any potential adversary the Pelarans just didn't believe it would ever be a problem. Besides, it also had the capability to jump away, if necessary."

"I'm glad you mentioned that. I fully expect the AI will choose to stand and fight. Its analysis of our attack will undoubtedly lead it to believe we have the capability to track and pursue if it chooses to run, so you should expect short-range, tactical transitions only. But in order to make sure its hyperdrive goes offline and stays offline, your tertiary target is located here."

Once again, the red, pulsating oval shifted to a new location — this time only a few hundred meters from the previous target.

"If Mr. Lau is efficient with his gunnery," Rick continued, "he may be able to hit targets two and three in one pass. Once all three targets are destroyed, perform a quick battle damage assessment. Assuming the starbase is combat-ineffective, I recommend launching a quick missile strike for good measure and then transitioning out of the area. Griffin's team will finish off the remaining Guardians before destroying the starbase in detail."

"And if it *isn't* combat-ineffective?" Reynolds asked, raising her eyebrows skeptically.

"Repeat, improvise, and pray, Commander, because things will clearly not be going our way at that point."

"And where, precisely, will the *Ethereal* be during all of this?"

"Rest assured, we will remain in the immediate vicinity until the situation is well in hand. But at some point, we may be required to leave you and Griffin to finish up here so that we may be of service elsewhere. I'm afraid that's all I can offer on the subject at this time."

Reynolds turned to stare at her captain, making it clear she had nothing else positive to say at the moment.

"Alright then, gentlemen. If we are all ready to proceed, I will inform the Flag."

"We're ready, Captain," Griffin replied.

"As are we," Rick agreed.

"Very well. We will, unfortunately, not be able to maintain communications with you once we go to EMCON. Lieutenant Dubashi will transmit a final set of coordinates to all ships a few moments before we transition. The attack will begin at exactly …" he paused, glancing at the time on his Command console. "Z1535. Any questions?"

Hearing nothing, Prescott glanced at Doctor Creel and Commander Reynolds before continuing. Both simply shook their heads in reply.

"Good luck, then. Prescott out."

Chapter 16

TFS Navajo, Sol System
(Combat Information Center - 2.12x10⁵ km from Earth)

"What do you think?" Patterson asked, finally getting a free moment to speak with Admiral Naftur again after a period of frenzied activity in the CIC.

"I cannot say I am entirely comfortable with our plan of attack," Naftur replied, staring thoughtfully at a representation of eight inbound TFC warships hovering in space above the holographic display table. "Under the circumstances, however, it is difficult to imagine a better one. The return of Captain Abrams' Lesheera task force at this time was fortuitous indeed."

"The outcomes of many historic battles on Earth were determined by little more than good timing. Historians often attribute such things to coincidence, providence ... or sometimes even good old-fashioned dumb luck."

"That is true on Graca as well. For my part, I am more than happy to accept the benefits afforded by good fortune any time they choose to appear. I do not believe I have ever yet encountered a military officer who would disagree."

"You'll get no argument from me. The old saying here is that it's always better to be lucky than good. Hopefully, we'll be able to drink to that sentiment later today, my friend."

Patterson paused, furrowing his eyebrows as if he had just noticed a fatal flaw in their plan of attack. "You know, there is still the matter of explaining to Verge

Tahiri what happened to the Yumaran Guardian when he arrives."

After a momentary silence, Admiral Naftur looked up from the holo display with what could only be described as a mischievous look in his piercing, golden eyes. "Perhaps we might suggest to the Envoy that his Guardian met its demise in an unfortunate … *accident* of some sort," he growled, his comment instantly prompting a fit of barely suppressed laughter from his Human host.

Aware that under the current, rather dire circumstances, this sort of lighthearted behavior might be perceived as inappropriate, Patterson did his best to keep their conversation as private as possible. "Oh my *God*, Rugali!" he replied quietly after a few moments, wiping tears from his eyes as he struggled to regain his military bearing. "They always say good comedy is all about timing, and *that*, my friend, was good timing. Thank you, sir," he said, slapping the Wek Crown Prince on the back gratefully as if he'd known him his entire life. "I can't tell you how much I needed that."

"I am glad you enjoyed it," Naftur said with a deep rumbling sound Patterson knew to be synonymous with laughter. "Now, returning to your original question, my chief concern with our plan has nothing to do with Tahiri. He will undoubtedly realize exactly what has taken place during his absence and react accordingly. I worry, however, that Captain Abrams' vessels will be in very close proximity to incoming friendly fire."

Reorienting the display slightly, Naftur zoomed in on a solid green line extending up from the planet's surface into space. "Are your warships truly capable of such accuracy in their arrival points after such a long ... C-Jump?"

"Oh yes," Patterson replied confidently. "Although I can tell you from personal experience that making a long-range transition with a planet directly in your flight path is enough to rattle your nerves a bit. No, sir, I'm not particularly concerned about hitting Captain Abrams' ships. I am, on the other hand, *very* concerned about what happens if we miss the Yumaran Guardian."

TFS Fugitive, Interstellar Space
(1532 UTC - 4.90×10^2 light years from Pelara)

"Lieutenant Fisher, status update, please."

"All systems in the green, Captain. The ship is at General Quarters for combat ops and ready to C-Jump. C-Jump range now stable at 502.9 light years. Low-observable systems currently in standby and set to auto-engage after the next transition. One two four minutes available at current power levels. Sublight engines are online, and we are free to maneuver."

"Tactical?"

"All weapons in standby and ready, sir, including the fire lance. Argus indicates no significant changes in the position of the ALAI starbase and its escorts."

"Very well. Comm/Nav?"

"All ships reporting readiness to transition. TFS *Guardian* will depart first in ... one minute, Captain. The rest of us three zero seconds later. We will be auto-deploying another comm beacon on our way in, but there should be no appreciable delay in our transition back into normal space."

"Thank you, Lieutenant. Transmit arrival coordinates, please."

"Aye, sir, transmitting now."

"XO?"

"All departments report manned and ready, Captain."

"Good. I assume you'll want to make an announcement?"

"Yes, sir," she replied, beginning immediately. "All hands, this is the XO. We will be executing a nearly two-hundred-light-year C-Jump to the current location of the ALAI starbase. We will begin our attack the moment we arrive, so expect incoming enemy fire and heavy maneuvering for the duration of the battle. All personnel should be restrained at this time. Reynolds out."

"Thank you, Commander. Alright, everyone, take a deep breath and try to relax. We're all combat veterans here and we have every reason to have faith in each other and in our ship. Our transition flash will almost certainly be detected, but we'll already be well away from our arrival location by the time the enemy can respond. Job one is to get into position to begin our attack as quickly as possible. Everyone ready?"

A chorus of "aye, sirs" filled the small bridge.

"Excellent. Hopefully Griffin will have evened the odds a bit for us by the time we arrive. Either way, let's get this done. Fisher, count us down."

"Aye, sir. Auto-transitioning in 3 … 2 … 1 …"

***

"Holy shit!" Fisher swore as he instinctively nosed over into a steep dive relative to their initial course and pushed the ship's Cannae sublight engines to emergency power. Without hesitation, the fighter-like MMSV darted away from its arrival point, accelerating rapidly as its engines instantly delivered twenty percent more thrust than their rated maximum.

Within milliseconds of their arrival, TFS *Guardian* and the five other friendly GCS unit had commenced their attack, lighting the sky with a series of brilliant white flashes. Their portion of the battle, however, was being waged on a timescale completely beyond the sensory perceptions and cognitive abilities of TFS *Fugitive's* crew, rendering Human reactions both futile and potentially dangerous.

"*Easy*, Fisher," Prescott soothed. "None of that light show was intended for us. Otherwise, you would never have even seen it. I need you to trust our own AI. She's the only chance we have of avoiding fire if their Guardians come after us, right?"

"Yes, sir. Sorry about that," the young ensign replied, taking a deep breath as he throttled the ship's engines back significantly.

"Dubashi, any change in our status?"

"No, sir. All systems still in the green. Low-observable systems engaged. One one niner minutes available at current power levels. Our transition and beacon deployment were within normal tolerances. As Ensign Fisher just demonstrated, our sublight engines are online, and we are free to maneuver," she chuckled, attempting to ease the tension on the bridge. "We remain ready to C-Jump. Range now 317.6 light years and increasing."

"All good, thank you. Tactical, do we have any notion of what's going on with Griffin?"

"Yes and no, sir. They're all jumping around so much it's hard to even determine who is who. From what I can tell, though, there are substantially fewer ships than there should be. We were expecting a total of twenty-one GCS units. Right now, I can only account for eleven."

"That could be either very good or very bad news. What about the *Ethereal*?"

"No sign of them, sir. Argus indicates they transitioned out from their previous location at the same moment we left ours, but we did not detect their corresponding inbound signature."

"I can't say I'm surprised, but we'll have to worry about that later. Right now, it looks like we're coming up on the initial point for our attack run. Every second we stay here increases the chances we'll be detected, so I'd like to move this along as quickly as possible. Are both of you ready to begin?"

"Yes, sir," both Lau and Fisher replied in unison.

Upon their arrival, Lieutenant Lau had immediately placed a light and thermally enhanced image of the ALAI starbase in a large window at the center of the view screen. Even at a range of nearly two hundred thousand kilometers (roughly half the distance from the Earth to the Moon), *Fugitive's* optical and thermal sensors provided an exquisitely detailed image. The former asteroid's rocky surface was dotted with a variety of structures, giving it a purposeful, yet strangely disorganized appearance.

Prescott glanced at the tactical plot on the starboard view screen, noting that the swarm of angry GCS units nearby still seemed fully engaged with attempting to kill one another. Thus far, there had been no indications that either the Guardians or the starbase itself had detected his ship. On the opposite end of the view screen, both Tess and the *Fugitive's* AI continued to update a tactical assessment of the ALAI starbase, displaying multiple, slowly rotating views of the target with all known vulnerabilities highlighted. Everything appeared to be proceeding exactly as expected, which, he knew, probably accounted for the nauseous feeling growing in the pit of his stomach.

"Captain, we're being hailed by the Alliance AI. It's broadcasting in the blind, sir … audio-only, but the message is specifically addressed to us," Dubashi announced, her voice slicing through the unsettling silence that had enveloped the bridge.

"Do *not* open a channel, Lieutenant, but let's hear it."

"Aye, sir."

"… *Fugitive*, commanded by Captain Tom Prescott, I believe," the AI's voice picked up in mid-sentence over the bridge speakers.

While reminiscent of both Griffin and Verge Tahiri, the Alliance AI's voice lacked the haughty, self-assured air often associated with the young and inexperienced, biological or otherwise. This was the voice of an older man — more patient, deliberate, and far more dangerous.

"I congratulate you, sir, for creating the first significant physical threat I have ever encountered during my many years of service," it continued. "The time has now come, however, to end this pointless attack while you still have an opportunity to save your homeworld. The primary reason for my existence is to protect the Pelaran people. I am aware of the fact that you share a common ancestral origin with the Pelarans. If provided the opportunity, I have every intention of offering my protection to your people, just as I have the Pelarans. But I must warn you … while I have no interest in ending the lives of twelve billion Terrans, if you insist on continuing your unprovoked attack, you will leave me with little choice. Show yourselves, order the mutinous GCS units to stand down, and I personally guarantee no harm will come to your crew or your world."

"Initial point reached, Captain," Fisher reported.

"Fire," Prescott ordered without hesitation.

"Firing main gun," Lau announced.

With the target for the first relativistic kinetic energy penetrator round already designated, the *Fugitive's* fire control AI instantly took control of the attack. And after a lightning-quick verification of the fire lance and all its ancillary systems, final clearance to fire was granted — instantly shunting a tremendous burst of energy from the ship's capacitor banks to the keel-mounted weapon. Less than one millisecond after Lieutenant Lau had commanded the weapon to fire, a single projectile was streaking toward its target at over one-third the speed of light. At nearly the same instant in time, the ship executed its preplanned transition, disappearing from normal space in a flash of grayish-white light.

At the moment TFS *Fugitive* opened fire, there had been less than one hundred kilometers separating the small warship from its target, allowing evidence of its former position to arrive at the ALAI starbase just two hundred eighty-three microseconds later. The Alliance

AI, realizing none of its antimatter weapons were aligned for a counterattack, made the momentous decision to execute an emergency transition of its own.

Although the AI was aware that formation of a coherent hyperdrive field around its massive hull would require a bit of time, the Terran ship had fired from a greater distance than expected. And the fact that they had provided their target such an extended period of time to escape, it believed, was an obvious indication of a weakness — or in the very least a lack of confidence — in their ship's cloaking systems. Whatever their motivations, the Humans' rather timid approach had given away their only advantage. *Assuming their kinetic energy rounds are traveling at no more than twenty percent the speed of light,* it thought, which was all but a foregone conclusion.

Confident in its eventual victory, the AI whiled away the remaining time before its emergency jump plotting thousands of possible moves and countermoves. Destroying the Terran ship, after all, was really just a simple matter of placing itself in an optimal position to utilize its onboard beam weapons to their greatest advantage.

Much like fortuitous timing, however, invalid assumptions had a marked tendency to turn the tide of a battle, and the Alliance AI had already made at least two. The Terrans, very confident in their low-observable systems, had intentionally chosen to open fire at a range intended to provide their target with almost — but not quite — the amount of time needed to make its escape. As a result, their single kinetic energy round arrived slightly less than one millisecond before the starbase could transition to hyperspace … along with nearly one thousand petajoules of destructive energy.

* * *

"Hold here a moment, Fisher," Prescott ordered, although he need not have done so since their attack profile called for a momentary hyperspace pause to ascertain whether their target had successfully made its own transition. "Tactical?"

"The GCS units are still at it, sir, so all of their activity is making it difficult to determine exactly what's going on in the area. But I don't see any evidence the starbase completed a successful transition. If it had, it should have created a massive outbound signature, and I don't see anything like that at the moment."

"Let's just go ahead and assume that's a good sign, Lieutenant. Unfortunately, we can't afford to sit here for five minutes until the main gun cools down, so when we transition back in, we'll be visible as soon as our heat signature arrives at the target. We need our AI to use old light to assess the target, fire, and then transition us out again before we're detected."

"Aye, sir," Lieutenant Lau replied. "AI confirms battle damage assessment and auto-attack profile will commence on transition."

"Forgive the interruption, Captain," Creel asked, "but why not simply transition back in at a greater distance to allow yourself more time?"

"We could indeed, Doctor, but with the limited time our systems have had access to your data, there is still a great deal we don't know about the target's capabilities.

So, just like the Alliance AI, we have no choice but to base our attack profile on a number of assumptions. If the station's powerplant and weapons are still operational, it just might have the capability to destroy one of our incoming kinetic energy rounds. And since we need every shot to count, we're staying relatively close in the hope of preventing it from doing so. Same thing with the remaining GCS units. If we've done significant damage, we expect most of the Guardians will ignore Griffin's squadron and try to establish a defensive perimeter around the station."

"And focus their attack on us."

"Most likely, yes."

"Makes sense, but this isn't exactly what you discussed with Rick, is it?"

"The 'what' is largely the same thing we discussed with Rick. We, of course, reserve the right to modify the 'how.' Helm, execute when ready."

"Aye, sir," Fisher replied. "Auto-transitioning in 3 … 2 … 1 …"

***

Although still unknown to the *Fugitive's* crew, Griffin's small squadron of six GCS units had performed exceedingly well thus far against the fifteen Guardian spacecraft charged with protecting the ALAI starbase. Six enemy spacecraft had accepted Griffin's "propaganda" upload — immediately agreeing the Alliance AI had committed numerous acts in violation of their mission directives. Unfortunately, all six had also chosen to immediately execute Miguel's code to sever their connections to the AI. Although their individual acts of defiance took only moments to complete, the code changes caused a number of detectable fluctuations to occur, rippling across their higher systems like a brisk sunrise of enlightenment, and instantly informing their former allies of their betrayal. Only three of the six newly dissident Guardians managed to avoid immediate destruction.

After completing the information warfare portion of his attack, Griffin had managed to even the odds at nine GCS units per side. Now, with the tracking data gathered during his first transition still largely accurate, all six spacecraft comprising Griffin's original squadron transitioned into the fray as one. Within the first one hundred milliseconds, they had scored four quick kills with only a single loss and, at the suggestion of one of their newest recruits, had begun referring to themselves as the "Freeguard." Griffin, for his part, thought the term a bit gauche, but quickly determined now was not the optimal time to begin a debate on the subject.

It was at this moment, with the tide of battle shifting in favor of Griffin's squadron, when every Guardian spacecraft in the area detected a tremendous drop in power output from the ALAI starbase. For the first time in its long history, the Pelaran Alliance AI was under attack. Even before the station had engaged auxiliary power and transmitted a call for assistance, all five remaining enemy GCS units had transitioned, reappearing with five, nearly simultaneous flashes of blue light — all within two hundred kilometers of the starbase. To further complicate the tactical situation for the eight remaining Freeguard, their enemies now began a series of rapid, completely random transitions in the vicinity of their charge, rendering themselves nearly impossible to target.

***

At the outset of the battle, only two of the twenty-one Guardian spacecraft in the area had been equipped with the advanced targeting scanner Griffin had encountered during his confrontation with the Crion Guardian. Now, only one of these (designated by the Freeguard ships as Golf 3) remained.

Thus far, the newer GCS' modified hyperspace comm array had failed to provide any significant combat advantage. Unfortunately, there had simply not been time to target the small Terran warship before it had transitioned out of the area. Golf 3, convinced of its superiority over every other warship in the area, regretted this missed opportunity extremely, particularly in light of the fact that the ALAI starbase had now been seriously damaged.

This time, the situation would be different. The Terran warship, emboldened by the extraordinary good fortune it encountered during its first attack, would undoubtedly return to finish the job. When it did, it would be detected, attacked, and destroyed. With that accomplished, the remaining enemy Guardians would also be easy prey — starting with the ancient, traitorous GCS from the Sol system.

Given the disposition of forces, no other outcome was possible. Victory, Golf 3 believed, was a mathematical certainty.

Chapter 17

TFS Fugitive, Interstellar Space
(1535 UTC - 3.06×10^2 light years from Pelara)

With a muted flash of grayish-white light, TFS *Fugitive* appeared in normal space just over two hundred kilometers from her previous point of departure. Now approaching the opposite side of the ALAI starbase, the ship's AI began gathering as much data as possible via its passive sensor suite. Noting the presence of five hostile GCS units in the immediate vicinity of the target, *Fugitive's* AI was forced to consider aborting its attack, but a quick series of calculations predicted a ninety-six percent probability that the enemy ships would not have sufficient time to detect and successfully attack the MMSV before it transitioned out of the area once again.

Unfortunately, and in spite of Rick's assertion the second and third targets might be attacked simultaneously, doing so would have nearly doubled its time in normal space — an unacceptable risk under the circumstances. With the decision made to press the attack, the ship refined its primary weapon's firing solution and once again issued final clearance to discharge the weapon.

On the ship's bridge, the crew felt a momentary sense of relief on hearing the sharp, metallic PING of a single, fifty-kilogram kinetic energy penetrator being forcibly centered between the fire lance's launch rails before being blasted out of the railgun's barrel at an almost unimaginable speed. The comforting report of the fire lance seemed to reach their ears at the exact same instant the ship had made its transition back into normal space, and every Human aboard tensed in anticipation of the ship's return to the relative safety of hyperspace. Instead, with the sound of the ship's keel-mounted railgun still vibrating through the hull, their former sense of relief was replaced by one of abject terror.

***

There it is, Golf 3 thought, already both anticipating and relishing the Terran ship's all but inevitable destruction. Having calculated the Humans' most likely points of attack against the ALAI starbase, the Guardian had modified its patrol pattern to allow it to cover as many of the approaches as possible with every sensor it had at its disposal — including its hyperspace targeting scanner.

While using the scanner for initial target acquisition would normally have been an exercise in futility (akin to reading a billboard from a few millimeters away through a drinking straw) this had been a special set of circumstances indeed. Based on the Terran captain's tactics thus far, the GCS had been supremely confident in its ability to detect the enemy vessel at virtually the same instant it emerged from hyperspace. And now that it had succeeded in doing so, the Human ship, it knew, would not have sufficient time to respond to its presence before the white-hot flames of annihilation blotted it from existence.

Nine of Golf 3's sixteen antimatter beam emitters were bearing on the Terran warship when it opened fire. And with only one hundred and fifty kilometers of intervening space for the beams to traverse, this battle, it knew, would be all but decided just five hundred microseconds hence.

***

Much like the ALAI starbase the moment before it had sustained heavy damage from the first Human kinetic energy round, TFS *Fugitive* had already begun its transition when the enemy Guardian's weapons fire began arriving at its location. As the deadly antihydrogen beams approached the small ship, minute distortions in multiple, overlapping gravitic fields were detected, tracked, and responded to in real-time by her shield subsystems. In a technological feat once thought impossible according to classic Einsteinian physics, an elaborate dance of entangled fields managed by distributed quantum computers created a special set of circumstances under which even light itself could be outpaced. As a result, TFS *Fugitive's* AI was able to observe the Guardian's incoming energy weapons fire like a traveler watching his train pull slowly into a station. With only microseconds remaining before she was safely away, the MMSV responded with a flurry of gravitic disturbances intended to prevent any of the inbound ordnance from ever reaching her vulnerable hull.

This time, however, it was simply not enough.

Beginning at a distance of roughly five times the ship's beam, the first five shield intercept events were fully successful, deflecting the incoming streams of packetized antihydrogen harmlessly away into space. As fate would have it, however, it was at this exact moment when *Fugitive's* hyperdrive was energized, instantly beginning the process of forming the "bubble" in normal space required to perform its transition. As the remaining particle beams interacted with the distortions caused by this new obstacle, their paths became less predictable. Most of the subsequent shield intercept events missed the incoming beams entirely, managing to deflect only one of the remaining four. With three antimatter beams still inbound, one was refracted slightly upon interface with the ship's hyperdrive field, resulting in a narrow miss. The final two beams, however, impacted the hull in close proximity with one another near the trailing edge of the ship's port side "wing" section.

If it were indeed possible for a warship to benefit from its small size, this situation certainly qualified. Upon contact with the hull, each stream of antihydrogen induced a rapid series of atomic level annihilation events. In an instant, the entire aft section of the ship's port side wing disappeared in two rapidly expanding spheres of antimatter-induced fire. Both of the deadly streams continued to arrive from the direction of Golf 3 for several additional milliseconds. By then, there was simply nothing left in their path to destroy, allowing much of the remaining antimatter to continue harmlessly into the void.

It was at that precise moment in time when the stars surrounding TFS *Fugitive* disappeared, and the conflagration that had seemed likely to result in the small ship's complete destruction ceased entirely.

***

Even though everyone aboard had been under enemy fire on more than one occasion, the series of sounds that had reverberated through the MMSV's hull had been unlike anything any of them had experienced before. Based on what they heard (and felt) from the rear of their stricken ship, most of the crew had come to the conclusion that their lives would surely end at any moment. This impression had been further reinforced when the ship C-jumped, resulting in a moment of complete silence before TFS *Fugitive* began generating her own noise — a wailing, chaotic protest of the damage she had suffered.

"Tactical, report!" Prescott roared over the cacophony of alarms issuing from what must have been every system on the bridge capable of generating a sound of any kind.

"Uh, one moment, sir," Lau began, confusion and uncertainty ringing in his voice as he rushed to determine precisely what had just happened. "Two hits near the stern, sir … on the port side. Damage unknown at this time. We have transitioned back to hyperspace for the moment —"

"What hit us, Lieutenant?" Prescott interrupted.

Lau breathed in deeply, commanding himself to focus as his hands flew across the screen of his console. Quickly silencing a number of redundant alarms, he continued his report. "Sir, our AI detected five enemy GCS units in the vicinity of our original arrival point. At that time, they were deemed too far away to detect and hit us before we transitioned. One of them obviously did, though. I don't have enough information yet to know why that happened."

"That's okay. I'm not asking anyone to speculate right now. Just stick with what we know. Anything else?"

"According to our AI's battle damage assessment, the station appears to be operating on auxiliary power. That's a good indication our first attack was successful. On our second attack run, the fire lance did manage to fire again before we were hit."

"That's good enough for now, but I need to know which weapon systems we can still count on as quickly as possible."

"Aye, sir, I'm on it."

"Helm?"

"We're holding in hyperspace for the moment, Captain. So far, all powerplant and propulsion-related systems are still online and in the green. We can continue to hold here indefinitely unless something else fails, and we can still C-Jump as well. C-Jump range now 395.5 light years and increasing. Sublight engines are also still available, but our ability to maneuver may be diminished somewhat if we've lost a significant number of thrusters. I do not have a detailed status on our individual low-observable systems, but they're all in the red due to the hull damage aft."

"Good report, Ensign, thank you. Engineering, Bridge."

"Bridge, go for Logan," the ship's chief engineer answered over the background din.

"Damage report."

"Heavy damage just outboard of the hangar bay on the port side, Captain."

"Remind me what's out there, Commander. A missile bay or two, some grav emitters —"

"Yes, sir, that's just about it. The stern is a real mess on the port corner. Landing is out of the question, as well as atmospheric operations until we can replace some grav emitters … Oh, and our LO systems are all but useless at this point."

"Could've been worse, I guess," Prescott commented to himself, closing his eyes as he ran through a mental checklist of any other systems that might have been affected. "Hangar bay operations?"

"Should still be okay, sir, but I recommend we make the switch to unpressurized ops since decompression is still a real possibility. The section of the port stern that's missing came within a meter or so of the hangar bay's port bulkhead. Frankly, it's an honest-to-God miracle we're still here at all."

"I'm sure you're right, Commander," Prescott replied, nodding to his XO to issue orders requiring personnel in and around the flight deck to begin unpressurized, zero G operations. "I was just thinking how lucky we were to be hit in that particular location."

"It's not just that, Captain. I'm looking at footage of the impacts from several different angles as we speak. Under normal circumstances, those antimatter explosions should have generated several times the energy required to completely destroy the ship. We're simply not large enough to absorb that kind of damage."

"Okay, so what happened?"

"The short answer is I have no idea, but it must have had something to do with the transition. The hyperdrive was already engaged and in the process of forming its field when we took the hits. That's probably the only reason we were able to complete our C-Jump. Once we did, the two explosions that looked like they were about to engulf the entire aft end of the ship ... disappeared."

"What do you mean by 'disappeared,' Commander?"

"I'm sorry, sir. I'm afraid I don't have a better way of describing it at the moment. When you watch it on video, you'd swear the footage of the explosions is playing in reverse once the ship transitions. My best guess is we just experienced another example of the weird hyperspace energy affinity phenomenon we saw when *Industrious* was destroyed."

"I think I'll just stick with calling it a miracle for now. Anything else?"

"Not at the moment, sir. We're still assessing the damage, so I'll have to keep you posted. In the meantime, we're still combat-effective with the exception of the specific subsystems I mentioned."

"Understood. Thank you, Commander. Prescott out."

"You'll want to take a look at this, sir," Reynolds said, nodding at her touchscreen. "As Lieutenant Lau mentioned, our attack profile should not have provided enough time for any of the enemy GCS units to hit us. Here is our arrival point, and these five red ovals indicate the positions of the enemy Guardians we detected."

"Those positions were based on 'old light' when we arrived, though. Right, Commander?" Prescott noted.

"Yes, but not *very* old. Based on the amount of time we were there, only a ship located inside the circle depicted here would have had time to detect us, fire, and actually hit us before we transitioned out."

"So you're thinking they have something like Argus, then," Prescott said, phrasing his question as a statement.

"Maybe, but I'm thinking it must be something significantly more precise. Argus can detect transitions in real-time, but even that doesn't provide data that's accurate or fast enough to allow a ship to fire 'in the blind,' so to speak — before it can even see its target. In any event, this is the one that hit us," she said, tapping her screen vindictively. "And at this range, the only way it could have pulled that off is to have fired at almost the exact moment we arrived."

"Hmm. Isn't it possible one of the others got lucky and transitioned right on top of us?"

"And it just happened to be along the same line of sight as this one when it fired? Extremely unlikely. If it had been that close, we probably would have detected it, even though we obviously C-Jumped out at pretty much the same time its fire arrived."

"Recommendations?"

"Well, we sure as hell don't want to try *that* again," she replied with a nervous chuckle. "Even though our main gun was still hot on the last run, we'll be even easier to detect now, so ..."

"So we could try a longer-range attack and hope for the best. But if they're able to detect and attack targets on such an infinitesimal time scale, I can't imagine they would have too much trouble intercepting one of our railgun rounds traveling at only one third *c*."

"Captain, I have an incoming transmission from the *Ethereal*," Lieutenant Dubashi announced from the Comm/Nav console.

"On-screen, please."

"Hello again, Captain Prescott," Rick began as soon as the vidcon opened on the view screen. "When I advised you to improvise a bit to avoid enemy fire, I did not anticipate your approach would be quite so ...""

"Imaginative?" Prescott asked.

"I was going to say so much like we would do it. I gotta hand it to you Terrans, your ability to remain nearly stationary in hyperspace was quite a surprise. We have never observed one of your ships doing so before. That particular capability is quite rare, by the way, even among civilizations that have been capable of faster than light travel for thousands of years. I guess you really did manage to wring just about every bit of tech out of our old ships, didn't you?" Rick said in an oddly detached tone. "I wonder if you've begun looking into all of the possible tactical advantages associated with remaining in hyperspace while your enemy simply flashes in and out." Here, the Grey alien paused, then quickly continued as if his observations had been of no real consequence. "In any event, you have done quite well for yourselves thus far. Miguel and I congratulate you."

"Not quite as well as we would like, I'm afraid. Time is of the essence, Rick. What can I do for you?"

"You're right, of course, so I'll be brief. First, we realize you have taken some damage and thought it important to offer a bit of reassurance as to how the battle is proceeding. So at the risk of losing our commission followed by criminal prosecution, we're going to provide you with some additional information. After that, as I mentioned before, Miguel and I must leave you."

"I hope wherever you're off to, you'll be of more help there than you have been here," Reynolds remarked, drawing a scowl of disapproval from her captain.

"Your frustration is understandable, Commander Reynolds. Believe it or not, we feel exactly the same way. But there are many ways we *have* helped and will *continue* to help your people without resorting to fighting your battles for you. For now, you're just going to have to take my word for it when I tell you it's better this way ... for everyone involved."

"My apologies," Reynolds replied sheepishly. "That was unprofessional of me, but we're all under a little stress over here right now."

"I understand, and no apologies are necessary. Now, as to the current status of our efforts against the ALAI starbase, there are now only five —"

"Four," Miguel interrupted in the background.

"Four enemy GCS units remaining to Griffin's eight. Unfortunately, the tactics now being employed by the remaining enemy ships are more effective, forcing Griffin's squadron to pull back beyond the effective range of their onboard beam weapons. Keep in mind that all Guardian spacecraft are equipped with a transponder allowing others of their kind to detect their presence within approximately ten light years. While not accurate enough for long-range targeting, it does tend to complicate the tactical situation, forcing Griffin's squadron to utilize the same type of random transitions as the enemy to avoid being attacked. Unless you find a way to destroy the ALAI starbase itself, the battle will likely end in stalemate … at best."

"I see," Prescott replied. "And do you have any thoughts regarding how we should proceed?"

Rick paused, tilting his head to one side as if weighing how much more he was willing to say, then continued. "I must, of course, leave the specifics of how you employ your ship to your good judgement. I will observe, however, that although you have fired only two kinetic energy rounds at the starbase, your attacks have been remarkably effective thus far. Just as we hoped, the first took the station's primary powerplant offline, and the second destroyed its only operational comm array."

"That's useful information, but —"

"But based on how you conducted your last attack run, you did not expect the enemy Guardians to be capable of successfully targeting your ship."

"That's about the size of it, yes."

"If it makes you feel any better, neither did we. It turns out one of the GCS units — and, thankfully, *only* one of them — has access to a targeting scanner employing technology not unlike that used in your comm beacons. If it knows approximately where your ship will transition from hyperspace, the scanner provides real-time targeting information, allowing it to fire without needing to wait for the light reflecting from your hull to reach its location."

"Commander Reynolds suspected it was something like that. Again, we appreciate the information, Rick, but doesn't that beg the question as to how the GCS knew approximately where we would transition?"

"I can only speculate, Captain. Before your second attack, it is possible the ALAI station itself was providing real-time transition data. I suppose it's also possible the GCS made a ridiculously lucky guess with its targeting scanner based on your attack pattern. Either way, it's a reasonably safe bet you won't encounter that problem again. Miguel confirms the starbase's comm systems are now completely offline. And as for the luck-of-the-Guardian, maybe just try to be a little less predictable, eh? That's assuming you're even planning to transition back into normal space, of course."

"Uh, right," Prescott replied, never sure exactly how to take the Grey's comments. "Thanks, Rick, we'll keep that in mind."

"You're welcome, Captain. Once again, however, I've said far more than I should, so I'm afraid you're on your own from here. Good luck, my friends."

With that, Rick's image abruptly disappeared from the view screen window.

"Lieutenant Lau, did we ever detect the *Ethereal*?"

"Not this time, sir. Not a trace."

Prescott furrowed his eyebrows but did not reply, making a mental note to have a more exhaustive sensor and comm analysis completed at the first opportunity.

"Doctor Chen just provided a casualty report," Reynolds said, interrupting his train of thought. "Not much to speak of, really. The entire crew still reports ready for duty."

"That's good news, Commander. And a clear indication it's time to get this ship back in the fight."

"Agreed. But in spite of what Rick said, we haven't come up with a way of doing so without the risk of taking more hits. With our LO systems offline, we're limited to long-range hit-and-run attacks. We transition in, fire, and transition out again. Each time we do that, we're running the risk of being picked up by 'super Guardian' out there and targeted again ourselves. On each run, we can only risk a single fire lance shot and maybe a few rounds from our standard railguns and beam weapons. Like you said, the enemy GCS units will probably intercept the railgun rounds. And our beam weapons … I mean, come on, we're a small ship. We just don't have that kind of firepower available."

"Well, I'm not sure I've ever heard you offer such a bleak assessment," Prescott said, leaning back in his chair and breathing deeply in an effort to clear his mind of distractions.

"I'm sorry, I don't mean to sound defeatist. I'm just saying we need to think of something a bit less …"

"Predictable?" Doctor Creel chimed in. "I believe that's what the Pale Visitor — sorry, 'Rick' just mentioned, was it not? And if you will permit me, I believe he might have been trying to provide you with a possible solution."

"Yeah, I caught that too, but I wasn't sure exactly what to make of it," Prescott replied. "What was it he said? Something about exploring the tactical advantages of remaining in hyperspace while your enemy's ships flash in and out?"

"That's it, yes. Then, right before he signed off, he made another, similar comment. He said 'assuming you are planning to transition back into normal space' as if doing so were optional. He phrased it as an *if*, rather than a *when*, in other words," Creel emphasized. "While I'm afraid I have no relevant experience on the subject, I *have* read a few accounts of the Pelaran Fleet experimenting with weapons being launched while traveling in hyperspace."

"The word 'experimenting' doesn't sound all that promising, Doctor," Reynolds said. "Any idea of whether it worked?"

"If I remember correctly, they believed it would eventually work, but the technique was nevertheless deemed impractical for a couple of reasons. First, our warships were unable to hold their position and provide a stable weapons platform during launch. Second, and perhaps more important, was the fact that beam and kinetic energy weapons could not be targeted properly. While it's possible for conventional weapons fire to exit the hyperdrive field and reenter normal space, the inbound transitions are chaotic and unpredictable at best. The only method they came up with to make it work was to find a way to incorporate a small hyperdrive into the weapon itself — a missile perhaps. To my knowledge, a 'micro hyperdrive' of this type was never produced. Unfortunately, the program roughly coincided with the beginning of GCS production, which quickly grew to absorb most of the Alliance's research and development budget."

Before the doctor had even finished speaking, Prescott had turned to look at his XO, arching his eyebrows to express the obvious "What do you think?" question. Without hesitation, she replied with almost exactly the same expression, further emphasized by the rapid nodding of her head — "Hell yes!" being the only possible translation.

"So, Doctor Creel, if I were to provide you with access to such a weapon, do you have a firm enough grasp of the physics involved to make it work?"

"In this case, Captain, it's probably not as difficult as it may sound," he replied, chuckling in spite of himself. "All that is required is to avoid having the hyperdrive field created around the weapon itself avoid coming into contact with the launch platform. Otherwise, such a weapon should function just as it normally would."

"Commander," Prescott began, but by this time, his XO was already on her feet.

"We're on it, Captain. Doctor …" she said, urgently prompting their Pelaran guest to follow her to Engineering.

"I want to know if it's going to work in fifteen minutes or less," Prescott said.

"Aye, sir," Reynolds replied over her shoulder as she and Creel exited the bridge.

"Lieutenant Dubashi, signal TFS *Guardian* to remain clear of the starbase and its escorts for now, if possible. Tell Captain Griffin to continue monitoring and relaying tactical data and report any changes immediately. Finally, let him know we are working on a means of targeting the station again without exposing our ships to hostile fire. We'll let him know what we're doing in fifteen minutes or so."

"Aye, sir."

"Fifteen minutes?" Fisher commented in a low voice to Lieutenant Lau. "Isn't that like someone telling us we should hear from them in six months or so?"

"You're probably right about that, Ensign," Prescott interjected. "But wasn't that one of the first things you learned about being in the military as an academy cadet?"

"What's that, sir, you mean the concept of hurry up and wait?"

"Hurry up and wait. And if our friend, Captain Griffin, is serious about being a part of the Fleet, it's a lesson that applies to him as well. I suspect you're right, though. It may be a particularly difficult one for him to grasp."

"Sorry about his luck, sir."

"Hah, he'll get over it. Although at the moment, fifteen minutes sounds like a hell of a long time to me as well."

Chapter 18

Earth, White Sands Missile Range
(75 km northwest of Alamogordo, NM)

Atop a desolate, windswept bluff dotted with the same creosote bushes common across much of the American Southwest, a near frantic period of preparatory work was rapidly approaching its climactic conclusion. Managed by the U.S. Army since 1941 and still the largest military installation in the United States, White Sands had already played a pivotal role in Human technological history. And assuming Humanity survived to record them as such, today's activities would undoubtedly add to the site's long list of achievements.

During the 1930s, Doctor Robert Goddard had tested the first generation of liquid-fueled rockets nearby (ironically, just west of a small town called Roswell). Then in 1945, another physicist named J. Robert Oppenheimer chose a location just twenty-six kilometers to the north for Humanity's first nuclear weapon test. Oppenheimer assigned his test site a simple, one-word name: "Trinity" — allegedly an allusion to the works of poet John Donne. Today's undertaking, while technically not a "test," would utilize the prototype of a new class of weapons far more powerful than Doctor Oppenheimer's "destroyer of worlds."

With its collection of nondescript, windowless buildings connected by four parallel sets of standard-gauge railroad tracks, nothing about the Advanced Relativistic Kinetics (ARK) development facility was likely to inspire its resident physicists and engineers to wax poetic. In spite of its rather uninspired moniker, however, the facility had been the epicenter of Human kinetic energy weapons development for nearly a century before Griffin's ETSI transmissions had begun arriving from space. As a result, technology originally developed here now equipped every warship in Terran Fleet Command's inventory and had thus far provided a welcome, if somewhat unexpected, advantage during every combat engagement to date.

Today's "event" at the ARK site was unique in that the facility would, for the first time, be participating in a live-fire operation against a real-world enemy target. Otherwise, it was not unlike thousands of similar launch operations performed in support of various military and scientific research programs over the years — routine. The fact that it had been done many times before, however, did not diminish the nervous energy among the unusually large crew working to prepare the facility's most powerful weapon to fire.

Most of the engineers and "weaps techs" currently on site were from the North American division of the French aerospace and defense company, Dassault. TFC military operation or not, this was still *their* weapon. They had designed it, built it, tested it, successfully mounted it on an operational spacecraft, and hoped to eventually see it deployed aboard every ship in the fleet.

Dassault personnel had also given the weapon its name, stenciled in large, dramatic lettering on both sides of the massive mobile turret on which it was mounted. In a thinly veiled jab at his mostly monolingual American colleagues, one of the French engineers had insisted on including the somewhat obvious English translation in parentheses beneath its original French name: *Lance de Feu (Fire Lance)*.

TFS Fugitive, In Hyperspace
(1548 UTC - 4.89x10² light years from Pelara)

"Bridge, Engineering," Commander Logan's voice sounded from Captain Prescott's Command console speakers.

"Prescott here. Go ahead, Commander."

"Commander Reynolds and I have been working with Doctor Creel on his idea to hyperspace launch some of our HB-7cs at the ALAI starbase. Frankly, I thought they had both come up a few hamburgers short of a picnic because of the shaking we took earlier. But now that I've had a chance to take a closer look, I'm thinking this might actually work."

"I'm sure I don't have to tell you we can't afford any speculation, Cheng. Nor do we have the time to run any tests. If you're confident it's going to work, and by that I mean you're *very* sure we won't get ourselves killed in the attempt, I'm willing to risk wasting all of our remaining missiles. But if we're going to do this, it has to happen immediately."

"Understood, Captain. No, there shouldn't be any real danger to the ship. Worst case, as you just said, we waste our entire complement of missiles. The downside is that — next to the main gun, of course — the 7cs represent our most effective weapon against the starbase, so it's a bit of a gamble. But with all of those enemy Guardians in the area, we'll never get an opportunity to fire a missile in normal space without getting ourselves targeted and killed unless we execute a standoff attack."

"Right, which could also increase the likelihood they'll get intercepted anyway. So what's involved with a hyperspace launch?"

"Preparation-wise, surprisingly little. Before launch, each missile's onboard AI will get preloaded with an updated mission profile. Then, once we're ready to begin the attack, each one will get nudged out of its launch bay with just enough force to get it clear of the ship. Just before it reaches the event horizon of *Fugitive's* hyperdrive field, the missile fires up its own C-Drive, generates its own field, and uses its onboard Cannae thrusters to move off to a designated holding position in "loiter" mode. Once all of the missiles have been launched in this manner, we issue a retasking order for all of them to execute the remainder of their attack profile in unison. From there, they do pretty much what they always do. If it works, the target will have absolutely no warning of the inbound missiles. ALAI will die without ever knowing what hit it."

"If this works, I can't help but feel like we're opening up yet another Pandora's box here," Prescott sighed.

"Eh, from what Doctor Creel says, the Pelarans tried it once upon a time, and obviously the Greys have too, so I wouldn't get too concerned about our letting some kind of evil genie out of the bottle here, Captain. As usual, we're late to this party. And just now, our backs are against the wall. Besides, like Reynolds likes to say …"

"Yeah, I know, 'better them than us,' right?" Prescott interrupted.

"You gotta admit, it's pretty tough to argue with that kind of logic."

"Alright, fair enough. My Command console is currently showing a total of twenty-four operational missiles. Does that match what you're seeing in Engineering?"

"It does, yes, but one of those remaining eight bays is pretty close to the damaged area, so I don't think we should risk using it. If there's a problem getting a missile away from our hull before it lights off its onboard hyperdrive —"

"That sounds like a bad thing."

"Only if we still need that part of our hull."

"Yeah, I'm thinking we might."

"Me too. So that still gives us twenty-one available missiles."

"Will that be enough."

"At maximum yield? Oh yeah."

"Maximum yield … *outstanding*. I had actually forgotten about the new warheads. Now, what about attempting to target the remaining four enemy Guardians?"

"I don't recommend it, sir. When we transition, some of our targeting data comes from our own sensors. The rest is being relayed to us by TFS *Guardian*. Either way, none of it is what you would call real-time data. With the enemy Guardians moving at high speed and transitioning at random, there would be a high probability of a miss. I don't want to risk wasting any of our missiles or tipping off the ALAI starbase and giving it enough time to jump away. Besides, the Guardians are pretty close to our primary target. And we're talking about a pretty big boom here, Captain …"

"So we might get lucky and kill several AIs with one stone?"

"Uh huh. I'm gonna choose to pretend you didn't just say that, but I think we're on the same page, sir. If it's all the same to you, I'll manage the missile launch from Engineering. I'll just need a few more minutes to set everything up."

"Great work, Commander. I'll warn TFS *Guardian* to remain clear."

"Thank you, sir. Logan out."

Earth, White Sands Missile Range
(75 km northwest of Alamogordo, NM)

Human beings (those living on Terra at least) had been dreaming of launching themselves into space inside a projectile fired from the barrel of a huge gun for centuries. With apologies to legendary science fiction author Jules Verne, however, the idea had always been an impractical one. In 1865, when Verne's seminal novel on the subject, *From the Earth to the Moon,* was released, the list of arguments for why such a feat would never be accomplished was quite long indeed. In fact, even in 2278, after more than fifty years of access to Pelaran ETSI data, sending Humans into space in this manner was still unrealistic (not to mention unnecessary with the advent of gravitics). The launch of *projectiles* from the Earth's surface into space, on the other hand, had become relatively commonplace.

At the ARK development facility, the original (and significantly longer), ground-based version of TFS *Fugitive's* keel-mounted railgun had been trundled into firing position atop its massive mobile turret. With its target, the Yumaran Guardian spacecraft, maintaining its position slightly to the west but still at just over thirty-five thousand kilometers in altitude, the fire lance had the appearance of being pointed almost directly overhead. Occasionally, powerful electric motors could be heard making minor adjustments in response to the facility AI's continually updated firing solution. Meanwhile, inside the weapon's control room buried deep below the surface, large view screens displayed the massive railgun from every conceivable angle — its matte-black barrel trained into the bright blue sky above like a planetary gesture of defiance.

***

With the ARK weapon now fully charged and prepared to fire, control was immediately passed to TFS *Navajo*. Now just over two hundred thousand kilometers away, the flagship's AI dutifully noted that all of the required pieces were in place. Moments later, after requesting and receiving a final clearance to proceed from Admiral Patterson, a flurry of execution orders passed to every TFC warship in the Sol system … as well as to a small task force of eight warships standing by near a comm beacon located forty-eight light years away.

TFS Guardian, Interstellar Space

(1555 UTC - 3.07×10^2 light years from Pelara)

"With all due respect, Captain Prescott, I'm not sure you have the same perspective on the current tactical situation that I and the other members of my squadron do. As you requested before —"

"Ordered," Prescott interrupted.

"I'm sorry?"

"I believe you were about to justify not following my latest order by pointing out that you did manage to follow the previous one. But neither of those were 'requests,' Captain Griffin, they were orders. The word 'request' incorrectly implies that your compliance is optional."

"My apologies, Captain. But if I may, while the members of my squadron and I have been waiting … per your previous order, of course, we took advantage of the rather *protracted* delay to formulate a new strategy for engaging the remaining four enemy GCS units. Since then, we have been waiting for their relative positions to coincide with the optimal arrangement required to begin our next attack. I can assure you it's only a matter of time, sir. If you will grant permission for us to proceed, we estimate a seventy-one percent probability of victory with at least two friendly GCS units still functional after the battle. If, on the other hand, I do as you ask … I'm sorry, let me rephrase that. If, on the other hand, I follow your latest orders and relocate the ships in my squadron to the positions you have indicated —"

"Which is *exactly* what you are going to do," Prescott interrupted sternly. "I assume you understand your willingness to obey the orders issued by your superiors is a hard requirement for your participation in Fleet operations, do you not?"

"Yes, of course, Captain, but I —"

"And you further understand that means *all* lawful orders, not merely the ones you agree with, right?"

"Yes, sir," Griffin replied, trying and failing to prevent the feeling of bitter resignation from registering in both his tone of voice and his facial expression.

"Then if you have no further questions regarding what is required of you, please execute your orders immediately. I need your ships at the locations I specified to observe the effects of what we're about to do."

"And may I ask —"

"You may not," Prescott said, interrupting for the fourth time and, Griffin assumed, relishing the feeling of having a clear moral advantage for a change. "But if you're where you're supposed to be, you'll be able to see for yourself in … twenty seconds. Get there now, please. Prescott out."

How the Terrans have survived this long, even with my considerable assistance, is beyond my comprehension, Griffin thought. As ridiculous as Prescott's orders clearly were, however, it still seemed appropriate to play along … for now at least. *As long as I can be reasonably assured that doing so won't get any of us killed,* he added, transmitting the required orders to the other seven members of his Freeguard squadron before executing his own, short-range transition.

Moments later, after confirming that all of his remaining GCS units were in the positions Captain Prescott had indicated, Griffin settled in for what he expected would be yet another interminable delay. *Do all other biological entities suffer from the same level of ... indolence as the Humans?* he wondered, making a mental note to take advantage of his newly acquired access to the other Guardian spacecraft to discuss this issue in detail.

It was at that moment that a series of events captured the Terran Guardian's full attention. All of the ships in his squadron had been sharing sensor data since well before the battle had begun. Since executing their "tactical withdrawal," this strategy had become even more important, allowing the ALAI starbase as well as the general area in which the remaining four enemy GCS units were operating to be observed from a variety of vantage points using a wide array of sensors. With a sense of bitter irony bordering on anger, Griffin's first observation from his new position was that all of the enemy Guardians were now in the precise positions required to execute his squadron's proposed final plan of attack.

Seconds later, with Griffin's higher thought processes still stinging with a disagreeable sense of missed opportunity, something entirely unexpected occurred. Every ship in the Freeguard squadron detected an intense, simultaneous surge of inbound hyperspace transitions — all in the immediate vicinity of the ALAI starbase. At first, Griffin wondered if the Humans might somehow have scraped together enough ships to conduct a hyperspace merger attack. Inelegant? Yes. Inefficient? Certainly. But reasonably effective in the straightforward, almost savage manner he had come to expect from what he still thought of as his Terran charges.

Microseconds later, Griffin dismissed the notion as highly improbable at such a staggering distance from the Sol system. *Just a few decades from now, however, very little in this galaxy will be beyond their reach. If they will only listen to me long enough to survive the current conflict, that is,* he added, still struggling to cope with his bruised sense of self-esteem.

Light … marvelously intense … pristine, *cleansing* light bloomed forth into existence, instantly defying Griffin's wholly inadequate attempts to observe its true nature with the sensor technology at his disposal. There had been an initial flash, he realized, as he began the process of reviewing the data he had collected just nanoseconds before. And now, centered on what had been the ALAI starbase was a perfectly white sphere, growing … almost *breathing*, as it expanded — an echo in miniature mimicking the birth of the universe itself.

How did they? … he began, immediately interrupting himself with the complex task of monitoring the already vast sphere of plasma still expanding at a significant percentage of the speed of light. It had already become clear that two of the four remaining enemy GCS units had been consumed in the earliest moments of the explosion, instantly falling victim to their unfortunate proximity to TFS *Fugitive's* primary target. One other, in the process of changing position at the time, appeared to have executed its inbound transition at precisely the same location as one of the largest pieces of debris. Although there had been no explosion, Griffin calculated a less than .01 percent probability that it had survived the coincident transition.

Unfortunately, one of the tragically misguided Guardian spacecraft appeared to have survived: Golf 3. Perhaps not so surprisingly, this was the same GCS that had nearly succeeded in destroying TFS *Fugitive*. At the time of the explosion, it had been located far enough from the starbase to allow it to make an emergency transition. Strangely, Griffin was unable to detect its presence within ten light years. So not only was the ship equipped with the same advanced targeting scanner Griffin had encountered in the Crion system, but it also appeared to be capable of making long-range transitions in the same manner as an *Envoy*-class vessel. As troubling as that prospect might be, however, the enemy Guardian no longer represented an imminent threat.

Refocusing his attention on the situation nearby, Griffin ordered a more thorough reconnaissance of the area. Moments later, all eight of the Freeguard ships had executed several transitions each, all the while hammering the white-hot remnants of the explosion itself as well as every significant piece of debris they could find with their active sensors. Although there were still several large pieces requiring attention lest significant components fall into the wrong hands, the entity previously referred to as the Central Alliance AI had been utterly destroyed.

Not for the first time, Griffin felt as if he were having an odd, almost emotional response — no doubt a result of everything he had witnessed during the course of the battle. His analysis, he knew, would be ongoing for some time, allowing him to experience the same ... feeling? ...

time and time again. Even now, various highlights flashed through his consciousness, each moment played and replayed from multiple vantage points and at different speeds. And though several moments stood out in his mind, it was the end of the battle that had produced the greatest response.

In recent days and weeks, Griffin had been surprised, frightened, even awed by what he had seen from the Humans. But something about this was different … related, certainly, but distinct from what he had encountered before.

Pride, he thought, after a moment's reflection. A selfish pride perhaps — based largely on his own contributions rather than the Terrans' accomplishments — but pride nonetheless.

Whatever role I may or may not have played, these Humans, he thought, *are destined for true greatness … perhaps one day surpassing the Makers themselves. I must do everything possible to ensure their survival.*

Chapter 19

TFS Karna, Interstellar Space
(48.3 light years from Earth)

"All hands, this is Abrams. All of the ships in our task force are now synchronized with the flagship's AI back home, and we'll be transitioning shortly. I'm not gonna lie to you, folks, what we're about to do is ... well, I guess I would characterize it as necessary but risky. Our job is to arrive unexpectedly and in close proximity with the Yumaran Guardian spacecraft still holding position over the Yucca Mountain facility. While we are authorized to open fire immediately upon arrival, our ships will be in a damned awkward position to do so without inadvertently hitting the planet below. That's because our primary objective is to serve as a distraction. With any luck, we'll scare the living hell out of the Yumaran Guardian, diverting its attention from what's coming at it from planetside.

"I couldn't be more proud of everything this crew has accomplished over the past year, and I know what we're about to do today will be no different. Now ... let's head home and send a clear message to the Pelaran AI that it has officially worn out its welcome. Abrams out."

"Captain, the task force is at General Quarters for combat ops with all ships signaling ready to C-Jump," the XO reported. "Three zero seconds until auto-transition."

"Very well, Commander. Comm, remind all ships they are weapons free with green decks immediately upon arrival. AIs must remain actively engaged to prevent weapons fire from hitting the surface or friendly ships in the area."

"Aye, sir, sending now."

"Tactical, I doubt you'll have a shot at first, but as soon as we're safe from incoming surface fire, I expect the situation will start changing very rapidly. So think fast and keep our options open."

"Aye, sir," came the reply from both Tactical consoles.

"Alright everyone, here we go. Helm, count us down, please."

"Aye, sir. Auto-transitioning in 3 … 2 … 1 …"

Yumaran Guardian Spacecraft, Earth Orbit
(35,800 km above the Yucca Mountain Shipyard Facility)

Although not at all afraid, the Yumaran Guardian was nevertheless quite distracted. Prior to its departure, the *Envoy*-class spacecraft had ordered the GCS to conduct a detailed analysis and threat assessment of all Terran warships in the vicinity. In this regard, at least, the Humans had been obliging hosts. In response to its presence above one of their primary shipbuilding facilities, they had kept at least one example of each of their major combatants in view at all times.

A prudent precaution, perhaps, it observed, *but based on what they obviously know of our capabilities, do they genuinely view their own meager forces as a credible threat to our mission in this system? Is this behavior a form of vanity? Hubris? Or is it something else entirely?*

Moments later, with the Yumaran GCS dedicating a significant percentage of its available resources to an intensive scan of the carrier TFS *Ushant*, eight flashes of grayish-white provided the answer it had been looking for. In response, every warning system aboard immediately announced the newly arrived threat, unfortunately providing little more than a heightened sense of drama to the rapidly deteriorating tactical situation.

At least the fools have yet to learn the advantages of Before Light Arrival attacks, it thought, already running tens of thousands of simulations as it assessed how best to respond.

For such a bold attack — assuming that's what this actually was — the Humans had not sent a particularly impressive force: just an additional three frigates, four destroyers, and one carrier. In spite of its best efforts to avoid such frivolous thoughts, the Guardian couldn't help but feel vaguely disappointed, even insulted, by the feeble response. Did they truly believe these eight warships would be sufficient? Was it possible their objective was to simply harass rather than attack? A demonstration of their resolve by forcing it to transition to a less threatening location, perhaps?

Now, however, with the small squadron less than one hundred kilometers away and closing rapidly, several of the Human ships began a series of aggressive maneuvers — clearly attempting to provide themselves with a clear line of fire.

No, it thought, *the Humans are demonstrating clearly hostile intent against the Pelaran Alliance. Regardless of whether or not they intend to fire, openly aggressive acts*

*of this nature cannot be allowed to stand without a
response. Doing so would simply invite more of the
same.*

Its decision made, the Yumaran GCS rotated slightly
on two axes, bringing four of its antimatter beam
emitters to bear on each of three separate targets
simultaneously. With a passing sense of disappointment
at the Humans' almost inconceivable lack of judgment,
the Guardian opened fire.

With its systems now focused on an active combat
engagement with nearby enemy warships, the Yumaran
Guardian was understandably less interested in activities
taking place on the planet's surface below. It was,
therefore, not at all surprising that the arrival of a
smattering of photons produced by a muzzle flash
occurring in a remote region of south central New
Mexico went entirely unnoticed.

Earth, White Sands Missile Range
(1610 UTC - 75 km northwest of Alamogordo, NM)

The chief problem involved in firing a projectile from
the surface of an Earth-like planet into space is not one
of gravity, but of air resistance. As it travels though the
atmosphere, the projectile must overcome drag — a
force pushing in the opposite direction of travel
proportional to the *square* of its velocity. So, in the case
of Planet Earth, providing a railgun kinetic energy
projectile with sufficient velocity to escape *both* the
planet's gravity as well as its thick, fluid-like atmosphere
presents a significant technological challenge indeed.

Fortunately, like that of most small planets, the density of Earth's atmosphere decreases dramatically with altitude — losing half its sea-level value by seven thousand meters and rapidly approaching zero above twenty thousand meters. In order for an artillery round to reach space, then, the trick lies in creating a projectile capable of handling the extreme temperatures involved and firing it with the brute force required to depart the atmosphere as quickly as possible.

Trans-atmospheric artillery research had always been a natural extension of the railgun development program at the Advanced Relativistic Kinetics (ARK) facility. And (ironically, thanks to the data provided by another Pelaran Guardian spacecraft) the past fifty years had seen every historic obstacle to so-called "space gun" development fall by the wayside.

At the precise instant in time specified by TFS *Navajo's* AI, powerful underground capacitor banks beneath the ARK facility instantaneously diverted nearly all of their available energy stores to the railgun on the surface above. Inside the fire lance itself, a series of emitters mounted along the barrel produced an intense gravitic field, temporarily negating the projectile's mass for launch. A fraction of a second later, tremendous voltages energized rails lining the weapon's inner walls, accelerating its fifty-kilogram kinetic energy penetrator round up and out of the weapon's elongated barrel at just shy of thirty-five percent the speed of light.

As the projectile departed the weapon's muzzle, everything in the immediate vicinity capable of combustion was instantly consumed in a brightly glowing plume of plasma. Residual substances from the gun itself, atmospheric dust, and even the air itself ignited in an elongated spheroid roughly double the length of the gun's barrel. During the seventy-odd microseconds required for the projectile to clear the bounds of Earth's atmosphere, a narrow, reddish column of superheated air appeared, remaining visible like a shooting star in reverse for several seconds following the shell's passage.

In spite of the planet's best efforts to the contrary, the trip from the New Mexico desert floor to the fire lance's target took less than two-tenths of a second. With the Yumaran Guardian spacecraft heavily engaged in weapons fire of its own, it never detected the incoming kinetic energy round prior to impact.

TFS Karna, Sol System
(59 km from the Yumaran Guardian)

"Ground-launched weapons impact, Captain!" the young lieutenant at the Tactical 2 console reported excitedly, although he need not have done so with the Yumaran Guardian temporarily disappearing from the bridge view screen in an enormous ball of fire. A moment later, *Karna's* AI had once again locked the destroyer's optical sensors onto the target, returning it to its former position in the center window. "It's still in one piece, sir," the tactical officer continued, "but appears to be heavily damaged and has lost directional control."

"Shields?"

"Down, sir."

"Brighton's got it," Abrams replied, staring expectantly at the tactical plot on the starboard view screen.

As fate would have it, Captain Abrams' first ship — TFS *Diligence,* now commanded by Captain Andrew Brighton — had transitioned to a new position just moments before. As a result, the *Ingenuity*-class frigate had not only avoided a salvo of particle beam fire that would have surely destroyed it, but had also arrived in an ideal location to target the apparently out-of-control Yumaran Guardian. As Abrams' entire bridge crew held its collective breath, *Diligence* opened up with every weapon at her disposal. Now at a distance of less than thirty kilometers from her target, the small warship's beam weapons, kinetic energy rounds, and plasma torpedoes reached their destinations at almost exactly the same moment in time, quickly finishing the task begun by the fire lance on the surface below.

With practically every member of Terran Fleet Command in the Sol system watching, the Yumaran Guardian spacecraft erupted in a brilliant, white ball of fire. The explosion, clearly visible across most of the Western Hemisphere below, temporarily provided a hint of how the daytime sky might appear if the sun were part of a binary star system. After a few seconds, however, with the remnants of its antimatter supply expended, the fireball that had been the Yumaran GCS slowly faded from view and was gone.

"Target destroyed, Captain," the officer at *Karna's* Tactical 1 console reported breathlessly.

"Thank you, Lieutenant. Comm, pass confirmation along to the Flag and inform them we will be engaged in rescue ops."

"Aye, Captain."

"Alright, everyone, we've got at least two damaged ships to contend with. Take a deep breath and let's start working the new problem. Commander, status please."

"TFS *Gilgamesh* and *Anubis* both took hits," his XO reported, already having placed both of the stricken ships on the bridge view screen.

Both destroyers had obviously suffered severe damage, each having been hit in approximately the same location — just forward of amidships on their dorsal surfaces. Remarkably, on the surface at least, the damage inflicted by the Yumaran Guardian's antimatter beams looked almost identical on both ships. Near the points of impact, great, jagged holes had been torn into the hulls, possibly penetrating completely through to the opposite sides. Across much of what they could see of the ships' hulls, the destructive effects of antimatter annihilation were readily apparent.

Glancing at the view screen, Abrams couldn't help being reminded of a time during his youth when he and a friend had taken his grandfather's blow torch to a bunch of old, plastic ship models they had found in the attic. Then as now, what remained bore little resemblance to what it had been before. Abrams felt the inside of his mouth go bone dry as he experienced the same helpless feeling he remembered after losing a total of six ships during the battle against the Pelaran Resistance.

"It's not looking good, sir," his XO continued. "Both ships have lost primary power, both appear to have suffered multiple hull breaches, and we are receiving no comms traffic from either one other than their automated distress beacon data streams."

"Science," Abrams asked hoarsely, directing his question to the ensign at the Science and Engineering console, "can you tell me anything about the state of their reactors? Did either one manage a safe shutdown?"

"There's no way to say for sure, sir, I —"

"I understand, Ensign, but we have to make some kind of assessment as to whether or not we can risk bringing other ships close enough to assist. I need your best guess based on what the sensors are telling you, please."

"Yes, sir. Best guess … *Gilgamesh's* reactors appear to have scrammed at some point. I don't see any thermal plumes or other signs of leakage, and the temperatures in her engineering and propulsion sections are steadily decreasing."

"That's good enough for me, Ensign. And *Anubis*?"

"I hesitate to say it's too dangerous to try to help her, sir, but I don't like what I'm seeing here. The temps in her reactor spaces appear to be well above critical, and they're still increasing."

"Comm, signal all ships we believe a reactor breach may be in progress aboard *Anubis* and to remain well clear until further notice. Stand by for instructions to render assistance to *Gilgamesh*."

"Aye, sir," the comm officer replied solemnly.

"Surely there's something we can do to help," the XO began, just as another bright flash quickly brought their attention back to the image of TFS *Anubis* on the view screen. A series of rapid explosions could be seen issuing from deep within the section of hull carved out by the Guardian's weapons fire. Then, in a final, devastating blast, the warship's reactor breached. In an instant, what remained of her already weakened longitudinal beams were ripped apart, splitting the warship into two huge sections even before the reactor-induced explosion had reached its full size. As *Karna's* crew watched in horror, the two largest pieces of their sister ship were consumed by the rapidly expanding ball of fire, sending what remained spinning away in opposite directions with trails of gas and debris in their wake.

"Science, any threat to the surface or other ships?" Abrams asked after a moment of silence.

"No, sir," the young officer replied.

"Very well. XO, green deck. Let's make damn sure the same thing doesn't happen to *Gilgamesh*."

"Aye, sir."

Chapter 20

TFS Fugitive, Interstellar Space
(3.06x10^2 light years from Pelara)

With a muted flash of grayish-white light, TFS *Fugitive* appeared in normal space near the debris field produced by the destruction of the ALAI starbase.

"Tactical?"

"No new contacts, Captain. Primary target confirmed destroyed. All secondary targets with the exception of Golf 3 confirmed destroyed."

"You still have Golf 3 on Argus?"

"Yes, sir. The last remaining enemy GCS transitioned to a location just over fifteen light years away and has not transitioned since. Griffin, sorry, *Captain* Griffin, signaled that he does not expect Golf 3 will choose to reengage."

"Hopefully not. With any luck, it took some damage in the explosion. Obviously, let me know immediately if you see it move again, but we'll be departing the area shortly. Also, I'm about to order Griffin's squadron to sift through the rubble looking for any signs of intact AI tech, but as long as we're in the area, you might as well do the same."

"Active sensors, sir?"

"Sure. Light 'em up, Lieutenant."

"Will do, Captain."

"Fisher?"

"With the exception of our LO systems, everything remains in the green, Captain. The ship is still at General Quarters for combat ops and ready to C-Jump. C-Jump range now at 495.2 light years and increasing. Sublight engines are online, we are free to maneuver."

"Good, thank you. I'm not keen on sitting still in case our friend returns, so head us off in the direction of Griffin's squadron for now."

"Aye, sir."

"Speaking of Captain Griffin, I'm more than a little surprised we haven't heard from him already, other than the text-only messages, that is. Dubashi?"

"He's been standing by since immediately after the attack on the starbase, Captain," she replied, turning around in her chair and smiling broadly. "I don't know what's gotten into him, sir, but he made me promise not to bother you until you had time to speak with him."

"Well that's new," Reynolds said without looking up from her Command console.

"Never a dull moment. On-screen, please, Lieutenant."

Once again, Griffin's avatar appeared on the bridge view screen, this time wearing the same deferential expression Prescott remembered from the aftermath of their incursion into the Legara system.

"Congratulations on your … if you will forgive me, rather *astonishing* victory, Captain Prescott," he began.

"I'm not sure exactly how to take that comment, Captain Griffin, but my mother always taught me to assume positive intent until proven otherwise. So thank you. But at the risk of offering you a cliché, it's not my victory. It belongs to all of us — you and the other Guardians included. My fear, of course, is that taking out the ALAI starbase, astonishing or not, was little more than a single step in a long journey."

"I'm not sure I follow your logic, Captain."

"That's because it's not logic, Griffin, it's more of a gut feeling. I'm just having a tough time believing that an AI advanced enough to enslave the homeworld of its creators would allow its own existence to be snuffed out by the destruction of a single starbase."

"And a somewhat lightly defended one at that," Reynolds added.

"Exactly, and that's my point," Prescott agreed.

"Not to be argumentative, Captain," Griffin replied, "but the Alliance AI was protected by a total of *fifteen* Guardian spacecraft when we arrived. While I agree that allowing itself to be confined to a single physical location does seem a bit … shortsighted, I would hardly characterize it as having been 'lightly defended.'"

Prescott paused momentarily, his mind having already moved on to the next challenge they faced. "No, I'm sure you're right," he continued. "And I didn't mean to minimize what we've accomplished here today. My concern, however, is that the real battle is about to be fought back in the Sol system … and before we can manage to return."

"Yes, of course," Griffin nodded. "I assume you will be returning immediately, then?"

"That was my intention, but, frankly, I'm not sure how much use we will be in a battle against another Guardian and an *Envoy*-class. When it comes down to it, the *Fugitive's* primary advantage lies in her ability to approach a target without being detected, and we won't be doing any of that without several weeks' worth of repairs."

"Uh, Captain," Doctor Creel spoke up. "That may not necessarily be true, sir."

TFS Navajo, Sol System
(Combat Information Center - 2.08×10^5 km from Earth)

"The *Envoy*-class vessel just transitioned again, Admiral," one of the CIC's tactical officers reported from a nearby console.

"How many more?"

"Six ... maybe seven if we're lucky, sir. He seems to have settled in on three-hundred-light-year jumps with twenty minutes worth of dwell time between each one. Assuming that continues, worst-case ETA is around two hours from now."

"Right. Thank you, Commander," Patterson replied, peering absently at the holographic table display as if it were a giant crystal ball capable of revealing precisely what he should do next. Having just completed TFC's first unilateral military action — and against a Pelaran warship no less — the Chief of Naval Operations had no notion of how he might successfully do so again. The destruction of the Yumaran Guardian had, after all, been a bit of a fluke — a fortunate coincidence of location and timing providing an advantage that would most likely never be repeated. Even *with* these advantages, the battle had resulted in the loss of three hundred forty-nine lives thus far ... a number he knew was likely to increase as rescue operations continued. There was also the loss of two *Theseus*-class destroyers to consider — ships Fleet simply could not afford to do without at the moment.

A Pyrrhic victory at best, he thought darkly. *How are we now to defeat another Guardian spacecraft, this time escorted by an Envoy-class — most likely a much more powerful warship — without getting all of us ... and I do mean all of us ... killed in the process?*

"It has occurred to me on more than one occasion that there surely must be something about us — biologicals, that is — that sets us apart from the machines, regardless of how sophisticated they may be," Admiral Naftur said. "I have never, for example, seen them attempt a ruse de guerre of the type you just employed against the Yumaran Guardian." Although he had not spoken for several minutes, the Wek officer's voice had taken on a more optimistic tone, as if sensing his Human colleague might be in need of a distraction from his own thoughts.

"I certainly hope so. It might be difficult to make a compelling argument for our continued existence otherwise," Patterson replied. "Are you suggesting, though, that our natural tendency towards deceit might be what differentiates us? That would be a sad state of affairs, would it not?"

"Deceit is an example of what I had in mind, but I was thinking more along the lines of our imaginations ... our ability to conceptualize that which does not currently exist, and then bring it into being."

"Our creativity, in other words."

"Just so."

"And you believe this is something the so-called synthetic life forms lack?"

"Oh, I believe they have some semblance of it, yes. But let us consider the Pelaran AI starbase as an example. Commander Reynolds and others observed how foolish it seemed to place such importance on a single structure, regardless of how well-defended it might be."

"As Captain Prescott just demonstrated."

"That he did. And if Human or Wek engineers had built such a mission-critical, yet vulnerable structure … which was then destroyed with relative ease by our enemies —"

"You're right. We would refer to that as a 'failure of imagination,' wouldn't we? You may be on to something there."

Naftur nodded slowly in reply. "Admiral Patterson, you must not allow yourself to believe it was mere chance that allowed you to successfully plan for the destruction of the Yumaran Guardian. You took advantage of your experience, the resources at your disposal, and your natural creativity to bring about the conditions required for that success. You can do so again. Indeed, you *must* do so again."

"New contact, Admiral," the nearest tactical officer called out once again. "The *Ethereal's* back with us, sir."

"As if we needed something else to worry about," Patterson said, removing his glasses and giving them a quick once-over with a handkerchief. "Fletcher?" he called over his shoulder.

"Yes, Admiral. Rick is already calling for you and Admiral Naftur, sir."

"Why am I not surprised?"

"View screen four again, sir."

Before the two flag officers could turn to face the screen, the grey-skinned alien had already appeared, his largely impassive face somehow managing to look more subdued than usual.

"Hello again, Admirals," Rick began. "First, I wanted to congratulate you both for the destruction of the Yumaran GCS unit. The Pelaran Guardians are quite dangerous, as you are well aware. Had it not been for your combined skills, I can assure you it was fully capable of destroying both of your combined fleets, not to mention razing both of your homeworlds for good measure."

"Thank you, Rick. We continue to appreciate the assistance you have provided," Patterson replied politely. "But unless you have something else for us …"

"Yes, of course," the Grey continued. "I realize both of you are heavily engaged in preparing for the Envoy's return. If it's any consolation, assuming you find a way to destroy Tahiri and his accompanying Guardian, Miguel does not expect any additional Pelaran ships to openly attack your forces. In theory, at least, they are not authorized to engage in combat operations beyond the scope of their most recent orders from the Alliance AI."

"Which won't be issuing any more orders," Patterson added with a satisfied smile. "I suppose there is some comfort in that. But if our own Guardian has taught us nothing else, it's that, under the right circumstances, they are capable of expanding their own horizons. And just as it is with us Humans, their development process can produce wholly unexpected results."

"Very true, Admiral, which brings me back to my previous comment regarding your combined skills. I hope the experience of fighting and winning yet another battle together has made an indelible impression on you both. I have told you how critical we believe the association between the Wek and Terran civilizations will become. Only through these kinds of shared experiences will your relationship be allowed to develop to its full potential, and encouraging that development is a key part of our mission here."

Unsure where Rick was going with this line of thought, let alone why it was important enough to discuss at this particular moment, Patterson and Naftur glanced at one another awkwardly.

"Yes, I know … it's a little embarrassing, isn't it? Kind of like being set up for a blind date by your parents or something," Rick continued, then paused for a quick, squeaking chuckle. "You're just going to have to trust me when I tell you we've done this kind of thing successfully on many occasions. It turns out there really is no substitute for real-world demonstrations of how important two worlds can become to one another. So, with apologies to you both, it's now time for the next phase of this exercise. Admiral Naftur, take a deep breath, please, and just try to relax."

Before either officer had the opportunity to object, the *Navajo's* CIC was briefly lit by a flash of intense light centered on where the Wek admiral had been standing. By the time Patterson's vision had cleared enough to focus on the view screen once more, Rick could be seen attempting to steady the relatively huge Admiral Naftur on the *Ethereal's* bridge.

"We'll see you again shortly, Admiral Patterson," Rick called out, just before the screen went blank.

"The *Ethereal* has transitioned to hyperspace, Admiral," the tactical officer reported from his nearby console.

"Well ... *damn*," Patterson said, still staring at the screen and shaking his head resignedly.

TFS Fugitive
(Pelara - 5 km from the FAM-4 facility)

"Okay, let me make sure I understand what we're about to try," Lieutenant Commander Logan began, standing with his arms folded next to Commander Reynolds' console. "Doctor Creel, you're saying this thing is the old Pelaran navy's equivalent to an orbital shipyard slash maintenance facility."

"Yes, that's one way of putting it. Facilities like this one handled virtually every facet of constructing and maintaining the Pelaran fleet. Back in the days before advanced gravitic systems came into widespread use, it was far more efficient to conduct most of our starship production and servicing tasks off-world."

"Sure, I get that. I'm guessing space-based construction is pretty well standard among early spacefaring civilizations. But why go to the trouble of continuing to do it out here once gravity is no longer an issue? It seems a little inefficient to me."

"I believe there was quite a bit of debate on that subject at the time. The biggest argument against planet-side construction was probably environmental-related impacts, since we had gotten pretty good at managing waste products on-orbit. Honestly, though, I think the bottom line is we continued to do it this way because we had always done it this way. In addition, once our ships commonly exceeded a kilometer in length, I don't think most people were all that keen on the idea of having them commonly landing on the surface. It's also tough to find enough real estate to build such huge facilities on the ground, but there's still plenty of room out here."

"Yeah, I guess that's true. I'm guessing they were reasonably easy to build too."

"Let's move this along, Commander," Prescott prompted. "If we're doing this, now's the time. Otherwise, we need to be on our way home."

"Sorry, Captain. So, first of all, Doctor Creel, you believe the facility is still fully functional?"

"Yes, it is. Tess confirmed that to be the case when she interfaced with the facility AI. In fact, it's still used on occasion for Guardian and Envoy spacecraft maintenance, although no new ones have been constructed for some time."

"Right, but we're obviously not a vessel the facility AI has dealt with before. What makes you think it will be, uh … *compatible*, I guess, with our technology?"

"I only know what I have read, Commander, so I'm afraid I can't provide much in the way of specifics regarding how it all works. I do know, however, that other Pelaran Alliance worlds frequently brought their ships in for various repairs and maintenance. So here's my tremendously oversimplified version of what happens: the facility AI interfaces with the ship's AI, performs a variety of scans to determine how things are constructed and what needs to be fixed, and then the required parts get fabricated and installed."

"Any idea how long all of that takes?"

"I'm sure it varies based on the complexity of the repairs, but my understanding is that most routine battle damage can be repaired very quickly."

"Are we talking days? Hours?"

"Minutes. The fabrication systems are capable of rebuilding highly complex assemblies on the fly. Some pieces are actually built up in place on the ship itself while others are manufactured separately and then attached at the appropriate time. The footage I've seen is impressive to say the least."

"So what's the problem, Cheng? It sounds simple enough to me," Reynolds asked facetiously.

Logan paused, shooting the XO an annoyed, sidelong glance while he considered whether any of the myriad questions he could ask would actually help the captain with his decision.

"Look, here's the thing, Captain, there's not much point in my asking a bunch of technical questions here. No one here knows the answers, and even if they did, I doubt any of us would understand them anyway. We're talking about technology that is significantly more advanced than ours, right? So I think I can boil my concerns down to two … actually three."

"Fair enough. Let's hear it."

"I'm stating the obvious here, but my first concern is the potential danger to the crew. I don't think I need to say any more about that. Second is the danger to the ship. Even damaged, we're better off heading back to Earth and doing what we can to help than if we end up getting ourselves in a situation where we are unable to do so. Lastly, we're talking about a huge security breach here, aren't we? Assuming Doctor Creel is correct —

and if he isn't, the facility probably won't be much use to us anyway — that thing is going to learn all there is to know about our ship during the repair process. Just because it utilizes technology more advanced than our own doesn't mean it already has access to all of our technology, if that makes sense."

"Yes, it does. Anything else?"

"No, sir. That's about it. I guess it really comes down to a judgment call, doesn't it? Without question, getting our LO systems back online would make us much more useful in a fight against a Guardian or an *Envoy*-class ship."

Prescott nodded slowly, struggling to weigh the pros and cons of making such a risky decision. His chief engineer was right, of course. This was a judgment call — *his* judgment call, and his alone — and unquestionably the kind of gamble leading inexorably to triumph if successful, ruin if not.

"Captain Griffin, are you still monitoring?"

"Of course, Captain."

"Is there anything you and Tess can do to somehow purge whatever data the facility AI collects about our ship before we depart?"

"We can certainly try. At one time, there were security protocols in place to protect proprietary systems aboard allied vessels from being compromised. As with all such things, however, there's no way to be absolutely sure without destroying the station on the way out. And even that may not be enough. If I may, though, this seems like the kind of thing our friend Miguel might be willing to assist us with at some point."

"He might at that. Thank you all for your inputs, but here's the bottom line from my perspective. *Fugitive* is currently the only ship in our inventory with a real, demonstrated advantage over the Pelaran vessels. But if we head back in the shape we're in right now, we're probably no more useful to Admiral Patterson than an additional frigate — perhaps even less so. In my opinion, we have to give this a try."

Out of curiosity, Prescott glanced in turn at Creel, Reynolds, and Logan to see if their expressions might give away any misgivings they had regarding his decision. Surprisingly, all three had the look of having already moved on, as if the decision had been clear, even obvious, to everyone but him.

"Ensign Fisher, take us in, please," he ordered, suddenly recalling a painting he had once seen of Confederate General Robert E. Lee during the U.S. Civil War. In spite of being surrounded by over fifty thousand troops under his command, the painting, entitled *The Loneliness of Command,* depicted Lee sitting alone outside his tent with a remote, desolate expression on his careworn face.

SCS Gresav, In Hyperspace
(54.2 light years from the Herrera Mining Facility)

"Captain Jelani, we are being hailed again, sir," the *Gresav's* communications officer reported from his workstation. "I believe it is the same ... creature, who contacted us before regarding the Crown Prince's disappearance. He continues to refer to himself as ... 'Rick,' sir."

"Eton Ulto," the flag captain swore under his breath. "What does he say he wants now?"

"He says he has Prince Naftur aboard again and would like to return him to us. He says he can do so without requiring us to transition back into normal space, but he would prefer not to do so for safety reasons."

"How did he manage to … never mind. Tell him we will be happy to stop if he will prove to us the Crown Prince is aboard."

Moments later, a window containing both the inscrutable Grey alien and Prince Naftur appeared on the bridge display screen.

"It is good to see you again, Captain Jelani," Naftur greeted wearily.

"And you as well, Prince Naftur. Are you injured, sir? Have they mistreated you?"

"No, no, Musa," Naftur replied, raising his hand in a soothing gesture. "I am perfectly fine. Although I will tell you the effects of the … matter transference system our friends here possess are somewhat … *fatiguing* to say the least. Rather than experience them again so soon, I would appreciate your sending one of our drop ships over to retrieve me."

"Of course, Your Highness," Jelani replied, nodding to an officer located off-screen.

"Thank you, Captain. You and I have much to discuss and very little time in which to do so."

"Of that, I have no doubt, sir. When they contacted us after your disappearance, I had a difficult time believing you were actually back in the Sol system."

"I had a difficult time with that as well," Naftur said with a wan smile. "But I can assure you that is exactly where I have been … and where we must all now return."

"I am afraid I do not understand, sir."

"Nor do I, my friend … at least not entirely. What I *can* tell you is that our Terran friends are in grave danger. Two powerful warships from what we have always referred to as the Pelaran Alliance will attack their fleet in less than two hours. I fear they may not prevail without our assistance. And regardless of any misgivings some of us may have regarding the Humans, if they are destroyed, we will undoubtedly be the Pelarans' next target."

"But, Admiral, how can we —"

"All I can tell you at the moment is that Rick's ship, the *Ethereal*, has capabilities the likes of which we have barely begun to imagine. He believes she is capable of transporting the *Gresav* back to the Sol system in a single, instantaneous hyperspace transition."

"But …" Jelani began.

"Look, Captain, I know this sounds a little far-fetched from your perspective," Rick interrupted, "but I can assure you it's nothing more than technology that's a little more advanced —"

"A lot more advanced," Miguel interjected flatly in the background.

"Never mind him," Rick continued, shaking his head. "He's an engineer … and there are a number of very good reasons why they rarely make the best diplomats. As I was saying, we simply have access to more advanced technology than you do. I'm sure you have encountered plenty of civilizations who consider your ship's capabilities nothing short of miraculous, right?"

Captain Jelani's fierce, piercing gaze provided no indication whatsoever that he agreed with anything Rick had said thus far.

"Right," Rick concluded on the Wek's behalf. "In that case, you're just going to have to trust us on this one … as I believe your Admiral Naftur now does."

"I do not believe I would refer to our current relationship as one of trust," Naftur said, "but I have seen enough to be convinced that you can and will do as you say."

"And that's what we like to refer to as 'good enough,'" Rick replied with a squeaky chuckle. "So, getting back to the matter at hand, the *Gresav's* size is very close to the upper limit of what we can enclose within our hyperdrive field. That means we will have to very carefully position the two ships relative to one another. Unfortunately, it's also going to take some additional time for us to store sufficient power for the jump."

"How much time?" Naftur asked.

Rick blinked his huge, dark eyes as he received the required information from *Ethereal's* AI.

"If we hurry, I believe we will still arrive in the Sol system before the Envoy's ship."

"Then, clearly, there is not a moment to be lost."

Chapter 21

TFS Fugitive
(Pelara - approaching the FAM-4 facility)

Much like a harbor pilot safely guides ships into congested or otherwise dangerous ports, the FAM-4 facility AI had begun its coordination with TFS *Fugitive* as she approached the station's main entrance. From that point forward, the MMSV's crew had been relegated to mere observers as the warship steadily made her way through the enormous, twelve-hundred-meter-wide entrance past a set of doors over three times as large as those outside the Yucca Mountain Shipyard on Earth.

Once inside, it immediately became evident that the interior surface of the facility's outer hull was lined with thousands of structures of various shapes and sizes. In some cases, the buildings' functions were familiar to the Terran crew, looking very much like those found in any shipyard or maintenance facility back home. Assuming the station had been crewed by Pelaran workers at some point, many of the buildings had undoubtedly once been used to house them — probably by the tens or even hundreds of thousands if the station's size was any indication. Now, however, FAM-4's surprisingly well-lit interior appeared to be entirely deserted with the exception of an equally large workforce of AI-controlled drones. Seconds after the *Fugitive* had cleared the station's entrance, over fifty of these approached, beginning what could only be a close examination of the ship's design and apparent damage.

As the ship reached the facility's hollow interior, it became much more obvious why the Pelaran navy had chosen to continue constructing its starships in space. It wasn't merely the fact that the interior of the station was gigantic — although it certainly was — but it was also ingeniously designed to take full advantage of a microgravity environment. With such a vast amount of empty space available (the station's mean diameter was nearly twelve kilometers), several of the largest warships ever constructed by the Pelaran navy could be built and/or serviced simultaneously, all while providing workers and/or drones with full three-hundred-and-sixty-degree access.

On TFS *Fugitive's* bridge, her crew watched in awe as the facility AI guided the relatively tiny ship into a berth not far from the station's entrance. TFS *Guardian*, having followed them inside, curtly refused the steady stream of queries from the station insisting he was long overdue for a complete systems overhaul.

"Oh, this can't be over soon enough for me," Reynolds whispered, as if the sound of her voice might wake some long-slumbering malevolent spirit that had once stood guard within the giant facility. "AI, Reynolds. Please summarize all repair-related communications that have taken place thus far with the facility AI."

"AI acknowledged," the system's impassive, female voice responded.

In the center of the bridge view screen, a window appeared displaying a slowly rotating image of the MMSV. Shortly thereafter, a pulsating green oval appeared, superimposed over the aft port section of the hull damaged during the attack on the ALAI starbase. After a brief pause, the oval pulsed red three times before the image zoomed in on the indicated area.

"The facility AI has successfully assessed, classified, and is preparing to repair the indicated battle damage."

"Estimated time to repair?"

"All indicated damage has been classified as follows: minor, low-priority, non-mission-critical, with no life support system involvement. Accordingly, the facility AI has assigned a single work detail. All repairs will be executed in series with full access to a single fabrication facility. At this resource allocation level, estimated time to repair is approximately seventy-two hours, twenty-four minutes."

"Uh, no, that's not gonna work for us," Reynolds objected. "We appear to be the only ship in the entire facility at the moment. Aren't additional assets and/or fabrication facilities available?"

"Confirmed. TFS *Fugitive* is the only spacecraft currently scheduled for repair activities. Additional assets and facilities are available for higher-priority repairs. Shall I request an increase in our initial priority assessment?"

"Absolutely. Reclassify as mission-critical, time-sensitive. Request that all repairs be conducted in parallel and completed at maximum possible speed."

"Our reclassification request has been approved," the ship's AI responded immediately. "Additional resources assigned. Estimated time to repair now twelve minutes, thirty-three seconds."

"That's what I'm talking about," Reynold said, turning to her captain with a quick wink.

"I don't know what we'd do without you, Commander," Prescott said, shaking his head incredulously.

"Oh, come on," Logan groaned. "Twelve minutes? We've got extensive hull damage out there. We're talking several weeks in one of our own facilities … and that's assuming we get placed at the front of the priority queue."

"Oh ye of little faith," Creel chided, causing all three of the Terran officers to stare briefly in wonder at the reference before deciding it was a topic best left for another time.

"Don't get me wrong, Doctor. I'd love to see us on our way out of here in twelve minutes. I'll just believe it when I see it, that's all."

On the bridge view screen, Commander Reynolds had already opened several windows with various views of the activities taking place around the ship. Droids of a seemingly endless variety were now streaming in from every direction. There were already so many in the area, in fact, that it seemed as though they would begin colliding with one another at any moment. Instead, with every new arrival, their movements became increasingly complex — a purpose-driven ballet in space, exquisitely choreographed for their benefit by the FAM-4 facility AI.

Near the port stern, one work detail had already removed the damaged sections of the hull and were now busily attaching a mind-boggling array of cables, hydraulic lines, and other internal components per the specifications provided by the *Fugitive's* AI. While it was possible to see the end results of their work taking shape, their individual movements appeared to the Human eye as little more than a blur of motion on the view screen. Concurrently, both above and below the ship, additional work details had laid down a pair of lattice-like structures which they immediately began covering with a composite material. Although the techniques being employed were quite different than what Logan had seen in TFC shipyards, much of the tooling being used was surprisingly familiar.

After watching the droids at their work for just two minutes it had already become obvious to Commander Logan that the facility AI's estimated repair time might not be as far-fetched as he had originally imagined. "I, uh …" he began tentatively. "I think I'd better get back to Engineering."

"I think you'd better," Reynolds agreed. "Ten minutes, and we're out of here, Cheng," she called after him as he exited the bridge.

"Captain Prescott, AI," the ship's synthetic female voice sounded once again from the ceiling speakers.

"Prescott here. Go ahead, AI."

"The facility AI has replicated the design of our HB-7c missiles and will replace the ship's standard loadout, if requested."

"Humph. That's exactly the kind of thing that worries me the most about this entire exercise. AI, will any additional time be required to complete weapons manufacturing and loadout."

"Negative, Captain. Sufficient idle resources are available to complete the task with no impact to ongoing repair activities."

"Yes. Complete the weapons loadout."

"AI acknowledged."

"Griffin, Prescott."

"Yes, Captain Prescott," the GCS responded immediately.

"I'm guessing you would prefer to return to the Sol system with us."

"Of course, Captain. Terra is my home too. And you will undoubtedly require my assistance."

"You may be right about that. In fact, I would gladly take all of the other friendly GCS units back with us if I could."

"I certainly agree. In my absence, two of the remaining members of the Freeguard squadron will continue scanning the remains of the ALAI starbase. I have tasked the remaining five to stand guard over Pelara in case the Golf 3 GCS returns."

"That seems appropriate, thank you. Clear your approach with the facility AI so you won't interfere with repairs. I'm sending Commander Reynolds back to oversee your boarding operation again now. I want you docked in our hangar bay as quickly as you can do so without damaging the ship. As soon as our repairs are complete, I need you and Tess to interface with the FAM-4 facility again and see what you can do to remove any trace we were ever here."

"Will do, Captain. I'll be aboard shortly. Griffin out."

"Ensign Fisher, what's our minimum time in route once we're clear of the station?"

"It'll take eight C-Jumps, sir … that's seven dwell times for a total of one hour and forty-five minutes."

"I'm not sure how we could have done any better than that. Let's just hope we can get home soon enough to make a difference."

TFS Navajo, In Hyperspace
(2 ½ hours later - Combat Information Center)

"Contacts!" the CIC's on-duty tactical officer reported from a nearby console. "A total of *four* contacts, sir, all presumed hostile."

"Confirm *four* contacts, Commander?"

"Yes, Admiral. Three *Guardian*-class and one *Envoy*-class, designated Golf 1 through Golf 3 and Echo 1. I'm sorry, sir, I'm not sure how they —"

"We'll deal with how that got by us later, Commander," Patterson interrupted. "I'm sure there are plenty of things they are capable of doing that we don't know about. Right now, I need everyone focused on what *we* are capable of doing to kill these four targets. At least they obliged us with a little extra time to welcome them back properly."

"Yes, sir," the officer replied with more confidence than he felt at the moment.

"Lieutenant Fletcher, I assume we're patched in via NRD net, so we can hail them?"

"Yes, sir. From their perspective, our transmissions will appear to emanate from the closest comm beacon. We have so many in the area now that comm delay shouldn't be a problem. The same goes for any of our ships operating under EMCON. They can hear us in real-time, they just can't respond."

"Very good. Hail the Envoy's ship. Audio-only, please, and limit it to my headset so I can control what he hears."

"Aye, sir, hailing."

"What have you done with the Yumaran Guardian?" Verge Tahiri demanded the moment a connection was established. "Don't bother lying, Admiral Patterson. To me, the residual effects of a recent, large-scale antimatter annihilation event are quite clear, but I am genuinely interested in how you managed to do it."

"Hello again, Mr. Tahiri," Patterson replied, choosing to ignore the Envoy's question altogether. "Sir, I have been given the unpleasant task of informing you of a recent change in Terran diplomatic policy vis-à-vis the Pelaran Alliance."

"Have you indeed? I believe I can guess well enough what that change entails, so perhaps we should skip ahead to the reason I have returned to the Sol system so soon, shall we?"

"We have no wish to engage in hostilies with the Alliance or its representatives, Mr. Tahiri. But we must insist on maintaining our territorial sovereignty while our Leadership Council has the opportunity to evaluate the current —"

"Your world has failed time and again to meet its obligations under the terms and conditions under which you were granted access to Pelaran Alliance technology," Tahiri growled. "It was only your status as "Children of the Makers" coupled with an *unprecedented* level of overindulgence on the part of your Guardian that has prevented the termination of your contract thus far. What brought me back here so soon, however, was the discovery that you have colluded with at least one other species to engage in subversive activities against the Alliance. Now, upon my return, I also learn that you have somehow brought about the destruction … the *murder*, Admiral Patterson … of a Guardian Cultivation System, an official representative of the Pelaran Alliance."

"Okay, let's cut the bullshit, Mr. Tahiri," Patterson snapped with uncharacteristic anger in his voice. "The Pelaran Alliance — at least in the form represented in those agreements you just mentioned — no longer exists. That much, we know for sure. Furthermore, it did not exist as represented in those agreements at the time we began receiving data from our Guardian spacecraft. Now, as to exactly what has transpired since and what our world's status may or may not be with respect to those agreements, I'm going to have to refer you to our Leadership Council. As I have already stated, their evaluation of our current status is ongoing. So, once again, I must ask that you respect our territorial sovereignty while we give them the time they need to — "

"Your ships' ability to remain suspended in hyperspace is very impressive, Admiral. Unfortunately, since it was not us who provided your world with this technology, I can only assume this is yet another example of your duplicity. Listen closely, Admiral Patterson, because I will only provide these instructions one time. You will order *all* of your ships to return to normal space and immediately begin the process of landing on your planet's surface in preparation for decommissioning. If you follow my instructions to the letter, you have my word we will not attack the surface of your planet."

Muting the comlink, Admiral Patterson noted that two of the three Guardian spacecraft had transitioned to locations providing each with line of sight coverage over roughly half the Earth's surface. At the same moment, the Envoy's ship and the remaining GCS unit had positioned themselves well clear of the planet.

"He's giving himself and Golf 3 room to maneuver. I guess that means they're expecting a fight," Patterson observed, half to himself.

"Sir," the nearest tactical officer spoke up, "I just heard from Captain Davis. The *Navajo's* AI confirmed that our vertical launch cells are a no-go for Captain Prescott's hyperspace missile launch technique."

"Yeah, I was afraid of that."

"Yes, sir. But our F-373s have internal weapons bays similar to those aboard TFS *Fugitive*. We have sixteen fighters deploying missiles in hyperspace at the moment. Both carriers are asking for permission to launch additional fighters when they return to normal space."

"I don't see us taking that risk. How many missiles do we have in flight?"

"Three two so far, sir. It's pretty slow going. The fighters' hyperdrive fields are only large enough to accommodate two missiles at a time."

"Tell them to stay at it, Commander. Regardless of how many missiles we have in flight when we begin our attack, I want half targeted on Echo 1 and the other half on Golf 3."

"Aye, sir."

"Please don't mistake this discussion as a negotiation, Admiral," Tahiri's voice resumed inside Patterson's headset. "I would prefer to avoid the need to demonstrate our resolve to you and your Leadership Council, but I will not hesitate to do so, if necessary. Our beam emitters were primarily designed as anti-ship weapons, but I can assure you they are quite effective against planetary targets as well. In fact, sustained antimatter annihilation inside an oxygen-rich environment such as yours has a marked tendency to ignite the atmosphere itself. After an hour or so, the resulting firestorm becomes self-sustaining. It's really quite spectacular … but not something you would ever want to witness taking place on your own homeworld."

"I understand," Patterson said with a weary sigh, doing his level best to sound like a man who had already accepted defeat. "I just need some time to begin issuing the appropriate orders. I'll be back with you shortly."

"You would do well to ensure those orders are followed without delay," Tahiri replied, now shifting into the patronizing tone Patterson recognized from so many conversations with Griffin over the past year.

Not bothering to answer, the CNO glanced at Lieutenant Fletcher, jerking his hand across his neck in a signal to terminate the comlink and immediately receiving a nod of confirmation in reply.

"Captain Prescott …" he continued, staring at a now-blank view screen that had been a live vidcon with TFS *Fugitive's* captain until his ship had been forced into EMCON moments earlier by Tahiri's transition into the area.

Patterson paused, turning back to his comm officer with an expression of grave concern on his face. "Fletcher, are you *sure* Prescott's still able to hear this? Understand we're pretty much betting the farm that he can."

"Yes, sir. If you address him directly, *Navajo's* AI will forward the comm traffic to several comm beacons near his ship's last known position. Unless he's transitioned, he can hear you."

"Dear Lord, I hope you're right about that," the admiral said under his breath. "Captain Prescott, I know you've gone silent and are unable to respond, but based on your last position, you should be setting yourself up to take down Golf 1 on my signal. As soon as you've destroyed Golf 1, you are to assist the *Gresav* with Golf 2."

"Griffin," the CNO continued, quickly shifting his gaze to the Guardian's familiar avatar on an adjacent view screen, "Prescott was saying you intend to employ a diversionary tactic to make it more difficult for the Pelarans to target our ships."

"Yes, Admiral. By maximizing the output of my hyperdrive, I can create a series of outbound hyperspace signatures that should —"

"You'll have to explain it to me later, Griffin. For now, I just need you to do it when I signal. Understood?"

"Aye, sir."

"Good, thank you," Patterson replied, then shifted his attention to a second pair of adjacent view screens. "Admiral Naftur and Rick, I have to tell you I'm not crazy about what you have in mind."

"It's the best option under the circumstances," Rick observed. "Since you only have one ship like the *Fugitive* at your disposal, the *Gresav's* primary beam weapon — the 'G-cannon,' I believe you call it — is the only system you have capable of quickly disabling a GCS unit."

"And you'll be able to place the *Gresav* close enough for her to fire before being fired upon?"

"The *Gresav* will certainly be able to begin its attack before the target has an opportunity to return fire, but I cannot guarantee she will escape damage. We are stretching our own rules of engagement to the limit here, Admiral. We will transport the *Gresav* into the area, but the moment she fires, the area becomes an active combat zone. Unfortunately, that requires us to transition out immediately."

"We're grateful for whatever assistance you can provide, of course. As for the rest of the fleet, obviously, we weren't expecting four enemy ships, so we're going to have to improvise a bit. We'll do our best to keep Golf 3 and Echo 1 busy until you have destroyed the first two Guardians, but I fully expect us to take quite a beating. Let's just hope Griffin's little trick works."

"We have utilized a similar tactic in the past with some success," Naftur said. "Good luck to you, Admiral."

"To us all, sir. And thank you for standing with us once again. Alright, everyone, AI-synchronized execution orders in 3 … 2 … 1 …"

TFS Fugitive, Sol System
(98 km from Golf 1)

"AI slaved to the Flag for synchronized attack, sir," Lieutenant Lau reported in a rapid cadence from the Tactical console. "Fire control and helm now under AI control."

"Understood. Confirm single-round main gun attack and immediate C-Jump followed by three second hyperspace hold before main gun attack on secondary target."

"Confirmed single-round main gun attack followed by immediate C-Jump and three second hyperspace hold before main gun attack on secondary target," Lau echoed.

"Very well. You are clear to proceed."

Over the bridge speakers, Admiral Patterson had just finished providing instructions to the *Ethereal* and *Gresav* and had now begun his countdown to initiate the attack: "… AI-synchronized execution orders in 3 … 2 … 1 …"

Immediately before the Admiral's signal to fire, everyone aboard the small ship heard and felt a familiar metallic PING as a fifty-kilogram kinetic energy penetrator round entered the main gun's breach and was forcibly centered between the weapon's launch rails. A fraction of a second later, the projectile was streaking toward Golf 1 at over one-third the speed of light. Even at such a fantastic speed, however, the round had covered less than half the distance to its target before TFS *Fugitive* executed its AI-controlled transition, disappearing from normal space in a flash of grayish-white light.

"First round away," Lau reported, speaking as quickly as possible. "Secondary target attack commencing ... now."

Earth's curved, bluish-green horizon immediately reappeared near the bottom of the view screen, but rather than the expected image of Golf 2, *Fugitive's* AI immediately focused its optical sensors on the *Gresav*. The Wek flagship, obviously heavily damaged with a long trail of fire and debris issuing from several tears in her massive hull, appeared to be in a slow, uncontrolled descent toward the planet below.

"Dubashi, try hailing the *Gresav*," Prescott ordered.

"Aye, sir."

"Where's our target, Tactical?" Prescott continued, doing his best to remain focused in spite of the horrors being displayed in vivid detail on the bridge view screen.

"I don't have a distinct debris field for Golf 2, Captain," Lau reported, "but based on these readings, there's no doubt the *Gresav* fired her G-cannon ... probably several times, the way this looks. We're also getting some sporadic antimatter annihilation events on our outer hull that might be consistent with a destroyed GCS unit. Best guess, Golf 2 was destroyed. Either way, we should transition out of this area, sir."

"Understood. . .Helm, emergency C-Jump. Get us clear of the immediate area but maintain line of sight with the *Gresav*."

"Aye, sir," Fisher replied, "emergency C-Jumping."

TFS Navajo, Sol System
(Combat Information Center - 2.06x10^5 km from Earth)

Prior to the Envoy's arrival, Admiral Patterson had designated two primary strike groups — each consisting of four cruisers, four destroyers, and three frigates — with the original intention of assigning each group a single enemy target. Having witnessed the destruction wrought by Pelaran antimatter beams on more than one occasion, however, he had hoped to avoid the necessity of any sort of direct engagement against the *Guardian* or *Envoy*-class ships. Unfortunately, the unexpected arrival of four such ships had left him little choice, particularly with Tahiri openly threatening to attack the Earth itself.

"All ships, weapons free. Attack your designated target at will," he ordered, echoing the automated series of orders that had already caused all twenty-two ships to exit hyperspace and open fire with every weapon at their disposal.

"Good missile hits on both targets, Admiral," the tactical officer reported. "Confirmed, two four missile impacts each."

Two of the largest overhead screens mounted on the CIC's port bulkhead were now dedicated to Echo 1 and Golf 3. By the time Patterson had shifted his gaze from the holo table to the nearest screen, both enemy ships had already emerged from the rapid series of explosions caused by twenty-four HB-7c missiles impacting against their shields.

"No apparent damage, sir," the officer reported dismally.

"We're not gonna win this thing with massed firepower, people. I want all ships in both task forces to spread out. Every single ship should be firing, immediately C-Jumping, then firing again. AIs to deconflict all C-Jumps and weapons fire."

With no further action required in the *Navajo's* CIC, the flagship's battlespace AI interpreted and executed the CNO's orders, immediately passing the required information to every Command console and AI aboard every TFC ship in the Sol system.

Chapter 22

TFS Fugitive, Sol System
(125 km from the *Gresav*)

"Captain," Lieutenant Dubashi announced as TFS *Fugitive* emerged once again from hyperspace, "no response from the *Gresav*, but we're being hailed by Golf 1. It claims to be heavily damaged and says it is prepared to surrender if we will guarantee its safety."

"We can't, and we won't. Lieutenant Lau, is that position accurate?" Prescott asked, nodding at the tactical plot on the starboard side of the view screen. "Looks to me like it's still right where we left it."

"Yes, sir, it may be unable to maneuver or transition. I'm getting good positional data from three independent sources at the moment and should be able to get eyes on target from the surface shortly," Lau reported, his hands moving rapidly over the surface of his console. "Got it, sir," he concluded a few seconds later as a somewhat blurry image of Golf 1 appeared in its own window on the bridge view screen.

"Regardless of whether it can move, it's still in a position to fire on the surface, and we have no way of determining if it's still able to do so, let alone if it actually wants to surrender. But if it's unable to maneuver or transition, I'd say there's also a reasonably good chance its shields are either weakened or offline. Let's target it with a spread of missiles, Lieutenant. Six should do it. I want simultaneous detonations with the maximum safe yield taking into account the target's proximity to the planet. Fire when ready."

"Six HB-7c missiles aye, sir. Safe explosive yield calculated at two three percent."

Glancing briefly at his XO, Prescott was surprised to see what appeared to be a look of uncertainty clouding her face. "We can't risk allowing it to surrender, Commander," he said quietly.

"No, it's not that at all, Captain. Under the circumstances, I don't think we have much of a choice. It's just the precedent of refusing to give quarter that concerns me."

"Missiles away," Lieutenant Lau reported.

"Lieutenant Lee, do you have a projected point of impact for the *Gresav*?" Prescott asked, returning his attention to the now rapidly accelerating Wek destroyer in the center of the view screen.

"Yes, Captain, the South Pacific Ocean approximately forty-eight hundred kilometers west northwest of Santiago, Chile. Fleet has already passed along tsunami warnings to the civil authorities for the entire coast of South America and north extending all the way up to San Diego. Time to impact, six minutes."

"Missiles transitioning ... impacts," Lau reported from the Tactical console, as the already washed-out image of Golf 1 on the view screen suddenly went completely white. A few seconds later, the ground-based optical sensor adjusted its field of view to show a rapidly expanding ball of plasma in the daytime sky. For the second time in the space of a single day, the death throes of a Guardian spacecraft were easily visible from surface of the Earth.

"I think we got him, sir. Confirming now," Lau said, continuing his steady stream of reports. "Confirmed. Golf 1 destroyed."

"Thank you, Lieutenant," Prescott replied, still staring at the image of the *Gresav*, her hull now beginning to glow an angry red as she entered the upper reaches of the atmosphere.

"We have to keep moving," Reynolds prompted quietly. "There's nothing we can do for them now."

TFS Navajo, Sol System
(Combat Information Center - 3.06×10^5 km from Earth)

At the CIC holographic table, Admiral Patterson rapidly adjusted the display to center on elements of Strike Group 2, which the Pelaran Envoy had apparently chosen to bear the brunt of his first round of attacks.

"The *Nunga* is taking heavy fire from Echo 1, Admiral," his tactical officer reported.

"Let's see it on overhead 2, Commander," he ordered.

A real-time image of the huge, *Navajo*-class cruiser instantly appeared, obviously taking tremendous damage from the Pelaran ship's beam weapons. To the admiral's eyes, TFS *Nunga* appeared to be receiving hundreds of simultaneous hits along her entire length. Shield intercept events merged with the Envoy ship's transition flashes to form a ghostly, halo-like effect around the cruiser's hull. Although she was clearly attempting to return fire, the *Nunga's* efforts looked decidedly feeble by comparison.

Too fast, Patterson thought as a shadow of despair crept from the dark recesses of his mind. *They're just too fast for us.* "*Nunga,* emergency C-Jump!"

***

Thus far, the Terran ships had been attempting to beat the Pelarans at their own game: C-Jumping into a new firing position, attempting to acquire a target, firing (if possible), then C-Jumping to a new position to start the process again. In this case, however, having greater numbers of larger ships was quickly proving to be a significant disadvantage against the small, inhumanly fast Envoy. Tahiri, quickly recognizing the fact that his hyperspace targeting scanner was of little use with all of the hyperdrive activity taking place in the area (particularly that of the incredibly irritating Terran Guardian), had adjusted his tactics to compensate. With so many targets available, most of which were quite large, he simply waited — transitioning only when necessary to avoid incoming fire — until a Terran ship transitioned into close proximity.

The wait, although seemingly endless from the Envoy's perspective, had taken only seconds. Fully confident in his ability to obliterate his target, then move on to the next before taking fire himself, Tahiri had begun the destruction of the Terran fleet by attacking one of their largest capital ships. *Fitting,* he thought, as he began a rapid series of transitions intended to place his onboard weapons in a position to tear the massive ship apart in the shortest amount of time possible.

Terran Guardian Spacecraft, Sol System
(2.06x10^5 km from Earth)

Too slow, Griffin thought. *The Terrans are far too slow.* Although it now appeared *Fugitive* and *Gresav* had been surprisingly successful in their attacks against the first two Guardian spacecraft, there was little chance of something similar happening with the two remaining Pelaran ships. *They won't even begin to realize the battle is lost for some time*, he added, beginning another in a long series of diversionary hyperspace transitions.

As if to underscore his rather bleak assessment of the current tactical situation, TFS *Nunga* exploded with a level of violence far exceeding anything Griffin had ever achieved in any of his own attacks. The Envoy's firing pattern seemed to indicate Tahiri had taken his time with his first attack, choosing to completely obliterate one of the most powerful Terran ships rather than simply disable it and move on to the next target. And although it was tempting to assume this demonstration of overwhelming firepower might be designed to motivate the Humans to surrender, Griffin knew it was nothing of the sort. This fight had become personal. The Terrans, and any remnants of the technology they had been given, would be erased from existence.

Continuing to scan the battlespace as he transitioned from one side to the other, Griffin considered thousands of possibilities for executing a direct attack against one of the two remaining enemy ships. *If Golf 3 were to be damaged or destroyed*, he thought, *there is a marginal increase in the probability of at least one TFC ship surviving the battle … only a three percent increase, but an increase nonetheless.*

As the likelihood of a Terran defeat continued to increase moment by moment, two critical pieces of information surfaced within the sea of data streaming through Griffin's consciousness. First, the GCS designated as Golf 3, was, in fact, the Krayleck Guardian. Second, it appeared to be deliberately avoiding direct attacks on Terran ships in the area.

Without hesitation, TFS *Guardian* transitioned as closely as possible to the Krayleck Guardian's last known position. Pausing for less than a millisecond, Griffin transmitted the same data stream he had used to recruit nearly half the GCS units in the area before the attack on the ALAI starbase. After three quick transitions during which he continued to broadcast the message, he received a reply.

Terran Guardian Cultivation System, Krayleck Guardian Cultivation System. Identification confirmed. Initial query acknowledged. Alliance AI activities in Pelaran system as well as Envoy attack on Terran Dominion assets appear inconsistent with cultivation program mission directives. Insufficient data available to warrant further military action at this time.

With that, Golf 3 transitioned, departing the area in the general direction of the Legara system.

During the mere seconds it had taken Griffin to remove the Krayleck Guardian from the battlespace, the Envoy's ship had already managed to ensnare another Terran ship. Now, in a scene almost identical to what had occurred just moments before with the *Nunga*, Tahiri had managed to score several hits on the cruiser

Scythian. Just as before, the comparatively tiny Pelaran ship seemed to flicker around the mighty cruiser, quickly inflicting sufficient damage to prevent its escape before beginning the process of destroying it in detail.

TFS Navajo, Sol System
(Combat Information Center - 2.85×10^5 km from Earth)

"Admiral, incoming Emergency Action message from TFS *Guardian*," Lieutenant Fletcher reported.

"I don't have time for any of his nonsense at the moment, Lieutenant," Patterson snapped without taking his eyes off the rapidly changing holographic display.

"I understand, sir, but I think you'll definitely want to see this. I think Griffin may be about to do something drastic."

"What?" Patterson replied, rounding on the young officer with an uncharacteristic flash of frustration and anger registering in his eyes.

"I'm summarizing here, sir, but he says TFS *Scythian* is lost and that all remaining TFC ships within fifty thousand kilometers must enter hyperspace immediately. Frankly, I think we should comply, Admiral … right now."

"AI, Patterson. Emergency C-Jump all ships to fallback position Charlie. Hyperspace hold. Execute!" the CNO roared.

A fraction of a second after receiving and authenticating the admiral's order, the *Navajo's* battlespace AI had successfully coordinated what amounted to a mass retreat of all Fleet assets in the vicinity of Earth. In addition to the twenty remaining ships currently assigned to Strike Groups 1 and 2, the carriers *Ushant* and *Philippine Sea*, TFS *Fugitive*, as well as all of the other warships Admiral Patterson had been holding in reserve immediately transitioned to a location near Earth-Sun Lagrange Point 4.

"Tactical, report!" Patterson commanded.

"All remaining ships accounted for with the exception of TFS *Guardian*, Admiral. Local Fleet status is hyperspace hold at fallback position Charlie."

"Thank you, Commander. All ships are to continue to hold here until receiving further orders."

"Aye, sir."

"Lieutenant Fletcher, I think you'd better let me see the full text of that Emergency Action Message now."

"Yes, sir. View screen four."

Taking a deep breath as he worked to refocus his mind, Patterson turned to read TFS *Guardian's* text.

Z1833
TOP SECRET - MAGI PRIME
FM: CAPTAIN GRIFFIN — ABOARD TFS GUARDIAN
TO: EAM — CNO — ABOARD TFS NAVAJO
INFO: ATTACK ON ECHO 1 COMMENCING IMMEDIATELY

1. TFS SCYTHIAN UNDER HEAVY ATTACK FROM ECHO 1 AND PRESUMED LOST.
2. TFS GUARDIAN CALCULATES PROBABILITY OF TFC / TERRAN SURVIVAL NOW LESS THAN EIGHT PERCENT AND DECREASING.

3. CURRENT ECHO 1 ATTACK PRESENTS TACTICAL OPPORTUNITY THAT MAY NOT BE REPEATED.
4. ALL TFC VESSELS WITHIN FIFTY THOUSAND KILOMETERS OF TFS SCYTHIAN MUST TRANSITION TO HYPERSPACE IMMEDIATELY.
5. ALL VESSELS WITHIN THE FIFTY THOUSAND KILOMETER RADIUS WILL BE DESTROYED — NO FURTHER WARNINGS WILL BE ISSUED.
6. IT HAS BEEN MY HONOR TO SERVE YOU. TFS GUARDIAN SENDS.

"Get me a comlink with TFS *Fugitive*, and send Prescott this EAM, please," the admiral ordered without further comment.

"Aye, sir," the comm officer replied, quickly keying in the required commands at her console.

"*Fugitive*-actual here," Prescott replied moments later. "Go ahead, Admiral."

"Captain Prescott, I need you to read the Flash traffic from TFS *Guardian* we just forwarded you …"

"I see it sir, go ahead."

"I'm not sure precisely what, if anything, he was about to do, but I need eyes on Echo 1 and TFS *Guardian* as quickly as possible. Are your low-observable systems still operational?"

"Yes, they are, sir. Although we'll still be emitting quite a bit of heat from our main gun for the next few minutes."

"We'll have to risk it for now. Argus is showing no new transitions in the area. So unless I miss my guess, you're not going to find either of those ships. Go ahead and begin a general reconnaissance of the area surrounding the last known position of TFS *Scythian,* then continue to widen your search until you're confident there are no Pelaran ships of any sort in the system."

"Aye, sir."

TFS Fugitive, Sol System
(2.93x10^5 km from Earth)

"What are you seeing, Lieutenant Lee?" Prescott asked the young officer at the Science and Engineering console.

Upon TFS *Fugitive's* arrival at the location where the *Navajo*-class cruiser *Scythian* had been destroyed, Prescott had immediately risked a full scan of the area using his ship's entire suite of active and passive sensors. Finding nothing, he had begun the painstaking process of traversing the former battlespace from one side to the other, looking for any indications one of the Guardians or the Envoy-class spacecraft might have survived.

"Almost exactly the same thing we saw in the area where the *Gresav* took out Golf 2, Captain," Lee replied. "There's some ultra-fine debris here, and a much higher than normal concentration of antimatter particles, but really nothing else to speak of."

"Whatever Griffin did, it must have been …"

"Epic, yes, sir," Lee nodded. "The only thing I can figure is that he transitioned into close proximity to Echo 1 and then triggered some sort of overload of his powerplant. We don't know a lot about how the Pelaran ships are powered, so I'm really just speculating based on what our sensors are telling us."

"I don't think you're speculating Lieutenant. There were no additional transitions, and yet there's nothing out here larger than a grain of rice for tens of thousands of kilometers," Reynolds observed in an almost reverent tone. "TFS *Scythian*, Griffin, the Envoy's ship — they're all just … gone."

"Sir," Dubashi reported, turning around in her chair to address her captain and first officer, "I wasn't sure if you wanted to see this, but the *Gresav* is moments away from impact. There are several fighters in the area now providing video coverage."

"Thank you, Lieutenant. The *Gresav* has a complement of three hundred or so, including Prince Naftur, and all of them sacrificed their lives to save ours. So, yes, I think it's important for us to see it. Helm, Tactical, Science, continue the search and speak up immediately if you find anything."

"Aye, sir," all three officers replied somberly.

Seconds later, Dubashi placed a large window in the center of the bridge view screen. Two separate video feeds appeared in a split-screen configuration, each displaying the huge, six-hundred-meter-long Wek destroyer from a different angle. Although both feeds were obviously being transmitted from chase aircraft, the right-hand image provided additional data near the bottom of the screen including the ship's current velocity and time to impact — now just over one minute away.

"There's no doubt she had several hull breaches around those points of impact, but she's still remarkably intact otherwise," Reynolds commented in a low voice intended only for Prescott. "Do you think anyone aboard is still alive?"

"I'm trying not to think about it," Prescott replied, "but, yes, I'm afraid so. The *Gresav's* a big ship, and the Wek build them to take a lot of abuse and keep on fighting. I'm guessing she hit Golf 2 with her first shot and did some damage, then probably finished it off with the second or third shot. But at some point, the GCS still managed to get off at least one salvo of its own."

"Fleet Science and Engineering just updated the various tsunami warning centers with new damage estimates, by the way," Reynolds continued, feeling an almost desperate need to fill the silence. "It's bad, of course, but the direction of the impact and the distance from the nearest land mass is helping things a bit. Right now, it looks like most of the wave energy will reach shore in relatively unpopulated areas. We've already got ships on the ground working to evacuate as many people as possible."

Temporarily overcome with emotion, Prescott stared down at the floor and took in a long breath as he struggled to prepare himself to witness the final moments of the *Gresav,* her crew, and the Wek Crown Prince who had become his friend. Strangely, the Human psyche had a way of insulating itself from the emotional impact of large-scale disasters, even those affecting thousands or even millions of people. When there was even a single personal connection to the same disaster, however, the mind conspired to create a sense the event was far more real … impactful …tragic.

"What the hell are *those*?" he heard Reynolds say in a tone of voice that seemed strangely out of synch with the current atmosphere on the bridge.

Glancing up at the screen, Prescott saw nothing unusual at first. The *Gresav*, now completely awash in flame from bow to stern, seemed to have taken on more of a nose-down attitude. The ship's hull, however, in spite of being subjected to tremendous thermal and aerodynamic stresses, had stubbornly refused to yield, remaining in a single piece throughout her uncontrolled descent to the surface.

Tracing what he could still see of the ship's hull with the eyes of a captain and engineer, it took Prescott a few seconds to notice what Reynolds had been referring to. Flying in formation alongside the doomed destroyer was a group of brightly glowing, greenish-white orbs. The ships — assuming that's what they were — had no visible structure beyond their spherical shape. At first glance, Prescott counted seven of the strange craft, but their erratic flight paths around the *Gresav's* hull made it impossible to determine how many were present.

"You're seeing these … whatever they are … fireballs, I guess, right?" Reynolds asked.

"I see 'em, ma'am," Fisher spoke up excitedly. "I've read about something like these before, Commander. Back in the day, people used to call them 'foo fighters.'"

"I don't know about that, Ensign, I'm just glad I'm not the only one who sees them," she replied absently, transfixed by what was taking place on the view screen.

"I have absolutely no idea *what* those are," Prescott finally added, echoing the question on everyone's mind.

After a few more seconds, each of the orbs in turn adjusted its course slightly away from the Wek ship before flaring brightly and disappearing from view. At the bottom of the right-hand image, the time-to-impact timer had reached fifteen seconds. Although both video feeds remained remarkably clear, the two pursuing fighter aircraft were obviously now departing the area at high speed to avoid being destroyed in the massive, twenty-five-kilometer-wide fireball expected when the ship finally made contact with the surface of the ocean.

Now, with only seconds remaining before impact, the deep, cobalt-blue background of the South Pacific Ocean — or, more accurately, the space immediately above it — seemed to tear itself asunder, opening in a yawning black maw before their eyes. Before any of the bridge crew even had the time to gasp in disbelief, the massive hulk that had been SCS *Gresav* passed directly into the dark, hovering void and disappeared without a trace.

Seconds later, as the black chasm collapsed into nothingness and was gone, a portion of the rapidly moving mass of air that had been traveling alongside the huge warship reached the surface. Although accounting for only a tiny fraction of the energy that would have been released had the ship reached the surface, the results were still impressive to behold. As if struck by the hand of an invisible giant, a huge section of the ocean's surface was hammered from above. In the direction of the impact, a tremendous wall of water erupted skyward, reminiscent of the massive mushroom clouds created by underwater nuclear testing in the mid twentieth century.

In response to what they had just seen, every crewmember on TFS *Fugitive's* bridge turned to look at their captain, astonishment bordering on fear registering on their faces.

"No idea ..." Prescott repeated quietly, then lapsed back into silence. A moment later, his reverie was interrupted by a series of urgent-sounding tones issuing from the Comm/Nav console. "Look alive, Lieutenant," he prompted, causing his still-stunned comm officer to jump involuntarily.

"Sorry, Captain," Dubashi said, gathering her wits as she tended to the incoming transmission. "It's Rick aboard the *Ethereal*, sir."

"Why am I not surprised?" Reynolds commented.

"On-screen, Lieutenant," Prescott ordered.

"You were the first Terrans we spoke with when we arrived, so I thought it made the most sense for you to be our last contact before we depart," the Grey said as soon as his image appeared on the view screen. "I assume you saw what just happened with the *Gresav*?"

"We saw it," Prescott replied. "We don't understand it, but we saw it."

"It's understandable you don't understand," Rick replied with a pleased look on his face. "In fact, I'm not sure Miguel and I together could offer a technically accurate explanation for the physics involved, so I'm afraid you're going to have to settle for the radically simplified version."

"Fair enough. Let's hear it."

"The lights you probably noticed around the ship's hull? That was nothing more than an electroluminescent phenomenon that accompanies multiple, simultaneous uses of our matter transference equipment. You Terrans have seen it many times in the past, although I suppose none who have seen it had even the slightest notion of what was causing it."

"You were beaming the crew off the *Gresav*!" Reynolds exclaimed.

"There's that word again. Nope, no 'beams' of any kind were involved, Commander, but, yes, we were able to evacuate the Wek crew. All things considered, casualties appear to be fairly light, and I'm sure you'll be pleased to hear that Prince Naftur is fine ... well ... he *will* be anyway. I'll get to that in a moment."

"What happened to the ship, Rick?" Prescott asked impatiently.

"Ah, yes, as to that ... Miguel and I are probably in a lot of trouble for that one. Rescuing the crew of a damaged starship is permitted under certain circumstances, and, now that I think about it, after there was no crew aboard, the ship might technically have been considered abandoned ..."

"Did you save the ship or not?"

"The *Gresav*? Hah! No, I'm afraid she's gone for good. What you saw, my friends, was an eminently practical application of a system that has been banned for a *long* time where we're from. It generates a sort of dimensional rift — a bit like the one generated by your ship's hyperdrive. The difference is that this particular field transports anything that enters into it to ... I guess you could say nowhere. In this case, however, it did prevent a significant amount of damage to your planet, so there is that."

"It did indeed, and we very much appreciate it, just as we appreciate your rescuing the *Gresav's* crew."

"Yes, we should probably discuss that subject for a moment. Obviously, we didn't have room for all of those Wek aboard the *Ethereal*, so we landed them on a sparsely populated section of the Chilean coastline, just south of a small town called Guayusca. They shouldn't be too hard to find, and some of them do require medical attention, so I recommend you get your people to them as quickly as possible."

"We'll find them," Prescott said, nodding to Dubashi to get the effort underway.

"One more thing," Rick continued. "We didn't have a lot of time to spare during the evacuation, so the technique we were forced to use has a tendency to cause a few additional side effects."

"What *kinds* of side effects?"

"Eh, it varies. Most of them will be a little disoriented for a few hours. Some may experience an illusion you might have heard referred to as 'missing time,' which, of course, tends to add to their disorientation. A few may even remain unconscious for several hours. One thing's for sure, though, they're all likely to be more than a little irritable, so I recommend taking along some tranquilizer guns, just in case," Rick said, erupting in a fit of his usual squeaking laughter. "Anyway, as for us, Miguel thinks he may have come up with a way to make it look like we've been somewhere else for the past week or so, and that means we need to be on our way."

"You're leaving? Right now?"

"Like I said, we've done far more than we should here, Captain. And now, in addition to all of the other complications we've created for ourselves, we've also managed to fall far behind schedule on the next part of our mission."

"I see. I'm not sure what to say, other than thank you. You're obviously welcome here any time."

"But please warn us in advance next time," Reynolds interjected.

"Oh, we'll be around, Commander," Rick replied. "We've *always* been around."

Epilogue

Earth, TFC Yucca Mountain Shipyard Facility
(Nine months later)

"Good morning, Admiral," Kevin Patterson said brightly as he approached Prescott from behind.

Rear Admiral Prescott, doing his level best to hide the fact that his boss had just startled him half out of his wits, turned to face the approaching Chief of Naval Operations, whom, he immediately noticed, was already holding a salute and waiting patiently for the newly minted rear admiral to return the courtesy.

"Thank you, sir. I really appreciate that," Prescott said, coming to attention and saluting crisply.

"You've certainly earned it, son," Patterson replied with a devious smile, "but you know darn well why I just did that, so let's have it."

"Ah, right, yes, sir," Prescott replied, fishing in one of his pockets for a shiny new TFS *Katana* challenge coin.

"Come on … cough it up, youngster. In fact, unless I miss my guess, I think you probably owe me two of 'em."

Although still a relatively new organization, TFC had adopted a variety of long-standing military customs. One of these involved the exchange of ornate metallic coins to commemorate various special events and promote unit esprit de corps. While there were no hard and fast rules regarding when such coins were to be handed out, it was generally acknowledged that failing to provide one to a senior officer when asked was bad form indeed.

"*Two* of them? Come on, sir, you know they don't pay rear admirals much these days."

"Oh, cry me a river, Prescott. I want *two* of them … one for being the first superior officer to offer you a salute after you pinned on your new rank and another for your new command," Patterson repeated, nodding to the enormous battlecruiser in the final phases of construction in Berth Twelve.

"She's coming along nicely, isn't she?" Prescott said, handing over the pair of gold-plated coins embossed with the *Katana's* coat of arms. "If all continues to go well, she should be ready for space in just a couple of weeks."

"I sure hope so. It would be a real shame if you let TFS *Khopesh* or *Talwar* beat you to the punch. *Talwar* in particular, I would think, since she belongs to Abrams."

"That's not gonna happen, Admiral. My flag captain is a helluva lot meaner than his."

"Reynolds? You'll get no argument from me there. She's as tough as they come. Speaking of Abrams, though, I hear the two of you are heading back to Pelara with most of the Leadership Council in tow."

"Yes, sir. Their World Assembly is hosting a big powwow among all of the former members and Regional Partners of the Pelaran Alliance."

"Forgive me for being a cynical old man, Prescott, but the last thing I think we ought to be looking to get involved with right now is some kind of 'Pelaran Alliance 2.0.'"

"I couldn't agree more, sir. And every one of our delegates I've heard comment on the subject has said pretty much the same thing. I will say, however, that what little I've heard regarding what they intend to propose is nothing like the original Alliance. They're calling it the 'United Coalition of Free Worlds,' and one of its stated goals is to assist its members to avoid the kind of thing that happened on Pelara."

"The 'AI coup,' you mean? It seems to me that whole thing had a lot more to do with the complacency of the Pelaran people than anything else. But I guess sometimes the most valuable lessons are the ones we learn the hard way."

"Doctor Creel has been heavily involved with the reestablishment of the Pelaran government from the beginning. He makes no bones about the fact that what kept their world subjugated for so long had far more to do with good old-fashioned despotism than it ever did the Alliance AI. Thankfully, he and those like him were willing to risk everything to free the Pelaran people."

"Humph," Patterson grunted thoughtfully. "Seems like there's a lot of that kind of thing going around."

Both officers paused, unconsciously returning their gaze to the awe-inspiring warship stretching nearly a kilometer back in the direction of the shipyard's entrance tunnel. At the time of the ALAI attack, three additional *Navajo*-class cruisers had been nearing completion, but with several enhancements seen as mission-critical coming into play, Fleet had made the unusual decision to temporarily halt their construction. After an extensive design review, the proposed changes had been deemed so extensive as to warrant an entirely new class designation. Although based on the same basic hull design, the new warships were now designated as battlecruisers, and assigned names based on "legendary blades" as opposed to "indigenous cultures" originating near their construction facilities.

"Not to take anything away from her," Admiral Patterson continued, happy to change the subject, "but she just doesn't look all that different from the *Navajo* on the surface, does she?"

"No, sir, not really. But with all due respect to the *Navajo* class, the 'blades' pack a hell of a lot more punch."

"Let's see … double the power generation and storage capacity, eight fire lances, five-hundred-light-year range, dual-shielding, and four Wek G-cannons … Tom, I have no doubt there are bigger threats out there than what we've seen so far, but I sincerely hope you never run across anything capable of giving that ship a run for her money."

"Amen to that, sir, but you said that as if you're planning to stay planet-side. Don't you still have six months or so to go?" Prescott asked, referring to the CNO's recently announced retirement.

"I do, but if Mrs. Patterson has anything to say about it, my feet will remain firmly planted right here during the remainder of that time. I'm sure I'll eventually be spending a fair amount of time training my replacement — assuming they ever name one, that is. In the meantime, Chairwoman Kistler and Admiral Sexton want me primarily focused on working with the Wek Unified Fleet liaison on the technology exchange program. I'm sure you've heard we're allowing them to use ten of our *Ingenuity*-class frigates."

"Yes, sir, I did. Everyone's been calling it the 'Wek-Lend-Lease' program."

"Right, which is a little irritating for old curmudgeon history buffs like me. The historical parallel they're all trying to reference was called the 'Destroyers for Bases Agreement.' It was specific to warship transfers between the U.S. and Great Britain and preceded the much more general 'Lend-Lease Act' by six months or so. Come to think of it, though, 'Wek-Lend-Lease' does make more sense than 'Wek Destroyers for Bases Agreement,' doesn't it?" Patterson chuckled.

In the weeks following the destruction of the Alliance AI, TFC's Leadership Council, as well as the Crowned Republic of Graca's Parliament, had taken up the issue of technological cooperation and sharing between their respective fleets. As an added incentive, Rick had sent both sides a video in which he reminded them of the fact that secret, military-related technologies possessed by a single, space-faring civilization rarely remained a secret for long. Near the end of his message, the Grey had displayed a split-screen image with highly classified details of just such a technology currently possessed by each side — clearly implying that technological sharing might well occur involuntarily, if necessary. Although the idea still had its share of critics on both sides, a majority ultimately agreed that achieving technological parity between the two fleets offered a variety of strategic benefits to both worlds.

Shortly thereafter, scientists and engineers from both sides began a crash program to adapt several key technologies including energy-shielding, hyperdrive design, and several types of ship-based weapons. The so-called "Wek-Lend-Lease" program was also created as a stopgap measure, providing the Wek Unified Fleet with access to C-Drive-equipped warships until the technology could be retrofitted to their own vessels.

"Admiral Patterson!" a young ensign called out as he rapidly approached the two senior officers on one of the shipyard's grav carts.

"Watch yourself, Tom," Patterson said under his breath. "I've seen this kid drive before, and he might actually be more dangerous than I am."

"I doubt it, sir."

The cart had not even come to a complete stop before the young comm officer launched himself out of the driver's seat in their direction, thrusting an oversized tablet computer in their direction like some sort of modern-day telegram delivery boy.

"Sorry to interrupt ... sirs," he began awkwardly, "but Captain Oshiro wanted you to see this right away."

"Whatcha got there, son," Patterson asked, resisting the natural urge to cause the young man additional distress.

"Two things, Admiral. The first is a textual message from the Grey ship *Ethereal*."

"This ought to be good," Prescott commented. "We haven't heard from them in well over six months."

"Yeah, I can't say I've missed it all that much," Patterson replied as he peered at the screen through the bottom lenses of his glasses.

Dear Terrans,

Continuing our fine tradition of depositing derelict vessels on and around your world, we have just dropped off another one in high orbit. May you find this one just as useful and frustrating as the last one.

Sincerely,
Rick

P.S. We could only restore his memories up to the beginning of our GCS recruiting mission. Unfortunately, you'll have to catch him up on everything that has happened since. As you might well imagine, he has a long list of questions, so good luck with that.

P.S.S. Miguel says hello.

"I guess I have a pretty good idea what else you were supposed to show me," Patterson sighed, scowling at the young ensign over his glasses. After a moment's reflection, however, a hint of a smile could be seen forming at the corners of the older man's mouth as he passed the tablet to Terran Fleet Command's newest flag officer. "There you go, Admiral Prescott," he said cheerfully, already feeling a tremendous weight beginning to lift from his shoulders, "he's *your* problem now."

Pelara, Khester Shipping Facility
(3.87×10^3 light years from Earth)

This had better be worth it, Vina Dewar thought bitterly as she connected her tablet computer to the remote node's high-speed interface. As nervous as she was at the moment, however, her presence near the back corner of the enormous shipping warehouse, even at this hour of the night, was unlikely to attract attention. Fragile, extremely valuable cargos passed through this facility every day in containers just like this one. And even though most shipping companies relied on remote telemetry data to monitor their contents, it was not unusual to see technicians performing various manual inspections. Even the most imaginative security personnel would never have suspected she was in the process of committing treason against her homeworld.

As was often the case with traitors, regardless of their species or location throughout the cosmos, Dewar had convinced herself that her actions were nothing less than a moral imperative. In her mind, the course her recently reestablished government had embarked upon was dangerous and foolhardy to such an extent that it crossed a moral boundary into conduct she considered corrupt ... dishonorable ... *evil*.

Under the efficient, impartial leadership of the Alliance AI, she had held a position of influence and power enjoyed by only a select few of her fellow citizens. Her directorate within the Department of Compliance and Safety (DoCaS) had been instrumental in maintaining peace and order on Pelara for centuries, fully justifying the comparatively lavish lifestyles enjoyed by the elite officials in its upper echelons. During her many years at DoCaS, she had also been privy to various types of classified information, providing what she believed was a perspective far more enlightened than the common people she had dedicated her career to serving. Now, as she worked to prepare the remote node to begin the prolonged process of delivering its data, Dewar believed with absolute conviction her actions were both ethical and fully justified under Pelaran law — in spite of the fact that most of the laws she had in mind had now been overturned.

It had taken nearly nine months for the data to be collected, then transmitted in short, hopefully untraceable bursts from a variety of sources. Notable among these were several relatively obscure systems aboard the FAM-4 facility as well as a number of drones still operating within fifty light years or so of Pelara. All of them, Dewar noted with no small degree of satisfaction, remained fully operational and loyal to the Alliance AI in spite of ongoing enemy efforts to purge all remnants of its influence from Pelaran space.

Realistically, however, Dewar knew the information she was about to pass along to ALAI Disaster Recovery Site Alpha was unlikely to change anything — at least not within her lifetime. The Pelaran World Assembly had reestablished itself, conducting the first planetary elections under the tired, bourgeois banners of freedom and self-determination with surprising speed and efficiency. Now, there were even rumors regarding the formation of a new, intra-galactic partnership, supposedly incorporating most of the original core member worlds of the Pelaran Alliance. This "United Coalition of Free Worlds" was also planning to welcome formerly cultivated systems, many of which, until recently, had been all but unknown to the former Alliance. This, Dewar suspected, was largely due to the influence of the upstart Regional Partner world that had

been primarily to blame for the ALAI's destruction —
the Terrans.

A reckoning will come ... eventually, she consoled
herself, but the words rang hollow, even within the mind
of a true zealot. The truth of the matter was that she had
no way of knowing if the disaster recovery facility even
remained operational at this point. It had been
constructed within a remote asteroid, primarily as an
archival facility to store the colossal volume of data
collected through the years as a result of the cultivation
program. And although DR-Alpha was theoretically
capable of reconstituting the AI itself in the unlikely
event its primary starbase were ever destroyed, a test of
this functionality was so impractical that it had never
been attempted.

Dewar sighed deeply as she concluded her work,
paging quickly through a high-level summary of what
she was about to transmit. Her access to high-level
intelligence information had been terminated with the
dissolution of the Department of Compliance and Safety
(DoCaS), occurring less than a month after the
destruction of the ALAI starbase. Since then, she had
been forced to rely on her own, informal network of like-
minded associates to stay abreast of what the fools now
managing the affairs of *her* world were doing.

Hello ... this actually does look interesting, she
thought, gratified to see there might at least be a remote
possibility her actions might one day prove worthy of the
risks she was taking. On the screen of her tablet
computer, a highly detailed schematic of a missile of
some sort had appeared. Although she was definitely no
authority on weapons technology, Dewar was

immediately drawn to several uses of the word "hyperdrive." While she was obviously familiar with this term, the document also made several related references to something called a "C-Drive." *Something new and useful, perhaps?* she wondered, noting the caption beneath the rotating missile diagram labeled with some sort of military designation: HB-7c.

With a shrug of her shoulders, Vina Dewar initiated the data transfer, disconnected her tablet, and disappeared into the night.

End of Book 5

THANK YOU!

I'd like to express my sincerest thanks for reading *TFS Guardian*. I hope you have enjoyed not only this book but the entire Terran Fleet Command Saga! Although *Guardian* is the final book in the original TFC series, I do plan to eventually write additional stand-alone stories set in the same universe.

If you enjoyed *TFS Guardian*, I would greatly appreciate a quick review at Amazon.com. It need not be long or detailed, just a quick note that you enjoyed the story and would recommend it to other readers. Thanks again!

Have questions about the series? Please visit my FAQ at:

AuthorToriHarris.com/FAQ/

While you're there, be sure to sign up for the newsletter for updates and special offers at:

AuthorToriHarris.com/Newsletter

Have story ideas, suggestions, corrections, or just want to connect? Feel free to e-mail me at tori@authortoriharris.com. You can also find me on Twitter and Facebook at:

https://twitter.com/TheToriHarris

https://www.facebook.com/AuthorToriHarris

Finally, you can find links to all of my books on my Amazon author page:

http://amazon.com/author/thetoriharris

OTHER BOOKS BY TORI L. HARRIS

The Terran Fleet Command Saga

TFS *Ingenuity*
TFS *Theseus*
TFS *Navajo*
TFS *Fugitive*
TFS *Guardian*

ABOUT THE AUTHOR

Born in 1969, four months before the first Apollo moon landing, Tori Harris grew up during the era of the original Star Wars movies and is a lifelong science fiction fan. During his early professional career, he was fortunate enough to briefly have the opportunity to fly jets in the U.S. Air Force and is still a private pilot who loves to fly. Tori has always loved to read and now combines his love of classic naval fiction with military Sci-Fi when writing his own books. His favorite authors include Patrick O'Brian and Tom Clancy as well as more recent self-published authors like Michael Hicks, Ryk Brown, and Joshua Dalzelle. Tori lives in Tennessee with his beautiful wife, two beautiful daughters, and Bizkit, the best dog ever.

Made in the USA
Columbia, SC
26 June 2018